PRAISE FOR THE CAT (
AND *EIGHT h.....* .....

"Once I start one of Borton's books, I virtually inhale it."

— SHARLOTTE DONNELLY, AMAZON READER

"This series is great. I don't know what else to say about it except read it for yourself. You won't be disappointed . . I hope D. B. Borton never tires of writing about Cat and her friends. I know I won't tire of reading about them."

— SHARON WELLS, *MYSTERIOUS WOMEN*

"This is a very soft-boiled (one might even say COZY) series, written with humor but still exploring some serious issues."

— *THE PURLOINED LETTER*

"Caliban is a hot ticket . . . Borton writes like the gritty parts of Dorothy Parker with a light glaze of Betty Friedan over the top. Wonderful stuff."

— KATHY PHILLIPS, *THE DROOD REVIEW OF MYSTERY*

"With crisp plotting, brilliant timing, and an intriguing cast, Borton's books deliver excellent entertainment."

— ROBERT POWERS, *THE ATHENS MESSENGER*

"Read the entire series . . . Funny, witty, and interesting quirky characters."

— M. KAMP, AMAZON READER

"Cat's witty, sarcastic and an all 'round hoot."

— SANDRA HARDY, *READ MY LIPS*

"This gray-haired gumshoe and her extended family of tenants sashay through some very clever and well-developed plots with a wit and warmth you'll love."

— MARY ALICE GORMAN, *MYSTERY LOVERS BOOKSHOP NEWS*

Praise for *Eight Miles High*

"Great plotting, delicious characters. Highly recommended."

— MARGARET F. BAKER, AMAZON READER

"With a delightful protagonist, pitch perfect narrative and a colourful cast of supporting characters, this is another entertaining read and a worthy addition to the series."

— RUTH GILES, NETGALLEY REVIEWER

"This is an incredible mystery written so vividly you feel a part of the story . . . A mystery that is a page turner from start to finish."

— SKYE LINDBORG, AMAZON READER

EIGHT MILES HIGH

D. B. BORTON

©2007, 2021

Boomerang Books

8616 Toronto Court

Cincinnati, OH 45255

Originally published in paperback by Hilliard & Harris Publishers in April 2007

Print ISBN: 978-1-7363519-1-8

Ebook ISBN: 978-1-7363519-0-1

To Mary Jane Borton Carpenter
in loving memory
and to the courageous women of WASP

ACKNOWLEDGMENTS

First and foremost, of course, I owe a big debt of gratitude to the WASP and their chroniclers and archivists, especially to Caro Bayley Bosca (43-W-7) and Sherry Ringler. Archivists Tracey MacGowan and Dawn Letson and historian Katherine Landdeck, as well as KOW Nancy F. Hoing, helped me at the WASP archive at Texas Women's University. The scrapbook of Adeline Blank, the diary of Rene Nielsen, and the oral histories of David Lamb, Irma Story, Leona Golbinec Zimmer, Lorraine Zillner Rodgers, Betty Williamson Shipley, Alberta Paskvan Kinney, Andrea Shaw, Betty J. Clark, and Ann Craft Moss were helpful to me, as were the published letters of Caro Bayley Bosca (TWU Special Collections), Mary Anna Martin Wyall (TWU Special Collections), and Bernice Falk Haydu (*Letters Home 1944-1945*, Riviera Beach, FL 20003). Three other histories of the WASP were indispensable: Byrd Howell Grainger's *On Final Approach* (Falconer, 1991), Jean Hascall Cole's *Women Pilots of World War II* (University of Utah Press, 1992), and Molly Merryman's *Clipped Wings* (NYU Press, 1998). All factual errors are mine, not theirs.

I'd also like to thank Mike Whaley of Steen Aero Lab for providing me with detailed information about the Skybolt and answering my questions. And to the hangar pilots and mechanics at the Delaware Municipal Airport, thanks for all the enthusiastic suggestions for sabotaging an airplane.

To find out more or make a contribution, visit the National WASP WWII Museum, WASP on the Web or the Texas Women's University WASP archives.

I also owe a big debt of gratitude to my advance team, and especially to Karen Edwards, who made helpful corrections.

AUTHOR'S NOTE

The following is a work of fiction. While it draws on historical events and attempts to represent those events as faithfully as possible, the main characters are fictional and so are their crimes. The only crimes which are not fictional are those of calumny, persecution, reckless endangerment, abuse, sabotage, exploitation, and neglect perpetrated against the heroic Women Airforce Service Pilots.

The 8, the cube number of 2, represents the actual solidification of matter, which is followed by death and regeneration. The cube, symbol of the earth, has 8 vertices; death belongs only to the earth.

For the ancients, the 8 was the number of justice because it divided evenly into 4 and 4, then evenly into 2 and 2, then evenly into 1 and 1.

— E. ABBOTT, *ENCYCLOPEDIA OF NUMBERS*

Now, the idea is to fly at a great height where the air is rarefied, and therefore much less power is required to propel the machine through it … A voyage between New York and London can be made in about three hours by going eight miles high.

If war comes again, I look for the extensive use of self-propelled air vehicles carrying enormous charges of explosive which will be sent from any point to another to do their destructive work, with no human being aboard to guide them. The distance to which they can be sent is practically unlimited and the amount of explosive they can carry is likewise unlimited …. We have here the appalling prospect of a war between nations at a distance of thousands of miles, with weapons so destructive and demoralizing that the world cannot endure them. That is why there must be no more war.

— NIKOLA TESLA, INTERVIEW, 1919

1

SATURDAY, JULY 19, 1986

THE FLOOR PLUNGED. I hung suspended in space for a heartbeat, then dropped. The floor leapt, slammed my soles and jolted my spine. The shock threw me sideways and my shoulder struck metal. I thrust out a hand to steady myself, but I couldn't find anything to hang on to. The air was thickening with smoke.

A hand closed over mine and guided it to a metal bar. Nearby, below me, someone had opened a door and warm air and smoke rushed in. A flash of light caught my eye. Across from me, my photographer, who was also my business partner, was lowering his camera, his mustache twitching with what I knew to be a smile of gratification. If I could have released my grip on the bar that held me upright, I would have lunged at him and shoved the goddamned camera down his throat. Leaning against his leg was a golden retriever hard pressed at this instant to live up to his name, which was Happy. The wind flattened the dog's coat. He was wearing a harness and backpack, as well as an odd little helmet like a miner's helmet, with a light like a flashlight surrounded by tiny lights that glittered in the smoky air. Surreal. Maybe I was having a nightmare.

My eyes stung and watered. In my ear, above the roar of the single remaining engine and the rushing air, a woman's voice shouted, "Remember, count to ten and then pull." A hand guided my free hand to a cord dangling from the harness that bound my heaving chest.

The floor dropped again. My arm was nearly jerked from its socket as I tightened my grip in panic. Everything tilted.

Firm hands at my waist were pushing me toward the open door. Smoke blinded me. I clung to the metal bar.

But it was a larger, firmer hand that shoved me out, a deeper voice vibrating in my ear, "Time to go, Cat!"

I plunged, and in the three-count before I yanked the cord, I had time for one thought: I need me a new partner.

2

JULY 4, 1986

THE OFFICIAL PARTNERSHIP of Fogg and Caliban wasn't that old. It dated back six months to Valentine's Day, when Moses Fogg — friend, neighbor, tenant, and retired cop — announced that he had been licensed as a private investigator in the state of Ohio. This was a step that all of us at the Catatonia Arms, my residence and four-apartment real estate investment, had been urging him to take for some months in the interest of furthering my own career aspirations, but once he took it, you'd have thought the whole business had been his idea. Not that he wanted to do any investigating, private, public, or otherwise.

"I did it for you, Cat," he'd said. "I'll keep working on your training, but mostly I'm a consultant, hear? You want me, you can find me in the park, walking the dog and playing with my grandbabies."

If I wanted him, I could find him downstairs in the basement, puttering around with his tools or doing laundry, or upstairs in his apartment, snoozing in his Barcalounger, or over at Chuck's house, playing poker with other cops. His grandchildren mostly reached the age when senior companionship is viewed with consternation, not eagerness. I should know. My own grandkids would rather go to church than to Grandma's. The church has Nintendo.

This is not a situation I intend to correct. My goal in life is to become a private eye, not a perfect granny.

But I didn't have two years of what the state of Ohio considered "relevant experience." Years of tracking down my own missing kids or my late husband's car keys didn't count. A lifetime of reuniting wayward socks with their mates didn't count. A perfect record at hiding the gin bottle from the underaged didn't count. Nor did a finely honed ability to be dropped into any building on the planet and locate a bathroom within sixty seconds. Philip Marlowe could take a beating with a grimace and a litany of wisecracks. But he never experienced labor. We grannies are tougher than we look.

Interrogation of suspects. Gathering evidence. Surveillance. Lie detection. Skip tracing. Take it from me, Cat Caliban: if you've raised kids, you have a solid grounding in the skills required to become a successful private dick.

And thanks to my cousin Delbert, the teenaged computer nerd, I had the computer equipment to carry my investigations into the 21st century, assuming we survived the twentieth with a Hollywood cowboy in the White House.

I'd had everything I needed to launch my new career. But the state licensure board didn't see it that way. No, what I needed was an ex-cop with a P.I. license.

Moses and I made a pretty good team. Mostly, our arthritis didn't act up on the same days. Our obvious differences — he was male and I was female, he was Black and I was white — actually worked in our favor when we were trying to gather information from a variety of sources. He had experience on the police force, though he'd spent most of his time in Juvie, and a lot of good contacts. I had the aforementioned experience and my natural charm. When he tried to boss me around, I ignored him, and vice versa. Neither one of us took offense easily. We both had a sense of humor, although it can be difficult to activate plummeting through black space from 15,000 feet.

At the moment, I was not sanguine about my chances of logging two years of relevant experience for a P.I. license.

What got me here was a family cookout. The Fourth of July had come and gone at the old Catatonia Arms and we were all still recovering, or "in recovery," as Al, the Legal Aid attorney, would say when she was impersonating one of the many social workers with whom she has dealings. What we were recovering from was the War of the Flags, which had started when Moses, a veteran, had installed a flag mount outside his second-floor front window and inserted an American flag.

"I know my country ain't perfect," he'd said, "but it's my country."

And when Kevin O'Neill, his downstairs neighbor, had eyed it with open disapproval, Moses had added, "I've fought for the rest of y'all's right to put up any damn flag you want to."

To me, Kevin groused that Moses's flag hung down into what he called his "space." He dragged me outside to show me. "Look how low it hangs!" he said, waving an arm at it. "I live in a country that won't even let me marry the person I want to and people think I'm flying an American flag."

"I didn't know you wanted to get married. Who's the lucky guy?"

"You know what I mean," he said. "It's embarrassing!"

"Is there a country you can get married in?" I asked out of curiosity.

"That's not the point," he said sulkily.

"The point is that Moses put up with the red cellophane on the hall lights on Valentine's Day, and he hardly complained at all." Well, not to Kevin, anyway. "Let's have a little give-and-take here."

The next day Kevin installed a flag mount outside his window and in it, a rainbow flag that was twice as big as Moses's American flag. I knew that Kevin approved of the Rainbow Coalition, but I hadn't thought he'd felt passionately enough about it to fly its flag. Melanie Carter, Al's roommate, set me straight, so to speak.

"It's a symbol of gay pride, Cat," she said.

"So do you and Al want to get married?" I asked, again because I just wanted to know.

"God, no!" she said. "Kevin's a romantic, I'm a realist. Besides, my girlfriend's a lawyer. I wouldn't trust her to draw up the prenuptial agreement."

By the next day, the Catatonia Arms bristled with flags like Sputnik with antennae. Mel had hung her American flag upside down in their second-story front window to register her opinion of the current administration. In the side window, Al had hung an earth flag. Moses had added a second American flag to the side window in retaliation for Kevin's monster rainbow flag. The rainbow flag, meanwhile, hung so low that it attracted the attention of the youngest cat, Sidney, who climbed it up to Kevin's windowsill so that he could see in, leaving a trail of tiny claw holes behind him. Don't ask me what the appeal was; he'd been in Kevin's apartment many times and looked out, but he seemed fascinated by this new perspective and maybe by the opportunity to leave nose smudges on the outside as well as the inside of the glass. After several of these trips, the flag began to shred. Then Winnie the beagle noticed it, and in a playful holiday mood seized it between her teeth for a game of tug-of-war. The last I saw of it, the victor was disappearing around the house as fast as her little beagle legs could carry her, colors streaming behind her like Isadora's scarf. I guessed we'd find it when we dug potatoes in a few weeks.

I called a meeting of my immediate household to discuss our own contribution to the festivities. Since I called it at dinner time, I wasn't expecting much dissent, but I wanted to hear any objections now before I put the damn thing up and not after. Every furry little head was buried in its dish. Nobody even looked up to admire my purchase.

"I think it's apt, inoffensive, and tasteful," I said. "Plus, I found it in the bargain bin for $1.99. But if it offends anybody's politics or sensibilities, now's the time to speak up."

Not a tail twitched. Our United Nations flag went up.

Moses presented a new rainbow flag to Kevin, a slightly smaller one that didn't hang so low, and apologized on Winnie's behalf. Winnie looked contrite and, well, hangdog. Since cats are never contrite, I consider it presumptuous to apologize on their behalf, so I don't, and didn't.

On the Fourth, everybody went off to family cookouts that nobody except Moses and me were looking forward to. I went with Moses. He was my ticket to freedom from the annual cookout staged by my son-in-law's family, where everybody talked about their golf games and argued over the precise dates of notable family events that meant nothing to me. Besides, Moses had a sister, Ruth, who made killer potato salad, and a sister-in-law, Froney, who baked pies. And the Foggs never talked about their golf games, if they had any. Nobody passed around pictures of their kids so everybody could debate which relative they most resembled. And if anybody took pictures, they did it discreetly, without interrupting what everybody else was doing and making them pose for a group shot.

Of course, I had to take a little heat from my daughter Sharon, who claimed to be astonished and hurt that I didn't want to spend yet another Fourth of July discussing golf and watching unruly kids play with matches and explosives. But people who can't take that kind of emotional extortion should never sign on for motherhood in the first place.

So there I was on a hot summer day, a beer in one hand and a plastic plate in the other, closing the distance between me and the potato salad as three of Moses's male relatives discussed not golf but recipes for barbecue sauce, and his niece Pauletta shifted the three-bean salad to make room for a Jell-O mold. These were my kind of people.

One of the relatives, a burly guy who evidently appreciated his own culinary skills, was holding up thumb and index finger to indicate how much whiskey he added to his sauce, when his face changed. I couldn't see his eyes beneath his sunglasses, but he frowned and his forehead creased. I heard a sound I couldn't identify and turned to follow his gaze past a circle of lawn chairs under the shade of an enormous maple tree. The sound was coming from somewhere beyond the new fence that marked the border between clipped lawn and a pasture where two brown cows grazed and flicked their tails at flies in the afternoon heat. What I heard was too loud to be an insect. And insects don't cough.

Other people had turned now, too. Two women in flower-print dresses had raised their hands to shield their eyes and three little boys were running toward the fence, pointing up.

Now I saw it — a small plane, buzzing and sputtering, its wings wobbling, coming in low over the woods at the far end of the pasture. It was trailing smoke. I heard shouts as someone brushed by me and then everyone was rushing the fence. I dropped my plate and ran.

The cows appeared to grasp the situation and trotted toward the fence on the other side. The plane dipped alarmingly. Its landing wheels struck the ground with an impact I could feel through my sneakers. The onlookers gasped and cried out. It bounced two more times, its wheels digging furrows in the soft ground, and then it shuddered and stopped. Flames licked the nose. Dark smoke obscured the cockpit. For a heartbeat, no one moved or spoke. Then, the crowd cheered. We saw a moving figure climb out of the cockpit, but the fuselage and the smoke hid most of the pilot from view. The kids were swarming over the fence, while the adults surged through an open gate. I followed. The adults in the lead were warning the kids back, away from the plane, and the kids had stopped in their tracks, as if an invisible barrier prevented them from advancing. Kind of reminded me of that scene in *The Thing* when the scientists surround the flying saucer embedded in the ice.

I heard sirens in the distance, so someone must've spotted the plane in trouble and called the fire department. We still couldn't see the pilot, who remained on the other side of the plane. I saw one of Moses's brothers giving the tail a wide berth as he rounded it to check on the pilot. The fire truck roared up the drive and into the field. Two firefighters worked on the hoses while a third, the driver, came toward us, waving us back. The water from the hoses hissed against the hot metal. In no time, the flames disappeared, leaving only an acrid column of smoke rising above the plane's nose.

We still couldn't see the pilot clearly, although firefighters, pilot, and several of the male Foggs were holding a powwow on the far side of the pasture. When it broke up, the firefighters headed back to their truck and the men headed our way. With them was the pilot, who was a woman. She was fairly tall and slender and had an athlete's stride. She wore khakis and a white shirt with dark crescents of perspiration under the short sleeves.

"I am so sorry," she was saying to the assembled crowd as she approached. She was shaking her head. Her hair was light brown beneath considerable gray, short and curly. She ran a hand through it. "I couldn't be more sorry. I've interrupted your party. Really, I am so, so sorry." She glanced back then and added, almost under her breath, "Missed the cows, though."

That was how I met Toots Magruder.

Later, after Toots had phoned home and been plied with barbecue and beer, someone mentioned that Moses was a retired cop and that he and I had started a private investigation agency. She gave us a thoughtful look, and said, "Really? Now that is interesting." Shortly after that, she stood up and said to us, "I'm going out to check the plane. Want to come?"

I unpeeled my skin from the lawn chair I was sitting in, gave a self-conscious swipe at the grid marks on the backs of my thighs below my white denim shorts, picked up my beer and followed her and Moses. The sweat made my shirt stick to my back and plastered my short-cropped white hair to my head. My skin felt flushed from an afternoon in the sun. Just inside the pasture gate, I stepped in a cow paddy. Cat Caliban, ace detective.

By the time I'd scraped my shoe clean, Toots and Moses were standing beside the plane. Toots was holding a stick that she'd picked up in the yard. She was using it to pry open a blackened door on the pilot's side of the nosecone.

"Don't touch it with your hands, now," Moses was cautioning her.

I couldn't tell if she'd heard him or not. Once she had the door open, she fished a handkerchief — a man's handkerchief, from the size of it — out of her back pocket and, grimacing, unscrewed a cap. She poked at something with a stick.

"The investigators will want to see it just the way it is," Moses said, not lecturing her, just stating a fact.

She retracted the stick and examined the end of it, then held it out for us to look at. Stuck to the end of it were some black fibers.

"What's that?" I asked.

"Something that has no business to be there." She squinted at us. "I believe I need to hire a detective. Kind of providential, don't you think?"

3

JULY 11, 1986

MOSES DROVE. Since he drove like most ex-cops, I kept waiting for the little oxygen mask to drop down from overhead. Since he drove like most men, it took us twice as long to get there in spite of our ground speed because he refused to stop and ask directions. As an ex-cop, Moses knew the city well, but he'd had little experience with antebellum farmhouses in Anderson Township, well past the Cincinnati city limits. I kept pointing out possible informants as we blew past them.

"Well, you got the map, Cat," he'd say. "What does the map say?"

"Who can read the goddamned map at this speed?" I'd say. "There's wind currents and shit. I can't focus."

This was an old bone of contention between us. He maintained that I couldn't read a map to save my life and I maintained that at the speeds at which we traveled, map reading was an exercise in futility. By the time I found us on the map, I was looking at the past — where we'd been, not where we were. This kind of squabbling tended to ensure that we showed up most places cranky.

The house, when we finally found it, proved to be a large but unpretentious two-story building with white siding and a wide front porch. It was shaded by trees that had probably been planted as saplings when it was built, most of them maples. The porch needed a woman to sit on it and string beans, and maybe a sleeping dog dreaming of past hunts, but the worn wicker chairs were empty. Gravel crunched under the Fairlane's tires and pinged off its fenders as we wound our way around the house to the back.

"She said the shed, not the barn," I said doubtfully, pointing past a barn that looked to be the same age as the house. "Think that's it?"

A wooden fence stood between us and a boxlike prefabricated structure that appeared to have been set on the near side of a large field, which was mown. Beyond this near field was another field, planted in knee-high corn. Wider than a two-car garage, the prefab building wasn't what I would have called a "shed." As Moses cut the engine, we could hear the whine of an electric drill and a metallic banging over the hum of insects. "Must be," he said. "Somebody's in there."

We unlatched the gate, which was made, like the fence, of roof timbers, pushed it open, and approached the open door of the shed. Someone yelled, "Dad-*gummit!*" And a heavy projectile sailed through the opening and landed with a thud on the ground. I was in the lead, so it was my knee that felt the puff of air as the object flew by. I froze, and avoided collision with the long piece of metal pipe that followed the object, which proved to be a small mallet. I stepped back and bumped into Moses.

He said, "This be a good time to tell her we're here, Cat."

I cleared my throat. "Ms. Magruder?" I called. "Toots?"

Toots McGruder had made this appointment with us a week ago at the cookout before leaving town for a few days. But I had confirmed it with her the night before, so she knew we were coming.

Under the whine of the drill, the voice bellowed, "I could just scream!"

The drill stopped. I tried again. "Ms. Magruder? Toots?"

"Jeepers!" the voice said and we heard scrambling and a metallic crash. Toots Magruder rushed out. She wore brown coveralls. A few strands of gray hair had escaped from a flowered kerchief and lay plastered against a tanned forehead. She had a dark smudge across one cheek. Under the short sleeves of her coveralls, I noticed muscles that reminded me that in a drawer somewhere at home was a gym membership given to me by my daughter Franny for my last birthday.

"Tell me I didn't hit you with anything," she said, her face crumpled in consternation, fingers pressed to her cheeks.

"You didn't." I offered my hand.

Her grip warned me to find the gym membership before I challenged her to arm wrestle.

Moses had picked up the mallet and the pipe, which had smaller metallic cylinders welded to it at right angles.

"Here, let me take that." I saw Moses's eyes widen slightly when he felt her grip. At the cookout, we'd been part of a group introduction so neither one of us had shaken her hand before. "Part of the fuselage frame." She frowned at the pipe. "I know the darned thing needs to fit tight, but I just don't have the hand strength that I used to."

Moses understood before I did. "You're building a plane?"

She nodded. "My first. If it doesn't kill me, it won't be my last. It's a Steen Skybolt. Want to have a look?"

She's building a plane? Planes, as everybody knows, are built in huge factories. During the war, some women had in fact built planes; they had worn outfits similar to the one Toots was wearing and wielded drills and punch presses and rivet guns. When the war ended, they'd all been sent home to polish their appliances and throw Tupperware parties, whether they'd wanted to or not. I'd spent the war doing clerical work in a mill that had produced fabric for military uniforms, but I'd seen pictures of girls who'd had more glamorous roles in the war effort, and envied them. My peekaboo bangs had been small consolation for the mundane work I'd done, especially after Veronica Lake had changed her hairstyle.

But now one of my contemporaries was building airplanes in a cornfield in suburban Cincinnati? It didn't compute.

The shed had wide doors that were propped open. Inside, sitting atop a weathered set of wooden sawhorses, sat something that looked like one of my grandson's Tinker Toy constructions, except that the sticks appeared to be made of metal, like the one in her hand. The general shape reminded me of a soapbox racer, but it was much bigger — about the length of the Fairlane, but not wider. The idea of leaving the ground in something that size stopped my breath.

Behind the structure, under a window that stretched across the back wall, was a large workbench. Silhouetted against the light was a figure, its back to us. My first impression was that the figure was a space alien, perhaps visiting Earth on a student exchange program to learn about primitive flight. This impression was caused in part by a curious glow around the figure, about chest high, like the glow from E.T.'s heart-light and in part by the bulbous eyes visible in its profile.

"Hey! Stretch!" Toots shouted, loudly enough to shrivel my ears. "We got visitors."

The figure turned and waved. A small blue flame issued from something it held in its hands. It turned back, set the tool down on the workbench, and moved toward us, passing a hand over its face. As it moved into the light coming from the open doors, I could see that it was a tall young woman wearing overalls and a T-shirt. She also wore a baseball cap backwards, and perched on top of her head was a pair of dark goggles that protruded like a pair of insect eyes. She had mahogany skin, dark eyes, and high cheekbones. Her expression was open but incurious. She was wiping her hands on a red cloth.

"My co-conspirator, Darcy Livingston," Toots said with a wave of her hand. "Most folks call her 'Stretch.' I'll let you guess why."

In fact, everything about Darcy Livingston seemed stretched, from the long fingers of the hand she offered to shake to the long neck emphasized by her upright posture. I suspected that the relatively formless coveralls concealed a pair of long legs.

"I'm really her amanuensis," Stretch said with a widening grin.

"But I can't pronounce it," Toots said, "so we call her my partner."

Stretch shook hands with both of us. "Sorry," she said. "I've been welding."

"Stretch's the brains of the partnership," Toots said. "Studies aeronautics at MIT. Wants to be a systems engineer. I provide the practical experience — say, which parts you will need when you stall out at 6,000 feet and what you'd better be able to do with them."

"Looks complicated," I said. Everywhere I looked, I saw airplane parts — some nestled in boxes, some propped against the wall, a few sitting on old kitchen chairs, a card table, or a workbench. To tell you the truth, it looked like a crash site, only neater.

The two of them turned to regard their workspace as if contemplating it from a new perspective.

"Actually, we're building from a kit, so it's a lot like building a model airplane," Toots said.

"Only heavier," Darcy said.

"And tighter," Toots said.

"And requiring more expensive tools," Stretch said.

"And heavier tools," Toots said.

They grinned at each other.

"And you don't have to sniff airplane glue or use toothpicks," Moses observed.

Toots closed one eye and looked thoughtful. "I wouldn't swear to the toothpicks," she said. "We end up using a lot of tools that aren't regulation."

Stretch nodded and jerked a thumb over her shoulder. "We got somebody's ponytail band holding two pieces together in the back there. I think it's got a pink butterfly on it. And as for sniffing, the dope we'll use in the Stits process when we cover the wings should provide a pretty good high."

"What will it look like when it's done?" Moses asked. It occurred to me now as it often had before that Moses had been a good cop because he never rushed an interview. He was always willing to encourage people to talk about what interested them most. He'd never been a detective on the force, but he was a good one, and I'd already learned a lot by watching him operate.

Toots was holding out a handful of papers. "It's a Skybolt," she repeated. "It's a very popular model for homebuilts. It's a two-place aerobatic biplane."

I moved closer to Moses to see the unfolded brochure in his hand. It included several full-colored pictures of two-winged airplanes with propellers on their noses and two landing wheels. The front part of the plane looked kind of like a cartoon mouse on roller skates, skidding to a stop before he flew into the open mouth of a cat.

Moses raised his head. "Aerobatics? You mean like trick flying? You do that?"

Toots nodded, but Stretch spoke up with evident pride. "Toots is a champion. She used to appear in airshows all over the country."

"Jeepers," I said.

Moses walked around the Tinker Toy soapbox racer, admiring it and asking lots of intelligent-sounding questions about the horsepower and wingspan. To me, it looked kind of naked and fragile, like a baby bird that hadn't grown feathers yet. I averted my gaze, but couldn't find anything worth looking at. Airplane parts were about as fascinating as golf clubs, if you ask me. But Moses seemed riveted by the discussion of "chrome-moly," "air-craft-grade sitka spruce," "aileron linkages," "MacWhytes," a "fuel-injected Lycoming," and "bungee cord loops." The last term was the only one that made any sense to me, but all it suggested was that ponytail holder Stretch had mentioned. I hoped they weren't fudging the specs without testing to make sure that a ponytail holder would hold the landing gear on as well as a full-sized bungee cord.

"What color are you going to paint it?" That was my contribution. I noticed that the planes in the brochure were all painted differently, from the restrained but tasteful white one with a double red stripe along the side to a bright yellow one studded with black triangles to make it resemble an angry shark.

Toots laughed. "We haven't decided."

"We think we might jinx the whole operation if we pick a color too soon," Stretch added. "Kind of like painting a baby's room before it's born."

Eventually — and not a moment too soon from my perspective — the plane-building talk subsided and Toots took us into the house while Stretch raised her goggles and went back to work. Toots settled us on a rattan couch in a sunroom most notable for its decor. Everything in it, from the hummingbird wind chimes that hung near the sliding glass door to the model plane on the coffee table in front of us to the butterfly print covering the couch cushions, had something to do with flight. We accepted iced tea and assured her that we'd had no trouble finding her house.

To be polite, I reached for a cookie when Toots set a plate on the coffee table.

"Bad girl! Bad girl!" a man's voice commented and I turned, surprised, to Moses before I realized that the voice wasn't his. Behind him, I caught a flash of bright green in motion and saw a cage containing two parrots. One, the green one, was hanging from the side of the cage by one foot and eyeing me with one beady eye. The other, a gray one with red markings, was admiring itself in the mirror from its perch.

"Oh, Orry, hush up, for Pete's sake!" Toots said, presumably to the green parrot. "You're not getting that cookie. You're too fat already."

The parrot and I exchanged looks. "So's she," said his expression.

"That's Orvelle and Wilbur," Toots said with a wave of her hand. "Orvelle with an *e* because she's a girl. They're smarter than God and they're good mimics, both of them. 'Bad girl' was something Hal — that was my husband — used to say to the dog when she was a puppy. We needed to confine her to this room when she was in training. After Hal died, they made me jump every time they used his voice, but I'm used to it now.

"So, anyway —." She took a deep breath. "The fibers you saw at the crash site — they belonged to a piece of cloth stuffed into the oil filter port. Well, 'stuffed' is my word. The investigators, who are careful guys, said 'introduced.' It's a popular means of sabotaging a plane. Well, not *popular*, maybe. We saw a lot of it during the war. Eventually causes the engine to seize up. It's quick and easy, can't be detected on a pre-flight, if it's done right. And when the crash is investigated, even if they find anything left of the rag that was used, nobody can say for certain that it wasn't negligence and not sabotage. But I know my mechanic and this wasn't negligence.

"If that was the only thing — well, I'd wonder about who was hanging around the airport that had it in for me. But it's not. And the other things all have to do with the past. I mean, the ancient past, when we were young." She frowned. "I don't know about you, but I can barely remember back that far. If it weren't for the reunions ..." She handed me a photograph and Moses leaned over to study it with me.

"You have to start here," she said. "At least, I think you do. That's us. That's the Crazy Eight." She had a trace of a Southern accent, almost an afterthought.

I glanced up at her in surprise and she grinned. The black-and-white photograph showed eight young women in coveralls. Some wore caps with goggles perched on top. Two wore leather jackets. Behind them was an old airplane with propellers, bigger and more substantial than the plane that had gone down on the Fourth.

"Ever hear of the WASP?" she asked.

"Were they like the WACs?" I said.

"And the WAVES," Moses put in.

Toots nodded. "They were and they weren't. They never became part of the military — they remained civilian. Didn't even receive military benefits until more than thirty years after they were disbanded. Well, I should say 'we,' not 'they.'"

She sat down on a nearby hassock, but perched on the edge, knees apart, hands resting lightly on her thighs.

I looked at the photograph again and ran my finger across the line of laughing faces. I stopped on the fifth one. "You were a WASP," I said. Sometimes stating the obvious can keep a conversation going, as we trained detectives know.

"Yep, that's me — a member of the Women Airforce Service

Pilots. For God and country, and mostly because I was just crazy to fly. All the girls were like that. The lucky ones among us would have puttered our lives away in Piper Cubs, while the unlucky ones would've spent our lives dreaming if it hadn't been for the war and Jackie Cochran."

"I remember her," Moses said. "She was kind of like Amelia Earhart, wasn't she?"

"She was famous enough to have some clout," Toots said. She stood, picked up a photo album that was lying on an end table, and came toward us. "Scoot over," she said to Moses, nudging his foot with hers. He scooted.

She opened the album. "Of course, before the WASP there was the WAFs, the ferry service. Nancy Love started that. Then Cochran wrote to Eleanor Roosevelt and had a talk with General Arnold, and the WASP was born." She was flipping through the album. "Here," she said, and pointed to a picture featuring an attractive light-haired woman in a military uniform. "That's Cochran."

She leaned toward Moses and lowered her voice. "They couldn't stand each other, Cochran and Love, but that's another story."

She straightened. "Anyway, women from all over the country got to Sweetwater, Texas, any way they could, just for a chance to fly things they never dreamed they could fly."

"So, wait," I said. "They were pilots already or they weren't?"

"In the beginning, you had to have seventy hours of flight time going in. They kept lowering that, just like they lowered the minimum age requirement. It was thirty-five hours when I joined. But Cochran never wanted to start from scratch, with girls who thought they wanted to fly only to throw up all over the cockpit their first time up."

"But how did they get the training?" Moses asked. "And the flight time? Seventy hours seems like a lot for a woman pilot. I'm thinking of the Tuskegee Airman and what those guys went through to become pilots."

She turned to him. "Say, those fellas were terrific! They came through Harlingen once, flying B-25s. You know, they had to be perfect gentlemen, because everybody was watching them, just like Cochran wanted us to be perfect ladies for the same reason." She laughed. "They were a hell of a lot closer to perfection than we were!" She shrugged. "Well, what did they expect? A lot of us lied about our flying time to get in and then padded the log. Or we stuffed ourselves for a week before the physical to get our weight up. Or sat in the waiting room eating bananas. This one little gal I knew, her mother was a beautician and rigged up some kind of thing to lift up her hair and make her taller, so she just barely made the height requirement."

I scanned the photographs in the album, open on her lap. "Were there any Black WASPs?" I asked.

She turned to me. "No, there weren't. The Armed Forces weren't integrated at the time, Cat, you know, and we were Army in almost every way but the most important one. What I heard was that Cochran might've been willing, but she had too many other battles to fight. And, of course, Sweetwater was the South and a lot of the bases we'd be assigned to were in the South."

"But —." I picked up the original group shot again and put my finger on a face with Asian features. Surely not Japanese, I thought; there were no flight schools in relocation camps.

"That's Esther Chang," she said. "Her parents were Chinese. She'd actually tried to join the Chinese air force with some other young people a few years before Cochran created the WASP. The Chinese didn't want any girls. But Cochran did. Well, Cochran made her stay in school then, so she came later with my class."

It seemed as good a time as any to get out my notebook and start compiling a scorecard.

"I still want to know how the women became pilots in the first place," Moses said.

"Oh, yes. Now some of them took private lessons at local airports — you know, just saving up whatever they could from their paychecks and maybe flying on their lunch hours. But a lot of them had come through this government program, the Civilian Pilot Training Program, you could get into if you were in college, even in junior college." She shook her head. "I don't think the government started out to train women pilots, but then they made this rule that every flight class of ten had to take one woman and lots of those women became WASP.

"Anyway, so everybody did their basic at Avenger — that was the airfield at Sweetwater, Avenger Field — then after graduation, you either went on assignment or you took another training course somewhere else. I went to B-26 school in Dodge City, along with Chub Davenport, Maddy Vincent, Squeak Eckels, Bernie McLenahan, Esther, and four other girls from our class. We were 43-W-9. That means we were the ninth women's class in forty-three. After Dodge City, five of us got sent to Harlingen to tow targets. Harlingen was a flexible gunnery school. They had four WASP already there — well, three, because Shorty left to get married. Two of them were from the class just ahead of us — Lou Zimmerman and Tommy Thompson. Tex Fairweather was 43-W-7."

Stretch appeared in the doorway, wiping her hands on a red rag that was now so stained with black that I couldn't tell if she was wiping grease on or off.

"I'm off to WDS for some more flux," she announced. "Anything else you need, boss?"

"Petroleum jelly," Toots said. "Better buy a big one." To us, she said, "Cheap lubricant."

"You got it," Stretch said and disappeared.

She was going to fly a Tinker Toy airplane held together by ponytail bands and lubricated with Vaseline? What was she going to run it on? Witch hazel?

"Does Stretch fly?" Moses asked when she'd gone.

"Stretch? Oh yes, she's very good."

"Do the parrots fly?" I asked, brushing crumbs from my fingertips. I was still a little unnerved by the way Orry had watched me eat my cookie.

"Oh, yes," Toots said. "There are no clipped wings in this household."

JULY 11, 1986

So far, I was enjoying the history lesson, but we still had a lot of years to cover between 1944 and 1986.

Toots crossed them in a bound.

"So, we have this reunion coming up next week, at the Dayton Air Show?" She glanced at me to see if I'd ever heard of the Dayton Air Show and I nodded. I didn't know what went on there, but I pictured it in my mind as a kind of giant cruise-in for airplane buffs, held annually at the Dayton Airport. I pictured people walking around, admiring the paint jobs on the planes and sticking their heads under the hood now and then. I thought probably I could cut a coupon off a grocery bag for a discount on admission, the way I could for the zoo and waterpark.

"It's not an official WASP reunion — the big one's in Sweetwater in September — but smaller groups sometimes arrange a meeting there," she explained. "Tex Fairweather will be flying one of the B-26s and Esther Chang and her daughter will be doing aerobatics."

I sneaked a look at Moses. Was he thinking the same thing I was? People our age were going to be flying bombers and turning airplanes upside down? That sounded dangerous. I hoped their vision was better than mine. And not just people, I thought, women. What was it like to have a hot flash at 10,000 feet?

Toots nodded at the group photograph. "Except for Tommy Thompson, who went down in forty-four, everybody who is in that photograph was going to be there."

"Went down?" I said.

"Was?" Moses said.

She didn't say anything for a few seconds. Then she said, "We've been an amazingly lucky group. Esther and Maddy survived cancer. Lou's lungs aren't so good — you can tell that by the way she has to stop and catch her breath. Squeak was walking with a cane last time I saw her. And Maddy — well, Maddy was an alcoholic and maybe there was something else wrong with her, too. But we were all alive and kicking a week ago."

"What happened?" I asked.

Toots frowned in concentration and looked down at her hands.

"It was late Friday night, two weeks ago — the weekend before last, June 27th. Actually, it was the 28th, I guess, because it was after midnight when the phone rang. I was still up, but barely. I guessed who it was before I picked up the phone: Maddy. She lived in Seattle — her husband had retired from Boeing before he passed away — and once she started drinking, she couldn't seem to remember that she was several dang time zones away from Ohio. We'd had some strange late-night conversations before, but that was the strangest. 'It's me,' she said, 'Maddy. Listen, I've been thinking, and I think it's high time we let everybody know what really happened to Ethel, don't you?' 'What happened to Ethel?' I said. I had other things on my mind right then. 'Yes, you know, about that boy she went off with.' Well, that confused me even more. I met my husband in instrument school when I went back to Sweetwater in the fall of forty-four, but we didn't get married until after the war."

She must have caught some bewilderment on our faces, because she interrupted herself. "Sorry, I forgot. You don't know. Ethel's *my* name. Toots was what my family called me and it stuck. Anyway, hardly anybody went by their real name at Avenger.

"So Maddy said, 'I've been sitting here all night, watching all the flag-waving and those bastards making speeches, and it makes me so mad till I can't see straight. I think we ought to celebrate the Fourth in a different way this year. We ought to tell what we know.'

"'Maddy,' I said at last, 'who do you think you're talking to? This is me, Toots. *I'm* Ethel. And I don't have any idea what you're talking about.' Well, then we went through one of those comedy routines, you know — where the sober fellow says, 'I'm John,' and the drunk says, 'Who is?' And like that, until the drunk says, 'John! Listen, I'm glad you called!' I knew that it was going to be funny in the morning, assuming I got enough sleep, but at the time it was just frustrating. Finally, I said, 'Maddy, I think you've got your wires crossed. Maybe you mean Evelyn' — that was Tommy Thompson — 'or Esther.' She could have meant anybody. She got so confused when she was drinking. Well, I shouldn't say that. It's not really fair. We had some CO's who couldn't keep it straight, either — like mothers who keep calling their kids by the wrong name. But luckily the CO's didn't have to use our first names much. Anyway, I said to Maddy, 'Why don't you go to bed and think it over, and when you figure out, you call me.' And that was about it. I doubted that she'd remember anything in the morning, not even who she called and what it was about. So I didn't think anything more about it.

"Well, the following Tuesday — that was the 1st — I called Lou Zimmerman about something to do with the reunion because Lou was organizing things. And Lou mentioned that she hadn't heard from Maddy, and I thought that was funny, because I knew that the reunion must have been on Maddy's mind when she called, though she hadn't actually mentioned it. So I called Maddy after I hung up from Lou and got her answering machine and left a message. And I called her that night a few times and couldn't reach her. The next morning when I called, her daughter answered the phone and told me that Maddy had passed away on Monday."

She paused and looked at me, as if noticing for the first time that I was furiously taking notes. "Am I going too fast?"

"Maddy called you early on Saturday morning, the 28th, and she died on Monday, the 30th, right?" I asked. "You found out on Wednesday. I got it."

"I don't know if that's ever happened to you." She looked from Moses to me. "Somebody dying like that, when you've just talked to them. I mean, God knows we all probably expected Maddy to drink herself to death, but not two doggone days after we'd spoken to her. But I finally got around to asking the daughter — Jeanine is her name — how her mother died. She said her mother fell down the basement stairs. And we left it at that. What was the point in saying what we both knew — that Maddy was probably drunk or hung over? She lived by herself — her husband died about six years ago. I should have guessed she'd have an accident or burn the house down."

She stood, picked up her glass of iced tea, which she'd neglected until now, and began turning it nervously in her hands.

"I thought, I'd better call Squeak," she said. "Squeak and Maddy flew together."

"You mean, like a copilot?" I asked.

She nodded. "Sort of, except you're really just flying partners. When you're towing targets in a B-26, you do what's called a Lazy Eight — you make a left pass and a right pass. One pilot makes the left and one makes the right." She demonstrated, sketching the figure in the air with an index finger. "Well, Wednesday night I couldn't reach Squeak. I didn't leave a message because I didn't want to leave that kind of message on an answering machine. On Thursday morning, someone picked up the phone at Squeak's house." She hunched her shoulders and hugged herself.

"It was like déjà vu. 'I'm sorry to have to tell you,' this woman said, 'but my aunt passed away yesterday.' 'Oh!' I said. I was so stunned I didn't say anything for the longest time, so the woman started talking about the funeral and all, until finally I got my breath back and I said, 'But honey, how did she die?' And she said, 'She took a fall down the basement stairs.'"

5

JULY 11, 1986

MY PEN FROZE IN MID-STROKE. I shivered. Moses shifted on the sofa beside me.

Toots was looking at us. "So tell me I'm crazy."

Abruptly, she set the glass down on the table and collapsed into a chair set at right angles to the couch. "I know what you're thinking — it's just a coincidence. That's what I keep telling myself. It's just a coincidence. Maddy was an alcoholic and Squeak had a gimpy leg." She raised her arms in an expressive shrug. "Why shouldn't they fall down the basement stairs? I've fallen a time or two myself and I don't have their handicaps. If it hadn't been for that phone call from Maddy, I would have just thought it was incredibly strange that two old flying partners died the same way within a few days of each other — almost like twins, you know? How they say twins have the same experiences?"

I nodded.

"Did they keep in touch?" Moses asked. "Maddy and, uh, Squeak." He pronounced the names awkwardly. As a trained cop, he would have preferred to use last names, but he didn't have the cast list in front of him. "Were they close after they left the WASPs?"

"Well, closer than to anybody else in our group," Toots said, "but it's not like they talked all the time, no. Squeak lived in Florida and, like I said, Maddy lived in Seattle. See, how it worked was this." She began to count on her fingers. "Eight WASP means two flights, so they could train gunners around the clock, day and night. Before we came, there were only four WASP, but Shorty left to get married, so they needed five more to make up two flights, two planes to a flight. You usually flew with the same gal, so you were closest to her. Then you were close to the girls in your flight, because the other flight was sleeping while you were working. When we had time off, all eight of us might do something together, but it was wartime, so that didn't happen very often. And of course, we'd all been at Avenger together."

"Who was your flying partner?" I asked.

"Up until almost the end, it was Tommy Thompson." She leaned forward, plucked a loose photograph wedged between the pages of the open album, and handed me a photograph of a grinning brunette, dark hair parted in the middle and tucked behind her ears and a glint of mischief in her eyes. She was wearing pants, a leather jacket, and lace-up shoes. One foot rested on the wheel of a double-winged plane, a relative of the one Toots was building. I passed it to Moses.

"Why 'almost the end'?" he asked.

"She disappeared in December of forty-four. She was flying to Avenger from Harlingen for the last WASP graduation, and she just disappeared." She took the photo back from Moses and studied it with sad eyes. "The weather was bad, it was night. We thought maybe something went wrong with her navigational equipment and she couldn't see where she was and went down in the Gulf of Mexico. They looked for her, but they never found anything. Not a trace."

"How could she have flown over the coastline and not been spotted?" Moses asked.

I wasn't sure what he meant, but Toots knew and nodded. "Well, that was the big question, wasn't it? All air traffic within twenty miles of the coastline was supposed to be monitored. She was going out, not coming in, and she was in a military plane, a PT, but still she should have been spotted by somebody. But like I said, it was a bad night for flying."

"So Maddy and Squeak," I said. I wanted to get back to something I understood, like personal relationships. "They were in your flight?"

"Yes."

"That means —."

She nodded. "I'm the only one left."

"Do you feel like you're in danger?" I asked. Moses could have asked this question. He has more respect for feelings — what people sense but can't prove — than most men and most cops. But it sounded more natural coming from me.

Toots turned an unblinking gaze on me. "I just don't know. I can't imagine why. Maddy died on the 30th and Squeak died on the 2nd. On the 4th, I had to make an emergency landing because my plane was sabotaged. Before that happened, I sure didn't feel threatened. Now I don't know what to think." She sat back in her chair. "I guess that's what I want you to find out. The Seattle cops and the Fort Lauderdale cops have no reason to talk to each other. But you can talk to both of them and find out things I probably can't find out."

"So you want to know if the two deaths are connected," Moses said.

"And if they are, if they're connected to your engine failure," I said. "And if so, whether anybody else is in danger."

"You'd obviously like to know sooner rather than later," Moses said.

"Preferably before the reunion," I said, "which gives us a week."

She grinned at us. "Did anybody ever tell you that you two are so cute together?"

Moses and I exchanged a look. "Anybody ever tell you," he said, "that you looked cute in a WASP uniform?"

She laughed. "All the time, Moses, all the time."

6

JULY 11, 1986

"You don't expect to find anything, do you?" I asked Moses.

We were sitting in Arnold's, eating dinner and making plans. Arnold's was the oldest continuously operating bar in Cincinnati and drew a mixed clientele that included city council members and neighborhood artists. Kevin tended bar here, which explained where he got his encyclopedic knowledge of city politics and social gossip. Behind us there was a large, raucous group of sweaty middle-aged men in shorts and matching T-shirts making up for whatever calories they'd burned on the softball field. The shirts said "Pete's Tow 'n Go" on the back and featured a picture of a brawny truck towing a small car and looking like Captain Ahab with a minnow on the line.

Moses shook his head. "It's like she said — two old ladies fell down the stairs. It could happen any time — especially if one of 'em's drunk and the other has a game leg. The rest is just coincidence. I ain't going to speculate about her engine failure, but the National Transportation Safety Board will be working on that one. If there was sabotage involved — and that's a big 'if' — she probably just ticked off somebody at the airport."

"But we're going to investigate anyway 'cause we said we would."

"Sure." He took a bite from his hamburger, chewed, and swallowed. "We'll make a few phone calls."

This was good news to me, but I thought I'd better check to make sure. "We won't need to go look at the scenes."

"You going to eat that pickle?" His hand was already halfway to my plate and I shoved it in his direction. "Nah, I expect we can do all we need to do over the phone, unless the local cops got any suspicions."

I nodded and shook some more salt onto my French fries. I thought salt got a bad rap it didn't deserve and ignored any articles to the contrary offered to me by my daughter Franny, who subscribed to publications like *Mother Earth* and *Natural Health News.*

Moses watched me, eyes narrowed. "'Course, if the local cops do have suspicions, then we might need to run out there."

I knew running was not what he had in mind. I dragged a fry through a scattering of salt crystals.

"You got any problem with that?"

I didn't answer.

"You're not afraid to fly, are you?"

I don't know where he got the impression that I was afraid to fly, unless it had suddenly dawned on him that in the two years he'd known me, I hadn't flown once.

I could hear laughter and the dull clunk of beer mugs colliding behind me as Moses set down his burger.

"You're afraid to fly."

I looked up at him. "Let's just say, I'd rather have all my teeth pulled by a closet psychoanalyst while Barry Manilow sings in the background and the nurse gives an account of her favorite soap operas."

"I don't believe it, Cat! You ain't no shrinking violet. And besides, flying is safer than driving. If you compare the fatality rates —."

I held up a hand. "Do not use the f-word in a discussion about flying, if you don't mind. And while we're at it, the t-word is off limits, too."

That stopped him for a few beats while he tried to work it out. When his brow smoothed again, he said, "Now, Cat, if you just understood the aerodynamics of it —."

"Let's leave aerodynamics out of it," I said testily. "My stomach doesn't understand aerodynamics."

"See, when you get turbulence," he said, ignoring me and raising a hand, palm down, to demonstrate, "it's just like driving on a bumpy road." The hand wobbled. "It means that there's some holes in the road, it don't mean the road's disappeared."

"Hi, kids!" Kevin had chosen this moment to appear at our table, and since he was carrying two full mugs of beer, he was welcome. He set the beers down and took a chair. "Are we working on a new secret handshake?"

"No, I'm just explaining to Cat how planes fly," Moses said, abandoning the plane and reaching for the mug. "Did you know she was afraid to fly?"

Of course, Kevin knew it. No secret worth worming out was wormproof where Kevin was concerned.

Kevin winked at me. "Any reasonable person is afraid to fly, Moses. Getting locked into a tin can defying gravity at thousands of feet in the air with who-knows-what kind of bozo behind the wheel and enough flammable liquid aboard to burn down the Yellowstone National Forest. I call that scary, don't you? I mean, who knows what kind of day the pilot is having? Or whether he's the macho, ex-military type who welcomes the challenge of flying a 747 through rough weather."

"Yeah, but Kevin —," Moses began and the hand-plane came up again.

"And don't even get me started on the air traffic control system," Kevin persisted. "Do you really believe that in five years we've made up for all of those controllers Reagan fired? You read stories all the time about how much overtime those guys are putting in. And the mechanics? What if one of those guys is going through a messy divorce and has his mind on his wife's new boyfriend instead of the whatsis he's supposed to be tightening the screws on? You ever think about that?"

"You're a big help," Moses complained. The hand had gone back to the beer mug. "Anyway, you fly."

"Sure I do, but I don't enjoy it."

"All I'm saying is that planes just don't fall out of the sky," Moses said. "Even in turbulence, they're riding air currents, and the air currents don't go away. I don't think Cat understands that."

Kevin turned to me. "He's right, Mrs. C. Planes don't usually fall out of the sky. They crash on takeoff or landing, before the air currents get them up high enough." He flattened his palm against the tabletop, angled it up, lifted it off, bounced it a few times, cleared the edge of my plate, then crashed his fingertips into my French fries. "Do you mind?" He snagged a French fry and stood up. "I'd love to chat more, but I've got to go back to work."

Moses glowered at his back. Then he turned to me. "See, all I'm saying is that the principles of physics —."

I held up my own hand, palm facing down. "Forget it, Moses. Call it a phobia, okay? I'm not saying it's rational, although it's just as rational as your fear of taking me to the shooting range."

He opened his mouth to protest, then couldn't think what to say — or maybe he just couldn't think of anything to say that wouldn't end our partnership and put him out on the street with only his Barcalounger and his beagle for consolation. The softball players were singing, loudly and off-key.

"The point is, what are we doing tomorrow?" I said.

"Okay. How about if I call Seattle and you call Fort Lauderdale?"

"Suits me."

"Fine."

On our way out, Kevin waved us over to the bar. He had to shout to be heard.

"If you see Leon, tell him I like the one with the beagle puppy in the deerstalker hat — I think it's adorable — but it may not be quite the image you want to project."

"What?" I shouted back. Leon Jakes was a neighborhood business entrepreneur, whose mild retardation didn't explain his attachment to the most insipid line of greeting cards and stationery that a teenage salesman ever succeeded in foisting off on a gullible public.

"Your business cards," he said. "Tell him to save that one for the birthday cards."

7

JULY 14, 1986

Of course, the cop I needed to talk to was off for the weekend, so I didn't reach her until Monday. By then, Moses had already talked to the Seattle police and hadn't come up with anything.

"Blood alcohol level was high enough to make the accident plausible," he'd told me. "She died in the early afternoon, probably not on impact but not too long afterwards. There's nothing to suggest homicide — no bruising to suggest that she was pushed or struck."

"But there wouldn't have to be, right?" I asked.

"There wouldn't have to be. You wouldn't need to push that hard if she was already standing at the top of the stairs, especially if she was drunk and confused. But it doesn't seem very likely, Cat."

So I wasn't expecting much when I finally reached Detective Vasquez.

She was still talking to someone else as she picked up the phone.

"— Ask him again and this time, don't take no for an answer," she was saying. Into the phone she said, "Yes. Vasquez."

I introduced myself and explained briefly that I was a private investigator who'd been asked to look into the coincidental deaths of two women who knew each other and who had both died in falls only days apart. I'd been referred to her.

"What's the name?" she asked. She sounded neutral, neither interested nor annoyed.

"Betty Ellerman. Elizabeth Ellerman." I doubted she'd gone by "Squeak" in Fort Lauderdale senior social circles, but you never knew.

"Oh, yes. She fell down the basement stairs and broke her neck."

"So I heard." I waited.

She waited.

I cracked first. "And that's all there was to it?"

"She walked with a cane. We found the cane nearby. She wasn't too steady on her feet."

"So I gathered."

She said nothing.

"So tell me this," I said at last. "Who has basements in Florida? I mean, aren't you people practically at sea level? How can anyone have a basement?

"Mrs. Ellerman lived in a condo that was built on stilts, with the parking area below the house — kind of a combination garage and basement. There was a storage room adjoining the parking area, with a door at that level and interior stairs going up to the main part of the house, as well as stairs outside."

"A woman who walked with a cane lived in a condo with stairs to the front door?"

"When she became disabled, she had a small elevator put in from the garage to the living room."

"So what was in this storage room?"

"Tell me again why you're interested in this case." I found it an interesting response and wondered if I'd hit on the right question.

So I explained at somewhat greater length about the WASP connection and the woman from Seattle who had been Betty's flying partner and who had died of the same cause as Betty two days before Betty had died.

"The other woman died in Seattle, you say?" Vasquez said.

"Yes, Seattle." As in, about as far away as you could get from

Florida without leaving the country. But we were dealing with pilots.

"And the person who hired you is who?" Vasquez asked.

"She was the fourth member of this WASP flight based at Harlingen, Texas, during the war. She'd received a strange phone call from Maddy — that's Betty's flying partner — a few weeks before Maddy died."

"What do the Seattle police say?"

"They say that Maddy's blood alcohol level supports the coroner's conclusion that Maddy's death was an accident."

"Uh-huh."

"So what was in the storage room?"

"Nothing much. Just some old boxes and a trunk full of stuff that her daughter said her mother hadn't looked at in years."

"What kind of stuff? Did any of it have anything to do with the WASP?"

"Could be," she admitted. "If there was a reunion coming up, as you say, and if her old flying partner had called her to ask if she was going, that could explain why she opened the basement door to begin with. Maybe she wanted to find her old uniform — try it on and see if it still fit."

"Was there a uniform?"

"There was. A dress uniform and a jacket and a jumpsuit — you know, a one-piece thing like the coveralls mechanics wear."

"When you say 'why she opened the basement door to begin with —.'" I was groping here, but there was something in her voice. "Was that bothering you? I mean, it sounds like you didn't know what she was doing there."

She sighed. "According to her daughter, she kept the upstairs basement door deadbolted. For whatever reason, she didn't have much of a lock on the downstairs basement door — the one to the garage. So the upstairs deadbolt was supposed to keep out intruders who came in through the garage."

"Which means she didn't keep anything in the basement she considered valuable enough to attract thieves."

"Apparently not."

"And you'd like to know why she unlocked the upstairs door in the first place."

"Maybe you just gave me the answer to that question."

"Except that she usually used an elevator, you said."

"Except that, yes."

I persisted. "Was that your only question?"

There was a pause and then she said, "No, there were others, but they don't add up to much."

"Can you tell me what the others were?"

"I can, but I don't want you to go back and tell your client that Mrs. Ellerman was murdered. That's highly unlikely. In fact, the odds are staggeringly high that the deaths of your client's two old friends were a coincidence. It's an interesting coincidence, I'll admit, but stranger things have happened."

"I understand that," I assured her. "Look, we're not trying to sell the client an expensive security system or anything like that. We're a small, two-person partnership and we don't expect to find anything that warrants further investigation. Okay?"

"Okay."

"So your other questions?"

"Okay. Someone had looked through the boxes and trunk. Recently."

"Not Betty?" I asked in surprise.

"It could have been Betty," she said. "Whoever it was wore gloves, but that might have been because the boxes were so dusty and even mildewed."

"Tell me more about what was in them."

"The usual collection of old letters, diaries, photographs, clothes, memorabilia — probably the kind of stuff you've got stashed in your attic or basement."

She was wrong about that. Nowhere in my basement would you find a set of aviator's wings.

"So the only fingerprints were Betty's, but there were other marks in the dust that suggested someone had searched the boxes wearing gloves," I said.

"That's right. But Betty's fingerprints were old, which tends to confirm what her daughter said about how often she looked at the stuff in the basement. The other marks were new — no dust."

"What time of day did Betty die?"

"The coroner estimates late morning, sometime between ten and twelve. She hadn't eaten lunch."

"And Betty wasn't wearing gloves when she died, so even if she'd been downstairs earlier in the day, which could have explained the marks you found, she should have been wearing or at least carrying gloves if she was going down to look to the boxes again. But I'm guessing you didn't find any gloves anywhere in the house that looked like they'd been used on dusty boxes."

"Right," Vasquez agreed, "although she could have used and discarded them the day before, which was the day of her regular trash pickup. We can't be that precise about when the marks were made."

"And she had dust on her clothes, some or all of which could be explained by the fall."

"Right."

"And your other questions?"

"Just one. A neighbor saw a car parked in Betty's driveway at around ten o'clock that morning. We haven't been able to locate or identify the car or the driver."

"Did the neighbor see the driver?"

"Nope. Just caught a glimpse of the car. The houses are pretty far apart on that road."

"What kind of car?"

"White, mid-sized — that's all we know. Probably the most common type of car on the road. Common rental car, too. Fort Lauderdale rental agencies had a fleet of 'em rented out the day Ms. Ellerman died. We didn't even bother to check Miami."

Vasquez was a smart, careful investigator.

"Nobody else saw anything? Then or later?"

"It's not a very heavily populated road."

"But it bothers you. The car, I mean."

"On a scale of one to ten, about three."

"Given the Seattle case, you wouldn't care to bump that up a notch, would you?"

"Sorry, no." Her voice was definite.

I thought. "I wonder if you'd be willing to do two things, though," I said.

"If you're going to ask me to find out whether the search focused on WASP memorabilia, I'm already going to do that. In my spare time, you understand. I can't justify a homicide investigation. But even if the answer is yes, that won't necessarily get us anywhere."

"I know. But would you also check her phone records?"

"To determine what? That her old friend Maddy had called her? What would that tell us?"

"Not much," I admitted. "But it just might suggest that the two deaths were connected, don't you think?"

"Well," she conceded at last, "it might just make your coincidence even more coincidental."

8

JULY 14, 1986

I FOUND Toots and Stretch standing over a worktable improvised from an old door and two sawhorses. Both were attired in their preferred workclothes — a coverall for Toots and overalls for Stretch. The table had been set up outside the shed under some trees. Before them was a narrow wing-shaped wooden frame, too small to be an actual wing of the structure I could see through the open shed door. To one side of the small frame, an amber-colored jar weighed down a large piece of paper, the fold marks of which I could see when the breeze lifted the page. The same breeze ruffled Stretch's dark curls and brought me the heady scent of glue. Stretch held a steel file, its tip resting on the page as if marking her place.

I wondered how many steps it took to build an airplane and which step they were on now. From the looks of things, I'd have said that they had a few hundred steps to go. But then, I've never taken up sewing in spite of my mother's best efforts and a year of high school Home Ec because I had no visual imagination when it came to putting parts together to make a whole. Don't ask me why I thought I could overcome this deficiency to take up detective work, but I thought it had something to do with the less physical nature of the parts I needed to assemble in an investigation.

I told Toots what Vasquez had said about Betty's basement —

that someone had gone through boxes of stored papers and memorabilia. I asked her where she kept her own collection of WASP mementos and papers. When she told me that most of her WASP material was stored, as Squeak's had been, in the basement, I asked whether the basement could be entered from outside the house.

Toots sounded bewildered. "Yes, it can, though I hardly use that door anymore. But why would somebody be looking at that stuff? It's ancient history. Nobody's interested in that old stuff."

"I am," Stretch said quickly.

Toots grinned at her. "Stretch, I don't know how to tell you this, but you're hardly the man in the street, if you know what I mean."

"That's beside the point," Stretch said. "Lots of women are interested in women's history these days." She pointed her file at Toots. "That's why I keep telling you to put it someplace safe."

"Safe from what?" Toots asked. "You think we're going to be murdered in our beds because some desperados broke in one night to steal my Avenger flight log?"

"Listen to Cat," Stretch said, nodding in my direction. "Some of that stuff could be valuable. You don't know what some rich collectors might pay for it."

"You're right, I don't," Toots conceded. "Can't imagine. Especially since they didn't find it, if they looked through everything and left the whole shooting match behind. Cat says that Squeak's WASP stuff was still there, and I know mine is because I saw it down there yesterday."

"You don't know that," Stretch insisted. "Maybe they took something."

"But what on earth would they be looking for? They're welcome to my song lyrics, my overseas cap, my dog tags, my broken seatbelt, even my little vial of sand from Avenger Beach — the stretch between the barracks where we used to sunbathe. God only knows why I kept that. I wish they would take my letters home — I sound so young and naïve!"

"But those are all valuable artifacts!" Stretch's voice rose in apparent exasperation.

"To whom?" Toots spread her arms wide.

To my surprise, Stretch threw down the file, turned on her heel, and stalked off. She left me wondering why she so obviously cared about the WASP memorabilia. Was she the rare young person who really valued her roots? A latter-day aviatrix who was obsessed with her predecessors?

Toots turned to me with an elaborate shrug. "Kid takes things too seriously. What I've got is a bunch of junk that I would have thrown out ages ago if my mother hadn't stashed my footlocker in her attic for thirty years. Some of it means something to me, I guess, but to anybody else, it's trash. Well, that's how I look at it. I guess some of the gals are on a museum kick — Lou tells me to save all that junk in case they build a WASP museum someday. Honestly, I'd be too embarrassed! And I can't imagine charging somebody admission to gawk at my old uniform or my diary in a glass case."

I ignored this assessment. "How's the lock on your basement door?"

"If you mean the outside door, there isn't any. Well, there is one, but it hasn't worked for years. The wood swelled up so the door doesn't fit very well anymore. We always figured if anybody was that desperate for a garden rake or a box of nails they could have 'em."

"You don't have any power tools down there?"

"I have some, but the best ones are out here in the shed now. What's left in the basement might interest an antiques dealer, but that's about it. I'm not sure I'd even notice if something had been stolen."

"But you do have boxes of WASP stuff down there? Your uniform, for example?"

"Most of my photographs are in albums in the living room and my uniforms are up in the attic. The basement is pretty damp. I do have an old footlocker down there and it keeps things pretty dry. Like I said, I think there's still some flight logs and letters and stuff inside."

"Can we go down and take a look and see if anything looks like it's been disturbed?"

She agreed and soon I was squatting on a cracked basement floor, inhaling the earthy scent of mold mingled with the faint odor of paint thinner and brushing cobwebs out of my hair. What we had here was your typical Cincinnati-area basement, built over an underground river. Waterproof paint was peeling off the walls in large patches that resembled jigsaw puzzle pieces. Over the decades, dozens of cans of paint had accumulated here and were slowly rusting on rotting shelves, surrounded by piles of miscellaneous bricks, tiles, and stones, old storm windows and shutters, lengths of pipe and other detritus whose original function was now disguised by layers of rust and mold and dust. From an insect's point of view, the room was a booming metropolis. In the stillness, you could practically hear the mice holding their breaths.

Toots rested her fists on her hips and surveyed the room. "Well, all I can say is, if somebody was in here, the least he could've done was to steal some of that paint." She turned to me. "I'd like to tell you that somebody's wrecked the place, but I'm afraid it always looks like this."

Assisting us in our inquiries was an elderly gray terrier named Willie, who probably slept most of the time and had roused herself for the rare prospect of a visit to the basement. She had not been in evidence during my previous visit and I wished she weren't in evidence now. Apparently, her eyesight was poor, because she kept bumping into things and then barking at them as if they been lying in wait to spring upon her when she wasn't looking. She made little pawprints in the dust on the floor.

I sighed. "Hand me that flashlight, will you?" I was wearing an old pair of khakis and a T-shirt Kevin had loaned me. It was one of his Reaganomics collection and showed planes crashing into each other. The print read, "It's Departure Time. Do You Know Where Your Air Traffic Controllers Are?" "For inspiration, Mrs. C," he'd said, "on your case."

"If I get stuck down here, just call the rescue squad," I said. I put one latex-covered hand on the filthy cement and lowered my torso. "If you could just keep Willie from —."

But it was too late. By the time I laid my cheek against the back of my hand for a floor-level view, Willie was breathing the warm scent of dog biscuits into my face. I switched on the flashlight but all I could see was dog.

"I'll get her," Toots said, but as she lunged, Willie dashed off. When my vision cleared, what I saw was a retreating dog rump and lots of little pawprints in the dust. I shined the flashlight on the area just in front of the outside door. And saw footprints.

I pushed myself up to a sitting position and swiped at my cheek with one sleeve. Toots had collared Willie, who was barking furiously. She was dragging the dog in the direction of a washer and dryer, which looked pristine and out of place, huddled in an island of tidiness at the bottom of the stairs. I pushed off again, ignoring objections from my back, and got stiffly to my feet.

I skirted the area Willie had already disturbed and made my way along the wall. I knelt by the door. There must be some high-tech way cops had to show up the outlines of footprints in dust. If so, I'd put it on my Christmas list. I knelt down.

"What size shoe do you wear?" I asked.

When I looked up, she was clipping a leash onto Willie's collar over the dog's vociferous protests. The other end was wrapped around a post.

"Eight. But I haven't been near that door in years, Cat."

"How long ago did your husband die?"

"Let's see. It was six — no, seven years ago in August. That is, it will be seven years in August."

These footprints weren't seven years old.

"Do your kids visit? You have kids, right?"

"Sure, they come to town from time to time. But I can't imagine why any of them would open that outside door to get in here."

"Let's ask Stretch if she's been down here," I said.

"I haven't." Stretch's voice came from halfway down the stairs. "No reason to."

"Not at all?" I let my surprise show. I thought she seemed a little defensive. "You've never been in the basement before?"

"Well, sure," she conceded. She descended the stairs and turned in my direction.

"Watch your head!" Toots called out.

Once again, it was too late. We heard a thud and Stretch's exclamation, "Ow!"

"Oh, golly!" Toots said. "This basement wasn't made for tall people." She hurried over to Stretch and put her arm around the other woman's shoulder. Stretch was rubbing her forehead. "I ought to do something about that low beam — put flashing lights on it or something. Someday I'm going to get sued by a plumber or electrician. How bad's the damage, kiddo?"

"I'll live," Stretch said. Willie was doing her part for the cause by pawing Stretch's pantleg and yipping.

"Golly, I think you're going to have a bump in the same place as last time. That's the curse of being tall. Let me get you some ice," Toots offered, and when Stretch didn't object, headed upstairs to the kitchen.

Stretch crossed the floor to where I was kneeling.

"So you have been down here?" I asked.

"I've used the washer and dryer." She probed her forehead gingerly.

"Did you know that Toots stored some of her WASP memorabilia down here?"

Stretch shrugged. "She told me, yes, when she showed me the albums she keeps upstairs. She promised to show me the rest sometime, but we haven't gotten around to it. I told her that she shouldn't let stuff like that rot in some basement footlocker. It should be preserved. I can't seem to convince her that it's important historical material, especially now, when they're talking about this museum project. Maybe you can help."

I looked around and spotted an olive drab footlocker up against one wall. Four cardboard boxes, moldy and water-stained, sat next to it, topped by what looked like an old shower curtain that had once been aqua, a color favored in the sixties. A glance told me that whoever had been down here recently had focused his or her attention on this particular group of objects because the dust had been disturbed in a wide area in front of it. I glanced at Stretch's feet. She wore sneakers — long, narrow ones. I felt her eyes on me.

"So you knew that the WASP memorabilia was stored in a foot-locker," I said. "Have you noticed it before, when you were down here doing laundry?"

I wondered exactly what the arrangement was between the plane-building partners. Was Stretch actually living in the house? How had they met? Had they been friends before?

Stretch stepped closer. "Yeah, okay," she said. "I noticed it and guessed what it was. It looks like a military footlocker. I came over here one day to get a closer look — and bumped my head then, too, in case you're wondering. But I didn't open it and look inside, if that's what you want to know. I do want to see what's in it. I'm interested, that's all. But I can wait until Toots shows it to me."

I sat back on my heels. "Do you know why she hired me?" My quiet voice matched her own.

She nodded. "Two women who served with her at Harlingen died recently within a few days of each other and in the same way. She wants to know if the deaths are connected. Do you think they are? Do you think Toots is in danger?"

The concern in her voice seemed genuine, but she seemed to me an intense young woman and I hadn't yet identified the epicenter of that intensity. "Help me up," I said, holding out my hand. She boosted me to my feet with so much power that I damn near hit my head on a joist. I couldn't repress a grunt as my joints unlocked. "I don't know if the deaths are connected or not. My partner doesn't think so. I'd feel more inclined to share his optimism if I hadn't just seen a trail of footprints from the outside door to that damned footlocker."

Willie's capers had disturbed any other patterns I might have been able to see before, but the trail was definitely there. If there had been an intruder, it had been a woman with big feet or a man. As far as I could tell, there had been no dog except Willie, unless it was a dog with Willie-sized feet.

"I don't like this, Cat," Toots said behind us. She handed Stretch a lumpy towel, which Stretch pressed to her forehead. "Are you going to tell me that if I'd heard a noise down here and come to investigate, I'd be dead, to?"

I shook my head. "It's more complicated than that," I said. "If you'd come down to investigate you wouldn't have had somebody behind you to push you down the basement stairs."

"I see what you mean," she said. "So maybe they fell just because they were frightened. You know, like they heard something and they were scared, and that made them even less steady than usual. So they fell."

I wiped my gloved hands, black with dust and basement crud, on the seat of my pants and advanced toward the footlocker. "Is that what you'd do if you heard a suspicious noise in the basement? Unbolt the door and come down here?"

"I might," she said slowly, "but I'd bring a shotgun with me."

"And you think Squeak and Maddy would do the same?"

She considered. "Maddy would, no question. She might just grab the nearest Jack Daniels bottle and charge down there like she had a shotgun. In the old days, Squeak would've done the same." She folded her arms and leaned against the post that held Willie in check. "You have to understand, Cat. The kind of women who joined the WASP — well, we were used to doing things for ourselves. We weren't used to depending on men to take care of us. We had to depend on some men, of course, like the mechanics. But even then, you never knew whether the mechanic who serviced your plane was an NB — a nonbeliever, a man who thought women had no business flying. So we learned to take our pre-flights seriously — a heck of a lot more seriously than the cadets ever did.

"You asked what I'd do if I heard a noise." She shrugged. "I guess a lot of women would call the cops. But I honestly don't think that's the first thing that would occur to me. What if they came and found a squirrel running around down there? I'd die of embarrassment! What would you do?"

"Well, I live with an ex-cop," I pointed out. "Usually, I ignore all noises. With three cats and a dog in the house, I can't afford to be jumpy." I didn't tell her that the last time I'd investigated a noise in the basement, it had turned out to be three runaway children. But she was right. It hadn't occurred to me to call the cops.

"Well, Squeak might have felt differently once she couldn't get around so well. But somehow, I doubt it. When I think back on the risks we took when we were flying for the WASP, I can hardly believe it myself. But we didn't think about it." She shook her head. "Sometimes I think that all it took to be a WASP was stubbornness and a lack of imagination."

That was one way to put it, I guessed. And Moses would say that when it comes to flying, I have an overactive imagination. But you don't need an imagination if one of your cohort has just gone down, as Tommy Thompson had. I thought Toots was soft-pedaling the courage involved.

"That's funny," Toots said. "I could've sworn those boxes were stacked on top of the footlocker."

I squatted down and shined the flashlight on top of the foot-locker. The dust had been disturbed and in several places on the locker I could see four long parallel marks the size and shape of fingers.

"Come take a look."

Willie had finally subsided and flopped down in what terriers must regard as the "ready position." When Toots and Stretch moved, she stood up and gave a hopeful bark, but when they ignored her, she lowered her belly to the floor again.

Both women bent down and squinted at the marks. "I just don't get it, Cat," Toots said, shaking her head. "What on earth could they be looking for?"

"You tell me. Do you have anything in here that somebody might consider valuable — to someone other than a historian or archivist, that is?"

"Like what? A map to a buried treasure that says 'X marks the spot'? Cat, do you have any idea what our pay scale was like? We practically paid Uncle Sam for the privilege of flying his planes and letting kids shoot at us."

"Okay, how about something that somebody might consider threatening to them?"

"Like what?"

"I don't know," I admitted. I thought about wartime. "Suspicions that somebody was an enemy agent? Anything like that?" It sounded lame to me and Toots looked doubtful.

"There were instances of sabotage. Some of it was proven, some wasn't, but I don't remember a case when I knew who'd done it. German POWs worked at some bases, but not at ours. When things went wrong, unless a line had been cut or crossed, you never knew but what the gremlins hadn't gotten you. Either that, or the mechanics were careless, which amounted to the same thing."

"Gremlins?"

She nodded. "We blamed the gremlins for most things that went wrong. Oh, if your seatbelt suddenly came unfastened when you were flying upside down, or if the landing gear stuck for no apparent reason, or the radio went out, or you undershot the runway, we said it was the gremlins. That's why our mascot, Fifinella, was a gremlin — a good gremlin. Here, I'll show you." She reached out to open the lid. "Can I open this now?"

"Sure, whoever was here wore gloves anyway."

Stretch and I moved the boxes aside and I was glad I was wearing gloves. In a dust-free rectangular space on top of the footlocker, a name had been stenciled: Harold E. McGruder.

"Your husband?" I asked.

She nodded. "Some of his stuff is in here, too — mostly letters he wrote to me and letters he wrote to his mother."

"Weren't the WASPs issued a standard footlocker?" I was wondering how easy it would be to pick out a stash of WASP memorabilia in the average basement or attic.

She shook her head. "Just a B-4 bag — a canvas bag for RONs — remain overnights. Also a purse that was one of the first shoulder bags available."

The lid creaked on rusty hinges. Inside, I saw mostly papers, books, and a couple of scrapbooks or photo albums. Lying on top were folded papers that looked like letters. They weren't in neat piles, but neither were they scattered randomly and I could see the broken fragments of rubber band that had once held them together. There were also some scraps of fabric, something that looked like a broken strap, an old canteen, a pair of goggles, a cap like a bathing cap, a bedraggled teddy bear wearing wings pinned to his chest and a small pouch strapped to his back, a rusty pocketknife, dull with age, and a few other objects I couldn't identify.

"Jeepers!" Toots said, gently lifting the bear in both hands and studying him. "I wondered where you'd got to." She turned him so that we could see. "Fifi."

The flying bear was a her, not a him. I was going to have to monitor my assumptions.

"Does anything look disturbed?" I asked her.

"It's hard to tell, isn't it?" she said, squatting next to me. "If somebody searched this stuff, he was pretty neat."

"Or she," I said.

Toots was picking up letters, smoothing and stacking them. She turned her head aside to blow dust off the pile. "Would you know if anything was missing?" I asked.

She shook her head. "I doubt it." Then she reconsidered. "Well, I take that back. I'd know if my telegram of acceptance was missing, or my logbooks, or any of my graduation certificates. A few really special things like that — I'd know if they were missing."

"Is that your uniform?" Stretch pointed to a pile of blue cloth exposed when I removed some textbooks.

She laughed. "God, no! That's my zoot suit." She laid down the letters and picked up the article in question. "Take a look." She stood up and shook it out. It was a jumpsuit and it was enormous.

"It's kind of big," I said.

She grinned. "They never made separate ones for the WASP. We got the men's castoffs. We had to use a lot of safety pins just to keep from tripping all over them or catching the sleeves on things. See?"

She fingered a rusty safety pin. "But there was one thing we liked about them. Look! Pockets! Lots and lots of pockets!" She turned two of them inside out to show us. "A girl could get mighty hungry on a cross-country. And, of course, you needed a place to stow your sanitary pads."

"You had two," Stretch pointed to a second pile of blue cloth.

Toots frowned. "I only had one. I don't know where the other one came from. It's not like we hoarded them to take home and wear around the house after the war. And we had to pay for them if we brought them home with us." She grinned at Stretch. "You're the one who likes historical artifacts. Want one?"

"Sure!" Stretch said. "If you really mean it."

Toots held out the zoot suit to Stretch. "It's all yours, kiddo. Maybe we can find you a cap to go with it."

Stretch stroked the fabric and looked as happy as I'd seen her. She was like a Beatles fan who had just been presented with a John Lennon bath towel from the first American tour.

"So your dress uniform is upstairs?" I asked.

"Upstairs, in a closet, along with my general's pants. Unlike lots of the girls, I can still get into mine, so I take them to reunions sometimes."

"General's pants?" Stretch echoed.

"Khaki pants — our field dress uniform. Cochran ordered them once when General Arnold was supposed to visit and she wanted the girls to look spiffy. Arnold never showed up that time, but the general's pants became standard."

I smiled to myself. Maybe to Toots, the WASPs would always be "girls," whether they were twenty-one or sixty-one or eighty-one and whether they needed sanitary pads or Depends.

9

JULY 14, 1986

"Oh, I was going to show you Fifinella! Here she is." She handed me a patch showing a winged female figure that looked like Tinkerbell in a jumpsuit and goggles. "The Disney studio designed her. They had a picture of her over the gates at Avenger."

"Cute." But she had wings. Even I wouldn't mind learning to fly a plane if I'd been born with a set of wings. "She's a gremlin?"

Toots nodded. I handed the patch to Stretch, who stroked it and smiled.

"Well, would you do me a favor and look through this stuff to see if you notice that anything's missing?"

"Sure, I can do that," she said.

I commandeered a five-gallon paint tub, plastic and therefore rustless, and settled my backside on top of it. "When Maddy called, she mentioned somebody running off with a boy. So sabotage may not be the right angle. If she didn't mean you, who did she mean?"

Toots shook her head. "I've been thinking about it and thinking about it. I just keep coming up with more possibilities." She closed the lid and sat down on the footlocker.

"First of all, girls went off with boys all the time. She might not even have meant Harlingen, she might've been talking about Sweetwater or Dodge City. And even at Cochran's convent, girls went off with boys. Boys flew in or drove in for the weekend, or we met them in Abilene. I remember the time three B-29s landed at Avenger to pick up the girls two classes ahead of mine and take them to a dance. Golly, that was something!"

I refrained from commenting on a government that could afford to run such an extravagant taxi service but couldn't afford to pay women pilots decent wages. "Did you know any other Ethels?"

"I knew one, but she was a class ahead of me. I didn't know her well at all, so whether or not she ran off with a boy, I don't know."

"Let's focus on the Harlingen group for the moment, the Crazy Eight." I didn't think I could handle any more than eight possibilities at one time. I peeled off my gloves and fished my notebook out of my back pocket.

But the first thing Toots did was add a ninth and tenth. "Well, before we came, Shorty Evers resigned to get married to a sergeant she'd met. That would have been in March of forty-four, when we were finishing up at Dodge City. That's why they needed five of us instead of just four. And then after Tommy disappeared, Bernie McLenahan finished out the time with us. It was only for two weeks. That was right before disbandment."

"Any scandal attached to Shorty's resignation?"

"Not scandal, really, but of course, it was a big shock to everybody. I mean, to have made it through it through Avenger and B-26 school to boot, and then suddenly throw it all over to get married — well, it just didn't happen very often, that's all. And all the other WASP told her she was crazy and she'd never get another chance like this to fly, or at least that's what they told us they said. And Cochran was furious! But Shorty did it anyway. So that's one possibility." She hooked one index finger with the other, counting. "Though why Maddy would get a bee in her bonnet about Shorty after all these years, I don't know. She wasn't even there when Shorty left."

She tapped a second finger. "Esther was already married and her husband was a pilot stationed at Alamagordo before he was sent overseas. He came through Harlingen a few times and once or twice Esther went off with him."

She tapped a third finger. "Back at Avenger, Lou Zimmerman used to sneak off with one of the flight instructors, which was strictly forbidden, but honestly — some of them were our age and just darling! You can imagine what some of the girls said about Lou, especially the ones who washed out. But Lou was a good pilot and she made it through B-26 school. The guy she eventually married, Wes, was a gunnery instructor at Harlingen."

She unfolded a fourth finger. "Chub married another gunnery instructor from Harlingen, and after he was reassigned, he flew in to see her once or twice — from Georgia or Alabama, I think it was. Well, really, lots of girls used to do that with boys they liked. I did and so did Squeak."

She opened her hands in an expressive shrug. "But where in all that you can find a motive for murder, I sure as heck don't know."

"Is there anybody we can eliminate?" I asked. "You haven't mentioned Tex, for example."

"Oh, well, Tex." She smiled. "Tex wasn't the romantic type. There was this one story about Tex, though. She was from 43-7, two classes before mine at Avenger. Before she went to bomber school, she went to Love Field in Dallas, and there was this trainer there who was washing out all the WASP — actually trying to fire them. You understand, we were trained like Army pilots and we had to pass Army check rides in order to continue and graduate. But it often happened that we'd arrive at the base where we were assigned and they'd send us back to ground school and make us go through check rides all over again in planes we'd been flying for months. Anyway, this fellow tried to wash out Tex, for no reason that she could see, and she gave him a piece of her mind. And about that time, she ran into Jackie Cochran, I forget how, and she told Cochran about him and Cochran got that trainer reassigned." She grinned. "Now if Maddy had said, 'that boy she went off *on*' instead of 'that boy she went off *with*,' then I could believe she meant Tex. But I still can't see why anybody would care after all this time. Like I said, the trainer got reassigned, probably someplace where he didn't have to deal with women and was happy."

"Maddy called you just before the Fourth of July," I said. "She'd been watching speeches on television and she said it made her mad. How could that be related?"

"I'm not sure. You know that the WASP wasn't militarized until 1977, thirty-three years after we disbanded, although we were always told it would happen while we were in. Meanwhile, we paid for room and board and uniforms and laundry services. We paid our way to Sweetwater, and if we washed out, we paid our way to get home. If a WASP was killed in a crash, we took up a collection to ship her body home in a pine box. The government gave her family less than $200 for burial expenses. We didn't have life insurance. Even if we could have afforded it, nobody would insure us."

"No G. I. Bill either, after the war," Stretch put in.

"That's right. We were all supposed to go home to our kitchens and make Jell-O molds and tuna casserole. And buy appliances — lots of appliances, to keep the war boom going. And meanwhile, there was this committee — the Truman committee — that was trying to reduce our pay because we earned more than the WACs, who were being fed and clothed and housed at Uncle Sam's expense. You know what my take-home pay was at Avenger? Twelve dollars a month. Well, you can bet it made us mad! And thirty-three years is a long time to wait to be recognized for service to your country. So maybe that's what Maddy was so steamed up about."

Willie responded to the anger in her voice by standing up on her stubby little legs and barking.

Toots glanced at her. Then she gave us a wry smile. "Of course, at the time, all we could think about was how lucky we were. The country was at war and we were having so much fun."

Abruptly, she slapped her thighs and sprang to her feet. "Look at me! Making you sit down here on a bucket in the musty old basement when we could be discussing this upstairs with a drink in our hands!" She helped me to my feet. I felt a cobweb brush my ear and hoped the spider, alive or dead, hadn't landed in my hair.

"So what do I do now, Cat?" she asked, studying my face. "Do I call up all the WASP I know and tell them to go see if anyone's been looking through their things? Do I tell them not to stand at the top of their basement stairs?"

"And not to fly without checking the oil port for rags," Stretch put in. "Don't forget about that."

"Let me think about it and talk to Moses," I said. "It's still possible that what we have is a series of coincidences."

"And it's possible that somebody's bumping off WASP," Toots said. "And it's possible that it's one of us."

10

JULY 19, 1986

MAYBE YOU THINK I was replaying this conversation in my head after I yanked the ripcord. Maybe you think that once the parachute exploded overhead like a genie released from a bottle, I had time to reflect on the events of the past week. Maybe you think that after the parachute jerked me up and after the pain in my near-dislocated shoulders subsided into a steady ache, I applied my investigative faculties to the case at hand while drifting earthward like a fallen leaf, thinking, "This is quite a two-pipe problem." If so, you would be mistaken.

In the first place, the force of the exploding parachute slammed the harness against my chest like a blow and knocked the wind out of me. So for a few seconds there, I was fighting to get my breath. Once my lungs started working again, I unglued my eyes and forced them open. I couldn't see a goddamned thing. If there was a moon, it wasn't having much effect. By then, I was holding myself rigid with terror, waiting for the reverberant thunderclap of ten thousand pounds of metal striking the ground and straining to detect human voices that would tell me who was still alive. That I hadn't heard any of it yet convinced me that shock had turned me deaf as well as blind.

In the third place, I was falling backwards.

Backwards?

It never looked like this in the movies. In the movies, jumpers were always facing forwards so that they could see where they were going. Assuming that my eyes ever adjusted to the darkness, I could only see where I've been. Conclusion? I had a defective parachute — probably one as old as the plane. Any second now, the damp rot that had begun during typhoon season in the Pacific or the small hole gnawed in a rope by some starving French mouse on D-Day would reach its inevitable conclusion and I'd plunge to my death clutching a broken rope and a scrap of cloth.

Here lies — wait a minute! Had she called me "Caterpillar"?

Had she made it out? Had Moses? Tex? And Happy? Was he trained to pull the ripcord on his custom-made parachute? He probably followed orders better than I did, but could he count to ten?

In the fourth place, there seemed to be a typhoon building over Southwest Ohio. Gusts of wind caught me and hurried me along, but to where?

I screwed my head around and felt something give painfully in my neck. Were those moving gray shapes in the distance? Were they parachutes? Where was the plane? I screwed my head around the other way. I supposed that one could be deaf and still hear those little popping sounds that unhappy bones and joints made. I expected to see a conflagration that made a homecoming bonfire look like Cherries Jubilee. Nothing. I swung my head back the other way. By now, whatever muscles that were going to give way had already given.

I could follow with my eyes a trail of smoke, rapidly dissipating like the memory of a nightmare. My own eyes were still watering from the smoke inside the plane and I didn't dare loosen my grip on the parachute to wipe them. I blinked to clear my vision.

I could now make out, in the remote distance, a fire. From way up here above the eagles' nests, it looked tiny, but it was producing a cloud of smoke that would support the weight of a Mothra if he chose to climb it. My lungs were still fighting a smothering blanket of fuel and I couldn't tell if the acrid odor I was smelling came from inside or outside my body, or both.

I looked away from the light of the fire to adjust my vision, then followed the column of smoke up to a darker layer of clouds. In the space between the column of smoke and me, against the black of the sky, I did see some lighter shapes.

And then I saw a tiny flash of light. And another.

My goddamned partner was taking pictures.

11

TUESDAY, JULY 15, 1986

THE CAMERA HAD BEEN Toots's idea. In fact, the whole set-up had been Toots's idea.

"You'd better come to Dayton," she'd said, "whether I live that long or not."

"Dayton" was the Dayton Air Show, where a small group of WASPs would gather, reminisce, and probably do the same things men did at their army reunions, whatever that was. I suspected that it involved a lot of drinking, which was okay by me.

"'Cept she don't call them 'WASPs,' Cat, have you noticed?" Moses had once pointed out. "I guess that's because the 'P' stands for 'pilots.'"

I pondered this information. "So what do you call a single WASP? A WAS? A WISP?"

"I think they just use 'WASP' for both," he'd said, but I never got used to the idea.

That was after we held a council of war — Moses, Toots, Stretch, and I — at Toots's country club.

Actually, the war council was preceded by a round of golf.

Yes, golf. I, Cat Caliban, who have never had a good word to say about the game and plenty of bad words; I, who have declared that I would rather reorganize my sock drawer or pick knots out of the

Kitty Tease than follow a small ball around in the hot sun just to see if I could chase it into a gopher hole; I, who have left instructions in my Living Will not to pull the plug on me unless somebody has first tuned the television to a golf tournament to see if I rise up to protest. I played golf.

Toots had invited us for lunch — unless, she'd said, we'd like to come earlier and "get in a round of golf." "I wouldn't mind," Moses had said. He'd been holding the phone at the time, so I was only hearing half of the exchange.

"Wouldn't mind what?" I said from across the kitchen table.

He hadn't answered me. He'd listened some more and then looked up at me.

"Well," he'd said, "it's not her favorite game, but I think she'll come along."

"Not my favorite game?" I'd exploded when he explained the arrangements he'd made. "Not my favorite game? Moses, you know my position on golf!"

"See, Cat, that's just the way you do," he'd groused. "Other folks got likes and dislikes, you got a position. Think of it as a business meeting. You got to play golf with the client — every business executive knows that."

"No, *you've* got to play golf with the client. That's what partnerships are all about. You play golf, I play bridge. You play poker, I play canasta. You fly, I drive. Hot dog and mustard, not mustard and mustard. See?"

Nevertheless, on Tuesday, July 15th, a day that will live in the annals of sports history and certainly in the memories of the staff at the Parkside Country Club, I played golf.

"How about I just drive the cute little cart and wave at you on the fairway?" I whispered as Moses was lacing me into a pair of golf shoes that should have been registered as lethal weapons.

"N-O, no," he said.

"Wait until they find out I've never played anything but putt-putt."

"Come on," he said.

So I started out truculent and truculent was how I stayed. I dragged my little cleated heels every step of the way.

"Don't worry, Cat," Toots said, laughing. "Stretch's a beginner, too. She only started playing this summer."

To illustrate her incompetence, Stretch stepped up to the tee and belted her ball straight down the fairway. Today she was wearing minuscule denim shorts and a plain white T-shirt. Toots was wearing one of those floral skirts split into shorts underneath and a white cap. Moses, who never showed his knees in professional situations, was wearing a nice pair of gray slacks and a gray knit shirt. I was wearing khaki shorts and my frowny face. Also a T-shirt from Kevin's collection that showed a map of the United States with little planes flying over it like mosquitoes and read, "Support the Defense Budget: Give Air Traffic Controllers a Pay Raise."

Toots's enthusiasm mystified me. How could anyone who'd flown bombers and fighter planes be entertained by swinging a stick at a ball the size of an underdeveloped turnip? But there she was, extending her visor with a hand to follow the progress of her ball, a look of intense concentration on her face.

"Keep your head down, Cat," Moses said to me, over and over. "Don't scrunch up your shoulders like that — you gonna be sore by tonight."

"I'm already sore," I muttered.

"Don't choke up on the club like that, Cat," he'd say. "Use your hips and swing through. You pulling to the left."

"I can't even see the damn flag! How'm I supposed to aim the damn ball if I can't see the damn flag?"

"It's behind that rise. Just get the ball down the fairway, then you'll see it."

"They've got all those bushes and trees and shit in the way," I said, and watched the flutter of feathers which announced that I'd once again found two birds in a bush and tried to brain them.

"They're probably an endangered species," I said.

"They are now," Moses observed.

A few minutes later, I was down on my hands and knees, trying to blow the sand out from under my ball.

Moses came running up. "Cat, what are you doing? You're not supposed to do that."

"Well, how am I going to get it up over that cliff?" Behind him, I could see Toots laughing. Even Stretch seemed on the point of cracking a smile.

"Look, take this wedge," Moses said. "Now, when you hit the ball, you kind of lift it up and over."

"Forget it. It just rolls back down. Listen, Moses, can't we play Caliban rules?"

"What's that?"

"Well, when the kids were little and we used to go to the putt-putt, you were allowed to move your ball after you tried to hit it five times. You know, like if you'd done your best, but every time you hit it the windmill blade came down and knocked it away. You could move it to the other side."

He stared at me.

"We always felt, Fred and me, that the important thing was to try your best. Nobody could ask more of you than that."

"How many strokes you got on this hole?"

"Eighty-seven." Well, I'd lost count after that.

He sighed. "We're only on the second hole. You playing the wrong game, Cat. You should be bowling."

He bent down, picked up my ball, and placed it atop the cliff. I hit it into a pond. The ducks were not happy.

Next, it was, "Cat, get out of there! What are you doing? You don't go in after your ball."

"I'm not about to use another one," I said. "That's wasteful. Besides, look how many other balls I found."

On the green at last, my socks squishing inside my shoes, I discovered that golf resembled another game I was a little more experienced at.

Moses's jaw dropped when I whacked his ball into the underbrush — the first time all day that I had actually hit what I was aiming at.

"What did you do that for?" he asked.

"Revenge." I lifted the flag and scooted my ball into the cup.

Moses was staring after his ball. "You can't do that!" he protested. "Cat, this ain't croquet, it's golf."

I put my hands on my hips, letting the club drop. "How many strokes do you have on this hole?"

"Four."

"Well," I said with satisfaction, "now you'll have more. Maybe you'll acquire a little empathy."

"That's not the way it works!"

Toots was doubled over with laughter. Stretch said, "She's got a point, Moses. If you don't watch out, she'll creep up on you."

If I did, it would be to wrap the damn nine iron around his neck.

Toots's laughter faltered a little when I hit her ball into a clump of poison ivy. She cleared her throat then and said, "That was, uh — that was my ball, Cat."

"Well, they all look alike! How are you supposed to tell them apart?"

"Cat, if the ball is sitting in the middle of the fairway on a straight line to the tee, it ain't yours," Moses said.

"My shoulders ache," I said on the fifth hole.

"I told you —," he began.

"And my neck is stiff from looking down all the time," I said.

By the seventh hole my shoes had dried stiff in the sun, which was bright and hot.

"Now let's see if you can correct that slice," Moses said, picking out a club for me.

"I don't want to correct it," I said. "It gets me under the trees, where it's nice and cool."

By the tenth hole a veritable army of golfers had "played through," which for you intelligent non-golfers means we let them move ahead of us. When Toots handed me a cup of ice water, I thanked her, and said, "I've got so much sand in my mouth and my hair, I feel like I spent the day at the beach."

She nodded. "The first time I ever played golf was in Sweetwater. Talk about sandy! We used to joke that the whole course — heck, the whole town — was just one big sand trap. And the wind used to drive it right into your face. We learned to keep our eyes covered. We played tennis there, too, but some days you didn't even need a partner. You just hit the ball into that West Texas wind and it came right back at you. We were all scared we'd end up like Millie Vandelinter, who got this weird eye infection they couldn't treat. She was in sick bay so long she couldn't graduate with her class. She told us she could never see too well after that, but she memorized the eye chart so she could pass all her physicals and keep flying."

This story did nothing to decrease my fear of flying. I wanted to know if Millie was still flying around up there, but I was afraid to ask.

"Well," Toots said brightly, picking up a club and looking around. "All rested up?"

By eleven I couldn't concentrate for all the sweat trickling down my face and tickling the back of my neck. And either I'd developed a sympathetic blindness or the salt was affecting my vision. I whaled away at the ball, digging a foot-wide trench in the grass.

"You supposed to put back your divot, Cat," Moses said.

"How can I?" I said. "It's scattered all over the goddamn fairway." The only thing that hadn't budged was the ball.

On twelve I hit a house snuggled up against the golf course and the ricochet beheaded a few zinnias and almost took out the woman who was weeding them. If I hadn't been blinded by sweat, I was pretty sure that the expression I would have read on her face even at this distance was murderous.

"You supposed to yell 'Fore!,'" Moses told me, "not, 'Oh, hell!'"

"There's too many rules. I can't remember 'em all."

I didn't think I could make it to eighteen. I already had a score that was higher than my age and my cholesterol count added together.

On fourteen I saw another pond and aimed for it. By some miracle, I hit it. By now I knew that Moses's information wasn't entirely accurate because Toots had loaned me a gizmo with an expandable arm so you could fish around for your ball in the water. I took the opportunity to splash some more water around and soak my shoes to cool my feet down.

That kept me going for another hole and a half. On the fifteenth fairway, I allowed myself to slump until I was flat on my back, my eyes closed.

I felt a shadow on my skin. "Cat," it said.

I cracked an eye and saw Moses, upside down, then closed it again.

"What are the symptoms of heat stroke?" I asked.

"Incoherence," he said, "which you ain't got."

I heard the creak of his joints as he lowered himself. "Mel says golf courses are some of the most toxic places around," he observed, "on account of all the insecticides and fungicides they use on the grass."

"Thanks for sharing but that's the least of my worries at the moment."

The silence stretched.

"That's it," I said. "Enough is enough. Not another swing. I mean it."

"Okay."

My eyes popped open.

"Okay?"

"Okay." He put a hand under my elbow to help me sit up. "'Sides, I already won my bet."

"Your bet?"

"Kevin bet you wouldn't make it past four, Mel had seven, and Al had ten. I said twelve. I'm the closest. 'Course, I didn't figure on you lying down in the middle of the fairway, but it doesn't matter, 'cause we didn't bet on that part."

On my feet by now, water sloshing around inside my shoes, I said, "You mean, I could've thrown in the towel at four?"

He ignored the question. "See, Cat? I got faith in you."

He should have known better than to piss off a woman wearing cleats.

12

TUESDAY, JULY 15, 1986

I WAS TAKING a little siesta in the golf cart, my cleats hanging over the armrest, when Toots roused me. Moses wasn't speaking to me at the time.

"Come on, Cat," she said. "Time for your favorite hole."

"The nineteenth?" I asked hopefully. Even I knew about the nineteenth hole.

"Come turn in your shoes," Stretch called.

The shoe man gave them a quizzical look, but he took them, which was a great relief to me. I was afraid he'd make me buy them.

Moses was limping a little. "Wasn't even my idea," he complained when he caught me watching him.

The brisk air of the clubhouse turned my socks clammy inside my Adidas, but I didn't care. I had a piña colada to wet my whistle, a cushioned chair to cradle my stiff muscles, and a toothpick umbrella to play with. I zoned out while the other three replayed the whole damn game — a ritual I'd never understood. Hell, I was willing to bet that my fourteen-and-a-half holes had been more eventful than anybody's eighteen, and even I wasn't interested in talking about them.

Finally, about the time lunch arrived, they were ready to talk about the case.

"So, do you think Toots is in danger?" Stretch asked again.

"If you're asking whether somebody's going around killing former WASP," Moses said, "I doubt it. In the first place, we don't have any concrete evidence that Mrs. George's and Mrs. Ellerman's death weren't accidents, although we have some circumstantial evidence that links them, like the cause of death and their closeness in time. There's some evidence that in Mrs. Ellerman's case, someone had been looking through her WASP memorabilia. That person could have been Mrs. Ellerman, but whoever it was wore gloves, which might or might not suggest that it wasn't Mrs. Ellerman."

"The Fort Lauderdale police have confirmed that the trunk showing the most marks in the dust was the one containing papers and other things from her WASP days," I said. "The stuff inside showed some smears where someone with dirty fingers, dirty gloved fingers, had handled it."

"Because the Seattle police are unwilling to treat Mrs. George's death as anything other than accidental, I called Mrs. George's daughter and explained our concerns," Moses said. "She was very nice, even though she was skeptical, but said she didn't know where her mother kept anything she still had from her days as a WASP. I asked her to look anyway, and she called back later to say that she did find some things in an old suitcase in the basement, but although she saw some marks in the dust and a few marks on the papers, she couldn't be sure how recent they were. She also said that unlike Mrs. Ellerman, her mother did go down to the basement from time to time to look through her things — said when Mrs. George drank, she'd get nostalgic and go down to look through old love letters or photograph albums, maybe get out her wedding dress or her uniform. So we got nothing definite there."

"Except that somebody looked through my stuff, too," Toots pointed out, "somebody who wore gloves, and it wasn't me." Whoever thought all ladies have delicate appetites hadn't met Toots. She was putting away a hot roast beef sandwich with fries and eying every dessert that passed our table. You would have thought she was still obsessing about the minimum weight requirement. Maybe WASPs never got over that.

My own appetite was healthy enough. I found myself craving salt after losing so much of it to sweat on the golf course and I'd been gratified by the mountain of potato chips crowning my club sandwich.

Stretch, who had the most height to fill, ate like a runway model.

"That's right," Moses agreed, nodding at Toots. "If it weren't for that, I'd say we had squat."

"But since all three of you kept your WASP stuff in the base-ment, it's suggestive," I said. "It's possible that Maddy and Squeak were killed because they were in the way. What the killer really wanted was to look through their things in the basement."

"I'm beginning to thank my lucky stars Hal never got around to fixing that basement door," Toots said. "But whoever it was could have done that at Squeak's house without killing her, same way he did it at my house. Didn't you say that was an unlocked door from the garage into the basement storage room?"

"Right," I said. "So maybe Squeak heard him — or her — and went to investigate. Maybe that's what got her killed."

"But it doesn't explain how the killer sneaked past her and pushed her down the stairs," Moses said, "unless you think he stood in front of her, picked her up and dropped her."

Toots shook her head. "She would've clobbered him with her cane. And in spite of her nickname, she was no featherweight. For a WASP, she was kind of a pipsqueak, but for a normal woman, she was tall. And she'd put on weight over the years." She shook her head again. "I just don't see it. If she'd spotted an attacker, there would have been signs of a struggle and it doesn't sound like the police found anything like that."

"Yeah, so what we got is an unlikely scenario," Moses said, "and not a lot of active investigation. The death was ruled accidental, so there's only one interested detective, Detective Vasquez, who's doing any checking at all, and I gather she's doing it in her spare time, which she doesn't have much of. But she did check the phone records and found two calls between Maddy and Squeak. The first was on the 4th of July, just before midnight. It was short, so we're thinking Maddy called Squeak just before she called you, but Squeak wasn't home. She may have left a message, but if so, it had been erased from Squeak's answering machine. The next night, Squeak called Maddy, and that conversation lasted about twenty minutes."

Toots smiled ruefully. "She stayed on the phone long enough to find out what the heck Maddy was all hot and bothered about."

"Which could be why she's dead," Stretch said.

"But why? Over what? It's just crazy! Sometimes I think I'm crazy for wasting your time." She gave us an apologetic smile.

Then she turned to Moses. "You're a cop, Moses. What do your cop instincts tell you? Am I wasting your time?"

Moses ran a hand along his jawline and shook his head. "I'm keeping an open mind. There are things that don't add up and some coincidences, but coincidences happen, and could be we're missing some of the numbers that need adding. But if you turn out to be right in your suspicions, I'd rather know sooner instead of later. And there's still that sabotaged engine— that worries me."

"'That boy she went off with,'" Toots quoted, staring into space. "What boy? Who went off with him? Girls went off with boys all the time." She let out her breath in exasperation. "But for all we know, the two deaths may not have anything to do with that blasted phone call, not even if they turn out to be connected. The phone call could be a whatchacallit — a red heron."

"Red herring," Stretch corrected quietly.

"What we need to know," I said, "is who else Maddy called." I looked inquiringly at Moses.

He shook his head. "We won't get it from the Seattle police. They don't consider the death a homicide."

"Not even if an ex-cop called and asked them nicely?"

"It don't work that way, Cat. Not with phone records." To Toots, he said, "I need to make sure I understand this business about the flights. You told us you were closest to the other pilots in your flight."

Toots nodded. "The night flight. That was me, Tommy, Squeak, and Maddy. And then after Tommy died, it was Bernie McClenahan, but not for very long — maybe only two weeks. The WASP was disbanded around that time."

"Did you already know Bernie?" I asked.

"She was in our class. She'd been flying B-26s, towing targets in Laredo."

"Tell me about towing targets," I said.

Toots shrugged. "It's just the way it sounds. They attach these big targets to your plane with cables — you know, like some of the advertisements you've seen being towed over stadiums? You've got about eight thousand feet of target. A crew member — we flew with a crew of three — would let the target out when we were in position. And then the cadets shoot at them."

"From the ground?" Moses asked.

I was too stunned to unlock my jaw. My question was, "With live ammunition?"

"Either way," Toots said. "Trainees usually started on the ground in basic, then graduated to the air. They started with cameras, then moved up to live ammunition. In advanced, the B-26s attacked the B-24s, and the ack-ack boys in the B-24s shot at the target with fifty caliber ammo."

Moses frowned. "How often did they miss?"

"And hit the plane?" Toots grinned. "Often enough. One time Tex got her hydraulic system shot out and the manual controls froze up, so she had to land without wheels and flaps. That was the worst incident at Harlingen, I think. The gunnery positions were color-coded, so they looked at the target once you brought it down to see how the different gunners were doing."

"Sounds like it took a lot of nerve to tow targets," Moses said.

"Strength, too, when you were flying a B-26. Those darned planes had so much torque, you had to keep both feet on the rudder. When you were back on solid ground, you could barely stand up."

"I read somewhere that the Army pilots refused to fly them," Stretch said. "Is that true?"

"That's what I heard," Toots said. "The boys at Dodge City were afraid of the Widowmaker — that's one of the things they called the Martin Marauder, one of the few things that can be repeated in polite company, anyway. As originally designed, it was a hot plane, which meant you were coming in fast with short wings on narrow landing gear. So one day, they marched the boys out by the runway and made them watch a bunch of B-26 landings — all of them made by WASP. They didn't get too many complaints after that." She grinned. "The gals who did that were a few classes ahead of me at Avenger. I sure wish I could've seen it."

"Sounds to me like the WASPs could have stirred up a lot of resentment," I observed.

"Sure we did," Toots said. "And we weren't even trying."

"But that wouldn't explain why someone would want to kill them now, more than forty years later," Stretch said.

"That's true. Whoever's been searching the trunks and foot-lockers has been actually looking through the papers," I said. "We know from the marks they left on the pages. Any ideas?"

"I just don't know!" Toots said. "Do they think we were giving away military secrets in our letters home?"

"Or reporting on negligence or sabotage that resulted in a crash?" I suggested. "It could even, I guess, be in the form of romantic gossip — maybe somebody was dating a boy who was a saboteur? Could someone like that gain greater access to the planes by dating a WASP?"

"I don't think so. It's not like we took boys on romantic midnight strolls through the hangars. I mean, in the first place, it wouldn't be all that romantic. This was war time, remember. Most bases were active twenty-four seven. If you wanted to be alone with a boy, you took him off the base."

"You went off with him."

"Well, sure."

"Whatever they're looking for has to be important enough to them that they're willing to kill to get it," I mused. "Of course, silencing the women, or — what? Getting revenge on them? — might have been the primary goal of the killer. But even so, they're willing to stick around to look for something."

Toots tilted her head back and laughed. "I shouldn't be laughing, I know." She held up a hand. "Not if Maddy and Squeak were murdered. But —." She struggled to control her laughter. "I'm just imagining some guy — okay, I admit it could be a woman, but right now I'm seeing a guy — with surgical gloves on his hands, reading my letters by flashlight. Jeepers! Do you know what my letters are like?" She picked up a knife, held it like a pen, and began to write on the tablecloth. "Dear Mama, The weather is so hot here I'm about to melt. I am suntanned all over except for these white circles around my eyes where my goggles are and I look like a redneck raccoon! The food here is yummy. Tonight we had steak. But after I get out I may never eat a carrot again as long as I live! Tommy and I went to the lake on Saturday with two boys she knows who drove down from Abilene. Last week I started flying AT-6es. I love this plane! But I have to carry a pillow to sit on so I can reach the controls. Someone is playing a radio and I can hear Johnny Mercer singing "Deep in the Heart of Texas," but I wonder if he has ever been here. You can't see the stars for all the sand blowing around. Please send me my green skirt with the little blue flowers and my red sweater, even if Sally is wearing them. Lights out now! Lots of love, Toots."

We laughed.

"Or wait — how about this one?" She began writing again. "Dear Sis, I'm sorry you're having boy trouble, but you don't know what trouble is until you feel something creeping down your zoot suit and realize that on the first leg of a cross-country, at 5,000 feet, you're getting your period! And your instructor has the bluest eyes and the cutest dimples and you will not see a latrine again for hours. If you go to Bergman's and happen to see that lipstick I like —

Ravishing Red — please buy it and put it in the box the next time Mama sends clothes. Whoops! The wind is picking up and I have to go out and help hold down the planes! Bye for now, Toots."

We were all laughing, but my own laughter was not unmixed with horror. I made a mental note to pursue the topic of menstruation with Toots later — not because it was relevant to the case, but because I was having trouble imagining a happy ending to the scenario she described and I was hoping there was one. I was myself too newly liberated from periods to have forgotten the many embarrassing moments they had given me.

But Stretch, who should have had better reason than I had to be curious on this point, seized on the detail that related to aviation engineering. "Did you really have to hold down the planes, Toots?"

Toots held up two fingers. "Scouts honor. I wish I had a picture of that — a mob of gals in various states of dress and undress, some with scarves tied over their curlers, hanging onto those planes for dear life. But when those West Texas winds reached gale force, they could have picked up those planes and carried them off to Germany. And then what? Would they close down the WASP? Or just send us trainers that were in even worse shape than the ones we had? It was the fear of either of those two possibilities that sent us running for the planes whenever the alarm sounded.

"But you can see what I mean about the letters," she continued, hands spread. "What could anybody hope to find in the correspondence of a twenty-two-year-old that would inspire them to murder?"

"How about at Harlingen?" Moses said. "You weren't flying AT-6es there. Did you write about anything that could be considered classified information? Or about any incidents of negligence, for example? Anything go wrong there?"

Toots snorted. "All the time. But it was so routine, I don't think I put it in a letter. Nobody ever did get shot down by mistake, for example. Well, we had a couple of close calls and emergency landings. Some of those guys had terrible aim! I'd never have told my mother I took flak, but I might have told my sister. But like I said, if you're looking for some big incident, there wasn't one."

"Did you report on romantic intrigues?" I asked.

"Some. Like, you know, 'Maddy can't decide whether to marry Tony or not' — that kind of thing. Or 'Squeak's sweet on some major she met on a cross-country at Dodge City and she's trying to find a way to get there on her way home when we get disbanded.'"

"How about the girl who left before you came?" I asked.

"Shorty Evers."

"Shorty. You said Cochran was angry with her."

"She sure was! And I don't blame her, really. After all, Miss Cochran had fought really hard to get the WASP in the first place, and even then, she had to keep fighting. She made sure we got the best training available. When she thought we might be militarized, she made sure that a lot of the girls went to OCS."

"For officer training?" Moses said.

"Yes. And then, at the end, she sent a bunch of girls off to instrument school so that they could get their commercial licenses after the WASP was disbanded. You can see why Miss Cochran might have felt betrayed when a girl left after all the time and trouble invested in her. But Cat, Maddy and Squeak and I, we didn't really know Shorty — at least, we didn't know her well. She was in the class before us at Avenger, so we knew who she was, but that's about it. She was gone by the time we got to Harlingen."

I sighed. I didn't really think we were getting anywhere. Then a thought struck me.

"Is it possible that someone in your flight had some kind of valuable document in her possession?" I asked.

"Like what?" Toots frowned.

"I don't know. It might be something valuable for its blackmail value, like a marriage certificate or something. Or a medical report. Or it could be something valued for its signature."

"You mean, like 'Love, Squeak'?" Toots said doubtfully.

"I don't really know what I mean, I'm just groping. For example, if someone had a document signed by Roosevelt, Churchill, and Stalin, that would be worth a lot of money, right?"

"I guess so," Toots said, "but somehow I don't think Jackie

Cochran, Nancy Love, and Hap Arnold are in the same league. Those are the signatures a WASP would be most likely to have that would be worth anything."

"No signatures of Eisenhower, McCarthy, and Bradley, huh?"

"Not that I know of."

"Earhart, Cochran, and Love?" I asked hopefully.

"Sorry. Earhart's copilot was a WASP — she was a few classes ahead of me. If someone was looking for Earhart's signature, they'd start there, not with a flight from Harlingen."

"Besides," Stretch pointed out, "if someone had a document worth killing for, wouldn't the killer know who had it? I mean, it seems pretty unlikely that someone would hear a rumor about something that valuable and not know which one of eight women had it."

"That's a good point. Maybe it's not a document," Moses said. "Maybe it's a photograph. Or photographs."

I turned to him. "There's a thought."

"Of what?" Toots asked.

"I don't know," I said. "What might you have photographs of? For example, would you have any photographs of a crash site?"

"I don't, but some girls might. We had two crashes at Avenger when I was there."

"Suppose that one of those pictures could now be blown up to show something that might embarrass or incriminate somebody. That's what Moses is thinking, right, Moses?"

He shrugged. "I don't really know. I'm just speculating."

"Or suppose somebody suspected that her plane had been sabotaged. Might she have taken a picture to prove it?"

"Yes," Toots said slowly, "I know some girls who did that. But unless it was a picture of somebody pouring sand in the carburetor or cutting a hydraulic line or loosening the bolts of an instrument panel while twirling their mustache, I don't see what threat a photograph could pose, especially at this late date."

"Okay, maybe we'd better focus on imminent danger," I said, "since we don't know enough to explain what's going on, if anything. The question is, could Maddy and Squeak have been killed to keep them from attending the reunion? Was the killer afraid that Maddy would talk to more people at the reunion about whatever it was she knew? Was Squeak killed because the killer knew she'd been Maddy's partner, or because he or she found out that Maddy had talked to Squeak? And if so, does the killer know that Maddy talked to you as well? More importantly, does the killer know you didn't know what she was talking about?"

"Apparently not, since somebody sabotaged the Cessna," Stretch said.

"The what?" I asked.

"Cessna," Stretch repeated. "The plane Toots was flying on the Fourth. Somebody stuffed a rag in the oil port."

"How about that, Toots? How was that done?"

"Simple. You open the hatch, unscrew the cap on the filter port, and cram the thing in. It would take five minutes max."

"Jeepers," I said.

"Why use that method?" Moses asked. "Got any theories? Couldn't you just put sugar in the gas tank, the way people sometimes do to cars?"

"I don't know," Toots said. "Sugar or sand in the gas tank would work just as well. I hadn't thought about that." She looked at Stretch. "Professor?"

Stretch thought a minute. Then she said, "It would only work as well if they knew when Toots was flying next. If you put something in the gas tank and let it sit long enough, you won't be able to start the engine. During wartime, when planes were flying around the clock and you didn't care which pilot you killed, as long as you killed one of them, putting something in the gas tank made sense. But if you're after a particular pilot, and if you don't know how long her plane is going to sit before she starts the engine again, you'd be better off with a rag in the oil filter port."

"Which suggests a certain expertise in the art of sabotaging planes," I said.

"Whoever did it didn't count on your skill as a pilot, Toots," Stretch said.

"So you're saying it wasn't a WASP because a WASP would have known how well Toots can fly," I said.

Stretch hesitated. "If you really knew how well Toots can fly, you'd know what a gamble it would be to try to kill her in that particular way. It would be long odds that she couldn't save herself."

Moses said, "If the phone calls on the 28th had anything to do with these two deaths, we have a killer who's working fast."

"Yes, but maybe not someone who can devote full time to it," I said, "or we might have had another attempt on Toots already. Were you thinking that somebody doesn't want the WASP to get together at the reunion and compare notes?"

"I guess that could be it," he agreed.

"But we've had other reunions, Moses," Toots objected. "Plenty of 'em, over the years. And in fact, the big one is coming up in September. There will be lots more WASP there than at Dayton."

"But nobody called you up beforehand and said, 'We should tell what we know,'" I pointed out.

"Well, no," Toots said.

"You are being careful, right?" Moses said. "I mean, so far the killer, if there is a killer, hasn't shown much ingenuity or even guts. It doesn't take much to push someone down the stairs and even less to stuff a rag in an oil port. You set up a plane crash, you don't even have to be around to see it, just read about it in the paper."

"I'm keeping an eye on her," Stretch said.

"I'm being careful," Toots said.

"Check out your car before you drive it," Moses said. "Anybody who could sabotage a plane could cut a brake line in the car. I assume the crash investigators talked to folks at the airport where you keep the plane. You know what they found out?"

"I talked to the guys myself. They feel pretty bad about the whole thing. It's a small airport, so it's really a one-person operation, most of the time. There's a mechanic who works out of the building next door. But there's also a flight school that trains there. So keys to hangars and planes are sitting out where anybody can snag them. There's not a lot of security, hangar doors stand open, and nobody's expecting any trouble. It's not very common to steal a plane and they've got no reason to expect sabotage. Bottom line: nobody remembers seeing anything — or anyone — suspicious."

"How many women pilots do they see?" I asked.

"You mean, would a woman stranger attract more attention than a man?" Toots said thoughtfully. "Probably. But I can think of three, maybe four, other women who fly out of there, not counting the women students."

"A woman stranger wouldn't even have to look like a woman, Cat," Stretch said.

She had a point. If I saw Stretch and Toots in their work clothes with their hair covered, especially at a distance or silhouetted against bright sunlight, I wouldn't have been able to tell whether they were women or men.

"So what should I do now — wear a sign around my neck that says, 'I don't know anything — honest!'?"

"Why don't you start by calling up the other WASP from Harlingen?" Moses said. "Ask them if they're attending the reunion, chat them up, and then mention Maddy's phone call. Find out if anyone else talked to her, and if so, ask if they know what she was talking about. That's all you want to know. That way, we might find out something about who else she called and what she said, even though there might be one person she called who'll lie about it. And meanwhile, you can make it clear that you don't know anything."

"Gotcha," Toots said. "Find a way to tell them to take that target off my back. Though I have to admit, Moses, I really can't picture these women as killers. I mean, we went through a lot together. If we hadn't helped each other out, we wouldn't have made it. We all know that. Even if you didn't know a gal personally, if you knew she was a WASP, you felt connected."

"Will Shorty be at the reunion, do you think?" I asked.

Toots was momentarily distracted by some kind of dangerous-looking chocolate confection passing on her right.

"I haven't seen Shorty since Avenger," Toots said. "She never comes to these reunions. I don't know if anybody knows where she is."

"How about the others?" Moses said. "We could use a list of names and addresses."

"I can give you everyone but Shorty. And Tommy, of course."

"You don't have an old address for Tommy?" he asked. "That could be useful."

Toots scanned the ceiling. "Not unless there's something in the footlocker. I know I wrote a condolence letter to her parents at the time, but I doubt I'll find an address now. Anyway, I'll look. Stretch's been dying to get her hands on that footlocker anyway."

Stretch ducked her head in a surprising show of embarrassment.

Toots beamed at the waiter who had appeared at her elbow. She said, "In the meantime, live for today because tomorrow —."

13

TUESDAY, JULY 15, 1986

TOOTS SAVORED her first bite of some kind of chocolate cake that was covered with chocolate, decorated with chocolate, garnished with chocolate, and presented atop a sprinkling of powdered chocolate. If I'd eaten it, they would have had to call the EMS squad before my second bite. When I looked at it, I could feel my arteries contract.

Toots swallowed and pointed her fork at us. That was when she said, "You'd better come to Dayton, whether I live that long or not."

I thought the dessert she was eating might well do her in before our phantom killer caught up to her, but I really had no room to talk, with my own fork sunk into a piece of carrot cake cut for King Kong.

"This is my favorite way to eat carrots," I said when I ordered it.

"There you go," Toots had said. "Just eat a piece of that every night for supper and you'll have night vision like a cat's."

Now I said, "I'm only eating half. The other half I'll save for Kevin." Or for later, I thought, when Kevin wouldn't be around to lay claim to it.

Toots said, "See what you think of this. Cat can be a magazine writer, doing some kind of special follow-up article on the WASP for, I don't know, the AARP magazine or something. We've had tons of articles written about us."

"Really?" I was surprised. How come I'd never read anything about them? I'd gotten the impression that the WASP had been a well-kept secret.

"Oh, sure. During the war, there were a few reporters around. It's funny. We were supposed to be some kind of top-secret military operation and then this reporter from *Ladies Home Journal* shows up. We had to go out and sunbathe so the photographer could take our picture. There we were, tanned as shoe leather from PT and all the time we spent out in the sun and we had to go sunbathe! Not that I hadn't done some sunbathing when I first arrived at Avenger, but that hot Texas sun loses its appeal pretty darn quick. And then they'd have you sitting in the cockpit, putting on lipstick or powdering your nose, like you're headed out on a hot date instead of a grueling cross-country. And they'd label it something cutesy, like 'A WASP completes the final step in her pre-flight check.'"

"Okay, but have any articles been written since the war?"

"A few."

"There was some revival of interest in '77," Stretch said, "when the WASP was finally militarized. Right, Toots?"

I put down my fork in confusion. "Okay, wait, Toots said that before. How could the WASP be militarized if it didn't exist anymore? Or did it? Did they start it up again?

Toots shook her head. "We were militarized after the fact, so that we could collect veterans benefits. Even that wasn't easy. But we got a handful of senators and congressmen on our side — congressional representatives, I should say, since Patsy Mink was one of the first sponsors — and they eventually pushed it through."

"I guess I need to know this stuff if I'm going to pretend I'm writing about them, huh?"

"Oh, I don't know," Toots said. "Most of the writers I've talked to were pretty ignorant. Not all, but most. When the Navy started training women pilots, there was all this brouhaha about the first women to fly military planes. Well, that stirred up a few WASP, I can tell you, and you don't stir up WASP unless you're prepared to get stung." She turned to Moses. "So, Cat can be a writer. And Moses, you can be the photographer."

I looked at Moses. His arm was extended to pour cream into his coffee cup and he paused, cream picture in mid-air, and frowned.

"Why can't Cat be the photographer and I be the writer?" he said.

"Because women are more likely to open up to a woman than a man," Toots said, ignoring the frown. "If Cat's a writer, they'll take it for granted that she's going to ask questions. They'll answer more freely than they would if you asked the questions."

"I was in the military," he said, a little sulkily, I thought. He set the pitcher down.

"Doesn't matter," Toots said.

"It's a girl thing, Moses," I said.

He shot me a hostile look.

"Do you have some camera equipment?" she asked.

"No, but he knows where he can get some," I said helpfully.

At least I didn't have to hear about golf all the way home in the car.

"Just look on this as acquiring a new skill to help you in your career as a detective." This was one of the arguments he'd used to counter my objections to golf only a few short hours before.

"I don't want a career as a detective," he grumbled. "This is your career we working on."

"Okay. Just look on this as acquiring a new skill to help you in my career as a detective."

"I done too much acquiring already today. I acquired a limp and a set of cleat marks on my foot."

"I'm sure Paul will be glad to teach you," I said, clutching the armrests as Moses sailed over a bump in the road.

"Yeah, that's right. I forgot about him. And he's such a good teacher, too. Why, that sets my mind at rest, Cat. I'm glad you thought of that."

For the record, Moses's son Paul, an engineer, had tried to teach

Moses how to operate: an answering machine, a remote control, a microwave oven, an automatic teller machine, a Mr. Coffee machine, and a programmable VCR. He had failed at all of them. No, that's not quite true. Moses knew how to push the "Play" button on the answering machine and the VCR, the "Record" and "Rewind" buttons on the VCR, and the "Start" button on the microwave and Mr. Coffee. Beyond that, he was lost.

"That's all I need to know," he'd say. "Look here, what do I need that digital timer shit for? I can look up at the clock on the wall and tell when my food is cooked. And why should I want to be recording some TV show when I'm out playing poker or walking the dog? It ain't natural. If I want to watch it, I should stay home."

"You might surprise yourself," I said now. "You might enjoy photography."

He took a corner on two wheels in response and snorted.

"You've got — what? Almost three days? — to learn it."

After a minute he said, "You ain't off the hook, you know."

"Why? Have you arranged another golf outing for me?"

"Nope. You going to see Arnie."

"Arnie? Who's he?" I caught my breath as Moses passed a silver El Dorado so close I could count the driver's fillings when she opened her mouth in terror.

"A computer wizard."

"What's he got for me?" I asked suspiciously.

"Information," he said, grinning. "Information and education."

14

JULY 19, 1986

BUT LIKE I SAID, as I dangled in black space like Faye Wray on King Kong's pinky, somewhere between heaven and earth, I wasn't thinking of my recent past so much as the sixty-one years that had preceded it. The cattle on my grandparents' ranch in Texas. The brown mutt named Barney that I had loved to distraction until he chased one too many cars and got hit by a milk truck. The Sweet Sixteen party my parents gave me in the hope that I would take a hint and stop running wild and settle down. My typing teacher, Miss Grogan. The musty factory office where I worked at my first job. A youthful Fred Caliban herding three sleepy children trailing blankets and teddy bears into a dingy room in a motor court somewhere in the Ozarks. I even caught sight of my own teddy bear, Growler, who was named for the noise he made when tipped forward.

These were not so much memories as images, not chronologically arranged, flashing across my inner eye the way this experience has been described by so many people who have returned from the brink of death. But the growling was real enough, and when a vein of intense light suddenly moved across the darkness, I realized that what I was hearing was thunder. Fear of electrocution overwhelmed fear of falling. Wasn't I, after all, sailing along like a tail attached to an enormous kite? I looked down. Where the hell was a tall tree when you needed one?

Something grazed my legs, seemed to reach up and pull me down. It scratched at my arms and face. Instinctively, I kicked to free myself and plunged. Something hard whacked my elbow. I was yanked to a stop.

I hung in mid-air, fighting to still my heaving chest. Another movement and I might drop again, who knew how far.

I lowered my eyes. This, then, would be the tall tree. Any second, the lightning would find it.

I had often suspected that God was like my Great-uncle Mort, whose one deaf ear turned all communication into a comedy routine.

15

JULY 16, 1986

ARNIE KOVALCHIK HAD a small office in a dingy former warehouse in the low-rent district downtown. It smelled more like paint and turpentine, though, than mildew and dust, and as I edged past a large canvas sitting in the hall, my finely honed investigative intellect deduced that this was probably because there was at least one artist's studio in the building. The canvas depicted a three-headed woman from the shoulders up. One head wore a bridal veil, a second showed a pudgy, complacent face under an absurd hat decorated with fruit, and the third showed a pale thin face, apparently the same woman, with enormous haunted eyes and vampire teeth. Telling myself that his neighbor's work did not reflect Arnie's taste, I knocked on a door, which bore only his name, Arnie Kovalchik, in peeling black paint.

I heard a noise from the other side, which I took to be something on the order of "come in." I went in. The first thing that struck me was that Arnie had a terrific view of downtown Cincinnati. The second was that he had his back to it. He was sprawled in a chair in front of a computer not unlike the one my cousin Delbert had installed in my office at home, where it was gathering dust and cat hair. When I say "sprawled," I mean that the lower third of his spine was making contact with the seat of the chair. His keyboard was propped against his knees, which were bare below jean cutoffs, or more accurately from the look of them, saw-offs. Rimless glasses sat askew on his face, which was long, lean, and pale, and he wore earphones. His chin almost rested on his chest. He had a thin beak of a nose and a shock of black hair. I saw that he had a mouthful of something and I followed a trail of powdered sugar across a short stretch of black T-shirt to discover a donut in his left hand.

He looked up at me over his glasses. "Caliban?"

I nodded. "Cat." I was prepared to offer him a hand to shake, but he didn't seem prepared to take it.

He crammed the second half of the donut into his mouth, licked his fingers, brushed some of the sugar off of his T-shirt, pulled the earphones down to hang around his neck, and extended a hand, but it was palm up.

"Whatcha got?"

I handed him a folder. Inside was a short list of names and addresses, the Harlingen Eight plus Lorraine "Shorty" Evers and Tommy Thompson's replacement, whose name was Bernice McClenahan Smith. In the cases of Evers and Thompson, there were no addresses. For Evers, Toots had written only "California," because that was all she could remember about Shorty's origins. For Thompson, she had written, "father a diplomat — South America somewhere?" Toots had not, in fact, welcomed Moses's proposal that we do a little background checking on the people most immediately involved. Moses had assured her that this kind of investigation was routine and she'd finally consented, with the proviso that we would not share the results of our investigation with anyone, including her, unless we found something we thought might be relevant to the two deaths. I suspected that the background checks were just part of my training, as well as a way to get back at me for supporting his future career as a photographer. I didn't even know what I was supposed to be looking for. And have I mentioned lately that computers give me the willies?

Arnie had opened the folder and was studying its contents. He muttered to himself, at least I assumed it was himself he was addressing, since the low volume made his remarks hard for me to hear. They went something like this: "Ah-hah, ah-hah, huh? Uh-uh, nope. Mmmm — maybe. Maybe. Yeah, yeah, got that. Hmmm, doubtful." There were a few noises I can't replicate, as well as the tap of a pencil on the folder, the arm of his chair, and his front teeth. Sometimes he tilted his head for emphasis.

Left to my own devices, I pulled up a folding chair, sat down, and looked around. I couldn't identify all the equipment in the room. Thanks to my regular sojourns to the public library, I recognized a microfilm reader and maybe a microfiche reader next to it. I recognized the stereo system that sat atop the room's only filing cabinet — a nondescript beige affair whose drawers stood partially open, revealing file folder tabs like exposed bra straps. The trashcan was overflowing with little white Chinese food cartons and beer cans. Everything else looked high-tech and relatively tidy. A profusion of cables bridging surfaces and snaking around baseboards made me think everything was connected to the computer and therefore, to Arnie's fingertips.

But apparently, I was wrong. Arnie pushed himself up, bent down, and rummaged under his desk. He came up with a well-worn atlas of sorts, blew on it, and handed it to me, saying, "Okay. Here's what you do. You take this list of addresses, match the city names to counties, okay? Then you're going to take a little walk down the hall to Fletcher's, find the counties on your list if I got 'em in the archives, come back in here and look up the voter registrations to see if they include Social Security numbers. Okay?"

"All this equipment and I gotta use an atlas to match cities to counties?" I asked. I was more than a little suspicious. Maybe Moses had set me up.

Arnie shrugged and waved a hand to take in all of his machinery. "One day, all this stuff will get junked because we'll have twice as much information in a box smaller than your mailbox. One day. But today isn't one day. And you and Moses — you want what you want today." He turned back to his computer screen, signaling that our discussion had ended.

"Right," I said to his back. Ever resourceful, I cleared a small space on a nearby table by shoving aside an electric typewriter. Arnie didn't object and the typewriter had the forlorn look of a machine that got shoved aside a lot. I helped myself to a piece of paper that I found on the floor and began to look up cities.

My eyes were drooping when something furry bumped against one of my ankles. Glad of the distraction, I leaned over and looked down to see a small tawny longhair looking up at me, tail tucked around forepaws.

"Hello," I said. "Who are you?" I offered him a hand to sniff.

"That's Tesla," Arnie said. After a pause, he said, "You know who Tesla was?"

I mentally scanned my own files. "Something to do with electricity, wasn't he?"

"He developed the alternating current. Also the Tesla coil. You've heard of the Tesla coil, haven't you?"

"Maybe." I could have said, Cookie, when you're sixty-one, you'll realize that a lot of the things you've heard of in your life went into deep storage in your brain within seconds of the time you heard of them. I refrained. He'd find out soon enough.

But I could see why somebody who looked at this cat might be reminded of electricity. With his abundant fur, he was a generator on forepaws. In winter a casual pet like the one I was now administering would probably make the sparks fly.

"You've got the cutest little black spot on the end of your nose," I said to the cat.

"'Black spot'?" Arnie echoed. He swiveled around and looked at the cat, who returned his gaze unperturbed. For some reason, the sight of Tesla galvanized Arnie, who scooped up the cat, said, "Got that list finished?" and disappeared into the hall without waiting for an answer. I snatched up my list and followed him.

The cat struggled and Arnie bellowed. "Fletcher!" He passed through the open door next to the three-headed woman.

"Tesla's nose is black again," he was saying as I entered the room. "Look, it's bad enough you got this gloom-and-doom thing going on and I gotta walk past the weird sisters every time I go down the hall to take a piss, but now you're contaminating my cat. Look, man! He's probably getting poisoned every time he licks his nose."

The party being addressed was shorter than I was and gnome-like. Half a corona of reddish-blonde fuzz circled his head and stopped at small, rather pointed, ears. The fuzz continued again on the other side, where it spread over his cheeks and upper lip. A pair of large, round glasses perched on the bald top of his head, which emerged from his hair like a promontory rising from the mist. He had small, pale eyes, which regarded the cat and its owner in surprise, not, as I half expected, indignation. He wore tattered jeans and a blue T-shirt smeared with paint. He sat on a high stool in front of a large canvas in which black and shades of purple dominated. His sandaled feet were propped on a crossbar; I doubted they could reach the floor. In an extravagant gesture, he located his glasses atop his head and lowered them to his nose with both hands, one of which held a long, slender paintbrush. He studied the cat, who swung limply at the end of Arnie's arms as it made its own extravagant gestures.

"Hand him over," he said, reaching out with both hands. "I'll get it off."

Arnie snatched back the hapless cat and crushed him against his chest. "No way!" he said. "You'll use turpentine or something and make him sick."

"In the first place," said Fletcher, "he won't die from a little paint on his nose. See?" He raised an arm to his face and licked a streak of purple paint that ran from his elbow to his wrist. My face must have registered my disgust because he favored me with an elfish grin. "In the second place, it's stylish. Gives him a certain *je ne sais quoi*." He pronounced each word separately, as if inviting us to admire each syllable. "In the third place, it marks him as a cat of superior artistic taste, unlike certain people I could mention. And in the fourth place, I wasn't going to use turpentine, I was going to use my thumb." He presented this digit for our inspection. It didn't look too clean from where I was standing. I imagined Tesla after the thumb treatment appearing somewhat tie-dyed.

"Oh, forget it," Arnie said, dumping Tesla unceremoniously on the worn and pitted linoleum. He waved a hand in my direction. "Cat needs to look at the files."

Arnie pointed his brush in the direction of several tall army-surplus file cabinets against one wall. "Happy hunting. Just move anything that's in your way."

I did have to move one canvas. It was an impressionistic rendering of a skinny male nude, standing, shown from the back. The dominant colors were black and purple. When I returned to Arnie with my list, which was limited to those names for which Toots had any kind of address, I was rewarded with a noncommittal nod.

"Okay. How much time we got?" He scanned the sheet.

"Till the end of the day tomorrow," I said. "Or, at a stretch, Friday morning."

His head came up. "You don't want much, do you?"

I shrugged.

"Here's the deal. I can look at driver's licenses — that I got access to. The other stuff I need — voter registration, marriage licenses, maybe court records — that stuff takes time because I gotta ask other people to do the legwork. Like I said, one day, I'll probably be able to get everything just sitting here on my ass in front of the computer. But right now, I gotta find somebody to do that in, what, seven counties?"

I sighed. "Moses said to do the best you could."

"Yeah, okay." He waved a dismissal.

In the hall I passed Tesla, licking the large painting of the three women. He wore a thoughtful expression.

16

JULY 16, 1986

ON THE WAY home from my meeting with Arnie, which I thought of as more of an "encounter" than a meeting, I stopped at Graeter's for a mocha chip cone to take the persistent taste of turpentine out of my mouth. Graeter's ice cream serves this purpose admirably, possibly because the fat in the cream and the chocolate coats the tongue, or possibly because of a chemical reaction between the chocolate or mocha and some neurochemical involved in the senses of smell and taste. A Nutty Buddy doesn't even come close.

When I arrived home, I stepped over two sprawling cats and around a snoring beagle on my way to the back door, only to trip over a box in the hall. I barked one shin on a hard edge and recognized the box. It was an olive-drab footlocker with "Harold E. McGruder" stenciled on the top.

Kevin appeared at his door, wooden spoon in hand. Sidney, the third resident cat, was perched on his shoulder. Sidney's fur was sprinkled with powdered sugar like fairy dust. "There's a box in the hall," Kevin announced

I rubbed my shin and gave him a baleful look.

"I would have taken it in," he said, "but I was stirring constantly."

He would have taken it and if it had been the size of a shoebox.

Kevin had the strength of Paul Bunyan and his blue ox put together, but he followed a policy of using it only when necessary. He called this policy "conservation" and not "laziness."

Moses appeared at the top of the stairs. It seemed to me that he was now favoring his other leg. "You see the footlocker Toots brought over?" he asked. "You should move it before somebody else trips over it. I would have taken it in 'cept you know how my back is."

The front door opened behind me and Al walked in, with Mel close on her heels. "Hey, Cat!" she said. "Did you see the footlocker? I would have taken it in but I was in a hurry."

Mel offered no excuses. She simply squatted, hefted the footlocker, and waited for me to open the door. She looked around at everyone. "It's not that heavy."

Kevin trailed us in and Moses brought up the rear.

Kevin's contribution was to move a pair of sneakers so that Mel could put the footlocker down on the floor next to the couch. "Toots said she didn't find anything suspicious in there," he said, "but she thought you might as well take a look. Oh, and she didn't find what's-her-name's address, either."

"Tommy Thompson?" I asked.

"That's the one."

"She told you all this while you were stirring constantly?"

He shrugged and settled down on the couch next to the locker. "Let's see what you've got." He looked around for a place to park his spoon and ended up sliding it under the waistband of his jeans like a ninja warrior with his favorite knife.

I knelt down on the floor and Mel squatted next to me. Moses pulled up a chair.

The first thing I extracted was a broken seatbelt, one end torn and frayed. I felt the blood drain from my face as I set it aside. Kevin took it up and examined it with curiosity.

"Toots said there were some instructors who would pop a trainee's seatbelt when they were flying upside down, just to see how she'd react."

"You're making that up!" I was appalled.

"Nope." He leaned over and retrieved a small booklet from the locker. He held it up so we could see its title: *Jumping Sense.* "I guess it was like the final exam on this book. If you landed safely, you became a member of the Caterpillar Club."

"And if you didn't?"

"Probably you were inducted posthumously."

We canvassed the contents of the locker. Toots had clearly taken the opportunity to tidy things up, replacing the broken strings and rubber bands I'd spotted with new string. I found everything pretty interesting, so I could just imagine how Stretch had responded to it. Here was a transcript from the Chalmers School of Aviation, confirming the courses that Ethel Ann Ames had completed and the number of flight hours she had logged. Here was an ID bracelet for "Ethel Ann 'Toots' Ames" from "Cincinnati, Ohio." Here was a pilot's ID, which recorded two of Ethel Ann Ames's fingerprints — yet another reminder of the danger these young women had faced. Here was a telegram from Jacqueline Cochran informing Ethel Ann Ames that she had been accepted into the Women Airforce Service Pilots, and a set of instructions for reporting to basic training at Sweetwater, Texas. And nestled in one corner was the neatly folded blue jumpsuit, what Toots called her "zoot suit."

Mel was reading a small diary. "Hey! Did you know they had to wash the bed springs?"

I spent most of Wednesday morning going through the papers, and though they made interesting reading material, I didn't find anything that seemed to be worth killing somebody for. Sophie and Sadie seemed to find the scents fascinating, but if they learned anything important, they kept it to themselves. I sat on the couch in the living room, dropping letters in a loose pile on the floor when I'd finished reading them. Sidney wandered in, nosed around, then began wheezing and went into his hairball crouch, so I snatched up everything in his immediate vicinity.

In the afternoon I drove downtown to the public library to read everything I could find on the WASP. Sure enough, sitting hunched in front of a microfilm reader, I saw some sunbathing pictures and a few lipstick pictures. Like a lot of wartime press, though, the older stories were short on disaster of the kind I thought could be behind the recent killings. None of them mentioned sabotage. Either Jackie Cochran had wielded enough clout to demand stories that were upbeat, or the newspapers and magazines themselves had determined that it was bad for morale to dwell on catastrophe.

But outside of the women's magazines, the press on the WASP was less favorable and I discovered that they were no strangers to controversy. In late 1943, Representative John Costello of California had introduced a bill calling for the militarization of the WASP. Despite some reported complaints from male pilots, the bill had sailed through hearings in the Committee on Military Affairs, where only one witness was heard from: General Henry H. "Hap" Arnold. General Arnold, the unofficial Army godfather of the WASP program, had reported that because of a pressing need for ground forces and a lower air casualty rate than anticipated, the Army Air Force had recently suspended the training of 36,000 pilots. The WASP, he argued, who were being used to ferry planes and train gunners, should eventually assume all domestic military flying responsibilities, freeing up men for overseas combat roles. The men who were complaining that the women pilots had taken over their jobs, he contended, were pilots qualified to fly under less stringent Civil Aeronautics Administration requirements but not under stricter Army Air Force requirements — requirements met by the women pilots of the WASP. Or they were flight instructors whose services were no longer needed. The War Department concurred with this analysis in the form of a letter from Secretary of War Henry Stimson supporting the WASP militarization bill. The committee recommended approval and the bill went to the full House for passage. A similar bill was introduced in the Senate in March 1944.

But that spring, the tone of articles about WASP militarization became increasingly hostile. Male pilots' complaints about the women began to dominate headlines and take up more space. Then the Committee on Civil Service launched an investigation of the WASP program, which actually appeared to have been an investigation of male civilian pilots' complaints about the WASP program. I looked in vain for photos of committee members inspecting the facilities at Avenger Field or meeting with WASP trainers and pilots. Surely a congressional committee could find an angry male pilot to fly its members to Sweetwater, Texas. But if they had visited Avenger, the press hadn't covered it. The committee report, called the Ramspeck Report after committee chair Robert Ramspeck, found all of the allegations against the WASP valid. In a *New York Times* article, I read a sentence quoted from the Ramspeck Report: *The implication contained in the proposal, that it is now either necessary or desirable to recruit stenographers, clerks, school teachers, housewives, factory workers and other inexperienced personnel for training at great outlay of public funds as pilots for the military planes of the Government, particularly when there already exists a surplus of personnel to perform these identical duties, is as startling as it is invalid.*

"What the hell?" I said.

I felt rather than saw heads turning in my direction. I glanced up and caught the frown of a librarian. "Sorry," I muttered.

Don't ask me why I was so surprised. After all, I had grown up with sexism and had a healthy share of it myself, when I was being honest. Even now, I found it hard to imagine women fighter pilots, though I certainly knew they existed. But having spent some time around Toots and Stretch, I had gained a new respect for women pilots. I tried to imagine them as housewives and stenographers. I couldn't. The jumpsuit and overalls got in the way — or maybe it was the muscular biceps.

"So it was okay to recruit male pipefitters, tree trimmers, ditch diggers, salesmen, and business managers to train as pilots, I guess," I said under my breath. I cranked the machine to cover the noise. "Or force the military to lower its standards, just to make sure that the person in the goddamn cockpit had a —." The reel groaned in protest and I felt eyes on the back of my neck.

After the report was released, the press grew even more negative:

the WASP program was expensive and unnecessary, the women were incompetent, the graduation rate was low, and the fatality rate was high. Over and over again, I read that women were taking jobs away from more qualified men. Wounded pilots were coming home after collecting their medals and their honorable discharges and finding all of the flying jobs held by charming, perky, but unqualified "girls." Only a Dallas newspaper, published within striking distance of Sweetwater, had the courage to refute the unsubstantiated claims made by the Ramspeck Report, citing lower graduation rates and higher fatality rates among male AAF trainees than among the WASP.

Buried in the articles was a sentence that made me pause. "I'm a trained pilot," one Joe Maranda told a reporter angrily, "and they want to draft me into the regular Army? That's nuts!" I re-read the sentence and stopped on the word "draft." Was that what this was about? I thought back. It seemed likely to me that domestic pilots and flight instructors had been given draft deferments during the war. But if they lost their pilot jobs, that deferment would have disappeared. General Arnold claimed that what the Army needed was ground forces. Suppose the real impetus behind all of this anger was fear — the fear of losing a relatively safe domestic pilot's job and getting drafted for dangerous overseas combat. Suddenly, it all made sense to me.

The Ramspeck Report was read into the Congressional record by a Louisiana congressman with a flair for oratory. Costello, the sponsor of the militarization bill, had a less florid speaking style. The press hammered away at the bill. On June 22, 1944, the bill was defeated by nineteen votes — the first time since 1941 that Congress had rejected an Army Air Force recommendation. But by then, the Allies, with the support of air forces commanded by General Arnold, had successfully invaded the European mainland on D-Day. When Arnold returned to Washington, he announced that the WASP program would end with the current class. The following December, the last of the WASP packed their bags and went home, with no severance pay and no G.I. Bill.

I sat back and crooked my winding arm behind my back to stretch it. Obviously, the WASP hadn't been short on enemies, both foreign and domestic, during the war, but that didn't explain why someone would want to kill them off forty years later. I closed my tired eyes and tried to develop a fantasy in which a particularly angry former pilot, a good old boy from his Camels down to his cowboy boots, had been drafted after losing his deferment. After the war, his wife had joined the rush to the divorce court. He'd had a hard time getting a job, maybe because of a war injury or maybe because he drank too much to forget the war or maybe just because he was an incompetent jackass. He'd remarried twice, but wives number two and three had dumped him as well. None of his children liked him and the best he could expect from them, once they passed the age of mandatory visitations, was an occasional birthday card. Then, recently, he'd been diagnosed with cancer — maybe lung cancer, from the Camels. Or maybe it was some kind of cancer caused by exposure at the manufacturing job he'd managed to hold down all these years, even though every time he saw a plane flying against blue sky and white clouds, he told himself that he was made for better things. The cancer diagnosis made him drink more and drinking more fueled his bitterness, resentment, and anger. "It all started," he'd tell himself, tongue thickened by alcohol, "with those damned women!"

"Hey, lady," a voice broke in, close to my ear.

My eyes popped open to see a petite brunette hugging a spiral notebook, a thick textbook, and an arm full of microfilm boxes to her chest. Protruding from the notebook and pointed in my direction was some kind of writing implement topped by a pink puffball covered with spangles. Kind of made me nostalgic for the old chrome yellow Eberhard Fabers.

"Are you done with the machine?" she asked. "We got homework."

"No, I'm just resting my eyes," I said. "Not enough carrot cake."

A second pre-adolescent appeared, her blonde ponytail set so high on her head that it reminded me of a blonde volcano. She carried a minuscule red plastic purse hardly big enough for her library card, a ring binder, and a duplicate of the oversized textbook. She nudged the brunette.

"Over there. That guy's leaving."

The two departed and left me to my research. I knew the fantasy was a no-go. Even if my fantasy pilot had been training at Harlingen when he'd been redeployed, it hardly seemed likely that he'd do the kind of research necessary to hunt down eight women pilots after all these years, just to exact some kind of twisted revenge.

But then I remembered a story Toots had told — something about a trainer who had gotten into trouble with the WASP. It had something to do with the one called Tex, something about a complaint to Jackie Cochran that had resulted in the trainer's reassignment. But that had happened at Love Field, ironically enough. Because I had some roots in Texas myself, I happened to know that Love was in Dallas. Dallas was half of a very big state away from Harlingen, but I supposed the distance was closer if you were a pilot. But even if the trainer was still pissed off after all these years, wouldn't he have started his killing spree with Tex? I remembered from the list that Tex lived in Texas, but Toots hadn't mentioned any other accidents or fatalities, so I assumed that Tex was still alive and kicking. In fact, I'd probably meet her in — what? — less than forty-eight hours. I eyed the piles of little brown microfilm boxes and sighed.

17

JULY 19, 1986

I HUNG IN THE TREE, thinking about Tex. She'd still been trying to fly the plane when we jumped.

"Don't worry about Tex," Toots had shouted in my ear when I'd turned to look over my shoulder as Toots pushed me toward the rear of the plane. "She's a pro."

But even pros met their match, if they lived long enough. Had Tex met hers? The air didn't seem smoky and I couldn't smell a fire, but then, the wind might have been carrying smoke away from the crash site.

Gusts of wind rattled the branches of trees and the branch I was hanging from swayed. My heart shot to my throat. When the lightning flickered, I turned my head slowly, trying to get my bearings. But all I could see was tree and parachute. I was afraid to look down.

My hands were still clamped to my parachute — to those strap thingies that hold you suspended from the umbrella part. I knew it couldn't do me any good at this point. It occurred to me that if the damned thing wasn't ripped, I might not be seeing much of the tree at all. The branch swayed again, gently, and I felt something sharp poking me in the behind — probably a branch I'd broken off in my crash landing. Probably, the branch had been dead already, which was why it had broken when my feet made contact with it. Maybe, in spite of the leafy shapes I could make out against the glimmerings of light, most of the tree was dead. Wasn't lightning attracted to dead trees? I should have paid more attention in the sixth grade.

A flash lit up the sky. When I opened my eyes again, I heard a rumble of thunder, low and ominous.

Time to start shouting for help. I opened my mouth and yelled, but even I could barely hear my voice over the rising wind, the trees, and the thunder. I shouted a few more times, but unless my imagination was playing tricks on me, which was likely, the movement of my chest as I filled my lungs to shout was somehow causing me to slip lower in the tree. The sharp branch was now inscribing a small, painful semicircle on my lower back. I stopped shouting.

I took a shallower breath and tried to remember some of the breathing exercises my daughter Franny had taught me when she was in her yoga phase. It was no good. I couldn't remember. Lamaze breathing, I could remember, but panting was out of the question under the circumstances.

I tried a more reliable method of controlling my panic. "Let's play the Glad Game. Think of things to be glad about. You're alive — that's one. You didn't land in a river or on a hard concrete surface. You're still conscious." I paused, unsure of whether or not to be glad about that. "You landed in a nice, sturdy tree. You haven't been attacked by a rabid raccoon and no squirrel has yet chewed through your straps."

I stopped. I'd run out of things to be glad about.

I rejected "You're dry" because that was so clearly a temporary state and pointing it out seemed to invite trouble.

I stretched out one foot, then another, cautiously, tentatively, hoping to find a sturdy branch to stand on. I touched something solid and promising and began to explore it with the toe of my sneaker.

A crack of thunder made me jump and I slipped lower. My foot grazed the branch and then dropped.

I remained still and breathed.

And then I thought of one more thing to be glad about: I'd proven my point about the dangers of flying.

18

JULY 16, 1986

I STILL HAD a hefty stack of little brown boxes to work my way through and I couldn't understand why, if the program had ended in 1944. I knew some of it had to do with retroactive militarization, so I skipped ahead to the 70s.

In the 70s, I discovered that the cause of WASP militarization was opposed by some of the usual suspects — veterans organizations — and by some surprising ones, including President Jimmy Carter. Its supporters included Representative Patsy Mink, Air Force Colonel Bruce Arnold, son of the same General Arnold who had fought for militarization during the war, and, to my surprise, Senator Barry Goldwater, who seemed an unlikely feminist champion. The veterans had managed to kill two bills in committee, once in 1972 and once in 1975. But in 1976, the Air Force began training women pilots.

The Women's Movement had apparently sensitized the press, which now tended toward outrage that WASP pilots had been denied military status and benefits for so long. Now, they quoted members of organizations called the "WASP Military Committee" and the "Order of Fifinella," which suggested to me that the WASP themselves had developed some organization and political savvy. Even the *New York Times* ran articles on the first women's air force.

When I began to read comments from the WASP pilots, I realized that I was seeing something new: except for the lipstick-and-sunbathing curiosity pieces for the women's magazines, none of the newspaper articles from the 40s had ever quoted a woman pilot. That struck me as odd.

In 1977, Senator Goldwater threatened to attach a WASP militarization amendment to every bill he introduced if the Veterans Affairs Committee didn't move the current bill out of committee. According to news reports, several former WASP testified, as did their opponents from the VFW, the American Legion, and the Veterans Administration. Similar hearings were held in the House. In late October and early November 1977 — just nine years ago, I realized — the relevant legislation had passed both houses of Congress, and on November 23rd, President Carter had signed the bill into law.

Nine years ago. It was hard for me to imagine someone holding a grudge for forty years, at least a grudge that had suddenly erupted into violence this summer. But clearly the debates of less than a decade ago had stirred up some old resentments. Was there something going on now that I needed to know about? Stretch and Toots had mentioned a museum project. I couldn't see anyone getting riled over a museum, but maybe I didn't know everything I needed to know. I'd have to ask Toots about it.

At home I found a basketball game in progress in the parking lot out back. Kevin, Moses, Mel, Al, Leon, and Moses's friend Chuck were jostling each other to the rhythmic thuds of leather on cement. They were sweaty and intense. My boy Sidney was sitting on the sidelines, guarding the beer and waiting for his chance to be called off the bench. His tail twitched in excitement. Sophie had commandeered a lounge chair, where she was curled up, tail to nose, napping, and Winnie the beagle lay beneath her in the shade of the chair, panting. Maybe Winnie had fouled out of the game. Sadie was nowhere to be seen; she was the only small animal to have the sense to avoid large, out-of-control humans wielding hard objects. But after an afternoon of repeated cranking in an over-air-conditioned room, I thought it looked like fun.

"Here she is," Chuck shouted as I climbed out of my car. He was the biggest player on the court, tall and solidly built. "The woman who's gonna win the game for us. Come on, baby, join my team and save my sorry ass."

"You need me to block for you?" I said.

"De-fense what you do best," he said.

This was true. I couldn't shoot for shit. But if I moved around the court, my teammates usually found a way to shoot over me.

So I entered the fray.

Leon gave me the ground rules. He was tall and lanky for his age and surprisingly graceful on a basketball court. "Don't b-b-block nothing I p-put up, M-miz Cat. I'm on your t-t-team."

"Me, too," said Kevin.

"Me, too, said Mel.

"Yeah, me, too," said Moses.

"No, you ain't!" Leon objected indignantly. "They f-f-fibbing, M-Miz Cat. Don't listen to them. It's m-m-me —." He tapped his tie-dyed T-shirt, another second from the store where he sometimes worked. On the back, it said, "Northside Bowl-a-Bama." "— And Al and Ch-ch-chuck." He pointed at each of my team members.

"I don't know why you bothered to tell her all that," Moses said. He was leaning over to catch his breath. "She can't never remember who's on what team, anyway."

Kevin beamed at me. "That's why it's so much more fun when she's in the game."

"Y'all leave my girl alone," Chuck said. He draped a heavy arm over my shoulders. "We gon' run some plays make y'all sorry y'all showed up here today. Ain't that right, Cat?"

Leon ignored them all and continued the line-up. "And W-w-winnie on injure re-reserve," he finished.

"Awww—." I turned to look at her. She heard her name, raised her head, and thumped her tail. "What happened to Winnie?"

"She caught a dribble on the paw," Moses said. "She be okay."

"She's just pretending, anyway," Kevin groused, "to win over the crowd." That was how I knew it was his dribble that had injured her.

Sidney sauntered over and touched noses with her in commiseration.

"Come on, people," Moses said. "We playing, or are we just having a Kodak moment?"

I lasted half an hour until Mel threw an elbow that caught me in the chest as we fought for a rebound.

"Jesus, Mel, lighten up a little, willya?" I said. "I'm a foot shorter than you, for crissakes. Only way I'm going to beat you on a rebound is if you get clipped by a low-flying plane."

"Sorry, Cat," she said, and looked genuinely regretful. I retired to the lounge chair, where I scooped up Sophie and settled her on my lap. I reached for a beer.

"That's okay, baby," Chuck said. "Give 'em a chance to catch up."

Several people were keeping score, but since the scores didn't match up and were all wildly improbable, I didn't worry too much about letting my team down.

"Unless —," Chuck added. He turned toward Sidney. "Yes, I do believe it's time for our secret weapon." He reached down and lifted Sidney with one of his large hands.

"Oh, no!" Al protested. "Not the Sidman!"

"Yeah, how we supposed to defend against that?" Mel said.

Moses moved forward to guard Chuck and Sidney. Leon moved forward to set up a pick. Sidney dangled aloft, feet swaying, as Chuck dribbled and dodged. Then they ducked behind Leon. Moses bumped Leon and reacted as if he'd hit a brick wall. He made one of those air-releasing sounds, like "unhhh" as he fell backward. Chuck levitated and Sidney got one paw on the ball before Chuck released it and it sailed through the air and into the net.

"Yessss!" I shouted. I pumped a fist.

"Come on, Sid," Chuck said. "You want to hang on the net a little, like the pros do?"

He raised Sidney to net height and draped two paws over the

rim, which was lower than regulation height out of deference to my height and incompetence. Sidney hung on the rim long enough to get his thumpers tangled in the net, and then Chuck freed him and brought him down so he could trade high-fives with his teammates.

"Aw, man, he does it every time," Al complained in mock disappointment.

Mel and Leon were helping Moses up. I knew he'd hammed it up for Leon's sake and hadn't been as surprised as he'd pretended. After all, this was the way all of our games ended.

"Moses, you've got to stop running into those picks," Mel was saying.

Moses shook his head ruefully. "Man, I never see 'em coming." Then he patted Leon on the shoulder and grinned at him. "C'mon, man, I'll buy you a drink."

"You see Sidney, Cat?" Kevin asked. "He just flew through the air."

I nodded. "Only way to fly."

After dinner, Moses and I moved the lawn chairs to the front yard and traded information as the light faded. He had insisted on following up at the small airport where Toots parked her plane (was that right — "parked"?), but he hadn't learned anything more about who might have sabotaged it.

"Security's pretty loose, Cat," he said.

"Can Toots sue the airport for damages?" I asked.

"Probably, but she won't. You find out anything at the library?"

I filled him in a little on the history of the WASP and he said he remembered some of it, which surprised me, because I hadn't known any of it. Maybe I'd heard something about the congressional debates at some time, but I swear motherhood depletes your brain cells faster than anything, and once they give out, they're gone for good.

"Well," Moses said finally, "it's interesting, but it don't seem relevant to me."

"Me, either. But maybe there's more to the story than what I read in the paper."

"Usually is."

"What's your take on Stretch?" I asked.

"As what? A suspect in the sabotage?"

"I don't know," I said. "Is she living with Toots? We don't even know that. Where did Toots meet her? She seems to take a big interest in the WASP."

"That seems natural enough. She's a pilot, she's interested in the pioneers. A lot of young people don't care about that stuff — history and all."

"That's right. A lot don't. But she does."

"She said anybody who knew how well Toots could fly wouldn't have tried to kill her by putting a rag in the oil port," he said.

"That's what she said. You believe it?"

"Think so."

"Of course, it could be that the sabotage wasn't intended to kill Toots," I said. "Maybe it was just intended to scare her."

"So she'd run out and hire a couple of crack detectives like us?"

"Yeah, or say, 'Jeepers! Maybe I'd better go get that dangerous photograph I've been hiding and ask Stretch to put it in a safe place.' And then the saboteur would watch them to see where they put it. That's how Sherlock Holmes did it, more or less."

It sounded kind of dumb when I said it, but he didn't disagree. He just said, "Could be."

A silence fell. I knew he was avoiding going back inside because he'd have to face the camera equipment and instruction manual.

"I think I'll ask Toots about Stretch," I said at last. "And maybe I'll ask Arnie to add her to his list. We've got her real name — Darcy Livingston. Even if we don't have an address, she must have a pilot's license. And even though it probably isn't relevant, I think I'll ask Toots to tell me something about the fight over militarization." I'd have plenty of time since the next day I'd be riding shotgun when Toots went to Dayton to meet with Lou Zimmerman. "In the meantime, want to practice your night photography?"

19

JULY 17, 1986

IN THE END, he had to break down and call his son Paul.

"I don't see why I need all this equipment," he said later as he was soaking the ankle he'd twisted when he ran into Leon's pick. He waved a hand at the equipment sitting on or leaning against the coffee table and fanned himself with a thick booklet that look like a manual. "They got cameras now you can point and click. Why can't I use one of those? Or the Polaroid Leon gave us — why can't I use that? Why do I have to know how to use a light meter when I could get a camera that figures it out for me? If it's too dark, the flash goes off — end of story."

But soon I had my own problems. I said I was going to "ride shotgun," but that wasn't exactly the way it happened, unless sitting in the copilot's seat gripping the armrests in terror as clouds stream past the windshield constitutes "riding shotgun."

We'd started out in the car; that was okay. Toots was filling me in on our upcoming visit to Lou Pirelli Zimmerman and that's what I was paying attention to.

"Lou was one class ahead of me at Avenger," Toots said as she gathered speed in her venerable Volvo. "She was 43-W-8. I was 43-W-9. She was one of the founders of the national organization, the

Order of Fifinella. She was very active in the campaign for militarization. She's the one who got me involved."

"Is she still flying?"

Toots nodded. "So far. She's got a Comanche. But her lungs aren't so good, I don't think. She smoked too long. So I don't know how much longer she'll be flying."

"And you're going to see her about the reunion?"

"Yeah, we just have some logistics to discuss. Lou wants to go over the schedule before she prints it out. We could do it over the phone, but I'd rather do it in person. And golly, look at that sky! It's a perfect day to fly."

She slowed and turned the car into a side road. Through the dazzling glare of the windshield I saw the word "airport."

"They fixed your plane already?" I asked in a weak voice.

"Nope, we've got a loaner," Toots said.

A loaner? Like a rental car? My throat went dry. This was very, very bad news. In front of us, the small frame building we were headed toward was smaller than your average Hertz counter.

I followed Toots around as she went through something called a "pre-flight," emitting little bleats of protest.

"Maybe this isn't such a good idea," I said, as she looked the plane over.

She opened the little hatch in the nose, reached in and unscrewed something.

"Have you ever flown this thing before?"

She applied a large screwdriver to something I couldn't see.

"I mean, how do you know the guy who loaned it to you is as conscientious about maintenance as you are?"

She pulled the screwdriver out, pushed up her sunglasses, and studied it.

"Dayton's right up the road, right? It's not far." I turned hopefully in the direction of our destination, as if I could see it from where I was standing.

She lowered her glasses, returned the thing in her hand to wherever she got it from, and closed the panel.

I followed her to the tip of the nose, where she examined the propeller, reaching up and turning it with her hand.

"You've heard about the hole in the ozone layer, right?"

I bent as she crouched to inspect the wheels.

"Right?"

She stood up and looked at me for the first time.

"I think I have a heart condition," I said.

She nodded. "It's called 'fear.'" She grinned at me. "We have nothing to fear but fear itself. Come on. I promise not to do any tricks with you in the plane. Scouts honor."

"What about sabotage? That's not nothing," I objected. She had opened the cabin door on the passenger's side. "What about crash-landing in a cow pasture? What about that?"

She put her hand on my elbow and guided me firmly. "In you go," she said.

"What about the air traffic controller shortage?" The seat was comfortable enough but it was already too far from the ground, in my opinion.

"Irrelevant here," she said, reaching across me. "It's a general aviation airport. There are no controllers." She snapped my seatbelt and my heart jumped at the sound.

"What do you mean, 'no controllers'? Who gives you permission to take off?"

"Nobody. I just notify all of the pilots within range and they let me know if they're in the way." She shut the door.

This sounded pretty slipshod to me. When she opened the door on the other side, I opened my mouth to say so, but she cut me off. "Look, Cat, nobody wants to run into anybody else. And there's not much traffic to control. Look around."

I looked. The sky was cloudless, except for some very high, thin clouds in the west. There were no planes in sight. Or so I thought until I followed a white line and realized that it was a jet trail. Then I saw another. Then a third. I couldn't actually see the planes, but something was moving up there.

"Look!" I said urgently, grabbing her elbow as she settled into her seat. I wanted to make sure she saw them. "I see three planes."

Toots glanced up. "Cat, those are jets from Wright-Patt. They're up at maybe fifty-five thousand. Our max is thirteen-five. They're not even in the same city we're in, much less the same neighborhood. Now, sit back and relax." She was fiddling with the instrument panel. "Close your eyes if it helps."

"I could be having a heart attack." I put a hand to my chest.

"Breathe," she instructed. Then she put on the headset and started the engine.

"What if I have to go to the bathroom?" I said, but I couldn't hear myself anymore.

The little plane began to move. It bumped along like a Volkswagen beetle on a bad road. Didn't they put shock absorbers in these things? I closed my eyes and gripped the armrests.

Aloud, I said, "I get motion sickness, really bad. I'll probably throw up all over the instrument panel." This was the one I should've thought of before she put the headset on.

The plane turned slowly, then paused. I opened one eye and the runway winked at me dead ahead. I shut it.

Then we were zooming along. The sound of the engine drowned out the pounding of blood in my ears. The whole plane rattled and I flashed on images of the space shuttle *Challenger*, coming apart at the seams not six months ago.

Then we were airborne and climbing. I held my breath. I willed the plane upward.

We seemed to be leveling off when I felt a nudge. I opened my eyes. Toots was trying to hand me a set of earphones. I loosened my grip on one armrest and took it. One-handed, I looped it over my head. Her voice said soothingly, "Now, that wasn't so bad, was it?"

I nodded. I was well aware that this nod might be misinterpreted, but my jaw was clamped shut and I couldn't talk.

"You said you had some questions for me about the history of the WASP," she said.

Out the window, all I could see was sky. It was very blue. I didn't look down. I unclamped my jaw, opened it wide, and yawned. My ears popped and the drone of the engine grew louder.

"Um, I don't want to distract you while you're — um, driving."

Her laughter sounded like static in my ear.

"I've had an instructor flip the plane on me while I was whistling 'The Star-Spangled Banner.' I think I can handle a few questions."

A thought struck me. "You don't need me to read a map, do you?" Moses drove fast, but Toots was faster. I didn't want us to overshoot Dayton and end up in Albuquerque.

"Nope. The LORAN-C will navigate. Just sit back, relax, and talk to me."

"Well, I was reading up yesterday on the whole militarization thing."

"Uh-huh."

"Why exactly were the male pilots so stirred up? Was it just competition or sexism? Or did the draft have something to do with it?"

"The draft definitely had something to do with it, and I'm impressed that you figured that out. It sure wasn't a point made in the newspaper articles at the time. The pilots who were qualified for military flying and the flight instructors who lost their jobs when the Air Force cut back on pilot training — they all lost their draft deferments. That meant that they were drafted as potential ground troops, which is what the Army needed most at the time. They weren't too happy about that and neither were the cadets who were reassigned in the middle of their flight training. I did feel bad for those kids! I know how I would've felt if someone had shut down my program in the middle of training. One of the many good things General Arnold did for us when he shut down the WASP was complete all the training programs in progress.

"Of course, there were some gals preparing to report for training when he killed the program and they were notified by telegram four days before they were supposed to report to Avenger. Some of them were already in Sweetwater, most of them were on their way — at their own expense, remember. Some of them had sold their possessions — even their houses — to finance the trip. They'd quit their jobs. That was a sad day in their lives, I'm sure. If they made it as far as Sweetwater, they got transportation back to the base nearest their home. But that was it. Nobody refunded their travel expenses."

"But Cochran sent some of you to officers' training."

"Yep, even when she saw the end coming, she was hoping we'd be accepted as officers in other branches of the military."

"So the male pilots were really hostile."

"Not all of them," she said quickly. "Probably not most of them, once they saw us fly. We had a lot of support."

"Did you ever have any confrontations with them? I mean, one on one?"

"Sure, all the time. I mean, we didn't usually get into shoving or even shouting matches. Mostly it was snide comments aimed in our direction and we learned to ignore them. But some of us had shorter fuses than others. I remember Tex used to challenge them to arm wrestle."

"No kidding? Did she always win?"

"She didn't always win the arm wrestling, but she usually won some respect. She wasn't easy to beat."

"Avenger must have had a different atmosphere than most of the places you were assigned to afterward."

"Now there's an understatement, though we were exposed to some of the nastiness when we flew cross-countries during our Avenger training."

"How about at Harlingen? Was the environment especially hostile?"

"Not especially. There were a few sour apples, of course. But two of us ended up married to guys we met there, so that ought to tell you something."

"Do you remember any particular confrontations?" I asked. "Do you remember any male pilots who lost their jobs and deferments while you were there?"

I looked over at Toots and saw her squint with concentration. Her eyes were practically closed. My heart skipped.

"Never mind," I said hastily. "Forget I asked."

So far, I had to admit that the ride had been smoother in the air than on the ground, but I thought that was probably because of my shallow breathing.

"I don't remember anybody like that who was based at Harlingen," she said, opening her eyes. "It was a gunnery school, so any target towers we replaced had been replaced long before we arrived. We did run into a trio of jerks in a bar in Corpus Christi one night when we were all together — a pretty rare occasion. These guys were about to ship out from Camp Hulen in Matagorda County and two of them had been ferry pilots. They were drunk and really obnoxious. One of them got in Tex's face, and as soon as his fist came up, she punched him in the gut. One of his buddies rushed her and she sidestepped him and tripped him, and he went sprawling. Number Three, who hadn't even been a pilot but seemed to feel that the honor of the US Army was at stake, pulled a switchblade out of his pocket and squared off with Tex. Tex reached over for a beer bottle, broke it off at the neck, and waited for him. But before he could move, Esther clobbered him with a full beer bottle.

"At that point, somebody — one of the onlookers — yelled, 'Hey, a Jap clobbered one of ours!' And somebody else yelled, 'Hey, that ain't fair!' All three of our attackers were down now, but the first guy was getting up. 'We play girls' rules,' Maddy said, and she yanked a tablecloth off a nearby table — not that this was the kind of joint that ran to tablecloths, generally speaking, you understand — and flung it over the first guy. I picked up the switchblade and threw it so it stuck in the wall. Some of the guys who were starting to get up to join the fight — I don't know on whose side — they saw the knife whizz past and sat back down. Squeak threw a glass of beer in Number Two's face, and Chub, who was wearing high heels, stepped on one of his hands.

"Number Three was getting up, shaking his head to clear it and bellowing with rage. Tommy moved in front of him as he stood and said, 'Don't you ever, *ever*, pull a knife on a WASP again!' Then she kicked him in the nuts. Lou was saying over all the noise, 'Girls! Girls! Remember Miss Cochran! Decorum, girls, decorum.'

"'In other words,' Esther shouted, 'cheese it before the MPs get here!' And she grabbed Tommy around the waist and Squeak by the hand and dragged them out. We all followed, with Tex bringing up the rear, watching our backs. I heard her say, in her best Texas drawl, 'We apologize for the disturbance, folks.' It was quite a night. When you think about it, those three had to be drunk to think they could take on eight WASP and win."

"They probably didn't have any doubt that they would win," I said.

But what had I learned? I'd already known that the whole idea of women pilots could make some men see red. Now I knew that if they started a fight with a group of WASP, the women could finish it. But I couldn't see one of those three men returning forty years later for revenge.

"Were emotions running as high when militarization came up again in the 70s?" I asked.

"Sure. Some of the male vets were incensed. Not all of them — we had some supporters, too. Like the *Stars and Stripes*. When they started covering the WASP debates, and their coverage was sympathetic, some vets were furious, so it was a pretty courageous thing for them to do."

"Any more physical assaults you want to tell me about?"

Toots laughed. "Nothing like that."

"So the Order of Fifinella was formed to lobby for militarization?"

Toots shook her head. "No, it was formed after disbandment. It was a service organization at first — the closest thing we had to a Veteran's Administration, and as usual, we had to do it ourselves. The idea was to spread news about employment possibilities. Miss Cochran had really tried to find work for us. She even offered our services to other Allies, but nobody accepted. The Order was also supposed to keep us informed about efforts to give us military benefits. I guess it was inevitable that the group would turn into an advocacy group. The Order of Fifinella approached its first congressional representative with a militarization bill back in 1947."

"But you didn't succeed until 1977?"

"Right, thirty years later," Toots agreed. "By then, the Women's Movement had changed things."

I nodded. "There's something that puzzles me, though. In the 70s, several former WASP testified and their testimony seemed to have been pretty effective at countering the charges of incompetence made back in the 40s. But why didn't any women pilots testify the first time around, when the charges were first made?"

"We weren't allowed. We weren't permitted to discuss our work, or even our training, publicly."

"Was it that top-secret?"

She shrugged. "It was supposed to be. We weren't supposed to tell our families how many girls were training at Avenger, for example, or give them any details of our training. Most of us did, of course, so my letters are full of admonitions not to tell anybody, as if my mother was going to run into a Nazi spy at the butcher shop and spill the beans. Keeping us out of the political battle was probably also part of Miss Cochran's campaign to make sure that we were always perceived as decorous young ladies. Or maybe she just wanted to keep us focused."

I imagined the Corpus Christi bar brawl and smiled.

"You're smiling," Toots observed. "Are you breathing?"

"A little," I admitted.

"Good," she said, "because we're about to land."

20

JULY 19, 1986

I HEARD the rain before I felt it. In the darkness, I couldn't even see it. Then a gust of wind blew me sideways and I felt cool water against my neck and hands.

I felt something in the parachute give and I dropped. I was still suspended, but how far from the ground? I didn't want to spend the night in terror only to discover, at dawn, that I was two feet from the ground. I didn't think I had that kind of luck, but whoever was in charge did, as I pointed out before, have a sense of humor.

I lowered my head slowly and tried to penetrate the darkness below me. I couldn't see anything past my white Adidas. Then a bolt of lightning flashed and I heard a deafening crack, followed by a boom of thunder and a crash. Someplace nearby, a tree had just been hit. So I wasn't hanging in the tallest tree in the neighborhood. But what if I was hanging in the second tallest?

After the tree exploded, there was an ominous silence. Even the rain fell quietly.

In that silence, I heard a new sound — the snapping of twigs. Something was down there and it was coming this way. Were there bears or mountain lions in rural Southern Ohio? I didn't think so. But as I reassured myself, I heard a distinctively animal grunt.

It wasn't a cat. Cats walk silently and they don't grunt.

Then my eyes made out a small, dim light moving on the edge of my vision below me. It appeared and disappeared, and it was surrounded by tiny, bright, sparkling lights. Fireflies? Fairies?

Another flash of lightning and peal of thunder disrupted my vision. I strained to see and hear and thought I heard heavy breathing. Then the lights reappeared just below me. The dull one cast a circle of light on the ground, which was still a long way down to somebody who had never in her life jumped off the high board at the neighborhood pool.

Then the circle moved and I found it trained on me. As my eyes adjusted, I saw that I had, indeed, been found.

Happy, the Golden retriever, gave a few excited barks. Unable to respond in kind because of my precarious position, I said softly, "Hey, guy."

Happy appeared to study me intently for a moment, not the least bit self-conscious about the combination of miner's helmet and space alien halo he had strapped to his head. He could tell at a glance that I wasn't the fashion police. He was beginning to figure out that I wasn't the human he'd been looking for, either. He sat down on his haunches and howled.

I knew just how he felt. If I was going to be rescued by a dog, I'd been hoping for a St. Bernard with a little keg of whiskey attached to his collar.

21

JULY 17, 1986

OKAY, I'll say it: the landing wasn't too bad. At least we were headed in the right direction. But half an hour later, we were still sitting in a pair of molded plastic chairs in the waiting area. I didn't object to the delay. The longer it took our ride to show up, the longer it would be before we'd have to take off again. Still, I was beginning to worry.

I'd already asked Toots about the phone calls to the remaining Harlingen WASP that she'd promised to make. None of them had received a call from Maddy, either on the 28th or between that night and the time of her death less than forty-eight hours later.

"I told them about the two deaths, how close together they were," she'd said. "And I told them about the sabotage to my plane. I had to. I told them all to be careful."

"How did they take it?"

"Well, if anybody thought I was nuts, they didn't say so. I told them what Maddy had said to me, about telling what we knew. I got a lot of interesting suggestions for what she meant by 'that boy she went off with,' but to be honest, none of them sounded very likely. I think you should probably hear them for yourself, though."

She looked at her watch again. "I can't imagine what's keeping

Lou. Chub was always late for everything except the flight line, but not Lou."

"Tell me about Stretch," I said. "How'd you meet her?"

Toots had twisted around to check the clock on the wall behind us. It probably read the same time as her wristwatch. She turned back. "I advertised for an apprentice in the Ninety-Nines magazine."

"The Ninety-Nines?"

"That's the biggest international organization of women pilots. It dates back to 1929."

"So why 'Ninety-Nines'? Why not 'Twenty-Nines'?"

"There were ninety-nine charter members when they named it — renamed it, actually. Earhart was president at the time."

"Was Stretch the only applicant for the apprentice job? Is it a job?"

"No, there were several applicants — not a lot, because it doesn't pay all that well and not everybody wants to move to Ohio for that kind of pay plus room and board. There was one local gal I interviewed, but she just didn't have Stretch's expertise. And Stretch had done her homework. She'd looked me up and mentioned in her letter how excited she'd be to work with a former WASP and acrobatics champion. It's not that hard to find out those things about me, but still, I was impressed that she'd bothered. She clearly wanted the job. And — well, she was an engineer from MIT." Toots grinned. "How could I pass her up?"

"Where is she from originally?"

"New Jersey, I think."

"That where she learned to fly?"

"I guess so. She's been flying since she was a teenager." She stood up. "I think I'd better call again."

I stood up, too. I wasn't sure who'd invented molded plastic chairs, but I was certain they hadn't used my buns to mold them.

"Do you have any other numbers to try?"

Toots shook her head. "She has a daughter in town, but I don't know the daughter's number. Her husband's retired."

While she was gone, I amused myself by reading the bulletin

board. The business cards advertised services from flight instruction to custom painting. Most of the notices I couldn't translate. There were quite a few airplanes for sale, and though none of them was obviously battered, burned, or scarred, I couldn't help wondering what was wrong with them. Flying didn't seem like the kind of hobby you gave up because you'd taken up something else, like stamp collecting, or even because you'd gotten busy doing other things, like coaching Little League. You didn't get a plane for a present unless you wanted one. One plane looked pretty much like another to me, whether it was a 1969 model or a 1984 model. It's not like they added tailfins or a sunroof to entice plane owners to trade in their older model for a newer one. So that had to mean that these planes were in some way unsatisfactory.

"Still no answer," Toots said behind me.

"Toots, what will happen to your Cessna?" I asked. "Will you fix it or sell it?"

"Too early to tell." She was reading the bulletin board over my shoulder. "The mechanics will have to take a closer look. The fire was confined to the engine area and most of that can be replaced. As long as the fire didn't compromise the structure, I'll get it fixed. I'll probably do some of the work myself."

I was going to ask her how dangerous it was to buy a used plane. Then it struck me that the plane we'd flown here in might be a secondhand plane and decided I was better off not knowing.

She looked at her watch again.

"Cat, I don't like this," she said. "I'm worried. Let's call a cab and head over to her house."

I nodded. "She could be lying at the bottom of her basement stairs."

"She doesn't have a basement," Toots said. "But she does have a plane."

The neighborhood was peaceful on this hot weekday in July. The kids must have all been at the pool, at a summer day camp, or inside their air-conditioned houses. The Zimmerman house was a modern two-story, with beige siding and matching multicolored brick, slate blue shutters, an attached garage, and a narrow covered porch set off by skinny columns. Flower beds stuffed with colorful annuals occupied most of the front yard. The house looked deserted. Toots rang the bell anyway. We heard it chime inside.

Toots bent to open the letter slot in the front door and peer inside. "Lou!" she called. "Are you in there? It's Toots. Can you hear me?"

Silence.

She rang the bell again for good measure. Then she said, "Let's go around back. I know where she hides the key."

I wouldn't have called the key "hidden" myself, given that it was placed under a conspicuous flowerpot in the first location a burglar would check, but maybe this wasn't a neighborhood prone to burglary. Toots fitted it in the lock, turned it, and frowned.

"What's the matter?" I said.

"I just locked it. It wasn't locked."

We looked at each other.

"So maybe she's home after all," I said. "She could be in the shower."

We went in. The house was inhabited by at least one smoker — that much was clear from the odor. We were standing in a tidy kitchen with green appliances and perky ivy wallpaper. There was a quarter-full pot of coffee in the coffee maker and I put the back of my hand on it.

I shook my head. "Cold." I checked the sink, but it held no coffee cups, so there was no way to tell how many people had drunk coffee this morning.

"You look around down here," she said. "I'll check the upstairs."

Lou couldn't have been hiding in the kitchen cabinets, not even the broom closet, not if she'd met the height requirement for the WASP. Still, I opened a few of the larger doors, just in case. I could hear Toots calling Lou's name as she climbed the stairs. Then I passed through the breakfast room and into the dining room and stopped.

The curtains were closed and it took me a minute to process

what I was seeing. There was paper everywhere. I pulled from my purse a pair of plastic gloves and set the purse down on the floor in the breakfast room. Then I crossed to the dining-room window, slipped on my gloves, and opened the curtains. I turned back and surveyed the room. My eyes fell first on a small electric typewriter on the dining room table, an island of order in a chaotic sea of paper. Then I spotted, on the floor nearby, an oblong trunk, about the size of a footlocker but in a contemporary red with faux-brass accents. Its lid was up and I guessed that it had once held some of the papers strewn about the room.

I approached the table and cocked my head, first one way and then the other, to read the papers. I could see parts of a mailing list, letters, and notes — some typewritten, most handwritten, several menus, several file folders, and a lot of forms that had been filled out. So this room was Lou's command center for the reunion, I guessed, and maybe for all her WASP business, whatever that was. Toots had said that there was a bigger reunion planned for September, so maybe Lou was involved in that as well. She was undoubtedly keeping track of more than eight women.

But the woman who kept her kitchen so neat would not have left her office looking like this. If this house were mine, I would suspect that animal mayhem had let loose in my absence. I flashed on a set of dog bowls on the floor in the kitchen by the back door. Where was the dog?

I went out into the hall and stood at the bottom of the stairs. "Toots!" I called. "Does Lou have a dog?"

No answer. Then I heard the air conditioning come on and decided it was better not to try to shout over it.

I climbed the stairs. At the top I called again. "Toots, where are you?"

I turned right, pushed open the first door, and found an empty bathroom.

"Toots," I called again. "Where are you?"

I thought I heard a muffled sound coming from the open door on my left. I walked toward it, then stopped dead. The door had been unlocked. Lou's papers had been disturbed. I should never have let Toots wander around by herself.

I should have taken up detective work when I was younger and my mind worked more quickly.

I thought of the gun in my purse downstairs.

"Toots." Again, I heard a muffled sound from the room to my left.

"I have something I want you to see," I said. "I'll go back downstairs and get it."

Toots could be in danger, I thought. The intruder could have a knife to her throat or a gun to her head, but it wouldn't help her if I got us both killed. I backed down the hallway. I needed a weapon.

I descended the stairs at a normal pace so as not to let the intruder know that I suspected his presence. I was rooting around in my bag when I heard a toilet flush upstairs. I looked up.

The intruder — I preferred this term to "the killer," at the moment — was trying to outthink me. He had decided to give me an explanation for Toots's silence: she'd been in the bathroom with the door closed. I'd seen one empty bathroom but a house like this one probably featured another off the master bedroom. I wasn't supposed to be thinking hard about it. I was supposed to be a suburban matron in her sixties, coming to visit her old friend Lou. I emptied my bag on the floor and found the Wilkinson Diane among the pennies, stray breath mints, bank deposit slips, lint, and other detritus.

Of course, it was just possible that Toots had been in the bathroom with the door closed and that the other noises I'd heard had been made by a dog. I'd seen dog bowls on the kitchen floor. But dogs don't lie quietly, even if they're confined to a kennel or a bedroom, and sleeping dogs wake up when you ring the doorbell or make loud noises. Unless they're dead. I slipped off the safety and reminded myself not to shoot the dog.

I glanced at the phone on the wall in the kitchen. I wanted to call 911, but I couldn't risk it. Even if I just left the phone off the hook, the intruder might hear the operator's voice and become suspicious. I picked up a random piece of paper and held it in front of the gun to conceal the weapon.

I began talking when I was halfway up the stairs. "Hey, Toots, I found the seating arrangement for the dinner and you're not going to believe who she's put at your table. I thought she knew that you and Esther don't get along." If the listener were a WASP, I hoped that my inaccurate account of their relationships wouldn't give me away. I kept my voice casual. "And me — she's got me next to some colonel. But she's put my cameraman between two WASP. That's no good. I'm the one who needs to get the story. I'm telling you, it's a good thing we came up here, because this arrangement stinks." At the top of the stairs, I looked around at the other doors off the hallway to see if they had been disturbed since I'd last been up here. If he were smart, he would've changed rooms. I didn't think I could afford to search all of them without tipping my hand. I cursed myself for not having paid much attention before. Then I caught a movement, just a slight one: the door across from the one on the left had budged, as if responding to an air current. Door Number Two it would be then. If I guessed wrong, I'd go home with the donkey and my opponent would win the all-expense-paid luxury vacation to Puerto Vallarta.

In the meantime, I kept talking. "I don't know why I can't sit where Maddy was sitting. She hasn't crossed Maddy out. My cameraman can sit next to the flight instructor." The intruder would have to get past me if he wanted to get out of the house. And I was holding a gun.

I paused outside the door and took a deep breath.

"Here, take a look at this," I said and pushed the door wide with my foot. I let the gun, still shielded by the paper, enter the room first, but I followed closely.

The movement came from my right. I whirled. Not a dog, a ski mask. And a lot of white. I fired. Something descended on me, blocking my vision. White cloth — a blanket? Just before my head exploded, I fired again. Then the white turned black.

JULY 17, 1986

"Quit that!" I mumbled.

Something soft was scraping my cheek. I tried to brush it away but my arm was like lead.

My head lolled and every scrape made it pulse with pain. "Quit that!" I repeated. I rolled away from it, onto my side, and drew my knees up. Time for another nap.

A sudden blast of sound. The pain shot up my spine and vibrated at the base of my skull. My eyes popped open. Inches from my eyes were two others, large, brown, and soulful. Something wet and cold and out-of-focus pressed my nose.

When my daughter Franny had been a humanities major at Ohio Wesleyan — this had been in between the psychology major at Kenyon and the art major at Syracuse — she'd read a book about hell which she'd recounted to me in great detail. Unlike most of Franny's reports, this one had stuck with me. It seems this writer, Dante, had created a place where everybody got punished in the way that was most appropriate to them and the sin they'd committed. Down at the bottom, where the worst sinners were, they were partially frozen in ice. I didn't know which sin of mine was being covered here, but I was willing to acknowledge that I couldn't think at the moment of a worse form of hell than to be frozen in ice and licked by a dog for all eternity. Unless maybe it was an eternal golf game.

The open eyes netted an enthusiastic reaction — more barking. After I closed my eyes again in pain, I felt more wet sandpaper on my eyelids. "Go away!" I muttered. In response, I felt a weight descend on my shoulder and a phalanx of nails scratched me there.

That was how I met Happy, the golden retriever.

I heard footsteps and my heart caught, though I couldn't exactly remember why I was afraid. But I had a gun in my hands; that much, I realized. So when the tall shape loomed over me, I tried to angle the gun in its direction.

"Don't shoot," it said. "I'm married to Lou."

Lou? "Do I know her?" I asked.

"I don't think you've actually met." The man crouched and took the first step on the road to friendship: he pushed the dog away. "Back off, Happy."

I felt a light touch on my shoulder. "Where are you hurt?" he said. "Is it just your head?"

I surveyed my aches and pains and decided that they were, in fact, concentrated in my head — on the right side, above and behind my ear. "I think so."

"Then let's sit you up," he said. He slipped an arm around my shoulders and lifted me upright. I groaned. He propped me against a bed. There was a bedspread puddled around me on the floor, and if this guy would just take the dog and go away and leave me alone, I could lie down again and pull up the bedspread and sleep.

To cheer me up, he said, "You shot the attacker. Did you know that?" He gently extracted the gun from my hand. "There's a trail of blood all the way to the back door."

I didn't say anything. I didn't really remember an attacker, to tell the truth, much less a back door. I thought it was best to keep quiet until I got my bearings, especially if I'd plugged someone. It was best not to admit anything prematurely. There was also a broken lamp lying on the floor next to me. Maybe I'd shot that as well.

"The ambulance is on the way," he said.

Automatically, I said, "I don't need an ambulance." Ambulances meant hospitals and hospitals meant sick people and sick people carry diseases you were likely to catch if you hung around them. I avoided hospitals on principal.

"We'll see," he said. "Now I have to go back and check on Toots."

Toots? Now there was a name that sounded familiar. "I know her," I said.

"That's right," he said encouragingly. "You came with her. In the plane."

I frowned. That seemed unlikely at best. But when I felt the fear welling up in my throat, it felt familiar. Had I actually let someone talk me into taking a plane ride? Or was I still unconscious and having a nightmare? Visiting an alternative reality in which Cat Caliban was a daredevil who laughed in the face of danger? I had shot someone, he said. I didn't think I'd ever shot anyone before. Shot *at* them, yes, but actually hit them? I didn't think so.

"Do I have to go back with her in the plane?" I asked.

"Not if you don't want to," he said soothingly. "Now, you just sit here and wait while I check on Toots."

"I'll just take a little nap."

"No, you can't go to sleep. Not right now. You have to stay awake until the medics check you out. I'm going to leave Happy with you. Hap, you're in charge, understand? She can't go to sleep. Don't let her go to sleep."

Happy barked and I winced.

"Ssh," the man said. "We have to be quiet, okay?"

The dog woofed softly.

"That's right. Good boy."

He left the room. The dog came and sat next to me, then leaned into me. Soft ears brushed my cheek.

"Okay, I get the picture. I have to stay awake. If I don't stay awake, they'll cart me off to the hospital."

Happy woofed.

I freed the arm he had pinned against my side and slipped it around him. "So, Happy, know any good jokes?"

My new best friend thumped his tail.

23

JULY 19, 1986

IT OCCURRED to me as I dangled in my tree, gazing down at Happy's upturned face, that he must have a low opinion of my intelligence. I'd only known him for three days, and twice during that time he'd found me in crisis. He must wonder how I've managed to stay alive as long as I have.

Of course, that state of affairs could change at any second. If I fell, would he try to cushion my fall? A cat, who will always choose self-preservation over loyalty or some crack-brained notion that its purpose in life was to serve humankind, would run away, no question. But would a dog? I imagined myself flat on the ground with a broken neck. My last words would be, "Now I know."

A gust of wind caught my branch and whipped it upward. I bobbed like a yo-yo and felt myself slipping, then falling. I heard wind, rain, and barks like gunshots.

I felt the shock of contact as my feet struck the earth. I let my knees flex, then pitched forward into a roll. When I stopped, I was lying flat on my back, eyes shut. Something descended on me, covering me — the parachute, I guessed.

Then I heard a kind of grunt and the parachute started moving. I felt needles of rain against my skin and something else, like soft sandpaper, scraped my cheek. Déjà vu.

"Now I know," I said aloud. Though to be perfectly honest, I didn't, not really. For all I knew, Happy could have spent those few brief seconds while I was plummeting to earth running around like a Keystone fireman with a net, trying to figure out where I would land. A golden retriever looks big on the ground, but from the air makes a very small target.

I opened my eyes to be blinded by the light — one big light, with sparkles on the periphery. "Enough already!" I batted the dog away and conducted an internal survey. My neck didn't seem to be broken and I hadn't landed on it. I hadn't even twisted an ankle, I decided, although some small critter had taken advantage of the altered topography to crawl up my pant leg to get out of the rain. My head was throbbing like before, only worse for having been rolled on. "That's the way they do it in the movies," I told it. "Quit complaining."

Slowly, cautiously, I sat up. My wet hair sent small rivulets of rainwater down my forehead and into my eyes. I wiped my face with the palm of my hand and felt a familiar weight leaning into me. I stretched an arm tentatively and felt an objection from my sore shoulder. I stretched it further, breathed into the soreness, and felt it ease a little. I did the same with the other arm, then laid it across the dog's shoulders.

"So, Happy, know any good jokes?"

THE DOG now seemed content to offer physical and moral support without commentary and I was touched in spite of myself. He sat quietly and let me gather my thoughts, which were in serious need of gathering. An intruder had thrown a bedspread over me and then whacked me in the head with a blunt instrument, or so I deduced from the bedspread puddled around me, fragments of a lamp nearby, and the knot behind my right ear. By the time I remembered enough to worry about Toots, I heard her voice.

"— not going to the hospital for a bump on the head," she was saying. "Just get me to wherever Cat is."

They appeared in the doorway. Toots had gone pale under her tan and she was leaning heavily on the man who was married to Lou.

"Cat! Isn't this awful? I feel like such an idiot."

"She's a little fuzzy," the man cautioned.

It hurt to tilt my head back and look up at her.

"Ease me down, Wes," she said. "Did you tell her about Lou?" He lowered her to the floor, where she settled herself in front of me, legs crossed, one hand gingerly touching the back of her head.

"She didn't seem to remember who Lou was," he said.

"I remember now," I said. "We came to meet with her."

"And we were waiting at the airport, remember?" Toots said.

The airport. So I hadn't hallucinated that part.

"But Lou didn't come, so we called a cab," I said.

"And the reason Lou didn't come was because she had an accident," Toots said. "Somebody ran a stop sign and hit her car."

I processed this information. "So there wasn't anything wrong with her car?"

"We don't know for sure," the man said. "She says she tried to stop, but the brakes didn't work. I don't know whether she's right about that. Maybe she thought she stepped on the brakes and didn't, or maybe she hit the gas instead."

"And we found the back door unlocked, and never even stopped to consider," Toots continued. "No, we just waltzed in here, making sure the killer knew that we were available. And then we split up, just to make it easier for him to pick us off."

"Except we're not dead," I pointed out. "What the hell did he hit us with?"

"A golf club," Wes said.

"We lucked out." The corners of Toots's mouth were twitching. "It was a wood, not an iron, and he didn't have much space to swing it in."

Somewhere, the scales of justice had tipped in favor of all the little birdies I'd nearly brained during my golf outing.

Then the paramedics arrived and close on their heels came the cops. We did some tough negotiating, but finally had the satisfaction of watching them wheel off their empty stretcher, leaving behind a pair of ice bags for the lumps on our heads.

By then, we were sitting at Lou's kitchen table. Wes, Lou's husband, had made us tea. I have never been able to understand this practice of giving tea to the sick or injured. Me, I'd been hoping for a gin and tonic, but none had materialized. Until we saw a doctor, we couldn't take anything stronger than extra-strength Tylenol, and it seemed to me that alcohol was what we needed. Fortunately, Wes had already left to pick up Lou at the hospital, so I didn't have to worry about hurting his feelings.

The cops took longer to get rid of and I couldn't blame them. Neither one of us was much help.

"I didn't see a thing, honest," Toots insisted. "One minute I was standing in a bedroom, looking around, and the next, I was waking up in a heap on the floor. I don't know where he came from, but I didn't see him coming."

But I had been expecting him, looking for him. And I was the trained detective. Surely, I could give them a better description.

"He was wearing a ski mask," I said. "It was red, with royal blue stripes."

The uniformed officer who was taking notes stopped writing. He and the plainclothes officer, who was asking the questions, looked at me expectantly.

"Fire-engine red," I said. "And the blue was like the color of this ice pack, only maybe a little darker."

The uniform didn't write anything. The other officer — Scott was his name — said, "You said 'he.' Are you sure it was a man?"

I started to shake my head, then thought better of it. "No, sorry. I had the impression that it was a man, but then, I was expecting a man."

"Because?"

When Toots nodded, I told him about the case I was working on — not all of it, but enough to clarify things a bit. I was relieved to find that I remembered most of what had been going on, even some details I left out.

"So even if this attack was connected to all that," Scott said, "you don't know for certain that the perpetrator is a man."

"No," I admitted.

"What gave you the 'impression' that it was a man?" He asked. "Build?"

I thought. "Not really. The attacker was tall, six feet or around there, but I don't remember anything else about his build. Maybe that's because he was holding the bedspread up. I just remember his mask and a lot of white, like a curtain. His hair was under the ski mask."

"Hands?"

"He was wearing gloves, or at least, a glove. I only remember seeing one hand. The gloves must have been white, I think. Not plastic surgical gloves."

The uniform made a note and I imagined him turning over my statement to the fashion editors rather than the news reporters: what the well-dressed house breaker is wearing.

"Big hands?"

"Sort of. But maybe no bigger than Toots's."

We all turned to look at her. She held out her hands for inspection. Scott took them in, then ran his eyes upward. His sigh was almost imperceptible.

"All WASP had to meet a height and weight requirement," she said.

And some of them are still using their hands, incipient arthritis or not, to build planes, I thought. But then I noticed her watch.

"Wait!" I said. "He was wearing a watch. A men's watch. Bigger than most women's watches, anyway. I must have caught a glimpse of it when he moved."

"Good." Scott nodded in the uniform wrote it down. "Any scars or tattoos on the wrist?"

"Didn't see any."

"After-shave? Cologne? Perfume?"

I started. "There was something, I think. Very faint. More masculine than feminine, I'd say. But I couldn't tell you what it was."

"Hand me that evidence bag, LeBrun." Scott unzipped the bag, which appeared to contain a crumpled tissue, sniffed it, and offered it to me.

I leaned forward, sniffed, and shook my head carefully. "That's not it, I don't think."

"We'll ask Mr. Zimmerman about any scents he wears," Scott said to LeBrun. To me he said, "Tell me again about going upstairs.

You'd heard a noise in the front room on the left and then went downstairs to get your gun."

I didn't want to dwell on this part. Technically, it was Moses, the former cop, who had a permit to carry a concealed weapon, but if the cops asked me about it, I intended to pretend that I thought the permit was attached to the gun, not the person. Of course, if I was that stupid, nobody would hire me to investigate anything. I kept my mouth shut.

"And then you came back upstairs with the gun. Tell me what happened next."

"I was pretending to talk to Toots about the seating arrangements at a dinner coming up."

"Uh-huh."

"And I stood at the top of the stairs and surveyed the hall and the three doors, trying to decide which one to choose because none of them was open all the way. I could see that he wasn't in the bathroom. The door was open and the shower curtain was open and the room was empty."

"So before, you thought he was in the other front room, the one where we found Mrs. Magruder," he said. "What made you pick the one you did?"

"Well, if it had been me, and I was just trying to get away, I would have changed rooms, hoping to sneak out behind me when I went into the other room. Did that make sense?"

He nodded.

"Of course, if he wanted to kill me, he'd wait for me in that first room. I didn't really have any way of knowing if he thought I was one of the women he was after or not. I just guessed."

"So why not choose the door closest to the stairs — the back room?"

"While I was standing there, I thought I saw the other door move slightly. I couldn't be sure that the one closest to me hadn't moved also. I was trying to see the whole picture. I was pretty sure, though, that the first door hadn't moved. So to me, that meant that something inside the room across the hall had moved that door, probably the bedspread, when he pulled it off the bed."

"Uh-huh."

"Wow!" Toots put in. "That was brilliant!"

"Yeah," I said. "So I walked in and let him throw the bedspread over me."

"Back up," Scott said. "You walked in how?"

"I said something like, 'You've got to see this,' and I pushed the door open with my foot. I was holding the gun in front of me in my right hand, like this." I made a gun with my hand and held it up, chest high. "And I held a piece of paper in front of it to screen it." I raised my left hand to illustrate. "And when I crossed the threshold, I saw him moving, to my right, and I turned and saw the ski mask and fired. I probably waited a few seconds too long, but I didn't want to shoot the dog by mistake. I knew there was a dog. And I didn't especially want to kill him." At the moment, the dog in question was curled up on the floor, his head on my feet, snoozing.

"I saw this white thing coming at me, and then all I could see was white, and I fired again, just before something hit me and I blacked out."

"I see," Scott said.

"I guess I just clipped him, huh?" I'd seen the trail of blood on the stairs and it was oddly reassuring. I didn't want to think that the bastard was holed up in somebody's garage or toolshed, bleeding to death.

"Probably," Scott said. "But then, a twenty-five caliber doesn't make a very big hole. We'll alert the hospitals, anyway."

"Lou will be happy to hear that, about a twenty-five caliber," Toots said. To me, she said, "They dug one of your bullets out of the wall."

The dog heard his name and lifted his head. Then he stood up and began barking and ran to the back door.

"Does he have to go out?" I asked.

But then we saw lights flash on the wall and heard a car in the drive.

"Speak of the devil," Toots said.

The dog scrabbled frantically at the door.

"We'll need you to sign a statement," Scott said, and he stood up.

"But I need to get home tonight," I said. By now it was mid-afternoon.

"Can you give us a couple of hours?" Scott asked. "Maybe stop by and sign the statement on your way out of town?"

My response was drowned out by ecstatic barking. Wes reappeared, supporting by the elbow a tall woman with wavy, mid-length pepper-and-salt hair and a brunette's complexion. Her left arm was in a sling and her wrist was encased in a splint. A dark purple bruise was visible on her arm; it disappeared under the short sleeves of her flower-print blouse. She was favoring her left leg, though what we could see of it beneath a tan split skirt was unmarked.

"Well, hell's bells!" she said, surveying Toots and me. "We better hope the other team looks worse than we do, 'cause it looks like we lost the damned fight!"

She had a deep smoker's voice, with a lot of breath in it.

There was a certain amount of commotion during the changing of the guard. Scott and sidekick left, Lou hugged Toots and shook hands with me while giving a dismissive account of her own injuries and exclaiming over ours, Wes offered to make more tea, and Happy circled Lou, contributing his own commentary to the din.

"I'd better see the worst of it first," Lou said. "Happy, put a sock in it! I'm fine."

She waved off Wes's arm and made her way slowly to the doorway of the dining room. She caught her breath. Then she said, "Forget the tea, Wes. I need a drink."

Wes said, "Honey, I don't know if you can. You're on pain medication, remember?"

"Lucky you," I muttered.

"Oh, hell, Wes, just fix us a drink, will you?" She turned to me. "Didn't they give you any pain meds?"

We shook our heads, winced in unison, and reapplied the ice packs.

"Well, you need a drink worse than I do, in that case. Can you call your doctors and get a prescription? Honey, why don't you bring us the phone before you take orders? These gals need some drugs."

25

JULY 17, 1986

So we called our respective doctors' offices and left our requests with the nurses on duty, both of whom scolded us for not going to the hospital.

I took a swallow of my lovely gin and tonic before I proposed a return to the other crime scenes. "I'd just like to take another look upstairs," I said.

They both tagged along, though Lou took the stairs slowly and wheezed. Happy stuck close beside her.

I hadn't yet seen the room where Toots had been attacked. It was the master bedroom. There was dark fingerprint powder on the doorframe. Blood on the carpet a few steps inside the room marked the spot where Toots had been attacked. Toots apologized.

"Well," Lou sighed, "at least you didn't die. Then they would have left a chalk outline on the rug."

"More likely they would have pulled it up and taken it in to look for trace evidence," I said.

Toots was looking around. "What is it we're supposed to be looking for, Cat?"

"Oh, I don't know." I studied the scene. "He attacked you from behind, right, Toots?"

"Must have. I never saw a thing."

"So he was standing about here. Lou, do you have another golf club?"

"Are you an investigative reporter, Cat?" Lou said, reminding me of my cover. "Is that why you carry a gun? Is it always this dangerous?"

"It can be," I said, hoping that would do as an explanation.

"Is she investigating the WASP?" Lou asked Toots, clearly thrilled.

"It's just a feature story," Toots said.

I watched Lou as she crossed to the closet, where the door stood ajar, and pushed it open. She retrieved a wood from inside and handed it to me. I took a few tentative swings. Then I handed it to Toots. "Let me see you swing, not like you're on the fairway, but like you want to hit somebody in the head with it."

"And don't you dare hit that lamp, Tootsie," Lou cautioned her. "The one in the other room was no great loss, but that one I brought back from England."

Toots took a few swings and looked at me. "Like that?" She put a hand to the back of her head. "I can't tell if it hurts because I moved it or if it's remembering what it was like to be on the receiving end."

"Let's see the other room." I led the way across the hall to the scene of my own debacle.

He'd taken a chance with me, though not much of one, considering the ski mask and the bedspread. I was sure he wasn't worried that he'd be called to a line-up of men wearing ski masks and holding bedspreads. A quick look told me what I needed to know.

"Lou," I said, "is Wes right-handed or left-handed?"

"He's a lefty. Why?"

"Can we get him up here for an experiment? We'll start in the other room. It's bigger."

"Sure," she said and went to call him.

When he appeared in the doorway, I waved him over. "Let's see you swing this golf club." I handed it to him.

He smiled. "Am I a suspect?"

Lou answered for me. "She's just conducting an experiment, honey. Watch the lamp."

"I've got a sore shoulder," he said, rubbing his left shoulder. "Can I do it right-handed?"

"I'd rather you didn't," I said. "Just do the best you can, but don't hurt yourself."

He swung a few times, wincing, and looked up at me. "Okay?"

I nodded. "Now stand here and do it." I positioned him where the attacker must've stood. "He was hiding behind the door when Toots walked in and then he stepped out and swung."

Wes raised the club and then cleared his throat. "Uh, it's kind of tight."

"If it hurts too much, don't do it," I said.

"That's right, honey," Lou said.

He swung awkwardly, without much momentum or power. He grimaced and rubbed his shoulder. You sure you don't want me to try the other side?"

"Let's try the other room instead." I tried to keep my voice casual as I asked, "What did you do to your shoulder?"

He and Lou exchanged glances. "He tried to move a filing cabinet down to the basement, after I told him not to. He hasn't been the same since."

"I'm usually careful with it," Wes added. "But when the hospital called today and said Lou had been hurt in an accident, I wasn't as careful as I should have been. Sometimes just turning my head around when I'm backing down the driveway can aggravate it and that's what happened today."

This time I positioned him just inside the door to the right, backed up against the bed. "Gee, I don't know," he said. "This is worse than the other room." He raised the club and pulled it back to swing, but he ran into the wall. He made another awkward swing. "Wait," he said. "Were you already down by then?"

"No," I said.

"Then he must have used his other hand, right?" Lou said. "That's what you're thinking, right, Cat?"

"No, I'm thinking that the only reason we're not dead after being hit with a golf club is that he couldn't swing very effectively in the space he had. Toots pointed that out earlier. We know he didn't change hands because of where he hit me — here on the right side." I touched the lump, which felt like a volcano.

"So he was left-handed!" Lou said.

"Like Wes here," Toots said. "So, Wes, you are a suspect." She gave him a disarming grin.

"But here's what I don't get," Lou said. "What was he after? Wes couldn't find anything missing. I wish he'd taken the damn television so we could make the insurance company buy us a new one, but no such luck. Instead, he went through the papers in the dining room like a tornado. Was he just frustrated that we didn't have a better television to steal or what?"

"I think there's more to it than that," Toots said. "I think he's looking for something."

And she told them about the other cases in which WASP memorabilia had been searched.

"So are you saying somebody could be bumping off WASP?" Lou said. She looked from Toots to me, incredulous. "Whatever for?"

"I really don't know," Toots said. "And we don't know any of this for sure."

"Hell, Toots, you couldn't buy a Timex watch with my wartime take-home pay," Lou said. "He can't think we're all rich. Anyway, you said he was looking for something. But what? My flight logs from Avenger? Oh, wait! I know! You remember that really sexy B-24 pilot I met in the OC? Well, we didn't call it 'sexy' in those days, but that's what he was, all right, and a really good kisser. He wrote his name and address down on a napkin, and after he left, they told me he was married. Maybe he's come looking for that napkin! That little two-timing Casanova probably can't even remember which one of us it was he flirted with, and that's why he's looking at everybody's things."

That was all this case needed — someone with an imagination even wilder than my own.

"Isn't this fun?" Lou said. "Just like being a detective. I wouldn't mind doing that kind of work. Don't you think it would be fun to be a detective?"

I touched the volcano again. "Heaps of fun," I said.

26

JULY 17, 1986

AT LEAST TOOTS's injury won me a ride home in a car. Toots couldn't locate Stretch, so I called Moses and he came to pick us up.

"I was kind of hoping to finish this roll of film, though, Cat," he said. "I think I got some good shots of Mel putting Kevin in a joint lock." Mel was a practitioner of aikido, a Japanese martial art, and Kevin was the only one of us who let her practice on him.

"Well, bring the camera along," I told him, aware of my audience. You can photograph the crime scene."

I introduced him to Wes and Lou as "my photographer," and luckily neither of them seemed interested in pursuing the subject with him. He scowled at my gin and tonic before lugging his equipment upstairs to take some pictures.

"Can I watch?" Wes said. "Here, let me help you."

"Sure," I said. "But he's trying out a new camera, so he might be a little awkward."

Nobody thought this an odd comment except me.

An hour later Toots and I had signed our statements, picked up our drugs at a nearby pharmacy, and were headed home again in rush-hour traffic that held Moses's speed to a sedate pace.

Toots and I told Moses the story of our day. When we finished, he didn't say anything at first. Then he said, "And what strikes you most about it, Cat?"

"We're not dead," I said.

Toots laughed, but I didn't and neither did Moses.

"So why are we not dead?" I continued. "Once we were out cold, he had plenty of time to finish us off. But he didn't. Why? Obviously, he didn't go to the house planning to attack anybody. If he had, he would have taken a weapon with him instead of picking up something he found lying around."

"And that suggests what?"

"Well, several possibilities that I can see. One, he went to search the house for something. We think he's looking for something, been looking for something. He didn't use a weapon on Maddy or Squeak, either. So maybe killing them wasn't part of his original plan. Maybe they just got in his way, or he saw the opportunity and took it. Or maybe he had a weapon and didn't use it because a better opportunity came along — he saw that he could make their deaths look like an accident. But maybe he never intended to kill anybody. A fall down the stairs isn't always fatal. Maybe he even knew that Toots could land her plane safely, although that seems more far-fetched as a means of just getting her out of the way for a while, because she wasn't in the way when he searched the basement. Even if he thought he needed to search the whole house, which doesn't seem likely, killing her in a plane crash seems pretty extreme as a strategy. So she must know something he doesn't want anyone to know. And that suggests that Maddy and Squeak knew it, too."

"But what?" Toots said. "And why didn't he kill me today when he had the chance?"

"I can't answer that," I admitted. "What about Lou's brakes, Moses? Do you think they were tampered with?"

"We'll have to see what the forensics team says," Moses cautioned. "Doesn't sound like anybody she knew was behind the wheel of the car that hit her. If there is a killer, and if there's only one killer, it would fit his M.O. I said this was somebody who's not comfortable with killing, not a pro. He's desperate enough to take somebody out if he needs to, but that only requires a little bit of courage. Could be that's why you two are still alive. Or maybe he thought he'd hit Toots hard enough to kill her."

"Or he panicked," I said.

"Or he panicked," Moses agreed. "But let's say he went in in the first place because he knew Wes was out of the house and since he'd fixed Lou's brakes, he knew she wouldn't be back anytime soon once he saw her leave."

"Imagine his surprise when we showed up," Toots said, "especially when we walked in."

"But how did he know Wes would be gone for a while?" I asked. "Toots? Any ideas?"

"No," she said, "not unless he does something every Thursday and the killer knew about it. I'll ask Lou."

"Wes took the dog with him," I said.

"Happy?" Toots said in surprise. "No, Happy would have been with Lou. Happy's always with Lou. Wes probably picked him up to take him home after the accident."

"Tell us about Wes," Moses said, glancing up at her in the rearview mirror.

"Wes?" she said. "What do you want to know about him? He's not really a suspect, is he? They're very happily married, as far as I can tell. Didn't you think so? They have four grown kids. They both like to fly. I mean, he wouldn't sabotage her car, surely."

"We don't even know if her car was sabotaged and the timing probably lets him off the hook," I said. "But we weren't out for very long. He supposedly went right home from the hospital when Lou sent him to find us. But even if we checked on the times and discovered that he took longer than he should have to drive home, we couldn't prove anything. He does have an injury that's causing him some pain."

"But he wouldn't have to sneak around to search his own house," Toots objected. "Besides, Lou explained the injury."

"You're right," I admitted. "I'm not at my best now, anyway. Forget it. Just tell me how they met. Did he know Lou when she was a WASP?"

"Well, sure," Toots said. "He knew all of us. He became a gunnery instructor at Harlingen after he washed out of flight training."

"He washed out? I thought you said he was a pilot."

"He is. But Army flight school was really tough, just like it was for us. Military standards were incredibly high. Lots of male civilian pilots couldn't meet them. Remember, the WASP trainees had already logged lots of flying time before they ever arrived in Sweetwater, but many of them still washed out. And sometimes trainees washed out for no good reason that we could see. Maybe the checkout pilot was having a bad day or maybe he didn't like your accent or your haircut. Maybe you got two such specimens in a row. I'm sure it was the same for the men, although I don't think Wes will ever be the pilot that Lou is. Don't tell him I said that, though."

"So he wasn't flying at Harlingen?"

"He was a gunnery instructor. Seemed like most of the guys in gunnery school at Harlingen were washed-out pilots, so that's probably what happened to Wes. He was probably sent to gunnery school and did well there, so he became an instructor. Talk about an attitude problem! I guess the Army figured that the flight trainees were at least used to spending their time in planes, so they turned them into aerial gunners and bombardiers once they washed out of flight school. We always thought, too, that maybe the Army decided to take advantage of all that pent-up anger — give them a machine gun or a bomb and let them blast away."

"At you," I said. I had turned around to look at her.

She grinned ruefully. "We thought it might explain about half of the flak we took. Of course, some of them were incompetent gunners, as well."

"And Wes was one of them," I said. "Not an incompetent gunner, an instructor, but still."

"Oh, I don't think he was one of the angry ones, if that's what you mean." She looked out the window. "After all, he retired from the Air Force — went to navigation school after the war. Ended up a colonel, flew as a civilian pilot. I guess he was disappointed, sure, but I've heard him say he has no regrets."

None that he's willing to share, I thought.

27

JULY 18, 1986

THE NEXT MORNING, we called on Arnie Kovalchik, and this time, Moses went with me. The day had dawned overcast, and when the first raindrops hit the Fairlane's windshield, I wondered whether the Dayton Air Show would proceed, rain or shine. Today was opening day and we were supposed to drive up with Toots and Stretch in the afternoon.

We were not arguing, for a change. This was probably because, out of deference to my throbbing head, I was maintaining silence. I suspected that Moses was silent because he was memorizing F-stops or whatever he had to memorize in order to pass himself off as a photographer.

The big warehouse was gloomy and smelled moldier on this damp day than I remembered. We stepped into the freight elevator and Moses looked around, frowning.

"You want to be afraid of something, be afraid of this thing, Cat," he said. "I don't see no inspection notice."

The elevator ascended laboriously, accompanied by not elevator music, but the clanking of chains and the groaning of poorly lubricated pulleys. At the third floor, we found Tesla the cat waiting for us. He licked his back toes nonchalantly, as if he could take us or leave us, now that we were here. Then he scooted ahead of us down the corridor and stopped in front of a painting leaning against the wall outside of Fletcher's studio. At least this nude was male, if you could say that about a figure with male genitalia, four arms, and a cabbage for a head.

"Tesla's his agent, I think," I whispered to Moses.

"Cat's got to have better taste than that."

"Maybe he's just breaking into the business."

"Ought to start a little closer to the top."

Arnie was sitting where I left him, wearing the same clothes. The same Chinese take-out boxes and beer cans were overflowing his trash can. He even seemed to be eating the same donut.

He and Moses exchanged the kind of minimalist masculine greetings that cool, macho types indulge in. We helped ourselves to two folding chairs and sat down.

"O-kay," Arnie said, peering through his glasses at a piece of paper. "Nothing on Thompson. She's listed as a casualty. If you want more on her, like who they paid survivor benefits to after the WASP was militarized in seventy-seven, I need a Social Security number and more time. There were seven Thompsons attached to the Foreign Service in 1943-1944, and six of them claimed permanent addresses in the DC area. Here's their names, you wanna track them down."

He handed Moses a list.

"As for Evers, there's four females named 'Evers' with pilot's licenses resident in California. Here's the list, be my guest, but my gut says you're wasting your time because a woman who was named 'Evers' in 1944 probably got married and doesn't go by that name now. 'Course, one of these could be related to her, since flying runs in families. On the other hand, could be she never flew again after the war, settled down and married a guy named Stephanopoulos and made babies and lives in Redondo Beach."

Moses took the list from him. I had to admit, I was impressed already.

"McClenahan Smith, Bernice Opal, sixty-six years old," he continued. "Lives in Iowa, owns her own home, registered Republican, no pilot's license. Pretty good credit rating now, don't know what her husband does — he's her second husband. Don't know if the first was a vet because, again, I got no social. Got into some financial difficulties, I think. Divorce recorded a year after her credit rating went south, back in 1953. Never been convicted of a felony."

Without looking, he reached out to place the paper on an extension of his desk, but missed. The paper floated to the floor, where Tesla the cat inspected it.

"Eckels Ellerman, Elizabeth Jane, deceased at age seventy-one. Lived in Fort Lauderdale, where she purchased her home in 1977. Registered Independent. Widow, one marriage, deceased husband was an Army Air Force vet, served in World War II and Korea. His estate valued at three hundred and fifty thousand, hers at just over three hundred. Estate goes to two sons. Excellent credit rating, never convicted of a felony. Let's see. Oh, yeah, estate includes a 1975 Beech 200 King Air, but no record of a physical after 1980."

Moses and I looked at each other. "Come again?" I said.

He looked up. "Which part?"

"The whole last sentence about a beach, a king, an heir, and a physical."

"A Beech 200 King Air is a plane, a single-engine prop, valued at around two thousand, twenty-five hundred dollars. But to maintain a pilot's license, you have to pass an annual physical, which goes on file at the FAA. So no physical, no license. That means Ellerman wasn't flying after 1979. Of course, she might not have been flying before 1979, since some pilots keep their license up even when they're not flying. Husband died in 1972, so she didn't buy it for him to fly. The sons don't have licenses. I checked. Capeesh?"

We nodded and that page joined the other one on the floor.

"Madeleine Margaret Vincent George," he continued. "Deceased at age sixty-six. Married twice, divorced both times. First husband is deceased, a Navy vet. Five children, two boys, three girls. Registered Independent. Looks like she retired from civil service — yeah, here it is. She worked for the Federal Home Loan Bank. Licensed pilot until three years ago, which coincides with an NTSB accident investigation. Crashed a Cessna 152 on landing, ruled pilot error, alcohol-related. Also has a DUI conviction, with six months' probation and a two-hundred-dollar fine. Credit rating not good, but not lousy. Hmm, involved in three civil suits — no, make that two. One was a countersuit. That one was over a fence put up by a neighbor in 1983. The other one —." He flipped the page up and read the one below it. "The other one was in 1978 and had to do with an unsatisfactory home repair — a new driveway, looks like. I see a lot of those."

I realized that despite the window unit that was cranking out cool air, I was sweating. It made me nervous to think how much information Arnie might be able to gather on me. This was only what he'd found in two days. In a week he could probably find out the color of my underwear and what was molding in the back of my refrigerator. Come to think of it, I might hire him to solve that last mystery.

Arnie tossed the pages, which separated in spite of the paperclip.

"Thelma Lee Fairweather, age sixty-five. Lives outside of San Antonio, Texas. Single, never married as far as I know, but I can't verify that. Registered Independent. Runs a flying school, dates back to 1964, property alone valued at one hundred and fifty thou. Shows up in four — make that five — NTSB incident or accident investigations, but two involve students of hers who were soloing. Not bad when you consider how long she's been in business. The others were ruled engine failures, so no pilot errors on Fairweather's own record. Flies these old planes — World War II era planes — apparently, so it's no surprise she's had a few engine failures." He shook his head. "Couldn't pay me enough to do that. But it looks like before she opened the flying school, she was a test pilot for McDonnell Aircraft."

It made my heart beat faster just listening to this account. Three engine failures? And she was still flying?

He flipped the page. "Police record isn't quite so clean, though. She was convicted of assault in 1970, although there must've been mitigating circumstances because she only got one year probation and a thousand-dollar fine, no jail time. Looks like she could afford it, though she could be property-rich and cash-poor. Seems possible with a flight school."

"You know who she assaulted?" Moses asked. "And with what?"

"No, but if you give me another week, I can find out," Arnie said. He looked at Moses over his glasses.

"I guess not. Not yet, anyway."

Arnie tossed the pages overboard and went on. "Verna Maude Davenport Burman, sixty-three. Lives in Abilene, Texas. Registered Democrat. Husband Charles Jackson Burman the Third, Army Air Force vet. I only know that because he's a public figure — serves on the city council, owns a local restaurant franchise. Both Burmans have active pilot's licenses. Three married daughters. Credit rating is iffy and they owe back taxes on a house valued at a hundred thou." He looked up. "Maybe the restaurant business isn't doing so well in Abilene."

"Do they own a plane?" I asked.

He shrugged. "Don't know. They're still alive, so I've got no probate. I got lucky on Ellerman because the probate hasn't been filed yet. But the heirs are already trying to sell the plane and my contact down there happened to find that out."

"The Burmans have any legal problems that you know of?" Moses asked.

"None that I know of, but they're going to have 'em soon if they don't pay off their taxes. Some places, though, sitting on city council can make some of your legal troubles disappear. Don't know if Abilene's that kind of town. Keep going?"

When we nodded, he added that page to the collection on the floor and looked over the next one. "Matilda Louise Pirelli Zimmerman. She's sixty-seven, lives up the road in Kettering, outside Dayton. Husband is Wesley Zimmerman, born Horst Wesley Zimmerman. Legally changed his name in 1942. You see a lot of that. People ditched obvious German names."

I was having difficulty imagining Wes as a "Horst."

"Also, if you joined the Army, they called you by your first name

— well, on legal documents and such. I imagine mostly they called you 'Zimmerman' or 'Private' or something like that. So sometimes you see a name change for that reason alone, especially if the guy got named for his uncle Woolrich or Philander and never used that name in his life. Zimmerman didn't start his service until 1943. Before that, he was in ROTC at Michigan State, finishing a degree in business. After, he stayed in the Army Air Force, later just the Air Force. I know all this only because I guessed that a pilot his age living in Dayton might be retired from Wright-Patt and I know somebody there. I got lucky.

"The Zimmermans have one son and two pilot's licenses. Never been involved in an NTSB investigation. Credit rating okay, though it took a hit in the early 60s. But they own their house and don't owe any back taxes on it, so their financial problems may be solved. She's registered as a Democrat. Oh, they were involved in a civil suit in 1965 over a business they'd invested money in, so that may explain the dip in their credit rating. Also they have two daughters and weddings are expensive. No criminal convictions that I could find. Questions?"

We shook our heads and he went on.

"Esther Susan Chang, sixty-five. Divorced, one son, one daughter. Active pilot's license. Lives in San Bernardino. Her credit rating is about where the Burmans' is, though like theirs, it's improved over time. Her corporation, which ran a flight school in San Diego, filed for bankruptcy in 1960 under Chapter 11. I couldn't find any record of a flight school in her name now, so she may have lost it or sold it along the way. I couldn't find any record of property she owns now."

"Know anything about the husband?" Moses asked. "When did she get divorced?"

He grinned at us. "I was hoping you'd ask. She didn't get divorced in either San Diego or San Bernardino counties, so what do you think I did?"

Moses frowned. "Nevada? Easy trip for a pilot."

"Bingo! She got divorced in Clark County — that's Las Vegas — from one Michael Allen Charleston in 1958."

"Which could have precipitated the bankruptcy," Moses observed.

"If you want to keep paying me, I'll find out," Arnie said.

"Wait, I don't get it," I said. "What does the divorce have to do with the bankruptcy?"

Moses shrugged. "Could be nothing. But could be that Charleston took off and left her with no money and no child support. We saw that all the time in Juvie. So suppose the flight school had been a sole proprietorship. Under those circumstances, first thing I'd do is move as much of the assets as I could out of the business accounts, especially if I'd been putting money into the business all along to keep it going. Then I'd incorporate, just to make sure that business creditors don't come after my personal assets."

"But she had to pay income tax on her profits before that, right? So how could she just transfer assets?"

"Well, what we really need is an accountant. I'm sure she paid her taxes on the business, but suppose over the years she'd invested money in it. She could legitimately claim to be the business's biggest creditor. If she was smart, she would have reported those investments as company debts all along, but she could always file amended returns. Or let's say the property was in her name — the field, the office building, the hangars. I don't know if that's legitimate from the county tax assessor's point of view, but we're just supposing here. She'd want to make sure to separate all of her personal assets from the business assets before incorporation. What do you think, Arnie?"

"I don't know about the property part," Arnie said. "But the other part sounds right. And if she was really smart, she might move some money into her kids' accounts. Then it would really be out of bounds."

"Anything else on Charleston?" I asked.

"Nope, I didn't come up with a social on him. You want me to keep digging?"

"Not yet," Moses said again.

"Okay, then," Arnie said. "Ethel Ann Ames Magruder, age sixty-four."

Jesus! She was older than I was by three years. If we'd been sitting together, you might've guessed we were around the same age, but as soon as we got up and moved, you would have sworn that Toots was younger. I had to start working out.

"She's a widow, husband was Harold Hunt Magruder, a surgeon."

Maybe that explains it: she had access to first-class medical care. It certainly explained how she could afford her expensive hobbies.

"You already knew he was a vet. Magruder's estate was probated in 1977, estimated value of about five hundred thousand. Three kids. Ethel Ann has a pilot's license. Two NTSB investigations, one mechanical failure and one weather-related."

Yow! And I'd flown with her?

"No bankruptcies, no convictions, no lawsuits that I could find. Clean as a whistle. She's been up to anything, she's kept it out of her own backyard. Oh, and she's registered Democrat."

He looked up. When we nodded, he dropped the page and moved on. "Last one. Darcy Elizabeth Livingston, age twenty-two. Comes from Princeton, New Jersey, originally. Graduated from Dana Hall School — that's private — in Wellesley, Massachusetts, 1982. Graduated from MIT in Aeronautics and Astronautics last June, accepted into the master's program in Engineering and Management. Registered Democrat."

He dropped the last page on the floor.

"And that's the lot. Want me to keep looking at any of 'em?"

Moses stood up. "Not yet. Where will you be tonight?" He stooped down and began gathering the papers into a pile.

He spread his arms in an expressive gesture. "Here or at my other office."

"He means Arnold's." Moses handed me the sheaf of papers. "We want him, we can call Kevin at the bar." To Arnie, he said, "Me and Cat are going up to Dayton this afternoon. Any of these folks that are still alive and still involved, we'll meet them there. Then we'll let you know."

Outside in the hall, I said dejectedly, "It's a lot of information, but it doesn't add up to much, does it?"

"If you mean it doesn't tell us what somebody's been looking for in old trunks and footlockers, no. But we didn't expect it to, did we?"

"No, but I feel kind of funny about investigating the potential victims. We don't, after all, think any of the Crazy Eight is bumping off the others, and we're no closer to figuring out who is. We don't even know which of these women Maddy was talking about when she said that they should 'tell what we know.'"

"You right, Cat," Moses conceded. "Still, it's good to know all we can about the potential victims. Might help us figure out who's next."

I looked at him. "So, have you figured out who's next?"

He grimaced. "Not yet."

I looked down at the pile of papers in my hand. In the middle of the top one was a dark purple paw print.

28

JULY 19, 1986

EVENTUALLY, I decided to try standing up. The dog appeared to approve of this decision because he circled me, barking, tracing little curlicues of light through the curtain of rain.

"The hat is swell," I told him as I eased myself up. "It would be even sweller if you had a waterproof map and a bottle of gin to go with it."

He must have taken offense, because he bounded off, leaving me alone in the dark.

"Hey!" I shouted. "Come back here with that light!"

He reappeared. I looked around for something to make a leash out of and spotted the sodden remains of my parachute. As I sawed with my Swiss Army knife at one of the lines that held the canopy, I said, "I don't know what you did with your parachute, but it was a neat trick."

The dog smirked at me. He danced away when I made a grab for his harness, but he might have just been teasing me, because he approached me again and sat docilely as I tied the rope.

"Okay. Here goes nothing."

And he took off, yanking the makeshift leash from a wet hand and knocking me back on my keister.

"Happy!" I called in my best alpha-dog voice. In the darkness, a light turned in my direction. I couldn't read his expression at this distance, but I could guess at it. Who was I kidding? Who was in charge here? The sodden senior citizen who had just fallen out of a tree? Not likely.

So I drew on my years of coaxing recalcitrant two-year-olds and said in a conciliatory tone, "I would really appreciate your help here, Happy. I think it would be a really good idea if we stuck together, but I can't run as fast as you can, so if we're going to make this partnership work, we'll need some compromise." Mostly on his part, as he and I both realized.

He trotted back in my direction and let me take hold of the leash. I wrapped it around my wrist.

"Now, please heel."

He didn't budge.

I looked around in the darkness. I couldn't see the stars for the clouds, so I had nothing to navigate by, even supposing I knew which direction to go.

"Okay," I said, and sighed. "I guess you know where you're going. Why don't you lead the way and I'll heel? Only please walk. Got it? Walk."

He barked, turned, and pulled me into the darkness. But he was walking, more or less.

"I know it's not my place to complain," I told him ten minutes later. I stopped to catch my breath and spat out a mouthful of leaves. To think that he spent all of his time in the company of a smoker. She couldn't have better lungs than I have. "But if I could just request a somewhat less rugged path. Or a path at all — that would be an improvement."

His head whirled as if he heard something. He barked excitedly and headed off again. "It better not be a rabbit," I groused. The leash was cutting off the circulation to my fingers down below and up above my shoulder was killing me. My head was still throbbing, my sneakers were heavy with mud, and I was soaked.

Then I heard the whistle. I hoped it belonged to somebody with an RV and a fully stocked bar.

Then I recognized the tune: "Sweet Georgia Brown."

We were nearly on top of him when I saw him. Happy's flashlight swept up the figure and onto the face of Moses, who was sitting on a fallen tree as if he had nothing better to do than sit in a clearing during a thunderstorm and calculate the wind velocity.

He grinned at me.

"Aw, Cat," he said. "You been retrieved."

29

JULY 18, 1986

The festivities began on Friday night at the bar on the patio at the Ramada, where Moses and I were occupying rooms formerly assigned to Maddy and Squeak. We'd driven up in the Fairlane, separately from Toots and Stretch in case we needed an extra car. Now we were staked out at a corner table with a view of the whole area. I was sweltering in a black pantsuit that I hoped made me look professional and Moses was looking cool in a blue tweed sports coat, gray shirt, and gray slacks. His gear was in a bag next to his chair.

Moses had frowned at me when I'd ordered a gin and tonic, but I'd said, "Nick and Nora do their best detecting under the influence of multiple martinis."

So he'd shrugged and ordered a beer, but said when the waitress left the table, "We dealing with a killer, Cat. You don't want another bump on your head or worse, you better keep a clear mind." Then he went back to his reading.

"Put the instruction book away, Moses," I said in a low voice. "The first guests are arriving."

Toots had spotted us and was wending her way through the tables, steering a tall strawberry blonde in our direction. Then I realized that all the women I met tonight would be taller than I was, unless they'd developed osteoporosis. You had to be at least five-four to be a WASP. It would be a little like hanging out with a women's basketball team, which I've done before. I was a pygmy among Amazons.

"Hey, you two!" Toots called. "I'm glad you could make it."

As she neared us, Moses stood. I gave the newcomers an expectant smile.

"I want you to meet Bernie Smith. Bernie, this is Cat Caliban, the writer I was telling you about, and her photographer, Moses Fogg. Why don't you sit down and chat while I check on things?"

I remembered that Bernie lived in Iowa and I thought she could have represented the state well in a Mrs. America contest. She had a full face with freckles covering smooth skin and large, intelligent brown eyes. She wore a little makeup, but it was restrained. She was considerably shorter than Toots and she had a lot of curly hair piled on top of her head, as if she were still trying to meet the height requirement.

"Gene — that's my husband, he'll be along any minute — will be thrilled to see you," she said to Moses, sitting down. She was wearing a flowered sundress with thin straps and she arranged her skirts gracefully on her lap. "He's always afraid these affairs will be one big hen party."

I liked her for trying to put Moses at his ease. She guessed he might feel out of place as one of the few males and Black people in this group and she'd made him feel welcome. Moses was rarely at a loss in social situations, however.

"Is he a photographer?" I asked. I figured we might as well know the worst.

"Oh, no! Not unless you consider pushing the button on an Instamatic photography, and I'm sure you don't." She smiled at Moses, who smiled back.

"And you're a writer!" she said to me. "That must be fascinating."

"We have a lot of fun," I said.

"Who are you writing this article for?" She asked.

"We're free-lance. We're hoping to interest *Modern Maturity*."

"The AARP magazine?" She beamed. "I read that all the time. I'll bet I've read some of your work. What have you written about?"

"Nothing lately. We do a lot of work for in-flight magazines." That sounded sufficiently anonymous.

Then my photographer spoke up. "The last piece we did for *Modern Maturity* was a piece on Frank Lloyd Wright houses."

I stared at him.

"Remember, Cat?"

"I remember that one!" Bernie said. "It was so interesting. And the photography was marvelous."

"Well, the lighting was kind of tricky, but I thought it turned out okay," Moses said. He was trying to look modest but instead he looked pained because I'd just kicked him under the table. He shifted in his chair to turn a shoulder on me. "We did a piece on senior weightlifters, too. Now we're hoping to do a series on senior athletes."

"Wow!"

"So, Bernie," I said, "did you know Toots before Harlingen?"

"Oh, sure. We were in the same class — 43-W-9. I didn't know her well, but I knew her."

"Where were you stationed before Harlingen?"

"At Niceville, Florida."

"Towing targets?"

"That, and testing and some ferrying, too."

"Testing?"

But at this point we were interrupted by a squeal. "Bernie Sue! I didn't know you were coming to this shindig!" A woman with recently permed, frosted blonde hair was galloping toward us, towing two men, one attached to each arm. The sun glinted off her large-framed glasses, which were gold with ornate little scrolls at the upper corner of each lens. She was speaking breathlessly in a very Southern accent. "But I ran into this handsome man in the lobby." Her voice rose as if for a question and she beamed at the man on her left. "And he told me he was already married — to you!"

"Chubby Lee Davenport, that is just like you!" Bernie was on her feet, hands on her hips, and she'd suddenly developed a Southern drawl. "Why do you have to have all the men? Why can't you leave a few for the rest of us girls?"

So this was Verna "Chub" Davenport Burman. I studied her with interest. She was probably chubbier than she'd been at twenty-one, but not by much, and I wondered how she'd gotten her nickname. She wasn't exactly a beauty, though she was handsome, but she radiated energy.

She let go of the men, stepped forward and threw her arms around Bernie, and said, "Kiss, kiss."

Introductions were made and the two men sat down next to Moses.

"Aren't they cute?" Chub said. "They want to sit together so they can gossip and trade secrets." She turned to Bernie. "But listen, wasn't that awful about Maddy and Squeak? I was so shocked when Toots told me."

Bernie nodded. "I guess we should expect to lose more of us as the years go on, but to lose two like that so close together —."

Chub's fingers brushed the back of Bernie's hand. "Honey, I know it! I want to grab every woman here and shake them by the shoulders and say, 'You take care of yourself and be careful, hear?'" Her eyes were wet. "The women in this room are so precious to me, every single one of them, even when I haven't seen them for years. There's so many memories in this room."

Bernie nodded and clasped Chub's hand. Neither of them mentioned the sabotage of Toots's plane, though I knew she'd told them about it. Maybe they didn't believe that it could be connected to the deaths of two old flying partners.

Bernie's husband Gene was a bland-looking man, several inches shorter than his wife, with thinning gray hair and a complexion that spent a lot of time in the sun. I noticed he had large, powerful hands, showing scars against the dark skin and a recent cut across the knuckles, marked by a wrinkled Band-Aid. He wore a gold men's watch on his left wrist, but his right wrist was encased in a splint. I was on the lookout for any male with an injury that could have been caused by a poorly aimed small-caliber pistol.

The other man, Chub's husband CJ, the city councilman, also wore a watch on his left wrist. He had a full head of curly brown hair flecked with gray and a florid complexion, like a man with high blood pressure. When he smiled or laughed, he showed a set of gleaming laser-cut dentures that contrasted with his skin tone. Though he was tall, his build was stocky and he'd added to it over the years. A green plaid sports coat was buttoned over his paunch, but he unbuttoned it as soon as he sat down. I scanned him for signs of an injury, but couldn't see any. He mopped a sweaty forehead and said, "I didn't think y'all had humidity up here in Ohio. You misled me, Chub."

"I said it wouldn't be as hot, is all," she replied. "And it's not. I didn't say anything about humidity."

"Chub, look!" Bernie said. "There's Esther. But who's she talking to?"

"Why, Bernie Sue, if you would put aside your vanity and get you some glasses, you would recognize her," Chub scolded. "That's Renie Waters."

"I don't think I know her," Bernie said.

"Sure, you do," Chub said. "She's the one who told that Link instructor to stick it up his tail."

"Oh, her. I never really knew her, just kind of admired her from a distance."

CJ Burman was talking with Moses and showing his teeth a lot. He was one of those hearty types who was always slapping people on the back or back handing them in the chest to make a point. I watched him raise his glass with his left hand. I hadn't seen any sign that he was in pain, but he could just be on strong meds and bourbon. Another man I hadn't been introduced to had pulled up a chair to join the men's circle, though Gene Smith didn't seem to be holding up his end of the conversation. Maybe he was in pain, or maybe he just didn't enjoy the company. He also drank with his left hand and he seemed to be managing okay, but I wasn't yet convinced that he was left-handed. Then he reached inside his coat and withdrew a pack of cigarettes. He seemed to fumble a bit with the lighter and frowned at it, but he got his cigarette lit.

The party was well underway. Lou and Wes appeared and dragged a second round table over to expand our group. Lou looked pretty good; she'd given up her sling but not her splint.

"Just a little car accident," she was saying to anyone who asked. "Really, I'm fine. How've you been?" Under her breath to me she said, "Thank God for pain pills, right, Cat?"

To Gene Smith, she said, "Look, Gene, we're a matched set!" She held up her splinted wrist. "How'd you get yours?"

He frowned down at his wrist. "Carpal tunnel surgery. Can't do a blasted thing with it. Doctor said six weeks, minimum, and I've got two weeks to go. I tell him it's got to be okay by harvest time, but he isn't making any guarantees."

Like many taciturn people, Smith seemed to grow downright chatty when it came to discussing his health. Me, I was just hoping nobody would notice how lopsided my head looked, and if they did, that they would be too polite to comment on it. I couldn't see the lump on Toots's head, but she had more hair than I did.

People left the group to hail newcomers, or bobbed up for hugs, or went off to the bar. The women clasped hands often and wept over their fallen comrades. Some had heard the news before they had arrived and some hadn't, but all of them seemed shocked. Gene Smith was displaying his splinted wrist for the inspection of the men's circle, pointing and gesturing as if explaining how the surgery was done. I saw a woman with a cane approach Lou, glance around, and slip Lou a folded piece of paper, which Lou slid into her pocket without reading. Curious, I thought; I wonder what that's about. Probably it was a donation to cover the open bar.

Reluctantly, I'd switched to soda water so that I could keep my head clear. Within the hour, I'd had seven different WASP sitting next to me and I hadn't yet gotten a word in edgewise, although everybody agreed that my work was fascinating. I'd seen two more women approach Lou in a surreptitious manner and their pieces of paper had joined the first in Lou's pocket. Maybe there was an election going on or maybe these women were just embarrassingly late with their dues payments. On the other side of me, Moses was adding to our writing credits and holding forth on various famous people and places he'd photographed. He had both shoulders to me now and his shins were out of range. Toots and Stretch joined us and I sensed a chill in the air.

"Oh, she's just mad at me for letting myself get clobbered," Toots whispered back when I asked. "She thinks I'm not paying attention."

"She ought to be mad at me for letting you get clobbered," I said. And when Toots didn't say anything, I glanced at her. "She *is* mad at me, isn't she?"

"She'll get over it." Then to someone who'd just shouted a question at her, said, "She doesn't get in until 6:30. I told her to come right on to the dinner."

As I listened to the voices around me, it seemed that all of the women's accents had drifted south, as if pulled by the magnetic field of Chub's voice or the ghost of Avenger in Sweetwater, Texas. Even Lou was drawling when she said, "Esther Sue, is that your granddaughter? She's adorable!"

The woman previously identified as Esther Chang had just arrived at our table, calling out, "Okay, who hid the hooch?"

Like the others, she was tall, but incipient osteoporosis had bent her spine slightly and she had probably lost an inch or two. Her black hair was pulled back into an attractive bun and her dark eyes sparkled behind her bifocals. She was dressed in a stylish, loose-fitting, light-green pantsuit. She was holding by the hand a skinny pre-teen with long, straight black hair and a shy smile.

Her exclamation brought gales of laughter from the other WASP. She added, "You'd better not let Killjoy catch you with it." This comment brought more laughter.

Toots said to the girl, "Don't mind us, kiddo. We're part of your granny's wild and crazy side."

"Is this Flea's little girl, Esther?"

Esther nodded and stroked the girl's hair. "This is Fly. She'll be copiloting tomorrow."

Flea and Fly? Esther seemed to be making up for her own pedestrian WASP moniker in the younger generations.

"Hey!" Chub was approaching Esther, pushing someone forward. This was a rather overdressed woman in her forties, wearing a silk suit and too much makeup. She had sharp features, dark hair in a blunt cut, with thick bangs brushing her arched and sculpted black eyebrows. "Guess who this is. Just guess."

"A cow," Toots said.

The woman looked startled but her smile remained fixed. "A what?"

"Cow," Lou said. "K-O-W. Kid of WASP."

"But whose kid?" Chub insisted. "Esther, you should get this one. You too, Bernie."

"Okay, I know," Esther said. "Bernie?"

"Do I get a profile?" Bernie asked. The woman turned her head obligingly. "Not Ronnie Pittman. Not Buzz MacAllister. I know!" Bernie slapped the table. "Shorty Evers."

"You got it!" Chub exclaimed. "This is Shorty's daughter, Isabel Yates. Isabel, this is Esther Chang. She was your mother's flying partner at Harlingen. Bernie Smith here was in your mother's class as well."

"I'm impressed," said Isabel Yates, shaking hands. "I'm usually told that I favor my father, not my mother."

Isabel was introduced around the table and then Bernie said, "Honey, is your mother deceased?"

One of the men — CJ Burman — was offering her a chair. She smiled up at him. To Bernie, she said, "Yes, I'm afraid my mother passed away in January from breast cancer."

There were murmurs of sympathy around the table. I saw Toots give Esther a quick look and remembered that Esther was a cancer survivor. Bernie glanced at Chub: another one lost. But before the subject could be pursued, dinner was announced.

On our way into the dining room, Moses said in my ear, "When you plan to start interviewing, Cat?"

"Oh, I don't know. Maybe when you run out of magazine articles to fabricate and give me some room to get a word in edgewise."

I saw him grinning under his mustache.

30

JULY 19, 1986

I was blinded by light.

"You land in a mud pit, Cat?"

When my eyes adjusted, I could see that Moses was leaning back casually on his log, holding up some kind of high-intensity flood-light from his camera equipment, taking in my bedraggled condition.

"Sic him, Hap!" I said and let go of the leash.

Seventy pounds of enthusiastic dog bounded across the clearing and barreled into Moses, knocking him off the log. "Hey!" he shouted as he tumbled backwards. He dropped the light and its beam raked the trees as it fell.

I stood over him, mopping hair out of my eyes so I could admire the spectacle of Moses, flat on his back, the muddy paws of a soggy golden retriever planted on his chest. Not that I could see much in the dark on that side of the log, just flashes of Moses's contorted face as Happy covered him in doggy kisses.

I grabbed Happy's leash and backed him off. Then I reached down and hauled Moses upright. He was considerably muddier and less nonchalant.

"What happened to the plane?" I asked.

He was cleaning mud out of his mustache.

"The plane," I repeated. "Did the plane crash?"

"I don't think so. I didn't hear a big enough noise."

"There was a lot of smoke, though." I could still smell it, but I could no longer tell whether the smoke was in the air or on me or both.

"Well, the engine was on fire. There was plenty of smoke before we jumped."

"Did everybody get out? I saw Chub and Esther jump. What about Toots and Lou and Bernie?"

"I followed the dog," Moses said. "Lou told me to whistle once I was on the ground and Happy would find me. I thought I saw two other jumpers, though, when the lightning flashed."

"I couldn't see anything. My stupid parachute was turned the wrong way."

"You supposed to turn it around, Cat. Remind me to show you how."

"I won't need to know. I'm never flying again."

"Now, Cat," he began.

But Happy suddenly picked up his ears, barked twice, and lunged, yanking me off my feet.

"Happy!" I heard Moses shout as I tasted wet earth and leaf mold. "Heel!"

"You can't tell him that. He's the only one who knows where we're going," I said, and spat.

Happy danced at the end of his leash, barking and whining.

"Lou must be calling him," Moses said. He offered me a handkerchief, but it was as muddy as mine.

"I don't hear anything."

"Could be a dog whistle. Come on, Cat. Let's go." The dog was already dragging him forward.

"She seems to have this emergency evacuation business awfully well organized," I said. I was having a hard time talking because we were on the move again.

"They've probably practiced," Moses said. He was trotting to keep up with Happy.

"Well, all I can say is that if you ever take Winnie up in a plane and throw her out the door with a parachute strapped to her back, our partnership is over."

At the door to the dining room, a small knot of women was forming around a distinguished-looking man. Lou waved us over.

"— can't join you tonight, ladies," he was saying, "but I look forward to tomorrow night."

He was a handsome man in his sixties who had aged well. His white hair set off tanned skin and blue eyes framed by laugh lines. He had an athletic build under an expensive gray suit. He wore an American flag on his lapel, but the reds and blues in his silk tie were muted. I recognized him, though I couldn't quite place him. I was sure I'd seen him on television.

Lou touched his arm. "Jim, this is the writer I was telling you about, and her photographer," she said. "Cat Caliban and Moses Fogg. Cat, this is Senator Jim Braverman, who's been a dear friend to us. He worked very hard to get the WASP militarization bill passed."

The senator clasped my hand in both of his and his eyes twinkled at me. "Lou's one of my best press agents. She and her fellow pilots did all the work. I just passed it on." He turned his twinkle on Moses and gave him the two-handed shake. "Mr. Fogg."

"He's being modest," Lou said.

The senator laughed. "Now that's one thing I'm rarely accused of." He passed his hand through his hair in a gesture that looked a little like modesty. "No, I've long cherished a high regard for these ladies. There are few causes I've supported with equal enthusiasm over the years." He glanced at his watch. "I'm afraid you'll have to excuse me. I'm late for another engagement. But I look forward to dinner tomorrow night. I want to hear more about your writing, Ms. Caliban. And your photography, Mr. Fogg. Lou, I'll see you in the morning." He sketched a wave and strode off, picking up two young people, a man and a woman carrying a briefcase and clipboard, respectively, as he crossed the lobby. They followed in his wake, chattering at him.

"He's a pilot himself," Lou was saying. "And he's become very active in the museum project. He thinks he can get us some congressional backing."

"He chairs the Armed Services Committee, doesn't he? That's great," Moses said. "Congratulations."

Moses and I were separated at dinner because Moses gave up his seat at the Harlingen table to Isabel Yates. The round tables seated twelve, so it was difficult, especially given the noise, to carry on a general conversation. At my table were Toots and Stretch, the Zimmermans, the Burmans, the Smiths, Esther Chang and her granddaughter Fly, and Isabel Yates.

"If Tex shows up, we'll just have to squeeze," Toots said.

"There are some extra seats at Moses's table," Gene Smith said, a little wistfully, I thought. He turned his head in that direction. "He might feel funny, surrounded by women."

"He likes being surrounded by women," I said.

"Besides," Isabel Yates said brightly, looking around, "we need some men to balance the table."

I wondered how many drinks she'd had out on the patio. I saw Toots and Esther exchange a look and grin.

"Tootsie Lou," Esther said, "behave yourself."

Even Esther seemed to have acquired a Southern accent.

"Okay," I said to Toots, who was seated on my left. "What's this

'Lou' and 'Sue' business? I happen to know that your middle name is Ann."

Esther leaned toward us. "Hasn't anybody explained that yet? When we were living in the South, we figured we should all have Southern names. Of course, Harlingen was so far south, it was practically Mexico, so maybe we should have had Mexican names. But we'd been hearing Southern accents ever since we moved to Texas, and so we started giving each other Southern names. My middle name really is 'Susan,' so we just use that. But most of the gals got a new middle name."

"That explains the Southern accents, too," I said.

"Well, I came by mind naturally, darlin'," said Chub, who sat on my right. "But the rest of them are just imitators, and bad ones, at that."

"I think we're pretty good, Chubby Lee, darlin'," Bernie said. She'd honed in on the conversation from across the wide expanse of table.

"That's *your* opinion, Bernie Sue," Chub said. "If y'all didn't think y'all were better than you were, you wouldn't ever have made it through flight school. But y'all can't talk Southern worth shit."

"I have a middle name," Isabel announced. Everybody looked at her.

Then Chub said, "What's your middle name, darlin'?"

"I'm told I was named for my father," she said.

"What do you mean, you were told?" Chub said. "Didn't you ever know your father, honey?"

"He was already gone by the time I was born," Isabel said. She seemed to relish the attention. What an odd woman, I thought.

The women around the table exchanged glances and I tried to read their expressions. I realized that they were shocked, and remembered that Shorty Evers had done what was to them unthinkable: she had turned her back on all of her training and left the WASP to get married. Now they were hearing that the marriage hadn't survived to see the first child born.

Esther was the first to speak. "I'm so sorry. I didn't know."

"Well, he left me his name, at least," Isabel said. "I suppose I should be grateful for that."

The drama of this statement was somewhat undercut by the intervention of servers, who were setting down salads. At my elbow, a voice said, "Coffee or tea?" Two women stopped at our table to whisper conspiratorially to Lou and Chub and leave behind folded pieces of paper.

Stretch nudged Toots. "Who's that?" she asked. When Toots turned to look, everyone at the table followed her gaze.

A lanky woman in jeans and cowboy boots was creating a stir as she made her way from table to table, headed in our direction.

"It's Tex!" Lou cried.

"It's Tex, all right," Toots said.

Tex Fairweather had the kind of bronzed, leather-like skin that comes with a lifetime of working outdoors. It was lighter around her brown eyes, a circumstance explained by a pair of sunglasses protruding from her breast pocket. Her hair, which was cut in a masculine, barbershop style, was brown streaked with gray and sun highlights. High up near her hairline on the right side, she wore a small gauze patch, secured with adhesive tape that had once been white and showing a crease that might have been made by a hat. She was lean, with hard muscle showing under rolled sleeves.

"What's her middle name?" I asked Toots in a whisper.

"Doesn't have one," Toots said. "At least, not one we use. Her real middle name was 'Lee,' 'Velma Lee.'" She shrugged. "Unless we were really mad at her, she was always just 'Tex.'"

"Ladies and gents," Tex said, smiling down at us.

Chub and Bernie hopped up to give her a hug and introductions were made. She had large hands, one of which closed on mine in a firm grip, and I noticed that she was wearing a men's watch — one with an extra circle of numbers and three smaller dials on its face. A pilot's watch? Was there such a thing? Isabel greeted her a little coolly, as if miffed to have her own story interrupted. CJ Burman offered her his chair, but Lou said, "Never mind, CJ. We can squeeze." Someone at the next table shoved a chair in our direction.

Bernie hooked it with her foot and dragged it over — one of the advantages of long legs. We all scooted sideways to make room at the table for another place setting.

"What are you flying tomorrow?" Chub asked her. Pilots, I was discovering, could be as single-minded as golfers.

"B-26," Tex said. "Just like the old days."

"A Martin Marauder?" Stretch asked, a little breathlessly.

"Yep," Tex said.

"Not a short-wing, though?" Stretch asked.

"That's the one," Tex said.

"Don't worry, kid," Esther told Stretch. "Tex doesn't have any widows to make."

"A lot you know about it," Tex said to Esther, and winked at her.

To me, Toots said, "The Martin Marauder, the short-wing B-26, was nicknamed 'The Widowmaker,' Cat, because it was so notoriously difficult to land."

Even the planes had nicknames.

"You told her a story about that," Stretch put in. "Remember, Cat? About the plane the cadets wouldn't fly? They redesigned it later."

I nodded, glad to be back in Stretch's good graces. Maybe the prospect of watching a woman in her sixties land a B-26 had lightened her mood. I caught Moses's eye two tables over and he nodded at me to indicate that he had registered the new arrival.

Someone set a bottle of beer in front of Tex. She raised it, saluted Lou with it, and drank from the bottle. Lou must've been her flying partner, I thought. How was I going to keep it all straight?

That was when a new voice cut through the chatter.

"Got room for one more?" it said.

All eyes turned. The newcomer was a brunette, her dark brown hair — too dark, I thought, not to show a sign of gray at her age — framed her oval face in waves that just covered her ears. It was rather an old-fashioned cut, like an advertisement for a Marcel. She was rather overdressed in a red chiffon pantsuit that matched her lipstick, with a flowing red scarf around her neck. She smiled at them expectantly. When nobody spoke, I glanced around at them. The men and Stretch were smiling cordially, Isabel was concentrating on her salad, and Fly was drawing on her napkin, but all of the WASP were frowning or wearing blank expressions. Then they began to glance at one another. Toots cocked an eyebrow at Lou, who shook her head slightly. Esther looked at Tex, whose frown deepened as she shook her head. Bernie and Chub looked at each other.

The woman put one hand on her hip. "Toots, I am so disappointed," she said, but she was still smiling. "Do you mean to tell me that you don't recognize your old flying partner after all these years?" She put a hand to her hair, self-consciously. "I know I've changed, but I'd know you anywhere."

All around us, conversation continued. Silverware scraped plates, voices rose and fell, laughter erupted, cups rattled against saucers. Our table was an island of silence.

Toots's expression was unreadable. Finally, she said, "Not — Tommy?"

The newcomer beamed at her. "Gone but not forgotten," she said. "I'm so pleased."

There were exclamations on all sides. "Tommy? Tommy Thompson? It can't be! I thought she was dead! Didn't her plane go down in forty-four? Is it really Tommy?"

"It's really me," she said, "back from the grave." She bent down and gave Toots a peck on the cheek, but Toots seemed too stunned to respond. Lou was the first to stand up and approach her for a hug, then the others followed.

Tex didn't move. "I don't believe it," she said. She took a long drink from her beer. Her expression said that she was telling the truth.

32

JULY 18, 1986

"Is it really her?" I whispered to Toots as Lou made introductions.

"It can't be," Toots said. "But why would anybody impersonate her?"

"To find whatever it is somebody's been looking for in everybody's collection of WASP papers?" I said. "Could it be Thompson? I mean, does it look like her?"

"Sure, I guess so. Right build, right hair color, right eye color. But it can't be her."

On the other side of Toots, Stretch was staring at Thompson. She wore an odd expression I couldn't interpret. Whatever her reaction was, it wasn't within the range of expected ones, given the circumstances, unless she thought the newcomer had sabotaged Toots's plane. But if she thought that, she could be right.

The men had finally decamped, in some relief, and there was some further scooting as we spread out again to fill the space. At some point, another woman dropped a folded paper next to Lou's plate and exchanged a meaningful look with her when she glanced up.

Thompson was saying, "It's a long, complicated story. I'll tell you the whole thing, but not now."

Dinner was served and little effort was made to keep a conversation going that could be heard by all the people at the table.

I opened a conversation with Chub on my right by asking about the food at Avenger.

"It was fabulous, wasn't it, Toots?" Chub said. "Really, Cat, I never ate so much in my life."

Toots nodded. "I think my mother got a little offended, I talked so much about the food in my letters home. I got the message and stopped giving her a daily account of the menu."

"But Cat should know that we didn't do much drinking at Avenger," Chub added.

"Who didn't?" Toots said.

"You didn't," Chub said. "None of us did, really. Well, there was that time Lola Sawyer hid a bottle of bourbon inside the swamp cooler, remember, Toots?"

"She was afraid Killjoy would find it," Toots said.

"But instead, Speedy Shiner retrieved it when Lola got stuck on a cross-country and had to RON, and we passed it around the bay that night," Chub said.

"I've never been so sick in my life," Toots admitted.

"That's because you weren't used to it," Chub said. "That's just my point. We were well-brought-up young ladies. "Well, most of us were." A cloud passed over her face. "Wherever Maddy acquired her drinking habit, it wasn't at Avenger."

"Truth is, you couldn't train like we did and do much drinking," Toots told me.

"Lord, no," Chub said.

"Who was Killjoy?" I asked. "Your CO?"

"Heck, no," Toots said. "She was one of Deedie's assistants."

"Leoti Deaton was the chief administrative officer at Avenger," Chub said. "And Killjoy was chief snitch."

"Were there are a lot of rules?" I asked.

Toots had been diverted by a question on the other side.

"Oh, sure," Chub said. "And you could wash out just by

collecting too many demerits. Some girls escaped by the skin of their teeth, I swear."

"Did you ever get in trouble?"

"Oh, sure," Chub said. "The worst trouble I ever got into was when I got lost in my PT."

"PT?"

"A primary trainer. It was bigger than anything I'd ever flown, so I kind of broke formation and went fence-hopping. That's when you fly real close to the ground, so you kind of jump the fences, you know? Darlin', I was having such a good time I forgot all about the formation and got lost. I finally landed in a field outside some little one-horse town where I could telephone the base to come get me."

"How many demerits did you get for that?"

But she was distracted by a woman who was standing by Lou, bent to whisper in her ear.

"Kit Warren!" she called. "Is your granddaughter still flying for the Navy? I hope you brought pictures."

I saw Lou glance at her watch and then at Chub. Chub folded her napkin and excused herself.

"What are those two up to, I wonder," Bernie said.

It was the story of my evening so far. I'd been asking the kinds of questions I thought a writer would be expected to ask while I figured out how to work my way around to something that would shed light on the two deaths and the sabotage of Toots's plane. But in this setting, I was going to have to be faster off the mark.

I sighed and reviewed what little information I'd gathered. If I were searching for a ski-masked assailant among those present, I had several prospects. Several of them sported obvious injuries. Several of them were left-handed. Several of them wore men's watches. But did I seriously suspect that any of them was capable of killing a WASP? Not really.

The lights flashed off and on, off and on, off and on. Luckily, my reflexes were a little slow and I didn't have time to throw Toots to the floor and cover her with my body — which wouldn't have covered much of her, anyway — when I heard not gunshots, but zither music. Then I saw Lou standing at a microphone at the front of the room. Next to her was a tall, turbaned and partially veiled figure in an outlandish get-up that appeared to have been fashioned from bordello draperies.

"Ladies and gentlemen, your attention please," Lou said.

All around me, people were craning their necks to see.

"We have a very special treat tonight," Lou continued. "Madame Zahara, the internationally renowned fortuneteller, has graciously condescended to pay us a visit. She had many invitations, of course, but she chose us over the brass and the fly boys because she felt that we were more spiritual and that our aura was stronger. Isn't that right, Madame Zahara?"

"That was our breath, Madame Zahara," somebody shouted from behind me.

But Madame Zahara nodded vigorously, making her gold earrings dance. In a voice with a heavy accent, she spoke into the mic. The accent was untraceable, largely because its geographic origins kept shifting. "I know an aura when I zee one. And I am alzo knowing a smart eleck when I zee one. So you be quiet, Tucker Palmer, or Madame Zahara zees a short shit in your future."

"What kind of shit was that?" someone else called.

"You don't need to ask Madame Zahara zat," the fortuneteller intoned. "You, Sadie Zeller, were the queen of the short shit. Zo pipe down! Madame Zahara knows all."

"That's right, Sadie," somebody said. "A third of the girls in your class got short-sheeted by you and some of us are here as witnesses."

Lou managed to wrest the mic from Madame Zahara and cut into the laughter.

"Madame Zahara will be passing among the tables while we have our dessert," she said. "You may consult her if you like."

"Is she expensive?" somebody called.

Lou fended off Madame Zahara and said into the mic, "You may certainly cross her palm with silver, cash, personal checks, travelers checks, or money orders. All of the proceeds will go into the WASP Museum fund."

"Doesn't Chub look great?" Esther said.

"I like the crooked lipstick," Tex drawled. "It adds an authentic touch."

There were six tables and we first caught Zahara's act when she reached the table next to ours.

"Ye-e-e-ss, ye-e-ss, Dodie Witherspoon, Madame Zahara can zee all," she announced. "Past, future, makes no deeference to Madame Zahara. I can zee zat movie magazine on your bed. Oh!" She clucked her tongue. "I can zee one, two, three — five wrinkles in your bed! And a picture of a boy — skeeny, too skeeny! Who eez zat? Jumble? His name eez Jumble? No, Sumper eet eez. Like the bunny rabbit." She passed a hand in front of her face and her eyes moved as if she were reading something there. "No, wait, Madame Zahara zees better now. Jumper eez zee name of ziss boy. Oh, Dodie Weezer-spoon, he eez a nice boy but I zee many geegs in your future. I zee a pop inspection and a lady who eez frowning at you. Madame Zahara haz not even mentioned your zoot suit, which eez, I am zorry to zay, on the floor. What a sad future you haff in store, Dodie Weez-erspoon!"

The group roared with laughter. Several people spoke at once and Madame Zahara seemed not to understand them at first. Then she said, "Past? Eet's her past?" She shrugged. "Past, future, eez all ze same to Madame Zahara. Time eez like a reever zat flows into ze zee, zat goes up eento ze clouds, zat rain down on ze reever — you get ze picture."

At our table, she descended on Tex first. She shooed Esther out of her chair.

"Oooh, ziss lady, she hass a very strong aura," she said. She clasped her hands together. "Madame Zahara loffs a good, strong aura. No, wait! Chust a minute! Eet eez not a strong aura zat Madame Zahara eez zeeing, but a strong arm. My mistek. You haff been arm-wrestling wiss men, and beating zem!" she accused Tex. "You must be very, very carful, Texass Fairweazer. Zere eez a very beeg secret zat Madame Zahara knows and eez going to tell you, so you will be more carful." She leaned forward and stage-whispered,

"Men don't like to lose to weemen. So take heed! You like too much ze danger."

I thought she was through, but she was just getting her second wind.

"I zee a man from your past," she continued. "Martin — Martin — Martin Marauder." She pronounced the last word as if it were a French surname. "He eez a big man —." She spread her arms wide and her bracelets clanked. Then she brought her palms together. "Weeth leetle arms. Beware zees man. Madame Zahara has spoken."

I was laughing along with everyone else, but I felt a frisson in spite of myself. I couldn't help taking seriously all predictions of doom that involved flying.

She turned to Esther next. "You, Esther Chang. Madame Zahara zees many years into ze future. Your daughter will fly like a bird, and her daughter, alzo. Madame Zahara has spoken. You weel name zees pilots for insects, Madame Zahara does not know why." She looked around her. "Aha!" She seized the hand of an astonished but thrilled Fly. "Zo! Your granddaughter, she weel look very much like zees young lady here, and she weel be ze best pilot in ze family." Fly blushed with pleasure.

"But Bernie McClenahan, for you, Madame Zahara zees only darkness — eet eez all around. Oh! Like a dark veil all around, up in ze air. And your heart, eet eez beating very fast in ze darkness."

"She must be talking about flying under the hood, Bernie," Lou said. She had been trailing Madame Zahara around, trying to prevent entanglements with her voluminous draperies.

"Oh, that!" Bernie said. "I'll say my heart was beating fast!"

Toots said to me, "That's how you learn instrument flying. You can't see anything but the instrument panel. Everybody's heart beats fast."

"And everybody hated it," Esther added.

"Tootzee Lou," Madame Zahara continued. "You I zee playing weez toys. Very beeg toyz. You are beelding somezing, no? A beeg toy. But beware! I zee you trowing a beeg wrench — a very beeg wrench — and crack!" She clapped her hands inches from Toots's nose and Toots jumped. "Zere goes ze rudder cable exit fairing." She shook her head sadly. "Eet weel almost make you to curse, Toots Ames. Madame Zahara has spoken."

She turned toward the next table, but Isabel spoke loudly. "What about me, Madame Zahara? Don't you have anything for me?"

Madame Zahara turned back. "You are ze daughter off a very fine pilot." Her eyes glinted and I realized that there were tears in them. "Your mozzer gave up efferyzeeng for you. Zat's all."

Tommy Thompson spoke up. "And me? What about me?"

"Your aura Madame Zahara cannot zee clearly yet," the fortuneteller said. "God weeling, eet weel become clear at a later time. But zere eez dess around you, Tommy Thompson. Madame Zahara feels zees." She thumped her chest with one fist. "You heff cheat dess once maybe, but dess eez a man, and he doesn't like to be cheated."

And she turned her back on us and moved on.

33

JULY 18, 1986

"That was quite a performance," I said to Moses in a low voice as the dinner was breaking up.

"Get anything useful out of it?" He asked.

"Two death warnings," I said, "if they weren't death threats."

"Toots?"

I shook my head. "According to Madame Zahara, Toots is only in danger of cursing, not being cursed. How about you? Learn anything from the guys at dinner?"

"Tell you later. Here comes the activities director."

"Want to change into something more comfortable, Cat?" Lou said. "We're meeting in the lobby in fifteen minutes."

I had been hoping for an evening in the bar so that I could talk to people one-on-one. I assumed we'd be hearing from Tommy Thompson and that everyone would be as eager as I was to find out where she'd been all these years if she hadn't been dead. What I was wearing was comfortable enough for the air-conditioned bar.

"Why?" I said. "Where are we going?"

"We're going to play putt-putt," she said with enthusiasm.

"What about your wrist?"

"Oh, I'll be fine." She looked at me with concern, "Do you have a headache?"

Of course, I had a headache. When someone whacks you upside the head with a golf club, you get a headache that doesn't quit. And even if I didn't have one, the thought of golf, even in a confined space, on a hot July night would have given me one.

"I'll be fine," I said, sighing, and turned toward my room in resignation.

"Kind of like getting back up on the horse after you been thrown, Cat," Moses observed. "Have fun."

I stopped. "What about you? Are you going?"

He shook his head. "The boys are playing poker. You got your gun?"

"Yeah, I got it. But I don't see how I can carry a purse through a game of putt-putt."

"Wear them cargo shorts with the big pockets," he suggested. "Just make sure the safety's on before you put it in your pocket."

"Won't they see it — the shape of it?"

"They're not looking for it," he said. "They'll see something, sure, but they won't know what it is. Wrap it in a hand towel, you don't want them to make out the shape. Wear something long and loose on top."

So half an hour later, there I was, preparing once again to chase a little ball around. On the plus side, I wouldn't have to walk so far and it would be easier to fish my ball out of the little ponds. On the minus side were the mosquitoes.

"Want some insect repellent, Cat?" Bernie was coating herself with a strong-smelling spray.

"Isn't this fun?" Chub said. She hadn't managed to remove quite all of Madame Zahara's lipstick and now Toots handed her a hand-kerchief and pointed. "Oh."

"Just like old times, right, Tex?" Esther said.

She had left Fly at the hotel, where the younger contingent was going swimming — a more appropriate activity for a muggy July night, if you asked me. Isabel had also stayed at the hotel, but Tommy Thompson was still with us, wearing short-shorts and a halter top — clothes she almost had the figure to get away with, even at our age. She was also wearing platform sandals, which struck me as the least practical footwear imaginable. I wanted to get closer to the ball, not farther away, and if they let me get down on my knees and use my club like a pool cue, I might finish the game in the next millennium without decapitating anyone in the vicinity.

Also in exuberant attendance was Happy, the golden retriever. This also had a plus and minus side. On the minus side, if he played, Happy would probably beat my score. On the plus side, he could retrieve my ball from the pond for me. Wasn't that what retrievers were supposed to do?

"Tex is even wearing her old watch," Lou said.

"Is that the same aviator's watch your father gave you?" Tommy asked, lifting Tex's wrist to examine it.

"Still ticking," Tex said.

"Can I see?" I said, and Tex obligingly held out her arm for me. "What's special about an aviator's watch?"

"It's got a compass and a luminous dial," Esther said. "And some of them, like mine and Tex's, have elapsed time indicators."

"You have one, too?"

"Sure," Esther said. "So does Toots. You have one, don't you, Chub?"

"Wouldn't leave home without it," Chub said.

"What about Bernie and Tommy?" I asked.

"I haven't flown since the war," Bernie said. "Got it all out of my system."

Tommy said, "I haven't, either. Couldn't at first, after the crash, then found I just didn't want to."

"The crash?" Stretch asked.

"Now, girls, we agreed that we wouldn't go into all that now," Chub said. "There will be plenty of time for that later. Let's play."

"Cat's an experienced golfer," Toots announced, and she and Stretch traded grins.

By the time I reached the windmill, I'd collected the following information. Like Toots, Lou and Tex could still fit into their WASP dress uniforms. Everybody could fit into their zoot suits. Tex was one of the few women, and fewer WASP, who could fly B-26s in exhibitions. Toots, Esther, and Esther's daughter Flea had all held the national women's title for acrobatic flying at some point. Bernie and her husband farmed and had ever since they married in 1947. Lou thought her husband, Wes, still harbored some resentment about having washed out of Army Air Force flight school, though he said often that if he hadn't washed out, he would never have met the girl of his dreams at Harlingen. Chub's husband CJ had been the handsomest young trainee at Harlingen and all the girls had been smitten with him except Esther, who was already married, Maddy, who claimed to prefer officers, and Tex. Squeak and Maddy had been practical jokers and their jokes had not always been well received. Tex, Squeak, Maddy, and Lou had all been smokers, but Lou was the only one smoking now and it showed whenever she put a hand on her chest and paused to catch her breath.

As far as I could tell, none of this had anything to do with murderous attacks on WASP in the present day. I wanted to ask about a boy one of them had gone off with, but Maddy's allusion to this incident in her telephone call had been too vague and I couldn't think of a way to work it into the conversation.

The women discussed Shorty Evers's failed marriage.

"Can you believe it?" Chub said. "To leave like that and wind up in divorce court so soon! Esther, you didn't know?"

Esther shook her head. "I never heard from Shorty after she left. She said that it would be a quiet wedding, just family."

"So you weren't invited?" I asked, just to be clear. I found myself wondering if there had been a wedding at all, but this possibility didn't seem to have occurred to any of my companions, so maybe it was just my suspicious mind.

"I couldn't have gotten off work," Esther said. She appeared to be concentrating on her stroke. She made contact with the ball and it bounced along the straightaway, slipped past a windmill blade, and reappeared on the green below, coming to rest within an inch of the cup. Happy had barked excitedly when he spotted the windmill and gone to wait below by the hole.

"This is his favorite part," Lou told us.

"And anyway," Esther said, "the wedding was in Oregon. You remember how it was during the war. People didn't make a lot of fuss."

"But Tommy caught a ride out to Colorado for Chip Forester's wedding," Lou said. "Oh, hell and blast!" She pried open the Velcro on her splint with her teeth and let the splint drop to the ground. She gave the ball a whack and it flew through the air and into the windmill, where it cracked against the wall. We heard the ricochet and then it popped out on the green.

"Yeah, but that was later," Esther said, "right before disbandment. Things got looser toward the end. And everybody was heading to Colorado for the Roosevelt thing. It wasn't the same as catching a ride to Oregon."

"The Roosevelt thing?" I echoed.

Toots said, "Roosevelt's son Elliott got married in Colorado that December, just before disbandment, so everybody who was anybody flew to Colorado for the wedding. Tommy had a friend stationed in Colorado who decided to take advantage of that wedding and schedule her own for the same weekend."

"Good thing Tommy went," Chub said, clapping Tommy on the back. "She had to land the damn plane. Remember, Tommy?"

Tommy shrugged. "I haven't thought of that in years. What I remember is the time a bunch of us borrowed a car and drove to Dallas from Sweetwater for Eileen Schultz's wedding. And then he was killed in action two months later. That was so sad."

"I'm just saying I think Shorty was rude to Esther," Lou said. "They were flying partners. And Shorty never even dropped her a line to tell her how it went."

"Well, I guess she had her own problems," Esther said.

"Did you ever exchange Christmas cards, Esther?" Chub asked. She tapped her ball and it sailed through the windmill, dropped onto the green, and rolled into the cup.

"I sent her a card or two, but I never heard from her again,"

Esther said. "I never even knew her married name, just knew the boyfriend's name was Charley."

"Well, I call that strange," Toots said. "I didn't know her well at all, but she seemed nice enough. And then she goes and cuts all ties with the WASP and nobody even knows how to contact her. And then, six months after she dies, her daughter shows up at a reunion. Don't you all think that's strange?"

"Maybe it's not her daughter," Bernie said. "Maybe it's an imposter!"

"Oh, it's her daughter, all right," Esther said. "Either that or a near relation. Right, Tex? Lou?"

"No mistaking that chin," Chub said. "Watch out, y'all! We're catching flak."

They scattered. The flak consisted of the ball launched by yours truly, which had smacked against a windmill blade and shot back in our direction.

"Damn!" Lou said, inspecting the blade. "I think she cracked it. I always thought those things were indestructible." Happy was standing on the other side, head cocked, still waiting for the ball to drop.

"I wouldn't stand there if I were you, Lou," Toots cautioned.

"Where should we stand?" Stretch murmured. "Riverfront Stadium?"

Tex retrieved my ball and handed it to me. "Here you go, Killer."

"You don't have to hit it hard, Cat," Esther said, "just tap it."

"Caliban rules?" I asked hopefully.

"No way," Toots said. "You can do it."

Tex squatted behind me. "When I say 'now,' give 'er a tap, okay, Cat?"

"I'm really good at Bingo," I said.

"Now!"

I tapped the ball and it rolled down the straightaway, missed the oncoming blade by a hair, and disappeared inside the windmill.

Once inside, it seemed to have a long think about its next move, then dribbled out onto the green and rolled past the hole to a corner, as far from the cup as it could get without jumping the boundary.

"All right!" Stretch gave me a thumbs up.

"Teamwork," Lou said "can't beat it."

Shocked as I was, long experience told me not to let go of my pessimism. I lined up my putt and sighed. When I moved the club, a cowboy boot appeared from nowhere and guided it toward the ball. The ball rolled obligingly toward the cup and stopped, less than an inch away.

I grinned up at Tex. "Thanks."

"Don't mention it," she said.

But I had a final assist from another new pal, who approached the ball, lowered his head, and gave one loud bark. The ball jumped, teetered on the edge, and dropped into the cup.

34

JULY 18, 1986

TOMMY THOMPSON TOOK a sip of wine. "Okay, I'm going to tell you what happened. But some of it's real hard to talk about. And there's some gaps in my memory, okay? Just so you know."

Moses and I exchanged looks. I'd retrieved him from the poker game, which was still going strong, because I wanted him to hear this story. We were sitting in a corner booth at the hotel bar, to which we'd added several chairs. All of the golfers were there, and when Moses had asked them who'd won, they'd all sworn, to a woman, that I had. I'd asked Tommy if I could take notes, but she had said that it would make her "too nervous."

"You remember I was going back to Sweetwater for the last graduation?" Tommy asked.

"That was just a day or two after you got back from Colorado," Toots said, nodding.

"I was dying to get back to Sweetwater and I told everybody I met," Tommy said. "So a few days after I got back from Colorado, I heard from one of the pilots passing through that they needed somebody to pick up a UC-78 in Mission, just up the road, and deliver it to Biggs — that was the big base in El Paso. 'Why don't you ask your CO?' he said. 'You could stop in Sweetwater on the way. They can't be in that big a hurry for those junkers.'"

"That's about right," Bernie said. "I flew those crates in Lubbock before I went to Niceville. The ones I flew were in terrible shape."

"Held together with spit and shoe laces," Toots said.

"Well, everybody agreed, and I caught a ride over to Monroe and picked up the plane."

"The air base at Mission," Toots explained to Moses and me.

"I wasn't more than fifteen, twenty minutes into the flight when I developed engine trouble," Tommy continued. "It was a dark night and I could hardly see anything. By that time it was raining, hard. And I took the plane down to look for a place to land. But there wasn't anything but water down there — miles and miles of water!"

She looked down at the table, her eyes widening, as if she were seeing it all again. Her hands hovered, palms down, fingers spread, just above the table.

Bernie whistled. To Moses and me, she said, "UC-78s were made out of wood. That's how they got their nickname — the Bamboo Bomber. Last thing you wanted was engine trouble when you were flying a Bomber. The whole plane would go up in smoke before you could climb out of the cockpit."

Toots frowned. "Were you flying on instruments?"

"Of course, I was," Tommy said, looking up. "I just told you, I couldn't see a thing up there."

"Then how did you end up over the gulf?" Toots asked.

"That's just it," Tommy said. "I don't know. I think somebody must have sabotaged the compass because as far as I was concerned, I was headed straight for Sweetwater. So I tried to turn around and head back the way I came, but without a compass, I didn't know which direction to go."

"Weren't you wearing your watch?" Toots asked.

"My watch?" Tommy echoed.

Tex held up her wrist. "Aviator's watch."

"Oh," Tommy said. "I don't remember. It's odd the things I don't remember and the things I do. I remember bailing out and the cold shock of the water when I hit — at least, I remembered it a long time afterwards." She shivered, but then, she was still wearing a halter top and short-shorts inside the air-conditioned bar and it made me cold just to look at her.

"But I still don't remember anything after that until I came to in a little house — a shack, really — on the Mexican coast. The man who owned the house was a fisherman and nobody in the house spoke any English. These were very poor people, completely uneducated — Indians, I supposed, from the look of them. I guess I'd been sick a long time before I woke up. My skin was peeling off in sheets from the sunburn." She brushed one arm with the back of her hand. "I had a cracked skull, a broken arm, a few broken ribs, and an infection that wouldn't quit. I kept asking for an ambulance or a hospital, but they kept shaking their heads and giving me tea to drink and fixing up nasty-smelling poultices for my injuries. I still have a scar on my arm where the bone broke the skin." She hunched her right shoulder forward and pointed out a place on her arm. The light was dim, but I could just make out a jagged white line on her upper arm above the elbow. "See?"

She looked around at us until she was satisfied that everybody had examined the scar. "I remembered that my name was Evelyn and that I'd been flying a plane. But why I'd been flying a plane I didn't know. I didn't remember Harlingen, I didn't remember Sweetwater or the WASP, I didn't remember anything. There was a lot of talk about the '*guerra*' and then I remembered something about the war and connected the word to the war. Honestly, I was just lost and confused all the time."

She shivered again and then scanned our faces. "It's hard to explain what that's like," she said slowly, "not to know who you are or where you belong, I mean, to people who haven't been there. And if you're sick and in pain and — oh, hot and dirty and isolated because you can't communicate with anybody, you just kind of give up and let everything wash over you. I did, anyway.

"Then one day — I really don't know how long I'd been there — they picked up my mattress, the father and several young men who could have been sons or brothers or nephews or whatever, and put me in the back of a cart. 'Finally,' I thought, 'they're taking me to a hospital. Somebody will call the nearest American consul and I'll find out who I am and go home.' But instead, they took me to a convent, where I was given a bed in a sick ward. Some of the sisters there spoke a little bit of English, at least, but the doctor, who only came once a week, didn't speak any. The nuns were kind and took good care of me and called me 'Evelina.' I just kind of drifted along."

She shrugged and took a sip of wine. "I got used to the place. It was wartime and nobody had time to come looking for one lost American girl."

"The Air Force went looking for you and so did we," Tex said. "Between us, we logged a lot of hours, about half of them over the Gulf of Mexico. We never found any trace of your plane."

"Oh, Tex, I didn't mean it that way," Tommy said. "I know you looked. There probably wasn't anything to find except an oil slick covered with ash."

"So when did you contact the consulate?" Chub asked. "After the war?"

Tommy nodded. "Long after," she said. "I stayed at the convent for eight years. By then I'd remembered a lot of what happened and I knew who I was. But when I wrote to my parents, I found out they were both dead. I had a sister and a brother. My brother was living in Tennessee, but we weren't really very close. I wrote him to tell him I was alive and where I was, and after that we exchanged Christmas cards every year. I saw him at a family wedding a few years ago. My sister was living in France, and it wasn't until I decided to go see her that I had to get everything straightened out at the embassy so that I could get a passport. I spent some time with my sister, then decided to move to Los Angeles. I had money from my parents' estate and I'd always wanted to live in Southern California. So that's pretty much the story of my life. I was waiting in a small regional airport one day last month and happened to pick up a copy of the Ninety-Nines newsletter. I read the notice about the reunion, so I decided to come and surprise you. And here I am!"

Chub slung an arm around her shoulders. "Oh, darlin', we are so glad!" she said. "You surely are a sight for sore eyes."

Lou smiled, too, but Esther, Tex, and Toots didn't appear to be in a celebratory mood. Stretch was staring down at her lap, as if embarrassed by the tension in the group. Bernie's smile was uncertain. She hadn't known Thompson well and would take her cue from the others.

"Oh, Toots!" Tommy said, and for the first time there were tears in her eyes. "I know you're mad at me for not tracking you down earlier. I suppose I could have done it somehow."

"The VA," Esther supplied, nodding.

"Oh, Esther, that's not fair," Chub chided her. "You can't just call up the VA like directory assistance and ask for somebody's address. You know it doesn't work that way."

"Well, Chub, the truth is, I didn't try," Tommy said. "My life was so different after the war. Sweetwater and Harlingen — those were just faint memories. They hardly seemed real to me. And then, when I read about the reunion —." She raised her hands to her head and narrowed her eyes. "It was like this. Part of me just rose up from the dead. And suddenly, there wasn't anything I wanted more than to see all of you again."

Chub's eyes were glistening too, now. She took Tommy's hand and gave it a visible squeeze.

"Let's drink to reunions," Lou said.

And since nobody could think of an objection to that, we did.

35

JULY 19, 1986

"So is she or isn't she?" I said to Moses. "Inquiring minds want to know."

We had opted out of midnight water polo with the WASP and were sitting in my hotel room, having a nightcap. Okay, I was having a nightcap; my photographer was slumped in a chair across from me with his eyes closed.

"You think they're safe out there?" I fretted. "What if somebody throws a hairdryer into the water?"

I looked down from my window onto the pool in the courtyard two floors below, which was bustling with activity. Happy was running alongside the pool barking. I couldn't tell if he was refereeing, coaching, or cheerleading. But as I watched he took a flying leap and landed in the middle of the game. My mistake.

"Cat, these women wearing me down," he said. "I need my beauty sleep."

"I know just how you feel," I said. "Come on, Moses. Stay awake for just ten more minutes and then you can go off to beddy-bye. Is she or isn't she?"

"Thompson?" He grunted. "Toots and Tex and Esther don't think so, so I vote no."

"But they think she could be?" I said.

He opened his eyes. "She could be," he agreed. "They all think she could be. You heard Tex test her Spanish?"

I nodded.

"Her Spanish is good, according to Tex," he said. "But she knows it doesn't mean much. Nobody in their right mind would come up with the cockamamie story about living in Mexico all those years if her Spanish wasn't good. Tex worked with the Mexican Air Force after the WASP disbanded. Instrument training. You know that?"

"No. I also find Thompson's selective memory loss highly suspicious, don't you? She remembers some things, but not others. And sometimes, she just seems to be faking it. I couldn't tell if she remembered landing that plane in Colorado or not, could you? And when Chub mentioned the time she tried to make dinner for that boy she liked and Tommy had to cook it for her. Remember that? She laughed along with everybody else, but she didn't add anything, did she? And yet, she was the one who brought up the dog that Lou adopted and the hair dye incident. And she remembers several run-ins with Killjoy, the CO's assistant."

"Tex seems to think she knows more about Avenger than Harlingen," Moses said.

"Maybe, but she remembered the bar brawl in Corpus. She remembers saying something about drawing a knife on a WASP, which agrees with what Toots told me. She remembers the emergency landing when they were towing targets in bad weather. She seems to remember several of the officers from Harlingen and she brought up one of the mechanics by name."

"There's no doubt that if she's an imposter, she's well prepared," Moses said.

"But why would anybody want to impersonate a WASP? Because they're still looking for something is what I said, but could that be true? What do you think?"

"I think your ten minutes is up." Moses stood up.

But as he reached for the door, somebody knocked on it. I looked through the peephole. "I think we're about to go into over-time," I said and opened the door.

Stretch stood there, glancing nervously down the hall.

"Can I come in?" she said.

I opened the door wide and she slid past me.

"Oh, good, Moses is here," she said.

"Have a seat," I said, but she was already lowering her lanky frame into the chair I'd just vacated.

"I have something to tell you," she said. She looked from Moses back to me. "But you can't tell anybody. Not yet."

"Okay," he said. "Shoot."

"That woman is not Tommy Thompson, as she claims." She paused dramatically as if expecting us to protest or express shock.

Because —," I said mildly.

She took a deep breath. "Because Tommy Thompson was my aunt — my great-aunt." Again, she paused.

Moses was running a hand along his jaw line, where his five o'clock shadow had lengthened into a short beard.

"You knew your aunt?" he said.

She stared at him. "No, she was dead by the time I was born."

"Uh-huh," he said.

"I've seen pictures of her, of course."

"Uh-huh. And this woman couldn't be that woman, forty years older."

She didn't answer directly. "She said she went to visit her sister and sent Christmas cards to her brother, and that was all bullshit! They never heard a word from her."

"Was she right about her parents being dead?" Moses asked.

"Who knows?" Stretch said, standing and throwing up her hands in exasperation. "She didn't exactly give us a clear timeline, did she? They were killed in a car accident in Morocco in 1950. But they weren't her parents, they were my great-grandparents."

"And why should we believe that you are who you say you are?" I asked.

She blinked. "Oh," she said. Her hands fell to her sides. "It never occurred to me that I'd have to prove my identity. I've been too worried about concealing it."

I asked the obvious question. "Why?"

"Why," she echoed. She sat down again. When she spoke again, she spoke quietly. "I've always been fascinated by my Aunt Tommy. I wanted to fly, ever since I was little, and the idea that my great-aunt had done it, someone who was my grandmother's age, was so amazing to me. It was like having Amelia Earhart in the family. The WASP was — oh, I don't know how to put it — this incredibly romantic ideal. An air force of women who were as good as the men. I had some pictures of them. I even had a picture of the Harlingen group, with her handwriting on the back, so I knew who was who. When I was a teenager, I'd study their faces to figure out how they did it — how they made it through Army flight school, when so many women failed."

"How did you get them, these photographs?" Moses asked.

"My grandmother had some photographs and letters — things her sister had sent her — and after she died my mother gave them to me. But Mother didn't know what had happened to the rest of my great-aunt's things. My grandparents had inherited my great-grandparents' rambling old house in Montgomery County, Maryland, and I used to fantasize about finding a trunk in some long-unused corner of the basement or in a storm cellar or maybe buried somewhere on the property, like a hidden treasure."

She leaned back and smiled at us. "Time passed. I learned to fly. I went to college. I was accepted at MIT in the Aero-Astro program. And then, low and behold, one day I picked up a copy of the Ninety-Nines newsletter and saw an ad for a summer assistant to help a woman named 'E. A. Ames Magruder' build an airplane."

"Did you know who she was?" I said.

"Oh, yes," she said. "You see, Toots wrote my great-grandmother the nicest letter after my Aunt Tommy disappeared. I still have that letter. From that letter and from my aunt's letters, I had always known that Ethel Ann Ames had been my aunt's flying partner.

Once I saw her perform at an air show in New York. I was twelve at the time and my great-uncle took me. It was probably one of her last performances — she was in her early 50s at the time. So when I saw that ad, I couldn't believe my luck." She gave an embarrassed laugh and looked down at her hands in her lap. "Well, I guess I thought it was fate, not luck."

"You still haven't explained why you didn't tell Toots who you were," I said.

She sighed. "Well, first, of course, there was the racial thing."

I felt my forehead crease. "The racial thing? You thought she might be racist?"

"Not exactly." Her eyes shifted to Moses.

"There weren't supposed to be any colored WASP," he said.

"Oh, and your aunt was —." Big duh, as my grandkids would say.

"Passing for white," Stretch said. "A lot of these women made sacrifices, Cat, just to get the training and have the experience. She thought she could pull it off and she did. She was light-skinned and she came from a very cosmopolitan, upper-middle-class family. Her father was a diplomat in the Foreign Service. She didn't think she could join the Tuskegee Airmen, like her brother did, and pass for male." She grinned. "But I'll bet she entertained the idea."

"You didn't think Toots would believe you?" I asked.

"Oh, I don't know," she said. "I thought it might come as something of a shock. And there would be ramifications. Somebody would have to rewrite the history books. Not that I think that's a bad thing — for all I know, Great-Aunt Tommy might not have been the only Negro WASP. It wasn't something she could talk about in her letters home."

"Sure," Moses said.

She looked down again and frowned. "But there was something else. I guess I wanted to prove myself to my aunt's old flying partner. I wanted her to respect me without knowing about my connections."

"Well, you certainly accomplished that," I said.

"I always planned to tell her," Stretch said earnestly, "just not yet. But with all that's been going on, this Tommy Thompson impersonator gives me the creeps." She shuddered. "It gave me chills to hear her describe her so-called accident, because it could so easily have happened that way for Aunt Tommy. Except that you don't lose consciousness when you're floating around in the Gulf of Mexico and wake up in a fisherman's hut. That's crap."

"Does she look like your aunt?" Moses asked. "We've only seen one picture of Thompson and not a very good one at that."

"Well, that's kind of creepy, too." Stretch leaned forward. "The photographs I have are old black-and-whites, of course — the ones from Sweetwater and Harlingen. But I also have a studio portrait of my aunt taken when she was twenty — four years before she died. And I can certainly see the resemblance — especially in the nose. My aunt had a narrow nose, with just a little bump in the bridge — here." She touched her own nose. "You'd think an impersonator would come up with a story about how she broke her nose in the crash and they reconstructed it or something. But this woman has that bump."

"So what if she was telling the truth, except for the part about contacting the family?" Moses said. "Isn't that possible?"

Stretch shook her head. "It's not her. It just isn't. It's such a goofy story, anyway."

"I'll grant you that," Moses said.

"I know!" Stretch jumped to her feet. "It's the Spanish!"

"Tex seemed to think her Spanish was good," Moses said.

"But that's just it!" Stretch said. "She said she couldn't communicate with anyone at first or understand what they were saying. But Aunt Tommy had lived in Brazil for five years as a kid when her father worked for the embassy there."

"So she probably knew some Portuguese," Moses said, "but that's not Spanish."

"But they're close enough," Stretch insisted. "The accent might throw you at first and some of the vocabulary. But you would certainly know what a '*guerra*' was, even if it was pronounced differently. And I'm just not convinced that memory loss covers the situation. You don't just forget a language you speak fluently, do you? Don't you see? You couldn't possibly be as lost as she claims to have been."

"Maybe she misrepresented some things," Moses said. "I expect she lied about a few things, even if she is Thompson. Most people do when they give accounts of themselves. Especially if they're trying to explain why they didn't get in touch with the authorities."

"But I'd know if it was her!" Again, she put a fist to her chest. "Believe me, I'd know."

Moses sighed. "You're probably right, but we can't be sure until we do some checking. In the meantime, we should try to figure out what this Thompson person is up to if she isn't Thompson, and maybe if she is."

"First, let's be clear about something," I said and turned back to Stretch. "You haven't been searching people's WASP collections for something, have you?"

Her eyes widened in alarm. "God, no! I wouldn't harm any of these women, I swear!"

"I didn't ask if you'd killed anybody, just if you'd searched their stuff."

"No, it wasn't me." Her expression changed. "But that reminds me of something! Lou has a room on the first floor of the hotel here where she's storing things for the museum. She encouraged the WASP to bring things they'd like to donate." She looked at us. "Do you think it's secure?"

"It's probably locked," I said. "Isn't it?"

"I would guess so," Moses said. "The hotel wouldn't want to be responsible if something disappeared from the room." He looked at his watch. "Anyway, it's now almost one in the morning. I don't know about you two, but I need my sleep. I think we should check with Lou in the morning."

"Is it that late?" Stretch said. "I'd better get back to the room.

Toots will wonder what's happened to me. And I don't like to leave her alone right now."

Moses followed her out. I called him back. When he stuck his head in the door, I raised my eyebrows at him.

"Not now, Cat, don't even suggest it. Overtime is over."

36

JULY 19, 1986

I DON'T KNOW who invented the breakfast meeting, but I know who promotes them. The promoters are the kind of people who bound out of bed at sun-up and jog or do push-ups and sing in the shower. They feed the cat before the cat has even had time to think up nefarious schemes for waking them up, much less feeding her. They watch morning news shows on television while they eat their breakfast and make their kids' lunches. They are clear-headed enough to remind everybody of everything they have to do that day. They leave the house whistling. They arrive at their first meeting on time and turn down the assorted carbohydrates intended to placate those who are attending under duress. In short, morning people.

I am not a morning person. And I wish the damn morning people would all drop dead and leave the rest of us in peace so that we can suffer through our first waking hours without them. I especially wish it when called upon to attend a goddamn morning meeting.

At 7:30 the next morning, I was balancing a cinnamon roll, a muffin, and two donuts on a small paper plate and glowering at Esther Chang as she arranged her paperwork in front of her on the table. My photographer was shooting some pictures, to the delight of the morning people in the room and the disgruntlement of every-body else.

To my surprise, Senator Braverman arrived, trailing the two assistants, who did not look like morning people. He kissed Esther on the cheek, waved at a few people, shook his head at the male assistant, and sat down at Esther's right. Three rectangular tables were arranged in a U and Esther was seated at the center of the connecting table. Lou was setting down a stack of papers at the place to Esther's left. She looked pale and I was wondering if the events of the last two days were catching up to her. Then I overheard some-one's account of an all-night poker game that started after the water polo game had ended and discovered one likely source for Lou's morning funk.

About twenty women were milling around. Some appeared to be seriously hung over. Toots and Stretch were there, and Chub. Just as Esther was starting to call the meeting to order, Tex sauntered in. She didn't pay any attention to the food table. She took a chair at the foot of one table, straddling it after she turned it around. She wore a different button-down shirt today, but the same jeans and boots and a clean gauze patch. I noticed that Esther was wearing a large watch today and guessed it was an aviator's watch like Tex's. Esther, her daughter, and granddaughter were scheduled to fly today at eleven.

Esther, still seated, called for introductions, and one by one, we introduced ourselves. Each WASP identified her class at Avenger and the place or places she was stationed afterward.

"I believe most of you already had a chance to meet Cat Caliban and Moses Fogg last night," Esther said. "Moses will be walking around here at our meeting and for the rest of the weekend, taking candid shots. He's told me to tell you that if you don't want your picture taken, you should just let him know. But he has agreed to let us have all the photos we want for the museum, so I hope you won't object."

"Will that be for the 'Then and Now' gallery?" somebody asked.

"God, there's a scary thought," said another. From her husky voice, I put her in the hung-over contingent.

Moses tried to look genial and busy. I thought his costume was over-the-top and I'd told him so, but he wouldn't listen to me. Surely no photographer these days would need to haul around as many bags as he had hanging from his shoulders or wear a vest with as many pockets. You would have thought he was the still photographer on the set of a Cecil B. DeMille epic.

"Just so you know," Esther said after the introductions, "the museum committee consists of myself, Chub Davenport Burman, Chip Ferrier Santos, Ruth Pittman Brown, and Flash Gordon Jackson." She nodded at each woman in turn. "Junior Littletree Staley and Muriel Fry are also committee members, but they couldn't come this weekend. They'll be at Sweetwater in September. Lou Pirelli Zimmerman serves ex officio as president. And then there's Jim Braverman, our honorary member."

The senator flashed a smile but passed up the opportunity to grandstand, which earned him points in my book.

"Chub, you want to give the treasurer's report?" Esther said. "It's coming around, I think."

The prospect of treasurer's reports constitutes another good reason to skip morning meetings. How anybody can concentrate on numbers, much less the minutiae of expenditures for paperclips and stamps, before ten o'clock in the morning is a mystery to me. I looked down at my purple ditto and crossed my eyes as Chub read it to us. My advice would be to let us read it for ourselves and start the meeting an hour later. But, as usual, nobody had asked my advice.

"The treasurer's being modest," Esther said when Chub had finished, and smiled at her. "What she didn't point out was that Madame Zahara's fortune-telling brought in over one hundred and fifty dollars last night for our building fund. I think she deserves another round of applause."

There were applause, cheers, and a whistle or two.

"Jim, maybe you can report now on where we are in the appropriations process," Esther said.

"Sure," he said, "be glad to. Well, I'd better begin with an apology. We got a late start on this thing and the language is drafted, but as you probably know, not much happens in Congress between now and election time. We spend most of August working in our constituencies and we adjourn October 1st, which is the beginning of the fiscal year." He brushed the hair off his forehead. "It might still be attached to another bill, but we all feel — those of us who are working on it — that we'd rather have more support lined up when we introduce it."

"Who else is working with you?" someone asked.

"Well, as you know," Braverman continued, "your old friend Senator Goldwater is retiring this year, but he's been active in the cause. In the House, Pat Schroeder, Charlie Stenholm, Olympia Snowe, and Lindy Boggs have agreed to co-sponsor. Senators Kassebaum and Glenn are working with Barry and I in the Senate. If any of you ladies see John at the Air Show or at dinner tonight, feel free to introduce yourselves. He may need you to shake a few hands. I can say that we've encountered no major opposition to the idea, so it will largely depend on the economy and the state of the budget when the measure comes to a vote. Timing, as usual, is everything, and difficult to control. But we'll do our best." He passed a smile around the room. "We're optimistic."

"Thanks, Jim," Esther said. "We really appreciate all your hard work."

"My pleasure," he said, rising. "Now, speaking of work, I'm afraid you'll have to excuse me. Enjoy your day."

Esther directed our attention to another purple ditto.

"You can see here what's already been donated and what we still need," she said.

"We own a B-26?" someone asked.

"Tex got that for us," Esther said. "It's a junker, but fine for our purposes. She's storing it for now."

"We don't actually have to demonstrate the Link trainer, do we?" Bernie asked.

"Sure, Bernie," Toots said. "We were saving that job for you."

Someone else said, "But you can demonstrate flying under the hood if you'd rather."

"I don't have a pilot's license anymore," Bernie said complacently. "One of you will have to do that."

Esther waited for the laughter to subside, then continued. "As you can see, we also have a BT-13 and and AT-6 in storage. But we could really use a UC-78."

"I had one," someone said, "but it went up in smoke."

"I had one," someone else said, "but the termites ate it."

"Now, those are big items, I realize," Esther went on. "But truthfully, we need anything you have to offer — diaries, letters, zoot suits, uniforms, sand from Avenger Beach, old parachutes, anything. Whatever we don't use will go to Texas Women's University in Denton."

The buzz in the room grew louder as women proposed items for the museum's collections — an immunization record, sulfur pills and salt tablets, a cockpit pillow, a crash bracelet, a slide rule.

"How about a pair of socks I knitted on the flight line?" someone proposed.

"God, we should have a whole room devoted to things we knitted," somebody else said. "Socks on the flight line, sweaters in the ready room, scarves on cross-countries —."

"How can you tell a WASP from an Army Air Force pilot?" someone called out.

"She can knit!" several voices chorused.

Someone asked, "What if we brought things here to donate, Esther?"

Esther nodded and raised her voice above the din. "We have a storage room here in the hotel on the first floor. If you ask at the front desk, they'll unlock it for you. I'll show you after the meeting."

The meeting turned into a brainstorming session about the museum and what it should contain. Finally, it seemed to be winding down. Esther asked, "Any questions?"

Tex raised her hand. "I'd like to know why there are natural gas rigs on the land we're supposed to have bought in Sweetwater a year ago." Her tone, as always, was mild, not accusatory. "And I'd like to know why the land is registered to an outfit name of Westex Corporation instead of to us."

Esther frowned. "There must be some mistake. Have you been there?"

Tex nodded. "Two months ago."

Lou said, "You must be mistaken. You must've been looking at the wrong piece of property."

All eyes were on Tex.

"Out past the landing strip, where Nellie Peterson crashed her AT-6," Tex said. "That's what you told us, right?"

"That's right," Esther said. "Couldn't you be mistaken about the exact location?"

"I know where Nellie came down," Tex said. "You said we bought twenty acres. These rigs look new. Thing is, even if I was mistaken, the county courthouse has no record of any property owned by us. I checked."

Esther and Lou turned to Chub, and then so did all the other eyes in the room.

"Well, I can't understand it," she said. "There must be some mistake. But I'll ask CJ. He handled the purchase for us. I'm sure there's a reasonable explanation. We bought the land."

Lou glanced at Esther. Esther said, "We'll check on it and get back to you. Thanks for bringing it to our attention, Tex." But none of the three women in charge looked thankful. They looked worried.

Tex waved a hand in acknowledgment.

"Now, if there's nothing else —?" Esther scanned the group, obviously hoping there wouldn't be. "Let's watch some flying!"

But the meeting broke up with less enthusiasm than confusion.

"I sent a hundred dollars," I heard one woman saying in a low voice to another. "That's a lot of money for me. I hope they haven't thrown it away."

The other laughed. "I don't think there's any chance of that happening. Still, it's troubling. Tex isn't very often wrong."

I joined Toots, Stretch, and Moses, who were having their own conversation, sotto voce.

"Don't they say that murders are usually committed over sex and money?" Toots was saying. "If you'd asked me an hour ago, I would have ruled out money because nobody has enough to kill over. Now —."

"Property and mineral rights can add up to big money," Stretch agreed.

Moses and I exchanged glances. I noticed that he'd dumped all the camera paraphernalia he'd been toting and was rubbing one shoulder.

"It doesn't feel right," he agreed.

"It doesn't explain what piece of paper somebody's been looking for in twenty-year-old collections, though," I pointed out. "You won't find a deed or a mineral lease in somebody's basement — unless it's an old one. Is that possible, Moses?"

He shook his head. "I don't know much about it."

"Esther's going to show everybody the storeroom. I think I'll just go take a peek."

I followed the small mob that was following Esther and a desk clerk like a tour group. I heard grunting and creaking behind me, which indicated that Moses had picked up his gear and was following me.

"Cat," he puffed in my right ear.

"No," I said. "It's your costume."

"I carried your golf clubs."

"Don't even remind me."

Then I heard Esther gasp. "Jesus!" She said.

There was a beat of silence and then the buzz began. I elbowed my way through the heart of the crowd to where Esther and a very pale young desk clerk stood staring down. I looked.

"Jesus!" I said.

The figure of Tommy Thompson lay sprawled on the floor, about two yards inside the door. She was wearing the red outfit in which she'd made her grand entrance the night before, its scarf buried in an ugly line around her neck. Her eyes were open and she was very dead.

"Call the police," Moses said to the young man. "Cat, you and Esther keep everybody out." He was already extracting a camera from a case around his neck.

"Shouldn't you feel for a pulse?" Esther asked, her voice quavering.

"No point," Moses said. He was squatting down, several feet from the body, inspecting it. He leaned first one way, then the other, but he avoided making contact with anything in the room. He never put a hand on the floor, I noticed. He took several photographs.

I had spread my arms to form a barrier. I heard Esther making soothing noises to my left. There was no hysteria, only curiosity. That struck me — the absence of noise. Nobody screamed, they didn't even shout. Then it came to me: these were WASP. At one point in their lives, all of them had faced danger daily. Many had probably witnessed death. Without Army status, they had been trained Army pilots. Nobody was going to faint now.

But I heard the question passed from mouth to mouth: "Who is it?"

And that, it seemed to me, was the critical question.

37

JULY 19, 1986

TOGETHER, Moses and I talked to a Detective Kroup of the Dayton Police Department in the abandoned meeting room as the staff cleared dishes and put chairs away behind us. It turned out that Lou actually lived in the city of Kettering, a Dayton suburb, so Kroup wasn't with the same outfit that had investigated the recent break-in and assaults, though he said he'd talk to the Kettering detective.

Kroup was a burly guy with thinning red hair and an impressive and distracting red handlebar mustache. His note-taker was a brunette with a ponytail and a very serious expression. Kroup and Moses seemed to hit it off right away, although he expressed a healthy amount of skepticism when we told him our story.

"Let me get this straight," he said. "Two elderly women on opposite coasts fall down the stairs and die. And because they were flying partners forty years ago, you thought their deaths might be connected."

"No, our client thought their deaths might be connected," Moses said. "She hired us to find out."

"Oh, your client," Kroup said. "That would be Ms. Magruder, the lady who pays you to investigate her fantasies."

I had already spent an hour in a meeting I hadn't wanted to

attend at a time of day I preferred to sleep through, so I had a short fuse.

"You know, your sarcasm would strike me as a hell of a lot more relevant if we weren't sitting here discussing the third death of a WASP assigned to Harlingen to have occurred this month, and to be discussing it in the context of a known assault on a fourth Harlingen WASP, and two sabotage attempts involving WASP vehicles." Okay, I didn't know that Lou's car had been sabotaged and I didn't know if an airplane technically constituted a "vehicle," but if he started critiquing my prose, I was liable to grab his mustache by its handlebars and rip it off.

"You have a point," he said, "although I'm guessing we have no confirmation yet on any sabotage. Could be these women are just unlucky."

"Yeah, you could be right," I said. "After all, during the whole time they were risking their necks for their country, they were told they'd soon be Army officers, only to get sent home with nothing. And maybe living together forty years ago synchronized their luck along with their menstrual periods. And the perp who clubbed us was probably just looking for a piece of notepaper."

He grinned at Moses. "She always this testy?"

I stepped on Moses's answer. "Question. I saw a footlocker in the storage room. I saw some other stuff as well, but our perp seems to be interested in paper. Had the footlocker been searched?"

Kroup looked back at me, then at Moses again.

Moses said, "See, that's how come she gets away with being testy. She's smart. Ain't always right, but she's smart."

"Nothing in the footlocker besides a couple of books," Kroup admitted. "Some letters and papers were gone. Ms. Chang and Ms. Zimmerman don't exactly know what was in there. They'd been using it to collect donated papers."

"So he scooped everything up and walked out with it."

"The room was almost at the end of the hall and there's an exit door right there," Moses said. "He — or she — didn't have too far to walk. Even if he was staying in the hotel, he wouldn't want anybody to remember seeing a guy carrying a stack of papers later. Did you get an approximate time of death?"

"Preliminary estimate is she'd been dead between five and eight hours," Kroup said. "But the night man on the desk says he locked the room at midnight. Says he stuck his head in, but the lighting was dim. He turned off the lights at the switch by the door and locked it. So she was probably already there by then, he just didn't see her."

"The room had been left unlocked?" I asked.

"Apparently, people had been going in and out all day," Kroup says. "Way I understand it, they were expecting people to leave things there, not take 'em."

"So she played golf with us, then sat in the bar and told her story," I said. "We got back to the room around 11:30. She wasn't wearing the red outfit last time we saw her, so she'd gone back to her room and changed into it, which suggests she was meeting somebody she wanted to dress up for."

"In a storage room?" Kroup sounded skeptical.

"He'd probably have to have a good line," I said. "Or be good-looking. You don't always need a good line if you're sexy."

"Yeah, Kroup, so round up all the sexy men in the hotel and talk to 'em," Moses said. "'Course, you already started with the top of the list."

I frowned at him. "I said 'or.' It's possible he had a good line. It's even possible he wouldn't strike us as sexy now but in his youth, he was a dreamboat."

"You keep saying 'he,'" Kroup pointed out. "You got any particular reason to assume it was a man? I believe you said before that you weren't sure whether it was a man or a woman who attacked you, Ms. Caliban. You change your mind about that?"

I sighed. "No, you're right. No reason to assume that a woman wouldn't dress up to meet another woman. It wouldn't even have to be a romantic motivation. I got the impression that Thompson — or whoever she was — liked to show off her figure. She might even want to make the other women jealous."

"Well, from what I've seen so far, a lot of these women could compete with her in that department," Kroup said. "They're a good-looking bunch of women. And there are plenty who'd have the strength to strangle somebody. Some of 'em shake hands like they're arm-wrestling." He rubbed his right hand with his left and I smothered a grin.

"But I want to go back to 'whoever she was,'" he continued. "Any theories on that?"

Moses and I exchanged a look. We hadn't told him about Stretch's claim to be Thompson's great-niece, only that she'd left my room about 12:45. When the cops had arrived at the hotel, Esther, the desk clerk, Lou, Moses and I had all been put in a room together with a minder to make sure that we didn't coordinate our stories. Toots joined us shortly afterward. The desk clerk had been interviewed first, then Esther, who was flying at eleven. Even in a homicide case, the Dayton cops apparently believed that the Dayton Air Show must go on. So we were the tail end of the parade.

"Not really," Moses said. "She could have been who she said she was."

"If she wasn't," I said, "she was somebody who was on the scene, at least at Avenger and maybe at Harlingen. She could have been another WASP. She could have been anybody from a flight instructor to a kitchen worker." A thought struck me. "Maybe she was somebody who washed out of flight school. She seemed to remember more about Avenger than Harlingen. Whether she could have washed out after Avenger, I don't know. You'd need to ask one of the pilots."

"But it sounds like you think whoever killed her believed that she was Thompson," Kroup said.

"Looks that way, doesn't it?" Moses said.

"Until I'm up to speed on these other cases, I don't know how it looks," Kroup said. "You'll be here until tomorrow afternoon, right?"

"In Dayton, yeah," Moses said. "Here or at the air show, I guess. We're just following the WASP around."

"Okay," Kroup said. "I'll have statements for you later. Stay out of trouble."

"I thought homicide detectives were supposed to suspect everybody," I said to Moses as we crossed the hotel lobby. He was lugging the camera bags again and jogging. "He didn't seem to suspect us."

"Probably checked up on us before he talked to us," Moses said.

"Oh."

"Come on, Cat, shake a leg," he said as I trotted to keep up with him. "I want to see Esther fly."

38

JULY 19, 1986

MOSES and I couldn't talk while Happy was setting the pace. We could barely get our breath. Moses still had one camera case slung over his shoulder and he was using the flashgun to illuminate the roots as we tripped over them in the mud and wet leaves as we slid.

A tree branch lashed my face. My ankle buckled and I yelped. "Hold up a sec, would you?" I called as the light disappeared into a thicket.

I heard Moses yelling, "Whoa! Whoa, boy!" But I deduced from the receding sound that it was having no effect. And then, Happy's barking covered all other sounds.

I dragged myself to my feet and limped on. I was now encouraged by the sound of another voice. It was saying, "Good dog, Hap! That's my good puppy! What a good dog you are!"

I broke out of the trees and found myself on a mown stretch of ground next to a cornfield, where I could see a partially lit reunion scene between Happy, Lou and Moses. Lou's legs were muddy below her uniform skirt and her hair had been restyled by Mother Nature, but otherwise she looked unscathed. She had a heavy-duty flashlight in one hand and something small and boxlike that I couldn't identify in the other. She was still wearing her splint. She wasn't wearing her shoes or her parachute harness. I was the only one besides Happy who was still wearing a harness.

"Cat!" she said when she spotted me. "Are you all right?"

"Just peachy. Do you girls always have this much fun when you get together?"

Lou had bent to extricate Happy from his harness. She looked up at me over her shoulder. "Well, we're not as young as we used to be. We used to have more." Then she straightened and raised something to her mouth and said, "Base to units one and two. I've collected a dog, a journalist, and a photographer."

"If they're in any kind of shape at all," a tinny voice said in response, "you beat me. All I've got is ten pounds of mud and five chiggers."

"Is that Toots?" I asked.

"That's Toots," Lou said.

"I got two dogs trailing me," another tinny voice said. This time it was Esther's. "I think they know where I'm going."

"Where's Bernie?" I asked. "And Stretch?" I was fumbling with my harness with wet, slippery fingers.

Lou reached out and did something that made my harness go slack. I wriggled out of it.

"Stretch should be somewhere between us and Toots. I don't know where Bernie is," she said, and grimaced. "Poor planning on my part. I ran out of dog whistles and walkie-talkies."

"What about Tex?" I asked. "Did the plane go down?"

"She must have landed okay," Lou said. "A B-26 makes a hell of a noise when it crashes and I didn't hear anything like that. Can you walk on that ankle? Because if not, we can send somebody back for you."

"I'll walk," I said grimly, unnerved by the prospect of being left behind and collecting a canine entourage of my own.

"I'll stay with you if you want to stay, Cat," Moses said.

"I'll walk," I said again.

Moses put an arm around my waist and I leaned on him.

Lou slipped on her shoes. "Remind me never to jump again in

pantyhose and heels." She picked up a bag she'd been carrying on the plane and threaded two arms through the straps to make a back-pack. Then she took the camera bag from Moses and slung it around her neck. She had exchanged my parachute line for an honest-to-god dog leash that struck me as nothing short of miraculous out here in the wilds.

"Ready?" she said. When we nodded, she spoke into what I now saw was a walkie-talkie. "Base to unit one. Give a whistle, Toots." When Happy turned his head, she said to him, "Nice and steady. Go find Toots."

And Happy barked once and began a sedate march.

"Why do I get the feeling I missed the drill?" I grumbled as we started forward.

39

JULY 19, 1986

"SO, WHAT ARE YOU THINKING?" I said to Moses as we sped toward the Dayton airport. From his ground speed, he must have been thinking that if he broke the sound barrier today, everybody would blame it on the air show. "You do think it was Thompson the killer went after, right?"

"Looks like it."

"Do we have any foolproof way to establish that the victim wasn't actually Thompson? I guess we'd have a hard time coming up with fingerprints to match after all these years.

"Depends on whether anybody has her pilot's ID or whether her license is on file anywhere. I imagine those had fingerprints."

My stomach clenched. A pilot's ID would have fingerprints because in case of a crash, the body would be so mangled that it would be hard to identify.

"From what Stretch said, assuming she's telling the truth, that doesn't seem likely," he said, "but we should ask."

"And we probably can't establish her race definitively, can we? I mean, if we can establish that Stretch is telling the truth about that."

Moses shook his head. "Best bet would be dental records. That's assuming she got any dental care while she was a WASP and assuming that those records still exist. They weren't military records at the time, so they may not. My guess is, Kroup will check on that."

"That would tell us that she wasn't Thompson," I said. "It won't tell us who she was. But if she wasn't Thompson, they'll surely find something in her room to tell them who she was."

"You'd think so. But that's not our concern. Our concern is to protect the women who are still alive."

As one of my shoulders slammed against the car door on a turn, I said, "Well, we can't protect them if we're killed in a car crash on the way to the air show."

"I don't know why you always complaining, Cat. I'm trained to drive at high speeds."

"Yeah, but this car doesn't have a siren and flashers," I pointed out. "Anyway, you have any new insights on what the killer is looking for in the WASP papers?"

"Can't think of anything worth killing three people over."

"How about a marriage certificate? I've been thinking about that. People got married in a hurry in those days — sometimes on impulse. One reason why the divorce rate was so high after the war."

"You thinking about someone who conveniently forgot they were married after the war? Maybe never told his second wife about the first? It doesn't sound like much of a reason to go around killing people, unless, of course, the second wife was an heiress. And why now? Oh — because of the museum."

"Sure. Everybody's looking through their old papers."

"And you think the killer thinks somebody's going to find this paper one day soon and say, 'Oh, look! Here's the marriage certificate I got when I married that cute, sexy what's-his-name. I wonder where he is now?'"

"It's just a thought," I said. "Maybe it would be too much of a public embarrassment for somebody — like CJ Burman, say. He's a city councilman. Maybe he wants to run for the state legislature. Or better yet, how about Senator Braverman? Maddy did say something about patriotic speeches. If the press finds out he's a bigamist, his political career is over."

Moses appeared to be mulling it over. Either that, or calculating speed and distance so that he could hit the next three traffic lights on green. "It's got potential," he said at last. "But seems to me a birth certificate would be more likely."

"You mean Braverman might have an illegitimate kid nobody knows about?"

"Could be. An illegitimate child carries more weight than a poor first marriage in wartime. For one thing, you got a birth certificate, you got a claim on inheritance."

"I see what you mean."

"Look at Isabel Yates," he said. "She's dying to tell us who her daddy was."

"She is?"

"Sure. She says she's named for her father, remember? She couldn't wait to tell us her middle name. Then Thompson shows up and spoils her big moment."

"Wait, you're saying she's illegitimate? Shorty Evers left the WASP to get married. Everybody says that, but I wondered."

"Everybody says it, but nobody witnessed it. Just think about it, Cat. You're a woman in 1944 who survived Army flight training and B-26 school. There's a reason why hardly anybody quit after that."

"But if she was pregnant —."

"You know what it was like back then. What would you have done?"

"I would have told my best friend and flying partner first thing."

"And if you didn't do that?"

"Gone across the border for an abortion?"

"Maybe, but not everybody could bring themselves to do that."

"But then why would the birth certificate be among anybody's WASP papers?"

He shrugged and then grinned at me. "That's the weak part of my theory."

"You think it's one of the men here? Wes or CJ? They were both around at the time. Or Braverman?"

"Gene Smith was around, too. He's a farm boy from Iowa, but he worked as a mechanic at Harlingen."

"Really? But I thought he was Bernie's second husband."

"He was. Ran into her at the Iowa State Fair in the mid-fifties after she'd divorced husband number one. His wife had died of cancer."

"You find that out at the poker game last night?"

He nodded.

"I wouldn't mind playing poker now and then. It would be better than golf."

"More expensive," he observed, "unless you're good."

I tried to contemplate the implications of this new bit of information. I'd pretty much eliminated Smith from consideration on the grounds that he wasn't connected to the WASP except by marriage. But now, it seemed, he was. And who would know how to sabotage a plane or car better than a mechanic?

"So getting back to the question," I said. "You think one of these men is Isabel Yates's father and she's come to Dayton to confront him?"

"Could be, but it wouldn't have to be. Could be she's looking for her father, trying to track him down. Maybe she knows his name but doesn't know how to find him. Could be she came here hoping to get more information about him. But you can tell she expects to surprise the WASP, maybe even shock them. She expects them to recognize the name."

"Well, if this is about inheritance, that lets out CJ and Esther's ex-husband, if we can trust Arnie's information."

"Not everybody has access to Arnie's information," he reminded me.

"So not everybody knows that the Burmans and Esther are in financial difficulties. Point taken. And speaking about money, what do you think is going on with the museum property? You think Tex was right about the gas drilling? And could that happen without the owners' knowledge?"

He shook his head. "Somebody had to have leased mineral rights to the drilling company."

"Is that worth a lot of money?"

"Can be."

"So you think the owner of record — Westex, was it? — is what? A bogus company?"

"I think that if CJ Burman handled the property purchase on behalf of the WASP, he's got some explaining to do. In the meantime, like I said, our priority is to protect the women while they're here, try to keep 'em alive if we can."

At that, we turned off onto a side road and the Dayton airport came into view — a view unobstructed by trees. I looked up and saw, against the cloudless blue sky, a small airplane plunging to earth.

"Oh, my God!" I seized Moses's arm. "That's Esther and she's going down!"

40

JULY 19, 1986

MOSES SLAMMED ON THE BRAKES. Behind us, a horn blared.

I watched in horror as the plane plummeted. Then, it turned. The nose pulled up and the little plane climbed again. The car behind us was still honking.

"It's a stunt, Cat," Moses said. He was using his explanatory voice, the patient one he, the professional, uses to impart arcane knowledge to me, the novice. But we both knew he'd been as terrified as I was. "Esther is a stunt pilot. That's what stunt pilots do."

"Tell me she doesn't have her granddaughter with her," I said.

"I believe she does."

The car behind us had pulled around, the driver glaring. We proceeded at a more sedate pace.

I watched as the little plane banked then swooped down low and began to roll, its wings turning like fan blades.

"I'm not going to enjoy this, am I?"

"Don't look, then. You here to interview WASP, so interview WASP."

I noticed that he left one of his camera bags behind and took it as a sign that the morning's activities had already put a dent in his enthusiasm for authenticity.

I was wilted by the time we walked from the parking lot past the main building to the airstrip, where all the action was. I found it impossible not to watch what was going on in the sky. When I next looked up, two identical planes were arcing toward the ground side by side, trailing fat plumes of red and blue smoke. At the same instant, they pulled out of their dives and, facing opposite directions, completed the two loops of smoke. In fact, as I looked around, I saw that red, white and blue were the favored colors of the airshow decorators.

We spotted our group easily because it was the rowdiest. Folding chairs and a table had been set up under a tent — our only protection from the July heat. Talking meant trying to drown out the enthusiastic voice coming over the loudspeaker.

"That gives the term 'generation gap' a whole new meaning!" he bellowed.

I turned to see the two planes whizzing by, side-by-side, one slightly higher than the other. The wings appeared to be inches apart. I shut my eyes.

"In fact, I'm told that the youngest Chang, Esther's granddaughter Ellen, is flying with her mother today!" the announcer boomed. "Let's hear it for the flying Changs!"

Thunderous applause made me wonder if it was time to take some more painkillers yet.

Someone touched my arm. I opened my eyes to see Toots, looking at me with concern. "Come sit down, Cat," she shouted close to my ear. She guided me toward a folding chair. When the noise died down from a roar to a din, she added, "And don't worry! They've been doing this for years. They hardly ever run into each other."

I gestured at the crowd of chattering women and men. There were more kids in evidence today, too — grandkids, I assumed. "I guess nobody's grieving much for Thompson," I said.

Toots followed my gaze. "I guess not. Well, how the heck can you grieve for somebody you grieved for forty years ago? Even if that woman was Thompson, and we're having a hard time believing that, we didn't know her anymore. It's complicated." She paused. "It just about broke my heart when Tommy died. I mean, we all accepted the danger. We took risks — we all did — every day. But it's different when your partner goes down. And it was worse not really knowing what had happened to her. I was sad for a long time. But now I'm grieving for Maddy and Squeak. It's not like I don't have room for her, I just don't have any sadness left to give her."

"I understand," I said. "You know, there's something I've been meaning to ask you. Why did Maddy use the name 'Ethel' when she talked to you? I haven't heard many WASP referred to by their real names. Everybody seems to use nicknames."

Toots smiled. "Maddy was probably the only one who remembered everybody's real names — or at least, used to. She used to pretend she was our mother and scold us. She'd say, 'Ethel Ann Ames, you pick up your shoes and put them away! And don't you give me that sullen look, young lady! You just wait till your father gets home!' And we'd say, 'Yes, Mom.' Or she might say, 'Verna Maude Davenport! You'd better put that diary away in a safe place where Killjoy can't find it! If Killjoy gets hold of it, all our gooses will be cooked!'"

My ears pricked up. "Why? Were the contents that dangerous?"

"Not dangerous exactly, but full of little things you wouldn't want Deedie to know, that's all."

She was facing the airstrip with a reminiscent smile when she said it and I was reminded that the concept of "danger" was relative.

"Those stunts that Esther was doing," I said. "Stretch said you used to be an acrobatic champion. Is that what she meant? Did you used to do things like that?"

"Oh, sure. After the war I used to travel around the country, doing exhibitions."

"But not now."

"Not now. You get tired of the circuit — at least, I did. Esther doesn't seem to, but then her family travels with her. That makes a difference, I think. And she doesn't do as many as she used to. She's well known, so she can pick and choose."

"Well, I need to get on with my interviews. They'll support my cover and maybe I'll get some useful information out of them. But this place isn't very conducive to talk, is it?"

Toots said, "There's some lag time between performances, like now, when the announcer shuts up and the planes aren't flying. You'll get some quiet time then."

But behind us, a tall, large-boned woman burst into song.

"The zoot suits that they give us they say are mighty fine,

you keep right on marching and they move along behind,

I don't want no more of Army life —."

And all around us, a chorus of voices joined in: "Gee, Mom, I want to go home."

"The airplanes that they give us they say are mighty fine,

the darn things can't shoot stages, they will not hit the line,

I don't want no more of Army life —."

Toots shrugged apologetically and sang along: "Gee, Mom, I want to go home."

My photographer, grinning, was taking pictures.

When the song was over, Toots said to me, "Why don't you ask some of the gals to show you the planes?"

"Are they parked?"

Toots laughed. "For most of them, their flying days are over."

So I rounded up Moses and we went for a walk with Tex, Bernie, Chip Santos, and Ruth Brown.

Chip was a wiry woman with shoulder-length flyaway hair tied back with a scarf. She was smoking some kind of aromatic cigarette. She pointed it at the first plane we came to — a big, four-engine plane. I knew it had four engines because there were four propellers. I was really catching on. This plane also had a gun turret on top, guns mounted to the sides, and a transparent nosecone. But my attention was drawn to a small oblong object hanging down near the front of the plane. It was painted to look like an angry shark, with a full set of pointy little teeth. The sign in front of the plane called it "The Flying Fortress" and you could see why.

"Now, there's a plane I'd love to have flown," she said. "A B-17. But my legs were too short. You girls ever fly one of those babies?"

"I flew them at Alamogordo," Ruth said, "but only as copilot. They wouldn't let a WASP pilot them."

Chip nodded. "I heard Love and Harkness were all set to fly one across the Atlantic until General Arnold got wind of it and grounded them." To Moses and me, she said, "Women weren't permitted to fly outside the continental US, not even if they were the head of the ferry service, like Love. And nobody was even supposed to know there were WASP at B-17 school. Very hush-hush. Imagine how it would affect the national morale if Americans knew that girls were flying the biggest bombers we had. How about you, Tex?"

"I flew them in Mexico," Tex said. We climbed a set of steps into the plane. To our left was the cockpit, with two of those semicircular steering wheels for the two pilots. I mentioned these because they were the only parts of the plane I could identify. The cockpit was studded with dials and levers and gizmos.

"How did your parents feel about you becoming a WASP?" I asked Chip.

"My father had to talk my mother into it," she said. "After that, it was okay. She knew I loved it."

"For me, it was the other way around," Ruth said. "My mother had to talk my father into it." She was a solidly built, full-breasted woman of medium height, but short-waisted, so her legs were disproportionately long. She had a cap of short white hair similar to mine. She wore a floral pantsuit and gold-framed glasses. She was nobody's idea of a bomber pilot.

Bernie said, "My parents just said, 'Whatever you want, dear, as long as you come back in one piece.'"

"How about you, Tex?" I asked.

"My parents both flew," she said, "so it was easy for me. When they heard about the program, they assumed I'd go. In fact, it was my dad who told me about it."

A thought struck me. "Ruth, did you ever have to copilot for a bad pilot, someone you didn't have confidence in?"

"Oh, sure. Well, let me be clear. If you didn't wash out of B-17 school, you were a good pilot. But you could have a bad attitude, you know? Especially if it went to your head. Some of these guys were real cowboys, so you didn't trust their judgment."

Moses took a picture of Ruth and Tex in front of one of the planes they'd flown.

Bernie said to me, "Tex will be in all the pictures. I bet she's flown every single one of these planes at one time or another."

"Look, girls, a Bombay Bomber," Chip said. "We all flew these, right?"

This, then, was the wooden airplane that Tommy Thompson had been flying when she disappeared — the UC-78.

"Did you hear about the shipment of UC-78s somebody donated to the Guinea Pigs at Ellington?" Ruth said.

To us, Tex said, "She's talking about the first class of women ferry pilots, who trained in Houston."

"These planes were falling apart from termite damage," Ruth said.

"I've heard stories about the junk they flew at Ellington," Chip said.

"Did any of you know Thompson?" I asked. I was still trying to wrest some useful information from this tour. "Before, I mean, in Sweetwater."

"Sure," Ruth said. "She was in my bay. She was a lot of fun. She had a great singing voice, so we loved to hear her sing in the shower. She bought this pair of red cowboy boots, but she wouldn't wear them when it was hot or when it was going to rain. We used to say that we could forecast the weather by looking at Tommy's feet."

"So was it Tommy — the dead woman?" Chip asked. "I didn't know her. What do you think?"

"I thought it was Tommy at first," Ruth said, "but now I don't know. She had the right build and the right nose." She turned to me and touched the bridge of her nose. "You know how some people have kind of a bump right here. Tommy had it and that woman last night, she had it too."

"Lots of people have those," Chip said.

"Can you think of anybody at Sweetwater who looked a lot like Tommy?" I asked.

"Oh!" Ruth stood still for a moment, her stare unfocused.

"What?" I said.

She shook her head. "It's gone. There was something there, but I lost it. When you said, 'anybody who looked like Tommy,' I had a memory flash, but it's gone."

"Tex?" I asked. "Can you think of anybody who looked like Tommy?"

She shook her head, then said, "But I'm not good with things like that."

The announcer started up again and I said, "Do you want to get back to the show?"

Chip shrugged. "We don't really come for the show. It's just an excuse to get together."

Bernie said, "There are a few stunts worth seeing, but we learned to do a lot of that in training."

"You did?"

"Sure. Loops, snap rolls, slow rolls, vertical reverses, inverted flight — we started doing those in PT's," Chip said.

"After all, if your engine stalls out at 8000 feet, that better not be the first time you've experienced a spin," Bernie said.

Moses asked, "Are there any World War II-era planes here on display that weren't flown by WASP?"

The women looked around. "No," Ruth said. "WASP flew everything the Army had. Bombers, pursuit planes, cargo planes — you name it, we flew it. We attacked formations and let them shoot at us in the air, we let them shoot at us from the ground, we staged dogfights, we ferried planes, we strafed ground troops, we flew night missions without lights for searchlight training, we flew cargo all over the country, we flew personnel, we flew weather-checking missions, and we flew as instructors and test pilots."

"Test pilots?" I echoed.

Chip grinned. "After planes were repaired, we checked them out."

"Or if somebody had recommended a plane be retired," Bernie said. "Some WASP test pilots had the authority to say whether a plane should be mothballed or flying."

"And some of the planes that had been repaired —," I said.

Chip's grin broadened. "Got sent back to the shop. Of course, the mechanics looked at them first, before we flew them, to make reasonably certain they'd come back in one piece if we took them up."

"But sometimes they were wrong," Ruth said.

Bernie shrugged. "We were young and crazy. Oh, look! A B-29!"

I have to admit, one bomber looks pretty much like another to me. This one was sleeker than the B-17. Whereas the B-17 was bristling with guns, not to mention that shark, this plane had a single modest gun turret. Whereas the B-17's sign labeled it "The Flying Fortress," the B-29 was apparently "The Superfortress."

"Dodie Witherspoon flew these at Salinas," Ruth said. "Be sure and ask her to tell you her story, Cat. Salinas was a super-secret B-29 base. But a lot of male pilots at the different bases were refusing to fly these bombers."

"Didn't they catch fire on takeoff?" Chip asked.

Ruth nodded. "The cowl flaps were bad, so by the time they did their checks and taxied, the engines were already overheating. The way the guys were taking off, they barely had enough speed to get off the ground, they were so afraid of overheating the engines. But some WASP like Dodie who had trained in Florida were taught to do the check before they turned the engines on, so without a run-up, the engines didn't have time to overheat. They sent Dodie and the others around on cargo transport missions to other B-29 bases so that the men could see that women could fly the B-29. Then some top brass NB got wind of it and nixed it. Didn't want women flying his bombers"

"Toots told us a similar story," I said, "but I didn't think it was about B-29s."

Tex said, "There are a lot of stories like that, Cat. I know the

WASP were called in to show men that women could fly the Jug, the P-47, when the men didn't want to fly it."

"We had so much fun," Chip said, her eyes sparkling. "And just think — after we paid for room, board, uniforms and laundry, we had twelve whole dollars a week left over to buy war bonds with!"

41

JULY 19, 1986

BY THE END of the day, I had collected a notebook full of stories, a sunburn, and permanent hearing loss. What I wasn't sure I'd collected was any useful information.

"It would make more sense to me if one of the WASP had turned into a serial killer and was bumping off people who had defamed them, belittled them, prohibited them from flying planes they were clearly qualified to fly, sabotaged their planes, attacked them in the newspapers, or even refused to serve them in restaurants because they were wearing pants," I said to Moses when we were back in the car. "That somebody is still attacking them makes no sense to me."

"I know what you mean, Cat."

He probably knew better than I did what I meant. As a Black man, he'd had plenty of opportunity to practice the same kind of strength and forbearance that the women pilots had had to develop. And I was willing to bet he'd entertained a few serial-killer fantasies of his own.

"I keep being struck by the force of emotion behind the sexism," I said. "I know it was a different time. I remember it well. But the anger they report being directed against them reminds me more of racism than sexism. I mean, I understand the scorn and contempt.

But the outrage and rage — that makes me think that men in general and male pilots in particular somehow saw the women's success as an attack on them and their abilities."

Moses grinned. "That's what Madame Zahara said and it was hard to tell whether she was talking about the past or the future."

"Speaking of Madame Zahara, do you know if Esther found out anything about the museum property? Chub didn't look quite as lively as usual today."

"There's an emergency meeting of the museum committee about an hour from now. It's just the committee this time, not an open meeting."

"Damn! It'll take a while for us to find out what happened. I don't suppose we could hide in a closet? Lou does think we're investigative reporters.

"I imagine Toots will tell us as soon as she knows anything. Besides, I expect we'll have statements to sign waiting for us at the hotel."

"What did you think the consensus was on Thompson?" I asked.

He grunted. "Way I heard it, there was no consensus. Some folks seemed impressed by what she remembered, but we know that the Harlingen women were more impressed by what she didn't remember."

"How about the way Ruth reacted when I asked if she remembered anybody from Sweetwater who looked like Thompson? That seem to ring a bell for her."

"Yeah, but it's long odds she'll remember what it was about," he said. "And when she does, it will turn out to have nothing to do with a Thompson look-alike."

I turned the air conditioner vent so that it would blow full on my face.

"Why would anybody even want to fly a Superfortress? I don't get it. Where's the thrill in trying to get a mammoth hunk of metal like that off the ground? Especially one that tends to catch fire as soon as it's airborne. If you'd asked me a month ago, I would've put it down to machismo, pure and simple."

"Well, some folks like a challenge," he said mildly. "You like a challenge yourself, just not that kind of challenge. Different strokes for different folks, Cat."

I flipped the windshield visor down and stared at my reflection in the small mirror. I looked like what I was: hot, tired, windblown, sunburned, and cranky. I couldn't see the lump on the side of my head too well, but it showed in the creases in my forehead and the truculent angle of my eyebrows.

"Tell me it's happy hour," I said.

42

JULY 19, 1986

THE PRE-DINNER RECEPTION that evening was held in the lounge area outside of the banquet room. Dinner was to be a more formal affair than the night before and one look at the room told me that if we'd hoped for entertainment to rival last night's Madame Zahara performance, we were out of luck. Two senators, Braverman and Glenn, two representatives, one of them Patricia Schroeder, and various state dignitaries were expected. I guessed there were many similar dinners being held tonight in the Dayton area and hoped that they had enough dignitaries to go around. The governor and the mayor of Dayton, for example, must have gotten better offers.

But although the evening was more formal, Isabel Yates seemed determined to outdress the occasion. Tonight she was wearing something we might have worn to a cocktail party in the fifties, a backless black dress with a sequined bodice and a flared chiffon skirt. I took one look at her and felt a pang of recognition. She was what every woman I knew feared to become — someone whose clothes never matched the situation. She had put in an appearance at the air show in a full-length Hawaiian-print muumuu and left after two hours without making any particular effort to converse with anyone.

She stood on the fringes of the Harlingen group like Death at the wedding feast.

Bernie said to her, "Don't you look nice, Isabel! That backless dress makes me long for my girlish figure!"

There was nothing wrong with her figure now and a less self-absorbed husband than Gene Smith might have earned himself some points by saying so, but he left it up to Moses to say, "You look good to me now. I've seen all the pictures of you ladies in your twenties and you were all too skinny, if you ask me."

They all laughed and Toots said, "In those days, we were all obsessed with putting weight on. We were terrified we'd drop below the weight requirement."

"It's true!" Bernie wailed. "When I re-read my letters home, I realized that I reported on my weight as often as I reported on the weather! And you know, to a pilot, weather is the most important thing. It was embarrassing!"

"And now, we're obsessed with keeping it off," Toots said.

A subdued Chub showed up. CJ, an arm around her shoulder, was still smiling, but I thought his smile looked a little forced.

Esther introduced us to her daughter Flea, an attractive woman who stood several inches taller than her mother.

"There's a special program for kids tonight," she said in response to a question about Fly.

"I guess she's had enough of hanging out with Granny's friends," Bernie said. "But tell the truth, Flea. Was that Fly doing those slow rolls?"

Mother and daughter grinned at each other. "She was just dying to do it, so we let her," Flea said.

A harried Lou bustled up with a clipboard clutched to her chest. "Anybody seen Flash?" she said. "And p.s., don't ever let anybody put you in charge of seating arrangements!"

"Aren't we sitting with the same groups as last night?" Isabel asked, frowning.

"No, the tables are smaller and we have to spread out to fill the tables where our special guests are sitting," Lou said. She was scanning the crowd.

"Special guests?" Isabel asked.

"She means dignitaries," Bernie said.

"Then I should tell you my middle name now," Isabel said in a raised voice. "I told you last night I was named for my father —."

But the normally patient Lou cut her off. "Oh, all right, then! Tell us your middle name, for god's sake!"

The sharpness in Lou's voice made Isabel start. Then she looked around the group and found everyone's eyes on her. A slow smile spread across her face. "It's Charlene. My middle name is Charlene."

I heard a stifled noise and turned toward it, but Esther had started to laugh. She laughed so hard that her eyes watered and she put a hand on her daughter's shoulder to steady herself.

"What's so funny?" Isabel said, apparently caught off guard. She was gazing at Esther in bewilderment.

"I'm sorry, honey," Esther said. Flea, smiling, handed her a handkerchief and she wiped her eyes. "I'm sorry, really. But if you came all this way to tell me that my ex-husband was a two-timing bastard, you're wasting your breath. I found out years ago. That's why I divorced him."

"*Your* husband?" Isabel looked confused.

"Guy Charles," Esther said. "Isn't that who you mean?"

"No," Isabel said, and turned her gaze on the Burmans. "I mean Charles James Burman. That's who I mean."

Both Burmans were pale now. CJ seemed to have tightened his grip on Chub's shoulder. Then he smiled. "Well, gee, this is great news," he said. "I have a daughter I didn't know I had. How about that?"

I looked at Moses and he raised his eyebrows at me.

Bernie said in a quiet voice, "Honey, are you telling us that your mother didn't leave the WASP to get married? That she left because she was pregnant with you?"

"That's right," Isabel said.

Lou erupted. "Well, if that's not the stupidest thing I've ever heard! Why didn't she tell us? She could have told Esther, at least. We could have gotten her a Mexican abortion."

"Honey," Wes said, clearly uneasy, "maybe abortion was against her religion or her — her beliefs."

Lou rounded on him. "That's bullshit! No, I'm sorry, Wesley, but it is. There's only one reason why Shorty didn't get an abortion and that was because she was still mooning over that smooth-talking son of a bitch!" She pointed an accusatory figure at CJ Burman. "Sorry, Chub."

The finger swung back to Isabel, who looked almost as shell-shocked as CJ. "And I'll tell you another thing. Chub Davenport was a good friend to your mother — even took care of her when she had the flu. And there is no way on God's earth that your mother would have wanted you to waltz in here and try to ruin Chub's life for your own satisfaction. Not the Shorty I knew! Your mother must be turning over in her grave."

She shot CJ another venomous look. "Lucky for both of you, I don't have time for this bullshit, or I'd tell you what I really think of you!"

She turned on her heel and stalked off, smacking Wes with the clipboard when he tried to follow her. I think she was just trying to wave him off and didn't realize that she was armed, but she didn't break her stride. Wes followed at a safer distance now, rubbing his elbow.

Tex applauded her.

Isabel Yates burst into tears.

Chub shrugged off CJ's arm. When she turned away from him, Esther was there and she stepped into Esther's embrace.

CJ Burman spread his arms and said, "She never told me she was pregnant. How was I supposed to know? If she'd told me, I would've helped her, you know?" He seemed to be directing his defense at Moses, as if another man, especially another soldier, would appreciate the reasonableness of his position.

"Oh, CJ, dry up!" Esther said. "We've heard enough out of you for one day." And she led Chub off.

That left Toots and Bernie to comfort the sobbing Isabel, and Toots was scowling at her. Bernie glanced at Toots's face, heaved a deep sigh, and moved close to put an arm around Isabel. She made hushing noises.

"Does she think I had such a wonderful life, as an il-il-illegiti-mate child?" Isabel wailed.

Over Isabel's shoulder, Bernie rolled her eyes at us and patted Isabel's heaving back.

Gene Smith cleared his throat and raised himself five notches in my estimation. He said, "Can I get anybody another drink?"

Moses and I took Toots aside and asked her if she knew what had happened at the emergency meeting. Stretch tagged along.

Over my head, Toots looked daggers at the retreating form of CJ, who, left to fend for himself, seemed to have decided to re-visit the bar. She caught Tex's eye and nodded an invitation to join us.

"They're asking about the emergency meeting," she told Tex. "All I heard was that CJ was running some kind of scam."

Tex's more formal dinner dress consisted of black jeans and boots, a silver belt buckle, and a sequined Western shirt. She hesitated and I wondered how forthcoming she'd be with a journalist, but apparently, she trusted Toots's judgment. She said, "He offered to handle the purchase because he had so much more experience than Chub, and she agreed, of course. He set up a dummy corporation to purchase the land — a subsidiary of Burman Enterprises. Then he leased the mineral rights for five years. He had a more creative way of explaining it, but that's what it boils down to. He gave us some crap about the proceeds going into the museum fund and about the drilling company feeling more comfortable working with one of his companies than with a nonprofit organization, and he emphasized that he could deed the land to us at any time. But it was all smoke and mirrors. Esther told him she wanted a full account of profits and expenses associated with the property and that she expected every penny of profit to be repaid to the WASP with interest, or she'd sue his ass."

"I don't get it," Toots said, hands on her hips. "Did he think he wouldn't get caught?"

"The lease was short-term," Tex said, "and nobody else lives close enough to the property to investigate. Of course, I'm only one of the members who live in Texas and not the only pilot, either, but I don't think CJ has a hell of a lot of imagination — or a hell of a lot of smarts, either, if it comes to that. And he underestimated us."

"But what about Chub?" Toots asked. "Did she know about it?"

"Oh, who knows?" Tex said. "If they ever took a drive out there to look at the place, I'm sure he came up with something to tell her. Maybe he told her that the property wasn't exactly where she thought it was, though there's gas rigs all over the place down there. Or maybe he just talked her out of going to take a look. Chub's got her own problems. Got to be a lot of self-deluding going on just to stay married to the jerk for forty years."

"Well, I can't believe she knew and didn't say anything, so you must be right," Toots said. "I feel bad for her."

"Oh, she'll survive," Tex said. "Maybe she'll finally get rid of him. Anyway, that's what we do, we WASP, right, Toots? We survive."

Unless somebody pushes you down the stairs, I thought, but I didn't say it aloud.

43

JULY 20, 1986

IT WAS SLOW GOING.

Lou, Moses, and I limped along, picking up mud like mud magnets. Happy was the only one of us who was remotely — well, happy. Of course, he would have been happier if we'd been jogging, but with his mistress on the other end of the leash, he was content. Goldens, I've heard, are easy to please. To him, it was just another walk.

"You got any theories about what went wrong with that engine, Lou?" Moses asked.

"No," she said. "With a plane that old, could be anything. I'm a little surprised, though. Because the planes are so old, the mechanics usually go over them with a fine-toothed comb. You don't usually get that kind of catastrophic engine failure without some warning. And, of course, Tex is a very careful pilot."

She'd just parachuted out of a plane on fire and she was "a little surprised"? That phrase hardly began to cover my own intellectual and emotional response to the near-disaster. Moses was right, I realized. I resolved to quit drinking when I was working a dangerous case like this one. If I'd had a clear head, I would never have been persuaded to go along for the ride. Even if I cut back on my drinking, my instincts would take a firmer grip on my judgment.

We found Toots eventually. She was standing under a tree and she was soaked to the skin.

"This darned zoot suit!" she said. "We used to joke about drowning in them, but we didn't know what we were talking about. Look!" She pulled at some of the extra yardage in her pants leg and wrung out a stream of water. "I must be carrying ten pounds of water!

Lou raised Esther on the walkie-talkie and told her to use the dog whistle. Toots took up position on the other side of me and slipped her arm under my shoulder. We lumbered forward.

"Worth giving Stretch a yell now," Lou said. "Toots, you've got the best voice for it, unless —?" She looked from Moses to me.

Moses said, "Cat's forte is vocabulary, not volume."

I would have kicked him, but he was holding me up, so it would have been counterproductive.

So Toots belted out, "Hey! Stretch! Stre-e-etch!"

She was on the side of my head where the lump was and I thought the soundwaves might shatter it.

"Need some meds, Cat?" she asked when she saw me wince.

Lou turned. "I've got meds, too, Cat. I just didn't think."

Toots fished out some pills that were only slightly damp. "Hang on. Let me wring out my other leg and you can have some water to take those with."

"That's okay," I said, but Lou handed me a bottle.

I forgot my pledge instantly. "Is it alcoholic?" I said hopefully.

"Don't I wish," Lou said, sighing.

"Maybe Esther has a flask," Toots said.

Toots shouted again and this time, we heard an answer. There was a lot of shouting back and forth then and Lou got on the walkie-talkie to tell Esther we were taking a small detour.

"We're getting close," Toots said. "But where —?"

"Up here," came a hoarse voice, very close now.

Lou's flashlight beam raked the treetops until it found a large white mass, then dropped down to reveal Stretch hanging in a tree about forty feet up.

"This is so embarrassing," she croaked. "First time in my life I haven't been tall enough to reach something. I didn't want to release the harness because I couldn't tell what was down there. Plus, I didn't want to break a leg and pass out and maybe never get found."

We all studied the situation. Lou pointed at a branch about ten feet off the ground. "That's our best bet." Then she grinned at Toots. "Think we can still do it?"

Toots grinned at Lou. "I can if you can. I'd better go up. You can't climb with that wrist. I'm taking off this darned suit, though."

Lou handed the leash to Moses, who said, "I got kind of a bad back, but I'd be glad to help."

"We'll be okay," she said.

Toots was stripping off her zoot suit. Moses looked away, but I said, "It's all right. She's wearing pajamas."

Under the suit, she wore a pair of striped pajamas, also soaked, but more her size than the zoot suit. She tucked in the shirt and grinned at us. "Always saved time in the morning."

Lou extracted from her bag the parachute line I'd used as a makeshift leash, neatly coiled. She gave it to Toots. "This might come in handy."

Toots inserted her arm into the middle of the coil and settled it on her shoulder. Lou removed Happy's headgear from his head and fitted it onto Toots's so that she had a headlamp. Toots said to Moses, "I'm ready for my close-up, Mr. DeMille," and stuck a Swiss Army knife between her teeth.

But Moses already had his camera out.

Lou crouched and Toots sat on her shoulders. Then Lou stood up and positioned herself next to the tree.

"Come give us a hand, Moses," Lou said. "Grab her ankle. I can't hold on with this damned wrist."

He handed me the leash and the flashgun.

Slowly, Toots raised herself into a standing position. She reached up, took hold of the next branch up, muttered, "I could use some suction cups," and then pulled herself up.

"You be careful, Tootsie Lou," Lou cautioned.

But Toots was careful. The tree was wet and slippery, but she seemed to test every step and hold before she settled her weight.

"Ow!" she said. "Those zoot suits do provide more protection than PJs." Then she called out, "Cat and Moses, if I fall out of this tree and kill myself, you'll know that the killer is either Stretch or Lou, or maybe they're in it together."

Stretch seemed startled. "What?" she said.

But Lou just said, "Aw, quit your bellyaching! You're doing okay for sixty-four."

"That's easy for you to say," Toots grumbled. "I'll be off the beam tomorrow."

"I think it *is* tomorrow," Lou said.

Toots passed Stretch and stood on a branch just above her. "I don't think I can hold her weight," she called.

"Wet as it is, I wouldn't try," Lou called back. "Just drop her."

"Line coming your way, Stretch," Toots said, and added, "I hope."

She pulled off one of her sneakers and tied it to one end of the line she'd taken up with her. Holding herself steady with one hand, she tossed the line out. It dropped and the shoe struck Stretch on the head.

"You hit your target, Toots," Lou said.

On Toots's instructions, Stretch tied the line around her waist. Toots, straddling the branch she'd been standing on, reached around it and secured the other end.

"Okay, kid, let 'er rip," Toots called.

Stretch released some buckles on the front of her parachute and dropped. The line yanked her up short less than twenty feet from the ground.

Lou looked up. "You want us to get you down from there?"

"No, I got it," Stretch said.

I saw something flash in the light and she fell the rest of the way. On impact, she pitched forward and rolled.

"You bounced, Livingston," Lou said, giving her a hand up.

Toots's descent was slower, but at last everybody was on the ground and we were ready to move again.

"Sorry about that, Esther," Lou said into the walkie-talkie. "We had to go up before we could move out."

Esther's tinny voice issued from the walkie-talkie. "Isn't that always the way?"

44
_____

JULY 19, 1986

As Lou had said, the tables were smaller at dinner on Saturday night and the Zimmermans and Esther were sitting with the dignitaries instead of with the Harlingen group. Moses and I were seated at a table with Toots and Stretch, Bernie and Gene Smith, Tex, and Chub, who looked subdued. CJ Burman was nowhere in sight. Isabel Yates, I saw, had been exiled to another table.

"I can't believe how many dignitaries they got to come out for this," Bernie said.

"Well, it's an election year," Toots said, "though I guess they're not all up for re-election."

"Are we paying for their dinners, that's what I want to know," Tex said.

"Senator Glenn is the nicest man!" Bernie said. "And to think that he was the first man to orbit the Earth!"

"He was in Naval flight training when we were at Sweetwater," Tex said.

"Yes, we chatted a little about that," Bernie said. "And Jim Braverman was in gunnery school at Harlingen when we were there, Cat, as an instructor. Did anybody tell you? He says that's why he has such a high regard for the WASP."

"He probably shot up our planes," Tex said, "and now he feels guilty."

"Better than the ones who shot up our planes and didn't feel guilty," Toots said.

Tex rolled her eyes. "Lord knows there's plenty of those around!"

"I've heard he might run for president," Bernie said. "And just think — he's an honorary member!"

"I'd rather see Pat Schroeder run for president," Tex said.

Most of the dinner talk ran to reminiscences. I didn't really have to play the interviewer because Stretch had so many questions to ask and the smaller size of the group seemed to encourage her. Bernie sketched the layout of Avenger Field on a napkin and then, at Stretch's urging, a plan of the barracks and the bays, or six-person rooms. Between the barracks, she drew a row of rectangles.

"That's where we put our cots on hot nights," she said. Then she added a small squiggle. "And there's the snake we hoped we wouldn't step on if we had to use the latrine in the middle of the night."

"And where did you hide the hooch?" Stretch asked, leaning forward to study the sketch.

"Oh, I forgot something." Bernie took back the sketch and drew a stick figure outside the rectangle that outlined a barrack.

"Who's that?" Stretch asked.

Toots laughed. "That's Killjoy. When we had a surprise inspection, she stood outside and collected everything we threw out the window. If you were in her good graces, you could get your stuff back if you paid her."

"She accepted cigarettes and gas coupons," Bernie put in.

"But if you weren't in her good graces," Toots went on, "you never saw your stuff again."

"You said she washed out of the WASP?" Moses said.

"Yeah, she was a bad pilot, but a first-class snitch," Bernie said.

"Bernie's right," Toots said. "She missed her calling. She could have made a big contribution to Army Intelligence."

"Tell them about the time she read your letters," Wes said.

We heard several Killjoy stories. Then Tex said, "Once I was on the flight line and a storm blew up — one of those West Texas specials, out of nowhere. We were grounded. So I went back to the bay to get the letter I'd been writing. I saw —." She stopped. Her expression froze.

We all looked at her, then at each other.

"Well, what?" Chub said. The Killjoy stories appeared to have lightened her mood a little.

"My God," Tex said. "Could that be right?"

"What, for heaven's sake?" Bernie said.

"I saw someone I thought was Tommy Thompson going through Tommy's locker," Tex said.

I said quickly, "And it wasn't?"

Tex turned her gaze on me. "No, it was Olive Kilroy."

There were several beats of silence at the table and then all of the WASP spoke at once.

Toots said to me, "They had a similar build. They were both high-waisted, long-legged gals with broad shoulders. About the same height — maybe two inches taller than me."

"If you saw them at a distance, you might confuse them," Chub said. "I know I did once or twice. They both had shoulder-length curly dark hair."

"But if you saw them close up, you'd never mistake one for the other," Tex said. "When I caught Killjoy in Tommy's locker, she had her back to me."

I glanced at Stretch and saw in her face a still intensity.

"But Tommy had this little bump on her nose," Chub said, placing a forefinger on the bridge as Ruth had earlier that day. "She didn't like it, but I always told her it made her look distinguished, aristocratic. Killjoy had one, too, only less pronounced."

"But here's the thing," Tex said. "If you saw them both smile, you'd never confuse them."

Chub drew in her breath. "It *was* Killjoy! Lord, Tex, I had forgotten all about that."

"Because of her smile?" I was doubtful.

"The way she smiled at us last night," Toots said. "That's what we mean, Cat. It wasn't Tommy's smile. We all felt that at the time. But now, thinking back, I recognize that sly half-smile, like a smirk."

"It's just the way Killjoy used to smile at us when she was making trouble for us," Chub said.

"I didn't know Tommy well," Bernie said. "But I knew Killjoy. She had these perfect little teeth, remember, girls?"

"Except for her fangs," Tex said.

"Well, even those were perfectly even," Bernie said and the women laughed.

"You all believe that the woman who claimed to be Thompson was Olive Kilroy?" Moses leveled an index finger at each woman in turn and they each nodded, except for Toots.

"But why go to all that trouble?" Toots asked. "And risk exposure if we recognized her?"

Tex shrugged. "So she could finally belong. So she could finally be a WASP."

Chub said, "Tex is right. Olive wanted to be a WASP in the worst way. That's why she talked Deedie into letting her stay on after she washed out."

"She wasn't the only one," Toots said. "One of the nurses had washed out."

"Yeah, but she was a darling," Chub said. "Killjoy was a pill."

"She would have been in your class, right, Tex? 43-W-9?" Bernie asked.

Tex nodded. "She was one of the early washouts. I felt for her — we all did. She wanted it so badly."

"See, she didn't have many social skills," Chub said. "She had kind of an irritating personality. And you felt like you ought to feel sorry for her because she wanted so desperately to belong and she didn't have any idea how to go about it."

"But every time you'd try to feel sorry for her —," Toots began.

"She'd pull the rug out from under your feet and smirk when you hit the floor," Tex said. "You wanted to rip the smirk off her face with your fingernails."

"She was terribly jealous," Bernie said. "I guess she wanted her revenge on us because we'd made it and she hadn't."

"Well, 'revenge' is kind of a strong word," Chub said.

"Speak for yourself," Toots said. "I got five demerits with her name on them."

"She would have needed to find out something about Harlingen," Tex pointed out. "She didn't know a lot, but she did know something."

"I'll bet she found an informant," Toots said. "Maybe she even found him or her before she hatched this nutty plan to impersonate Tommy. Maybe that's what gave her the idea."

"But why pick us?" Chub said. Her forehead was creased in bewilderment. "There were seven of us stationed there, in addition to Tommy, that she would have to fool. She could have picked a place where only two or three WASP were stationed, maybe even a place where all the WASP who were stationed there are dead now or no longer involved with the organization. I mean, she looked like Tommy, sure, but is that the only reason?"

Toots said slowly, "I'll bet it was Tex she wanted to impress. Tex was in her class and she's one of the most respected flyers among us. She had more experience than any of us at the time. I do agree with Chub that she wanted to belong to a group, but I'll bet she picked us because she wanted Tex to acknowledge and respect her."

"Somebody's been eliminating the Harlingen WASP," I observed, working things out as I spoke. "Of the original eight, three are now dead, two of them very recently. Others, like Toots and Lou, have had accidents. Tex, as far as I know, hasn't."

Chub gasped. "You think Killjoy was bumping off WASP so Tex would respect her?"

"Not exactly," I admitted. "I'm not sure what I think. My biggest question is whether Olive Kilroy was killed because she was impersonating Tommy Thompson or because she was Olive Kilroy."

"First thing we need to do," Moses said, "is to contact the police and let them know that they should check the victim's fingerprints not only against Thompson's but also against Kilroy's, assuming the files still exist. Or check dental records?"

"Would you be willing to do that, Moses?" Toots said. She didn't explain why she'd asked one of the two men at the table, and that man a photographer, but nobody seemed to notice.

As Moses retreated, Chub said, "Boy! Y'all sure know how to help a girl forget her troubles."

45

JULY 19, 1986

THE EVENING'S entertainment featured a Come-As-You-Were party. Chub said she wasn't in a party mood.

"Besides, I suppose I should go and talk to that awful woman and find out what she wants from us," she said. "I hope she doesn't think her daddy's rich, because he isn't."

"Now, Chubby Lee, don't you dare let that Isabel ruined your reunion!" Bernie said. "You know you've been looking forward to the Come-As-You-Were party and we need you to lead the sing-along."

"Well, I'll come," Chub said, "but I hardly need a costume change. I was young and stupid then and I'm old and stupid now."

At Toots's request, we stopped by her room before the party. I was dressed in green khakis and a white short-sleeve shirt. Moses wore tan khakis, an olive-drab T-shirt, and an Army cap.

"It's the only part of my uniform I can still get into," he said.

I noted that he was only carrying one camera bag slung around his neck.

Toots and Stretch were trying to pin up their zoot suits.

"I got room for one more in here, Cat, if you're interested," Stretch offered.

"Lou's wearing her Santiago blues," Toots told me. "I told you she was nuts. Even if I could get into mine, I'd choose an oversized jumpsuit over a uniform and pantyhose any time." She nodded at Moses. "But it will make a good picture."

"Do they make you pay for these when you deactivated?" Stretch asked.

"Yeah," Toots said. "Can you believe it? They let us keep one summer uniform and one winter uniform. Everything else we were supposed to turn in or pay for. And we ponied up and deprived some size-44 recruit of the pleasure of wearing a jumpsuit that would actually fit him."

Then she turned to us. "So, what's your thinking on what's going on around here? Any ideas?"

"Probably not anything that you haven't thought of," Moses admitted. "It's weird that somebody would try to impersonate a dead WASP. It's even sad if she finally got what she wanted all her life only to be killed as a result. But is it related to the other killings in any other way? I doubt it."

"You think the killer thought she was Thompson," Toots said. "I guess that's a relief because it lets most of us off. We didn't think she was Thompson."

"You weren't sure, though," I said. "Maybe the killer couldn't afford to take a chance."

"Suggesting that Maddy really meant 'Evelyn' when she said 'Ethel' — the boy Evelyn went off with? 'Evelyn' was Tommy's real first name," Toots said. "The killer moved pretty quickly when she appeared on the scene."

"Tommy Thompson and Maddy were in the same flight, right? Tommy and Maddy and Squeak? And you were the fourth?"

Toots nodded.

"You think the killer will try again soon, then?" Stretch asked. "To take out Toots, I mean."

"As far as we know, Bernie hasn't been threatened," I said. "So it could refer to something that occurred before Bernie arrived in Harlingen."

"But what about the burglary at Lou's," Stretch asked, "and Lou's accident?"

"As far as we know, Lou didn't cause the accident," Moses pointed out. "We don't know why her brakes failed. So the accident could have been an accident. As for the burglary, we know that somebody has been searching for something in WASP papers. Lou's leadership role in the organization and the museum project make her a major collector of WASP papers and memorabilia. Could be our killer went to her house because they couldn't find what they were looking for elsewhere."

"If it's all connected to some incident that happened at Harlingen," I said, "let's remember that it was connected, in Maddy's mind, with 'flag-waving and speeches.'"

"It's possible she was listening to a lot of Fourth-of-July talk about 'our boys in uniform,'" Toots said. "I don't blame her, really. I mean, we weren't ever deployed to a combat zone, but what about all the nurses who work? Their training was rigorous, you better believe. Their service always gets ignored. And when the men get praise, you'd think they walked to Normandy on water. When I think of some of the numbskulls and skirt-chasers and arrogant jerks who flew for the Army Air Force, my blood just boils."

"Yeah, so don't forget Isabel Yates, either," Stretch said. "Apparently, more than one woman 'went off' with CJ Burman."

"I don't know," Toots said slowly. "What do you-all think? You think somebody would kill several people just to keep that kind of thing secret?"

I shrugged. Moses said, "Hard to imagine, unless they became a conservative minister afterward."

"Or a politician?" Stretch offered.

Toots snorted. "Well, CJ is no minister and I don't know any WASP who is, either. I suppose you could consider him a small-time politician."

"Maybe he aspires to bigger things," Stretch said.

"Now there's a scary thought," Toots said.

"Of course, if there is a birth certificate somewhere that gives someone a claim on an estate," he said, "that could be a different story."

"You think that's what Isabel Yates is after?" Toots said. "If so, she's barking up the wrong tree."

"How do you know?" I said.

"Well, that's what Chub says and I believe her," she said. "She knows that CJ's had some setbacks and blames herself for letting him take care of the land purchase for us. She sees now that it was just too big a temptation."

"I don't know," I said. "Nothing we have so far feels like sufficient motivation. We must be missing something."

"Just be careful tonight, Toots," Moses said. "Keep your eyes and ears open. You too, Stretch."

"Don't worry," Stretch said. "I won't let her out of my sight. I'm her copilot."

When we arrived at the party, it was in the milling-around stage. There were lots of baggy blue zoot suits and tan khakis, which Toots identified as the "general's pants" or "GPs" after General Arnold, whose impending visit had once caused Jacqueline Cochran to devise an impromptu uniform. Several women wore white turbans — "Urban's turbans," according to Toots, after the Avenger commandant who insisted that the trainees keep their heads covered. Others wore hairnets, caps, or berets.

"No wonder they called it 'Cochran's convent," Stretch said.

Toots was our interpreter. Red socks meant that you had soloed in an AT-6. WASP rings had been fashioned by a Sweetwater jeweler out of Army Air Force insignia altered to look like the WASP ailerons. Red long johns sported by one reveler commemorated the standard-issue winter underwear. Two women wearing zoot suits had painted "Hands Off" on the capacious seats of their pants.

"The EOs — Establishment Officers — didn't have much sense of humor," Toots said. "They would have earned demerits for that."

Two women were wearing short pajamas and going barefoot. When Moses asked if he could take their picture, they told him that a canine camp mascot, Lady, liked to steal their shoes whenever they dragged their cots outside to sleep.

Lou was one of perhaps five women wearing the dress uniform of Santiago blue. They looked very professional, but the women in pajamas looked more comfortable.

Some of the men wore parts of uniforms as well, but few uniforms were complete and few men looked as if they could have fit into anything they'd worn in their 20s.

Some women had simply opted for civilian clothes — flared or pleated skirts, baby-doll sweaters, bobby socks, and saddle shoes.

"It used to drive some of the WACs crazy that WASP could wear civilian clothes to the OC," Toots said. "They considered it unfair competition."

And speaking of competition, there were contests. The first involved those wearing zoot suits. Lou announced that the object of the competition was to stuff the largest number of items inside your zoot suit. Esther, Toots, and Chub piled a table high with permissible items, everything from extra sweaters to toothbrushes, knitting needles and yarn, lipstick, compacts, sanitary pads, and fruit. There were several items that look like chains made out of folded money. Toots explained that whenever a pilot landed someplace new, she had someone sign and date a dollar bill — a "short-snorter bill" — that would be added to the chain. In addition, there was a large bowl of ping-pong balls.

"Come on, engineer," Toots said, grabbing Stretch by the elbow, "let's see what you're made of."

Lou instructed the seven contestants to empty their pockets. "We don't want anyone to start with an unfair advantage."

Moses had followed Toots to take pictures and I followed Moses.

Laughing, the women dug in their pockets and piled room keys, khakis, wallets, coins, handkerchiefs, small pill bottles and cases, pocket knives, lipstick, and pieces of paper on a nearby table.

"Hey, Toots," someone called and pointed. "You dropped something."

Stretch bent and picked up a small square of folded paper and unfolded it.

"What is it?" Toots said. "My laundry list?"

"It's that cheat sheet you made up for the Code test," someone said.

Stretch frowned, then seemed to catch her breath. "I can't read the handwriting very well, but it has Tommy Thompson's name in it."

"Must be Tommy's laundry list, then," Toots said with a shrug. "I knew I hadn't bought two zoot suits."

But Stretch didn't add the paper to the pile on the table. Instead, she handed it to me. She made eye contact. "Cat can hold onto it."

I smiled and slipped it into my pocket.

Toots won the competition, although the ample-breasted Sadie Zeller protested, saying that she ought to be given a handicap. But Stretch pulled Toots away when Toots was challenging Sadie to a re-match.

With her other hand she grabbed me by the arm and propelled us out of the room and down the hall toward the lobby, with Moses trailing behind.

"I'm the one who should be calling for a re-match," she grumbled. "I would have thought it was against the rules to stomp on the ping-pong balls and flatten them."

"WASP rules, kiddo," Toots said. "Anything goes as long as it gets you there."

We found a relatively quiet corner, although the sounds of a band tuning up in the lounge suggested that it would not be quiet for long. Stretch let go of Toots and held out her hand to me. I extracted the paper from my pocket and gave it to her. She unfolded it carefully. It was limp in her hand, I saw — not brittle, but soft with age. She laid it out on a table, flattened it with her hand, and leaned over to read it.

Toots was still smiling. "What is it?" she asked. "Something Tommy wrote?"

Stretch shook her head, her eyes on the page. "It's not her hand-writing."

Toots said, "And how would you know that it's not her hand-writing?"

Stretch slowly raised her head. Her eyes flicked to me, then settled on Toots's face.

"No time like the present, I guess," she said. She swallowed. "Tommy Thompson was my great-aunt."

"What?" The surprise showed in Toots's face. When Stretch didn't say anything, she said, "No fooling?"

Stretch looked down. She said in a small voice, "I knew you were her flying partner. I read about you sometimes. I went to see you at an air show when I was a little girl." She sounded very like that little girl now, the one who had thrilled to the stories of her daredevil aunt who had flown bombers during the war. "I told you that part. The part I left out was about Great-aunt Tommy. I read the letter you wrote to Nana and Grandpop when Tommy was killed. It was such a sweet letter. And then I saw your ad in the Ninety-Nines newsletter. I knew it was meant for me, but I was so afraid you'd hire someone else."

Toots frowned. "Well, that explains why you were so eager, I guess. But why didn't you tell me that Tommy was your aunt, for Pete's sake?"

Stretch still didn't look at her. "I guess there were several reasons. For one thing, you never knew that Tommy was Black."

Toots exploded. She raised her arms in a gesture of protest. "Well, what difference would that make? Hell's bells, I didn't care if she was purple, as long as she could land a B-26 with one engine on fire or a propeller shot off! Besides, she was my friend!"

Stretch looked at her then, studying her face. She said, "It was a different world in the 1940s — a segregated world. I don't know what it was like. I wasn't around. But I've heard stories about it."

Toots appeared to consider this statement. "Yeah, okay. It was a different world. You're right. I didn't have any Negro friends growing up. The only Black people I knew were the custodian at my school and George the Fish Man, who owned a little fish store we used to go to. The funny thing was that integration probably would have worked pretty well at Avenger. We were all so focused on flying, that's just about all we cared about. And everything was so new to us. I don't think I'd ever met a Jewish person in my life until I got to Avenger. See, most of us had never been anywhere, seen anything or anyone different from the places and people we'd grown up around. It wasn't like today. So everything was new. You kept trying to figure out what we had in common that made us survive and succeed, Stretch. But we didn't think we had anything in common, except that we loved to fly."

Stretch's eyes strayed back to the paper she was holding.

"Okay, right," Toots said. "You're Tommy's niece. Let's get on with it. Just don't expect any special privileges now. I still expect you to do the heavy lifting."

Stretch grinned at her, and then went back to the paper.

"Is it a letter?" Moses asked. He was lifting his head to find the best angle for his bifocals.

"It's not a letter," Stretch said. "It's more like a statement. It has to do with landing a plane, I think. Look, isn't that word 'landed'?"

The handwriting was a scrawl, almost impossible to read. The ink had faded, and this, too, made it difficult to decipher.

"I think it says, "On December 1st, 1944, when I was' — what's that word?" Stretch's index finger was following the words on the page and then stopped.

"'Copilot,'" Toots suggested. "Or 'copiloting.' The words just kind of trail off, don't they?"

"'— copiloting a B-26.' There's 'Harlingen' and that looks like 'Colorado,' but I can't make out —."

Toots interrupted her. "'En route from Harlingen to Peterson AFB in Colorado Springs,'" She read.

"Yeah, yeah, that's it," Stretch said. "'Copiloting a B-26 en route from Harlingen to Peterson AFB in Colorado Springs.'" She stopped where a circle of blue evidenced a drop of water that had obliterated the writing. "No way to figure out what went there. Then what's this?"

"C-O-L," Toots said. "Colonel Harding. He was a big shot. Must've been visiting the base at the time."

"'Colonel Harding, the pilot became' — what? Could that be 'ill'?"

Toots put her finger on the page. "'Became ill and WASP Evelyn Thompson landed the plane,'" she finished. She laughed and shook her head. "Poor bastard! The way Tommy told it, the copilot had washed out of B-26 school and he was training in navigation at Harlingen. That was just before we deactivated, when they didn't need so many pilots. No wonder he washed out! From his handwriting, you'd think he was illiterate. But this Harding character was one of those sexists who didn't really believe that women could — or should — be flying bombers. So he put a washed-out B-26 cadet in the copilot's seat and Tommy, who flew B-26s every day, sat in the navigator seat.

"The way Tommy told it, they were already over the foothills, climbing from four thousand up to five thousand feet, headed into the mountains, when the engine caught fire. Next thing she knows, Harding is clutching his chest — too much excitement, I guess. So he passes out in the pilot's seat and the kid in the copilot's seat looks terrified. Tommy shoved him out of the way and took the controls. She finally gets him to do the job he was trained for and find her an airstrip. She has to land soon or tell the guys in the back — the plane was carrying some brass to the Roosevelt wedding — to jump. She landed at Pueblo AFB. The pilot was still out, but he must've pulled through, because I read something about him later.

"Well, Tommy was already steamed. But the kid is terrified she'll tell everybody she landed the plane. Why wouldn't she? He begs her not to say anything — something about how his father would never forgive the kid the public humiliation, and blah, blah, blah. So she agreed not to, but she was so furious, she made him write it down. Must've just stuck it in her pocket and forgot about it."

"She didn't have much time to remember it," I pointed out.

"You said before that she disappeared on December 7th on her way to Sweetwater."

"That's true," she said.

Moses asked, "Would she have been wearing her zoot suit to fly to Colorado as a navigator?"

Toots shook her head. "She would probably have been wearing her winter flight suit for Colorado, with the zoot suit under it. She would have been wearing her GPs when she flew to Sweetwater for graduation."

But I was craning my neck to see the name at the bottom of the page. "Who wrote it?" I said

We all leaned in. There was a moment of silence.

"Well, dad-*gummit*!" Toots finally said. "Why didn't they teach those cadets how to write?"

"The second letter looks like a capital *j*," I said.

"This is impossible!" Stretch groaned.

"The last name starts with a *b*," I said.

"I'll vote for that," Toots said. "And it ends with one of those annoying squiggles, which could be anything — an *n*, an *m*, an *r*."

"Any of this ring any bells, Toots?" I asked. "Did Tommy ever tell you the guy's name?"

"Hey, Cat, I'm in the age category that's happy to remember our own names," Toots said. "If she did, it's long gone."

I hadn't noticed that Toots was having trouble remembering anything, but I knew what she meant. What are the chances that anybody would remember a name from a story someone told them forty years ago?

"Besides, what difference does it make?" she continued. "It's ancient history. Nobody cares about this stuff anymore. There are hundreds of stories like this one. The very first WASP death was what today we call a 'friendly fire' incident, I guess. She was shot down by a gunner at Camp Davis, flying a junky A-24 with a jammed hatch release. The instructor was General Arnold's son. I didn't even know that until years later. I'd always heard that the cause was equipment failure, pure and simple. They didn't want the public to know that the cadets were shooting us out of the skies. But if people find out now, it's no big deal."

"Maybe it's a big deal to somebody," I said. "Moses, do you think you can get Arnie on the phone?"

Moses nodded. "Ask him to check on the men?"

"We've got two hanging around here with a *j* and a *b* in their names. I'm wondering how a cadet gets invited to the Roosevelt wedding, if that's why he was flying to Colorado. Do you know what CJ's father did, Toots?"

"He was a big oil man, very important. Friend of the governor's and all that. He lost most of his money when the Texas oil business crashed in the 80s. But Tommy wasn't going for the Roosevelt bash, so the cadet might have had another reason for wanting to get there, too. Maybe he was just visiting his sweetheart."

"Sure. That's possible."

"But you said 'two'?" Stretch said. "Who's the other?"

"Senator Jim Braverman, of course," I said.

"But he's —," Toots protested.

"What? An honorary WASP?"

"Well, yeah," Toots said. "I mean, you don't fight for militarization just so your victims can get death benefits later when you bump them off."

"You have a point," I said.

"Besides, Tommy told me this kid washed out of B-26 school. I'm pretty sure Jim just got reassigned when they stopped training pilots."

"I'm still keeping an open mind," I said. "Moses?"

"Me, too."

He went off to call Arnie and we returned to the party. It wasn't hard to find. From halfway down the hall, you could hear the voices singing, to the tune of "Glory, Glory, Hallelujah!"

"When the war is over, we will all fly Cubs again,
When the war is over, we will all fly Cubs again,
When the war is over, we will all fly Cubs again,
Like heck we will, like heck!"

46

JULY 19, 1986

IT WAS ALMOST MIDNIGHT. The band was winding down. The dance floor was empty.

All of the dancers were slumped in chairs or draped over tables. Many of their costume accessories had been discarded. Several people were fanning themselves with Avenger Beach bingo cards. The two women who had shown up in red long johns had taken scissors to their costumes about an hour ago and now wore short johns.

Lou looked wilted, even though the uniform jacket was hanging from the back of her chair. She had danced a slow number with Wes and now had an inhaler pressed to her face. Toots and Esther looked worn out and even Stretch was yawning discreetly. Toots had opened her zoot suit down to her waist to show pink striped fabric underneath. Moses, a marathoner on the dance floor, had a hand on his lower back. He was wincing. I'd known it was a mistake to try to teach Stretch the jitterbug, but I'd also known that he wouldn't listen to me. And when I saw him roll her, hip to hip, across his back, I'd foreseen the consequences as clearly as if I'd been Madame Zahara herself.

Speaking of Madame Zahara, she'd drunk enough to float a Flying Fortress and passed her peak about an hour ago. She was now on the slow slide into depression. The alcohol she'd consumed was drawing out her Southern drawl until it sounded like a record played on the wrong speed.

I was trying to distract her, though I'd consumed a fair amount myself.

"Chub," I said, waving a hand in front of her face to draw her attention, "I want to ask you something. You remember that story about Tommy Thompson landing the B-26 in Colorado, right before she disappeared? She had to take over when the pilot collapsed and the copilot was too scared to land the plane when the engine caught fire. Remember?"

Chub's brow creased with exaggerated concentration. "I 'member, darlin'. She was on her way to Colorado Springs for that wedding."

"CJ was an officer, wasn't he?" I said. "Do you know if he went to the Roosevelt wedding?"

"He was a lieutenant, the rat," she said. "Lieutenant Rat."

"Right. Did he go to the Roosevelt wedding?"

"Now, let me think," she said. "I b'lieve he did, but I don't b'lieve he was on that flight. If he was, he never told me about the emergency landing." Her tongue got tripped up on the word 'emergency,' so it came out a little garbled.

"Did CJ ever go to B-26 school?"

"Oh, sure. But then he got sent to gun'ry school instead, when they stopped training pilots. Poor old rat! He had to train other little rats, never got to see the action."

"Do you remember the name of the kid who was copiloting the plane Tommy landed?"

To my surprise, she answered without hesitation. "Chip, darlin'. Or maybe it was Chad or Chuck — something like that. One of those little, teeny-weency short names."

I sighed. "Not Jim?"

"Not Jim and not Rat," she said with conviction. Then she said, "Lieutenant Rat had a mouse in every port. Some ports, he had more than one. I used to be proud he picked me out of all those mice. I guess I thought I was the big cheese. But now, lookin' back, I was just the one who got caught in the trap."

To my dismay, a tear slid down her cheek. Bernie, who sat on the other side of her, slipped an arm around her shoulder and gave it a squeeze.

"Now, honey, don't be that way," Bernie said. "You got to remember the good times. You had three lovely girls and now you have grandchildren."

"Maybe I've got more," she said. "Do you suppose that Isabel Yates has kids?"

"She's got two boys," Bernie said. She was smoothing Chub's hair.

"Two boys?" Chub gave way.

"Now, now, Chubby Lee," Bernie clucked. "Got a handkerchief in that oversized pocket of yours?" Both Bernie and Chub were wearing zoot suits.

Chub produced one and blew her nose.

Bernie looked around the table. "Goodness! This group looks dull. We need to help Chub take her mind off her troubles."

"I know what," Lou said. "Tex should take us to see her plane."

"That's a great idea," Toots said. "I haven't been inside a B-26 for forty years."

Tex looked up over her line of empty beer bottles and grinned. "I'm game."

There was a certain amount of confused activity while people searched for parts of their costumes or, in the case of the zoot suits, the contents of their pockets. Gene Smith had disappeared long before and Wes Zimmerman bowed out at this point, to get his "beauty sleep," he said. Lou followed him upstairs and returned with Happy. We hadn't seen CJ Burman since the reception. That left the WASP — Toots, Lou, Bernie, Esther, Chub and Tex — and their tagalongs, Moses, Stretch, Happy and me.

"Who's sober enough to drive?" Toots asked.

This was a matter that had concerned me. I was not volunteering.

"Esther doesn't drink and Tex is always sober," Bernie said. "You're sober too, aren't you, Lou?"

Lou shrugged. "More or less. Sure, I'll drive."

"Will it hurt your wrist?" Toots asked.

"Nah, it needs the exercise." She held up her splinted hand and waggled it to illustrate.

Nobody suggested that Chub was sober.

We drove the ten miles to the airport without being stopped by the police. As we followed Tex to the hangar, she suddenly belted out:

"I'm a flying wreck a-risking my neck

And a hell of a pilot, too!

A hell of a, hell of a, hell of a, hell of a,

Hell of a pilot, too!"

A short, bald man wearing mechanics' coveralls and an expression of astonishment popped out of a nearby hangar. Tex just waved at him and went on singing. Bernie, Toots, Esther and Chub lined up two by two behind Tex. Their attempts to march were hampered by Chub's position at the front and her inebriation. Esther kept bumping into her. They joined in the singing.

"Like all the jolly good flyers,

The gremlins treat me mean,

I'm a flyin' wreck, a-riskin' my neck

For the good ole 318th!"

Moses looked at Stretch and shrugged. They lined up and fell into step.

Lou waved to tell them to go ahead. "I can march, sing, or breathe," she said to me as we brought up the rear. "But I can't do more than one thing at a time anymore."

Happy was barking and dancing. "Okay, pal, go join in the fun," she said and unclipped the leash. When he stood and looked at her, she said, "Go on! It's okay, I'm coming." So he dashed off and circled the parade like an overeager drill sergeant.

At the entrance to a large hangar, Tex nodded at a security guard and he nodded back. Inside the mammoth building were six planes.

I recognized them from the one on display the day before, but now that they weren't parked next to Fortresses and Superfortresses, they looked bigger.

"That must be Tex's," Bernie said, pointing.

Several of the planes featured designs on the pilot's side, just back of the transparent nosecone. One of them showed the gremlin Fifinella with a yellow rose between her teeth. Underneath were the words, "The Yellow Rose of Texas."

We clambered up the drop-ladder through the hatch. I gave Chub a push from behind while Bernie and Toots pulled her up. As the women had done the day before, the WASP gravitated to the cockpit and began speaking a foreign language. Moses snapped some pictures.

Then I heard something I could understand.

"You know what I wish, y'all?" Chub was saying. "I wish I could go up in this baby! For old time's sake!"

"Me, too!" Lou said and sighed.

"Take us up, Tex," Bernie pleaded. Her eyes glittered in the dim light from the hangar. "Pretty please?"

Tex laughed. "What, now?"

"Sure!" Bernie said. "Why not? It's all ready to fly in the morning, right?"

"Please, please, please, with sugar on it?" Chub said.

Happy barked his approval.

My heart froze in my chest.

Moses cleared his throat. "Y'all have been doing a lot of drinking. I don't think it's such a good idea." My hero.

Chub pouted. "Esther hasn't had anything, so she can copilot. And Tex can hold her liquor."

"We're all dressed up with no place to go," Bernie said, pulling on the sides of her zoot suit to make it balloon out.

This struck me as such a ludicrous thing to say that I would have laughed if my life weren't at stake.

Moses decided to appeal to reason. "Toots?" he said.

But Toots had been drinking, too, and besides, nobody who has once held a title for acrobatic flying should be considered a reasonable person, in my book. I saw the same glint in her eye that I've seen in Bernie's. This was getting out of hand. Suddenly, they were all twenty-two-year-old daredevils again, a gaggle of high-spirited, mischievous girls who had been trained to fly bombers.

"Don't worry, Moses," Toots said. "We'll turn on the lights."

This brought gales of laughter in which Moses and I did not share. The next thing I knew, Tex had gone off to file a flight plan, Bernie had gone back to Lou's car for Lou's "flight bag," and Esther and Toots were checking the parachutes.

Parachutes?

Tex reappeared at a trot and began to walk around the plane. She must have switched on another bank of lights because the hangar was more brightly lit now.

"I'm not going," I announced.

"Oh, come on, Cat," Chub said. "Don't be such a big baby. How can you write about us if you've never experienced what it was we did?"

"Easy," I said. "I'll interview you when you get back — if you get back."

Tex was climbing in and closing the hatch door behind her.

"Tex, Cat says she isn't going," Chub complained.

"Oh, come on, Cat," Lou said, taking me by the arm. "It'll be fun. Look how excited Happy is."

Indeed, Happy looked thrilled. But I didn't credit him with a lot of intelligence, either.

"It won't be a long trip," Tex said, apparently to reassure me. "There's a storm approaching from the west, but we'll be fine for half an hour or so."

Psychology had apparently not been part of the curriculum at Avenger.

"Oh, poot!" Chub said.

Esther was already sitting in the copilot's seat. Tex slid into the pilot's seat. Bernie handed me a flask.

"What's this?" I was hoping for a general anesthetic.

"Dutch courage."

I drank. Whatever it was, it warmed my veins and melted away my resistance. I felt my will go limp.

Tex and Esther had their earphones on. They were busy flipping levers and pushing buttons and speaking in tongues.

"I know!" Chub said. "I'll tell Cat a funny story to distract her. This one time, Lou and me were on this night run, with no lights, so they could practice with the searchlights."

Out of the corner of my eye I saw Toots shake her head no, but by the time I turned my head to look at her, she was smiling blankly. Chub stared at Toots for several beats, then her mouth snapped shut. "Never mind," she said.

"Toots, you'd better take the navigator's seat," Tex said, "at least until we're on the runway. Anyone want to ride in the nose?"

"I do! I do!" Chub said, raising a hand like a school kid. "If I can get down that low."

Esther stood up and moved aside and Chub disappeared somewhere near her feet. I shuddered.

"Where do we sit?" Moses asked.

"Here, on the bench in the bomb bay, till we take off," Bernie said. "Once we're up, you can go sit in the gunners' positions if you want to."

I can't describe where we sat because I had my eyes closed by then. All I can tell you is that it felt like a board — say, a bleacher at a Little League game.

"What if I throw up?" I asked.

"Aim to your right," Lou said. "I'm on your left."

After that, if anybody said anything to me, I couldn't hear it. I bounced along on my seat, wondering if this was what it had felt like to ride a covered wagon across country. Every jolt struck the base of my spine, then traveled up until it exploded inside the lump behind my right ear. I gripped the bench and clenched my teeth, in part to keep down everything I'd drunk and eaten in the past four hours. But when I felt the plane lift, it all rose in rebellion. I turned to my right as instructed and let go.

I heard a faint, familiar protest. "Aw, Cat!"

I could have done three loads of laundry in the time it took the plane to level off. I cracked one eye. Lou was trying to drag Happy away from a foul-smelling puddle on the floor to my right. Everybody but me was standing up. And everybody was smiling, I noticed, except me.

Lou leaned close to Moses, spoke, and pointed up. He nodded. He was wiping his camera case with his handkerchief. He took hold of a ladder bolted to the side of the plane and began climbing. Lou climbed after him.

Bernie offered me the flask and I took it, grateful. She leaned close and said, "Want to go sit in the tail gunner's seat?"

I shook my head. All I wanted was for this ride to be over, I thought. I hastily amended that thought: safely.

That was when all hell broke loose. Toots appeared with an armful of parachutes. She handed one to me and gestured that I should put it on. This must be part of the safety drill, I thought. Lou was backing down the ladder and Moses was coming after her.

"Where's Bernie?" Lou shouted.

I cocked a thumb toward the rear, but as she moved in that direction, Bernie reappeared. Then even Chub was there, looking more sober than she had ten minutes ago.

Then I smelled it. Something more than the heady odor of fuel. Smoke.

Lou was crouching to strap something onto Happy, who, for once, stood perfectly still. She gave him an affectionate pat and kissed his nose.

Esther appeared and she and Toots conferred. Toots nodded. Lou was passing things out but she skipped me. Somehow, I didn't think it was a set of aviator's wings to pin on my shirt to show what a good little passenger I'd been.

Toots took my hand and guided it to a pull-string dangling from my parachute harness.

"Count to ten and pull," she shouted in my ear. I felt her hand on mine as she guided it to something else. "Emergency release," she shouted. She held up ten fingers to emphasize the ten count. Then she raised her eyebrows at me. I stared at her. She nodded, gave me a thumbs up, and then a quick pat on the back.

The floor plunged. I hung suspended in space for a heartbeat, then dropped. The floor leapt, slammed my soles and jolted my spine. The shock threw me sideways and my shoulder struck metal. I threw out a hand to steady myself, but I couldn't find anything to hang onto. The air was thickening with smoke.

47

JULY 20, 1986

HAPPY FOUND Esther and her canine fan club playing soccer with a pinecone on a blacktop in front of a dilapidated building that once had been a small feed store. It was fronted by a narrow two-lane that might have been a rural route. It was lit by an ancient-looking yellow floodlight.

"I don't know who's still paying the light bill on this place, but I'm grateful," she said.

"Did Tex land okay?" Lou asked.

Esther shrugged. "She must have brought it down because I didn't hear a crash. You know Tex has land luck. But I hope she walked away from it."

"You go looking for a telephone?" Toots asked.

"Not yet," Esther said. "I was waiting for you. Nice of you to take your time about getting here. Gave me and the boys time to get acquainted."

"Sorry!" Stretch said. She was still embarrassed to have been the one stuck in the tree. I wasn't about to detail my own escapades.

Lou looked at the mutts — and they were all mutts. "I'll bet they know where we can find a phone."

"Are you sure you don't have one in your bag of tricks?" Esther asked her.

"I'll have one next time, I promise. And a bottle of hooch for Cat."

"Way I feel right now," Toots said, "she'd have to fight me for it."

"Me, too," Stretch said.

"Me, three," Esther said, "and I don't drink."

"We can follow this road," Moses said. "Looks like some lights up that way maybe."

Lou took a few steps in that direction, stopped, and said, "Let's do it. The dogs seem to think it's a good idea."

We followed the road, making slow progress. Every time we stopped, my ankle got used to immobility and protested twice as indignantly when we began moving again. When the group spread out, Toots said to Moses and me in a low voice, "Do you think the plane was sabotaged?"

"Seems likely," Moses said. "Tex is on the program and even I could have figured out which B-26 was hers."

Toots nodded. "And you think it's one of those two men."

"We'll see what Arnie finds out," Moses said.

"Are you mad at Stretch?" I asked.

She looked at me in surprise. "For getting caught in the tree?"

"For not telling you who she was." I said.

"Oh, that," Toots said. "I figured there was something going on with her, I just didn't know what it was. I figured she'd tell me in her own good time." She watched Stretch ahead of us, trying to match her long strides to Lou's shorter ones. "She's a good kid. I'm glad she's Tommy's niece — well, grand-niece. Makes me feel I got something of Tommy back."

She frowned. "You know what I can't forgive Killjoy for? Or whoever it was. The way she described the supposed 'accident' — well, it was probably pretty close to the truth. Tommy wasn't wearing her watch that night. I found it in the showers later. She was in such a rush, she just forgot it. If anything went wrong with the navigational equipment — that's the only thing that makes sense, given that they never found her plane — she wouldn't have any way of knowing until it was too late. No way to find out now who drove her from Harlingen to Monroe, unless somebody remembers. But whoever it was —."

"I suppose there was a way to sabotage navigational equipment on those planes," Moses said.

Toots looked at him over my head. "Easiest thing in the world. All you need is a magnet."

48

JULY 20, 1986

A VOICE ASSAULTED MY EAR.

"Rise and shine, Cat," it said.

"Wrong number," I mumbled.

The phone rang again. The voice said, "Come on, Cat! We got work to do."

"Look, I don't know who the hell you are or who this Cat person is, but if you call this number again, I'll report you," I said.

Next came a pounding on my door. I rolled over. It continued.

"I got donuts!" a voice called.

"Oh, all right!" I snapped. I swung my feet to the floor and scowled at the cane I'd acquired at the end of the evening's festivities. I tried putting weight on my foot. It hurt like hell. I must've tripped over one too many tree roots the night before.

"Take your time," the voice called.

That reminded me to look at the clock. Eight o'clock. Surely this was an optical illusion caused by the cocktail of meds now circulating through my system. When you go to bed at four, you don't get up at eight. Everyone knows this.

"Don't rush on my account," the voice called.

If I let him in, I thought, I could beat him with my cane. I pulled myself upright, limped across to the door, and let him in.

"How you feelin'?" he said, edging past me with a bag of donuts and a Styrofoam cup of coffee.

"I'd feel better if I was dead," I said.

"This'll get your blood sugar up." He set the bag down and took a seat. "You want to hear Arnie's report before or after you get dressed?"

I sighed. "Just get it over with." I limped to the table, fingered the bag open and studied the selection.

Moses eyed me. "You need to keep your strength up."

I extracted an iced jelly donut and a cake donut smeared with chocolate and coconut and set them on a napkin.

"Good choice," he said. "Well, first off, I didn't get a chance to tell you last night that they don't have any fingerprint records to match with the murder victim because all of the Avenger records were destroyed. After the war, apparently nobody was interested in them, so Deedie took them home with her to Wichita Falls. But eventually, since nobody asked for them, she tossed them out. So Detective Kroup was happy for a suggestion of prints to check.

"As to the men we asked Arnie to check on, Burman is, as Arnie indicated before, financially overextended, although he's paid off a few creditors and improved his credit rating in the past year. He's also a member of a prominent West Texas family with big political connections — his father, a veteran, served three terms in Congress during the 70s. CJ is said to be considering following in his father's footsteps, though the local political reporter thinks he has his eye on governor.

"Arnie couldn't find out in the time we gave him whether Burman attended the Roosevelt wedding, but his father was well-placed to receive an invitation. Burman senior served on the War Production Board during the war. Junior was awarded the Air Medal, don't know what year.

"If Burman wants to be governor, Braverman's sights are set higher. Insiders believe that he's preparing for a run at the White House. His father, also a veteran, was a senator from Vermont who served for a long time on the Senate Ways and Means Committee.

Braverman is a past chair of the Armed Services Committee and now sits on Ways and Means. Again, Arnie doesn't know whether he or his son attended the Roosevelt wedding. Son was awarded the Distinguished Flying Cross in 1945."

Moses looked at me over the tops of his bifocals. "That's it."

I nodded. I had bit into a jelly donut and was now spreading the jelly around with my pinky.

"You know," he said, "these just the kind of folks get away with murder, don't you, Cat?"

"I know."

"Even if we had anything on anybody, which we don't."

"Might be trace evidence, if the cops knew what to match it with."

He snorted. "You know what a high-priced defense attorney would do with that kind of evidence in court?" I started to say something, but he added, "That old statement won't amount to much, not even if the cops find a couple of handwriting experts to swear it was written by one of these men."

"More flight logs or passenger lists proving that he was in the right cities at the right times?"

He shook his head. "Circumstantial."

He was right, of course. There's a reason why prisons are filled with poor people.

"On the other hand," he said, "if we right about what the game is, it ain't over."

"Can we set a trap?" I asked. "Suppose we let it be known that we found Thompson's flight suit."

"And wait for him to come after it?" he ran a hand through his hair. "Depends. You want him convicted for stealing a flight suit or you want him convicted for murder?"

"Blackmail?"

His mouth turned down. "You want to set somebody up — say, Toots — so he comes after her while the cops wait in the closet and listen in?" He shook his head. "I don't like it. Too risky. You know how much time it takes for somebody to pull a gun and shoot? No time. And they don't usually stand around discussing their crimes once the gun is out, either, the way they do on television."

"He hasn't used a gun so far."

"That's true, but he's either getting bolder or more desperate," Moses said. "The Thompson killing was the first time he didn't try to make it look like an accident."

I sighed. "In that case, maybe we'd better take a chance. You seen Chub yet this morning?"

"Nope, or Shorty or Tex, either."

"Some people are probably sleeping in, after last night's ordeal," I said pointedly. "You think Tex will fly today?"

"Far as I know, it's still on. She said last night when we got in — well, this morning — that one of the B-26 pilots got called out on a family emergency, so they have an extra plane — one that doesn't have the Yellow Rose of Texas or Fifinella on the nose cone."

"Just so we're clear on this: I'm not going with her. Not today, not ever." I stretched and felt a stab of pain between my shoulder blades. "I think I'll call Chub."

Moses was putting the folded page of notes from his phone call with Arnie into his breast pocket. He stopped and looked at me. "Why? You need a good voice?"

"I need a fortune teller."

49

JULY 20, 1986

AFTER AN HOUR OF PLANNING, Stretch drove Toots, Moses, and me to the air show. We all looked the worse for wear, even Stretch, who kept making circles with her shoulders like a fledgling testing her wings. I was sporting a new bandage wrapped around my heel and ankle and brandishing a cane. The way Moses rubbed his right hip and lower back alternately, I couldn't tell whether the jitter-buging session or the late-night hike had done him the worse damage. Toots's contributions to the conversation were interrupted by yawns and when we parked the car at the airport, she said, "Is it nap time yet?"

She was drowned out by the thunder of planes overhead.

The morning was dedicated to World War II veterans and when I looked up, I saw that a mock dogfight was in progress. When one of the two planes looped backwards and began spiraling down, my donuts surged up from my stomach and I closed my eyes.

"It's just pretend, Cat," Toots said close to my ear and yawned.

I opened my eyes in time to see the falling plane pull out of its descent to the roar of the crowd and the loud approval of the commentator.

"Choreography looks more like a gunfight at the O. K. Corral than a dogfight," Toots muttered.

I was in no position to be critical. As long as nobody bit the dust, I was willing to applaud.

We made our way to the WASP tent, where we had to field expressions of concern and questions about what had happened the night before.

"Just one of those things," Toots kept saying.

I tried it out a few times myself, but I couldn't muster the nonchalance that Toots had.

Chip Santos clapped me on the back and said, "Guess you really have something to write about now, huh, Cat? Moses said he got some great pictures."

Then, just when I thought the talk about our adventures had died down, I felt cold liquid hit my head. Someone grabbed my free arm, apparently to keep me from falling.

"Hey!" I shouted, hunching my shoulders.

"Welcome to the Caterpillar Club!" a chorus of voices shouted.

I looked at Moses in bewilderment, but he was drenched, too.

Lou said, smiling, "After your first jump, when you become a member of the Caterpillar Club, you get thrown in the Wishing Well — like when you solo. But we don't have one here. So we improvised."

People cheered, clapped and hooted. "Okay, okay," I said and ducked my head to wipe water from my eyes onto my sleeve. "Just don't expect me to solo anytime soon."

There were more mock battles to be fought and the women mostly watched these out of the corners of their eyes as they conversed, breaking off now and then to offer a critical observation or recount some memory that the sight had triggered. I couldn't keep the planes straight. Suffice it to say that there were little, medium-sized, and big ones, with one, two, or four engines. They all seemed to have nicknames.

Someone said, "The B-26s are up next," and the conversation died down. Six planes appeared in formation, flying much too close together, if you ask me, which nobody did. Then, as if they were all bored with the casual danger of collision, one peeled off from the formation, climbed, banked, and dived for the middle of the group. Again, I closed my eyes. When I opened them again, the plane was below the group, apparently unscathed. It repeated this maneuver, then rejoined the formation and a second plane went through the same drill as the first. I wondered if the object was to come closer than the preceding pilot to imminent destruction.

The WASP watched the whole performance with cool detachment as spectators clapped and cheered on all sides. The planes made a final pass in formation, but the last plane swooped down on the WASP tent. I threw myself on the ground, which was softer than concrete but harder than you might wish if you'd fallen out of a tree and hiked a couple of miles the night before. When I raised my head, I was looking at a forest of legs. I was the only one on the ground. Everyone else was erect and laughing, but not at me. When I followed their waves, I saw the B-26 seesawing its wings as it gained altitude.

Moses peeled me off the ground and help me to my feet. "You okay, Cat," he soothed. "You just got buzzed, is all."

"Remind me never again to take on a goddamn pilot as a client," I said. "They've got a warped sense of fun."

There followed appearances by a couple of Fortresses and Superfortresses that could have taken out the city of Dayton among them and had enough firepower left to begin the assault on Cincinnati. But the WASP only paid them casual attention and I turned my back on them. If they decided to buzz us, I didn't want to see it coming.

A VIP lunch for perhaps two hundred was served under a tent on the airport grounds in the early afternoon. The WASP were seated together at adjoining tables, except for the Zimmermans and the Burmans, who were seated with official VIPs. Senator Braverman was at the Burmans' table and CJ appeared more animated and less hangdog than he'd been that morning, surrounded by WASP, while his wife was gadding about, working on our plan. When Chub's eye fell on him, which wasn't often, she looked at him as if he were a distant cousin whose name she couldn't quite call to mind.

Tex ambled in to applause all around and tipped her cowboy hat. She eased into a chair at our table, looking like someone who was accustomed to landing several burning bombers a day before breakfast. She was wearing a clean bandage on her forehead and I saw a new one on her left lower arm, just below the elbow. She swept her former passengers and her copilot with a glance and drawled, "Ladies — and gentleman. Glad to see y'all looking so bright-eyed and bushy-tailed."

Lou said, "I'd better loan you my glasses."

Just as I was taking my first bite, Toots said, "Oh, my God! Look who's here."

"Who?" I leaned back to get a better view.

"Don't you recognize him?" she said, as I scanned the faces to see who she was looking at. "It's Braverman senior — the retired senator."

Moses said, "The heavyset, white-haired guy with the tan sports coat?"

"That's him."

In spite of the giant fans turned on the lunch guests, I was dripping sweat on my plate. You couldn't have paid me enough to wear a sports coat on a day like this. The current senator was in shirtsleeves, as were most of the men, so it was easy to spot the one wearing the tan sports coat. As I watched him make his progress from one table to the next, I saw him shake hands with two dozen people, including Senator Glenn.

I glanced at Toots. Her face had drained of color. I nudged her with my elbow.

"Cold feet?" I asked.

It took her a few seconds to respond. Then she sighed. "No. Let's get it over with, if we can."

Half-melted ice cream was being set in front of us when the emcee started his announcements and acknowledgments. I clapped when everybody else did, which saved me the trouble of listening to him drone on. So I wasn't paying attention until I suddenly heard, "Madame Zahara!"

Madame Zahara swept onto the stage to thunderous applause and whistles from our corner of the tent and a mixed response from the rest of the guests. Clearly, word had spread to some extent, and I watched as the more puzzled applauders leaned forward to hear explanations from those in the know at their tables. In any case, the WASP enthusiasm was infectious and soon the smiles in the audience predominated.

The emcee was thanking Madame Zahara for condescending to repeat her performance for a wider audience today. Madame showed surprising restraint and inclined her head graciously. I hoped that the serious purpose of the current performance wouldn't dampen her enthusiasm.

I shouldn't have worried; Madame was a trouper. Soon she was down among the tables, holding Senator Glenn's hand and feigning astonishment.

"What eez zees?" she said, as her heavily penciled eyebrows disappeared under her turban. "Oh-h-h, John Glenn, Madame Zahara zees ze whole of ze world in your hand! And you — you are like a teeny, leetle bug, flying around ziss world like a bee around a z-z-z-zinnia. Ohh, John Glenn, you are a brafe man! I zee medals — a Flying Cross — no, many Flying Crosses." She frowned. "I zee from ze uniform zat eet's ze Navy. Too bad!" This sally was greeted by laughter and a few hoots from Army and Air Force veterans. "You weel go to outer space, and zen, you weel even go to Iowa. I zee mountains — Caucasus — een your future."

Glenn chuckled and said to her, "I'm afraid I've already been to Iowa, Madame Zahara. Would you advise me to go back?"

She considered a moment, her index finger crooked at her lips. Then she said, "Efter you fly again to ze outer space, zen perhaps, Madame Zahara would advise you to go again to ze Caucasus een Iowa."

Glenn enjoyed a hearty laugh at this advice and thanked her for her counsel, adding, "I'm afraid I'm getting too old to return to outer space, Madame, and that makes me too old for Iowa."

"Neffer too old!" She scolded him, an admonitory finger in the air and her earrings jangling. "Look at Madame Zahara —zo like a spring chicken, you would neffer believe she eez —." Here she paused for effect, then stage-whispered, "—zerty years of age."

Glenn feigned shock and applause accompanied Madame as she sought her next victim. She had gathered new information on the mayor of Dayton, an Army general, an admiral, a local congresswoman, and a television news anchor. Whenever anyone protested that her predictions had already come to pass, she would throw her hands in the air, raise her eyes to the skies, and proclaimed, "Past, future — eez all ze same to Madame Zahara."

Now, she drew a bead on Senator Braverman. He winked at her when she took his hand and began to study his palm, pleased to be in the spotlight. "Ohh, zo many flying people today! Like a convention of angelz. You weel alzo fly high up in ze sky — but not zo high as John Glenn, I zink." She frowned and leaned closer, then glanced up at him sharply. "I zee a wedding. Zees should be a happy occasion, no? But you weel not enjoy it. I zee a plane falling, falling, falling — out of ze sky. Somezeeng eez wrong weez ze engine."

Braverman froze. His eyes met hers and locked. "Zere eez a girl at ze controls. A tall girl, wees dark hair and a boy's name: Tommy."

Braverman laughed nervously and tried to withdraw his hand. "Now, Madame, don't go telling stories that might get back to my wife."

But Madame Zahara, who had once controlled 24,000 pounds of steel with a seventy-one-foot wingspan, still had a powerful grip and she hung on now.

"Zere eez a man on ze floor of ze plane, sick, very sick. Ziss man is ze pilot, but alzo a very important man. Ze plane — eet eez alzo very sick. You are very afraid, Jeem Braverman. You sit weez ziss man while ze dark-haired girl lands ze plane. Soon, she will be dead." Her accent began to weaken. "But before she dies, she makes you write somezing. She makes you tell how she landed the plane." Now, only the vowels carried vestiges of an accent. "You —." She nailed him to his chair with her eyes. "You have been looking for what she wrote. You have visited other women pilots, looking for this piece of paper. Some of them are dead, too, now."

"This is outrageous!" The outburst came from the senior Braverman, who rose to his feet on the opposite side of the table from his son. The emcee, who had been trailing Madame with a microphone, looked up, startled, but he was slow to register what was happening.

CJ Burman was the second to rise. "Chub," he said in a strangled voice.

Madame Zahara did not shift her gaze or react, other than to say, in a low, sad voice that had a hypnotic cadence, "No, it's true. All true. He's been looking for a piece of paper — this piece of paper." And she reached into the front of her peasant blouse and extracted what did in fact appear, from where we sat, to be a small piece of paper.

Burman was leaning across the table, supporting himself on his palms. "Jim," he said, "I don't know where she got it, I swear! I didn't tell her any of this. I swear!"

Madame Zahara stiffened then and turned to look at him. She stood and stared at her husband.

But I was watching the senator. His gaze moved to the red-faced man in the sports coat who was now bearing down on Chub, his expression pained. His son's eyes flicked to him, then dropped to the piece of paper in Chub's hand. He snatched it, leapt to his feet, and bolted for the open spaces outside the tent.

All around me, the WASP were buzzing angrily. Then, they were in motion. A group of them surged forward, and by the time I got to my feet, I saw them running flat out: Tex, Toots, Bernie, Esther, and Stretch. The sixty-year-olds were holding their own against Stretch. Lou had leapt to her feet to cheer them on.

Next to me, Moses muttered, "He's crazy. We'll probably never convict him. We don't have the evidence."

I said, "I don't think it matters. He's afraid he'll be convicted in the only court he cares about."

I looked back at Braverman senior. He stood motionless, his mouth open in a caricature of stupefied amazement.

Confusion surged around us. More people, some of them wearing security uniforms, had joined the chase, although the WASP were out of sight now. The emcee was trying to regain control of the crowd's attention, but his bleats were ineffectual. Most of us were moving toward the action.

Lou, wheezing, grabbed my arm. "This way," she said, moving away from the general direction of the crowd. "They'll all have to use the runways."

My ankle was relieved to be moving away from the crowd, but it didn't move any faster. I waved Moses ahead as Lou and I made slower progress toward the field.

The first plane to appear, low and climbing, was a twin-engine veteran — a boxy plane with two tails. I watched it climb and then turned my head to look back toward the runway. I lifted a hand to shield my eyes and squinted in the bright sun.

A dark patch in the shimmering waves of heat off the tarmac resolved itself into a plane. It grew taller as I watched, an optical illusion, as I realized, created by the plane behind it as it lifted off the runway. The second plane lifted off, then a third.

"Oh, no," I said involuntarily. "They're in single-engines and he's in a twin-engine."

Lou shook her head. "The Jugs they're flying are faster than the P-38 he's flying. Plus, they've got a higher ceiling. Don't worry. They know what they're doing. They'll bring him down."

"Let's just hope nobody gets hurt," Moses said, his arms crossed.

We watched until the planes disappeared from view.

A soft voice behind us said, "Could my mother fly like that?"

We turned to see Isabel Yates watching, a curious expression, sad and wistful, on her face.

"She could and she did," Lou said. "She was the best."

Tears slid down Isabel's cheeks and I wondered if it was the first time she'd fully realized what it was that her mother had accomplished, and what her mother had given up to bring her into the world.

"Here they come," Moses announced and we all turned back to

see four bright spots against the western sky where the afternoon sun glinted off their wings.

The three single-engines were herding the twin-engine in our direction. One flew above the twin-engine, as if trying to force a landing, but they weren't low enough to begin the approach, I didn't think.

Then, the twin-engine dropped out of the formation, plummeting, spiraling, nose downward. Behind me I heard screams of horror. The plane slammed into the tarmac. It exploded on impact into a fifty-foot-high fireball. The three pursuit planes leveled off.

As soon as the acrid smoke reached us, I felt my stomach clench as my brain registered the familiar, deadly odor. My hands, from where they had been pressed to my cheeks, dropped to my side and I turned away from the sight. Moses put a steadying hand under my elbow. In silence, he guided me to a chair in the shade of a small tent, deserted by its former occupants in the excitement. Lou followed.

"Did you know the old man would be here, Cat?" he asked.

I shook my head. "I may be smart," I said with a weak smile, "but I'm not clairvoyant."

50

JULY 20, 1986

Tex was the first to stand and applaud when Chub appeared in the hotel bar late in the afternoon. "Chubby Lee," she said, "you deserve a medal."

The rest of us hesitated, waiting for Chub's reaction, but when Chub blushed, apparently with pleasure, we joined Tex's standing ovation.

"Y'all are the ones who deserve a medal," Chub said. "The way y'all intercepted that P-38 and brought him back."

Esther frowned. "Couldn't talk him down, though."

"His choice," Tex said. "I can't feel sorry for the bastard."

"Me, neither," Lou said.

"Oh, I don't know," Bernie said. "A parent can put a lot of pressure on a kid. Some kids never get over it."

"Doesn't give him the right to make other kids and parents suffer," Tex said.

"I know," Bernie said. "I'm just saying you can understand it, is all. I do feel sorry for him, but I'm not trying to convert anybody."

"I feel sorry for Maddy and Squeak and their families," Lou said. "And us."

"Yeah," Toots said. "They would have loved to have flown one of those Thunderbirds."

After a moment of reminiscent silence, Toots said, "So I suppose it was all about that dad-blamed medal?"

I looked at Chub. "That's what CJ says," she said, and sighed. "Braverman got the Distinguished Flying Cross for landing that damned plane in Colorado and saving all those important lives."

"The plane that Tommy landed," Stretch said softly.

"That's right," Chub said. "She was so furious, she made him write that statement. CJ said that he was in a state afterward, terrified that she'd tell somebody and the story would get back to his father."

"They were buddies at Harlingen — CJ and Braverman — weren't they?" I said. "That's something I never thought about. Did Braverman wash out of flight school?" I remembered something Lou had said about the gunnery trainees — how many of them had washed out of pilot training. I wondered if the same was true of navigators.

"He made it through flight school okay," Chub said, "but he washed out of B-26 school at Dodge City, and at that point, they needed navigators more than they needed pilots, so he was sent to Harlingen. Of course, his official biography says that he was in B-26 school when he was 'reassigned.' That's part of the mythology about the famous emergency landing. I guess his father was pretty angry about that reassignment."

"The Flying Torpedo wasn't for everyone," Bernie observed.

"Yeah, but just imagine," Toots said. "My parents were horrified to learn that I was flying B-26s. And his father was furious that he wasn't."

"So, anyway," Chub continued, "some asshole of a general decides to put him in the copilot's seat because, after all, he's Braverman's son —."

"And male," Lou said.

"And male," Chub repeated, nodding, "which automatically makes him more qualified than some girl whose name he doesn't recognize who only flies B-26s to tow targets."

"And then the male chauvinist general goes and has a heart

attack," Lou said, "and that girl has to save his sorry ass. And worse, she doesn't even get the credit."

"I guess they mentioned the possibility of a medal right away after the landing," Chub said, "because Jim — he went by 'Chet' then, because his first name was 'Chester' — was sure that if Tommy heard about it, she'd produce her piece of paper."

"So he made sure she didn't hear about it," Toots said. She reached out and gave Stretch's hand a squeeze.

"Apparently," Chub said, "CJ and Braverman were old drinking buddies. Even though CJ was an instructor and Jim — I guess I should call him 'Chet' — was a trainee, they were the same age and they liked to debate politics. The story Chet told CJ was that he was hung over on the flight to Colorado Springs, and that's why he couldn't land the plane. I know it's not what Tommy said —."

"Tommy said he was terrified," Toots said.

"Braverman probably thought CJ would sympathize if he was hung over," I said, "though it was a long flight to Colorado in those days. Plenty of time to sober up, you'd think."

Chub grimaced. "I'm sure CJ believed what he wanted to believe. He knew that Chet was real anxious after the Colorado trip, and then suddenly, he wasn't, but he didn't know why. He says he asked about it, but Braverman just shrugged it off and CJ forgot about it. By the time Braverman was awarded his medal, he'd left navigation school and been reassigned. CJ says he forgot all about it. Maybe he did and maybe he didn't. Who knows? He must have heard about Thompson's disappearance. He says Braverman never told him the girl's name, but I don't know if I believe that."

"Years pass," I said. "Braverman becomes a senator, just like dear old dad. He supports WASP militarization and it salves his conscience. In fact, all of the WASP think he's a great guy. And then he catches wind of the museum project and hears that the WASP are collecting papers. And that makes him nervous, because by now, he's beginning to think that maybe he can achieve something even dear old dad couldn't achieve: the White House. After all, Reagan's second term will be over in '88 and the presidency will be up for grabs. And then, Maddy gets a bee in her bonnet and calls him. I'm sure we can check the phone records to see if she did." I glanced at Moses and he nodded.

"He sure moved fast," Esther commented. "I can't get my congressman on the phone that fast."

"Did Maddy work on the militarization campaign?" I asked.

Lou nodded. "Yes, she did. So she could have had a private number from that phone list."

Toots frowned. "So he says what? 'Let's talk this over, face to face?' Something like that? And then what?"

I shrugged. "We may never know. Unless — Chub?"

"CJ claims not to know anything about it," Chub said. "I think I believe him. He says Jim called him and asked him to look through my papers for anything with his name on it. I get the feeling he stroked CJ's ego some and said things like, 'Wouldn't it be great if I won the presidency and you won the governorship at the same time?' I do think that CJ's too big a coward to kill anybody and probably too big a coward to stand up to Jim when he realized what Jim had done."

"Braverman wouldn't have had any reason to confide in CJ," I said, "beyond what he'd already done when he was too young to be cautious. And it seems unlikely that CJ could gain access to WASP without arousing their suspicions. Braverman needed access, because even with Maddy out of the way, there was that pesky statement he'd signed and that might yet turn up. Then, too, he had to know if Maddy had talked to anyone else. Or if any other WASP who knew the story had connected the copilot Chet with Senator Jim Braverman. Braverman probably called up Squeak and told her he'd come to town and found himself with a few free hours. He suggested that, as a member of the museum committee, he'd like to come look at her WASP memorabilia. At least, that's how I imagine it."

"He was certainly a charmer," Lou admitted. "But he sure took some big risks."

"What I don't get is why he never contacted Toots," Stretch said.

"Is that because he managed to find her stuff and go through it without her knowing? But what if she knew the story?"

"I'm betting he was the one who sabotaged Toots's plane," I said. "That would have been the simplest solution to his problem. But he might have tried to contact you, Toots. He probably didn't want to risk leaving a message. I gather that both Maddy and Squeak were fairly housebound."

"Oh, sure," Toots said. "I'm not easy to get hold of. Stretch asked once if I didn't want a phone extension installed in the shed, but I said no. When I'm working, I'm working. I don't want to be answering the phone every ten minutes to tell somebody that I don't want aluminum siding."

"So in the end, he got the statement back, but he didn't think it would do him any good?" Esther asked.

"Oh, he didn't get the statement back," Chub said. "That was just a letter to my mother asking her to send my blue sweater and complaining about the West Texas sand getting in my hair."

"So he read it and realized that you still had the original and that's when he decided to commit suicide?" Esther persisted.

"Who knows?" I said. "I suspect he knew that he was doomed from the moment the subject was brought up in his father's hearing."

"Then why fly off like that?" Esther said. "Where did he think he could fly to?"

"Maybe no place," Toots said. "Maybe he just wanted to prove to his father that he could fly."

It was as good an answer as we were likely to get.

Toots turned to me. "Cat, after we'd narrowed the list down to two suspects, how did you know that the killer was Braverman and not CJ? Was it because of the medal he'd been given for landing the plane?" She gave Chub an apologetic look.

Lou said, "Oh, wait, Cat." Her raised index finger moved from me to Moses. "You and Moses — you're not a writer and a photographer?"

I saw Moses stiffen a little and grinned. "I'm a photographer," he said.

"And I'm a P.I.," I said.

"Then you deserve a medal for cracking this case," Bernie said.

"Not me," I said. "You're the ones who deserve medals — all of you — for all of the dangerous missions you completed during the war."

"That'll be the day," Tex said.

"Oh, they can keep their darned medals," Toots said. "I'm happy with my memories."

I glanced at Chub, who winked at me. "Past or future?" I asked.

Toots smiled and raised both arms. She settled one on Lou's shoulders and one on Stretch's shoulders and sighed.

"Both," she said.

EPILOGUE

September 1986

THE WASP HAD BEEN RIGHT about the true identity of the murder victim. She was not Tommy Thompson, but Olive Grace Kilroy, former assistant to Mrs. Leoti Deaton, chief administrative officer at Avenger. Fingerprint identification was inconclusive because the WASP records didn't exist anymore, but she was positively identified by dental records. Her sister confirmed that Olive had been obsessed with the WASP all her life, but the sister didn't seem to know anything about the planned impersonation.

After the war, Olive had worked as a secretary at Mather Air Base in Sacramento until she retired. She had never learned to fly. In her apartment, investigators found a scrapbook from her Avenger days, in the back of which were stuck several old newspaper articles about Tex, Toots, and Esther. They also found letters from several men and a nurse who had been stationed at Harlingen during the war. From the letters, they guessed that Olive had written, in the guise of a military historian writing a book about women pilots, requesting information about the WASP.

On a cloudless day in September, with just a hint of fall in the air, Toots and Stretch took off in their Skybolt. Moses and I went to see them off, and I have to admit that the little plane — red with silver streaks on its tail and wings — looked beautiful as it waggled its wings against the blue sky.

The WASP were gathering at Avenger Field in Sweetwater, Texas, for their biggest reunion ever. They would toast Jacqueline Cochran and memorialize Leoti Deaton, Madeleine Vincent George, Elizabeth Eckels Ellerman, Lorraine Evers MacBride, and even Olive Grace Kilroy. They would pay tribute to the thirty-eight WASP who had lost their lives in flight training or on active duty, and remember the ones they had lost since the war ended. The high point of the festivities, however, would be the posthumous awarding of a Distinguished Flying Cross by Air Force Colonel William Bruce Arnold, son of General Arnold, to Evelyn May Thompson for heroic action taken in December 1944.

Stretch and Toots both cried when the medal was presented to Stretch. Colonel Arnold shed a few tears, too. I know because I saw the pictures.

I wasn't there.

I don't fly.

Please rate and review this book at Amazon, Goodreads, BookBub, or your favorite book site. To learn more about my books and sign up for my mailing list, please visit dbborton.com.

LOOKING FOR YOUR NEXT GREAT READ?

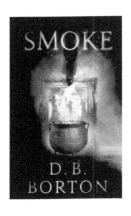

Late one night during the fiery days of the Iranian revolution, two figures slip into the Tehran Museum of Contemporary Art and steal twelve of the world's most valuable paintings. Here's what the thieves don't know: most of the paintings are fake.

Decades later, when she ought to be enjoying a sedate retirement from the field, Marge Smith remains on active duty as an agent of the secretive Quixote, Ltd. But now that she's broken her leg in a motorcycle accident, her bosses have sent her to a nursing home to recover. She doesn't know why, but she doesn't think it has anything to do with the geriatric production of Macbeth she's been inveigled to take part in—until one of the witches drops dead in the middle of opening afternoon.

Called in to work on a theft recovery, Marge is surprised to discover the surviving witches across the conference table, and astonished when she's handed a list of stolen paintings to recover. She knows these paintings; she once stole them herself.

Now Marge has several problems to solve. Who stole the paintings and how can she get them back? Are they the real paintings or another set of fakes? If they're real, how did they end up in a house in suburban Washington, DC? Was the third witch murdered for them? And how soon can she ditch the crutches? **Buy Now** to find out.

"The writing is wonderfully descriptive and often produces audible chuckles … Certainly one of the most unique books I've read in awhile … Fun and informative." Rosepoint Publishing

It's hard to be hard-boiled when your biggest fan and toughest critic is your twelve-year-old daughter.

Comedy meets mystery and history in the summer of 1961, when Houston is still a cowboy backwater—overheated, under-air conditioned, and plagued by daily downpours that bring the Gulf of Mexico ashore and wash crawdads down suburban streets.

P.I. Harry Lark is running a detective agency out of a seedy downtown office building when a well-dressed out-of-towner entangles him in President Kennedy's moon mission. LBJ and his Texas cronies are plotting to get NASA to build a space center in Houston, but somebody is out to stop them. Harry decides that he's working for the wrong side and gives his client the brush-off, but when a dead body shows up in his office, he discovers that he can't walk away. Then Harry is hired to clear a local civil rights group of involvement in a string of firebombings.

Meanwhile, Dizzy Lark and her pals are running a lost and found out of a suburban garage when they're hired to find a missing father who is supposed to be dead and buried.

What's the thread connecting a dead mobster, a missing father, torched buildings, and NASA's moon mission? Harry and Dizzy race to find out before the city goes up in flames.

If you like stylish, witty writers like Raymond Chandler, Robert B. Parker, Lisa Scottoline, and Elmore Leonard, you'll see why *Romance Reviews Today*'s Jani Brooks rates *Bayou City Burning* "a Perfect 10 book." You may agree with blogger Brooke Gunderman when she calls *Bayou City Burning* "one of my new favorite books!"

Will Harry and Dizzy save the city? Will Harry survive a month of single parenthood? **Buy Now** to find out.

ABOUT THE AUTHOR

A native Texan, Borton became an ardent admirer of Nancy Drew at a young age. By the time she was fourteen, she had acquired her own blue roadster, trained on the freeways of Houston, and begun her travels. She left Texas around the time that everyone else arrived.

In graduate school, Borton converted a lifetime of passionate reading and late-night movie-watching into a doctorate in English. She discovered that people would pay her to discuss literature and writing, although not much. Finding young people entertaining and challenging, she became a college teacher, and survived many generations of students. Later, during a career crisis, she learned that people would pay her to tell stories, although even less than they would pay her to discuss stories written by someone else.

Borton has lived in the Southwest, Midwest, and on the West Coast, where she planted roses and collected three degrees in English without relinquishing her affection for and reliance on nonstandard dialects. In her spare time, she gardens, practices aikido, studies languages other than English, and, of course, watches movies and reads.

www.dbborton.com

Made in the USA
Monee, IL
22 February 2022

91650876R00177